RAZOR SHARP

Books by Fern Michaels

Mr. and Miss Anonymous
Up Close and Personal
Fool Me Once
Picture Perfect
About Face
The Future Scrolls
Kentucky Sunrise
Kentucky Heat
Kentucky Rich
Plain Jane
Charming Lily
What You Wish For
The Guest List
Listen to Your Heart
Celebration
Yesterday
Finders Keepers
Annie's Rainbow
Sara's Song
Vegas Sunrise
Vegas Heat
Vegas Rich
Whitefire
Wish List
Dear Emily

The Sisterhood Novels:

Razor Sharp
Under the Radar
Final Justice
Collateral Damage
Fast Track
Hokus Pokus
Hide and Seek
Free Fall
Lethal Justice
Sweet Revenge
The Jury
Vendetta
Payback
Weekend Warriors

Anthologies:

Snow Angels
Silver Bells
Comfort and Joy
Sugar and Spice
Let It Snow
A Gift of Joy
Five Golden Rings
Deck the Halls
Jingle All the Way

RAZOR SHARP

FERN MICHAELS

ZEBRA BOOKS
KENSINGTON PUBLISHING CORP.
http://www.kensingtonbooks.com

ZEBRA BOOKS are published by

Kensington Publishing Corp.
119 West 40th Street
New York, NY 10018

All Kensington titles, imprints, and distributed lines are available at special quantity discounts for bulk purchases for sales promotion, premiums, fund-raising, educational, or institutional use.

Special book excerpts or customized printings can also be created to fit specific needs. For details, write or phone the office of the Kensington Special Sales Manager: Attn. Special Sales Department. Kensington Publishing Corp., 119 West 40th Street, New York, NY 10018. Phone: 1-800-221-2647.

Zebra and the Z logo Reg. U.S. Pat. & TM Off.

ISBN-13: 978-1-4201-0684-8
ISBN-10: 1-4201-0684-8

First Kensington Books Hardcover Printing: June 2009
First Zebra Books Mass-Market Paperback Printing: October 2009

10 9 8 7 6 5 4 3 2 1

Printed in the United States of America

Chapter 1

Cosmo Cricket looked at the Mickey Mouse clock on his desk, a gift from a grateful client. Because, as the client put it, what do you give to a man who has everything except maybe a part of his childhood to remember? For some reason, this particular clock meant the world to him and not because Mickey Mouse was part of his childhood—because he hadn't really had a childhood, at least not a normal one. Someday, when he had nothing else to do, he'd figure it all out. He wished he could remember the client, but he couldn't. Mickey told him it was the end of the workday. But the city that he lived and worked in, one that never slept, was about to come alive just as he was about to head home.

This was always the time of day when he sat back with a diet drink and reflected. On his life. On his work. On his past. And, on his future. He never reflected on the present because he knew who he was and what was going on, right down to the minute, thanks to Mickey. He'd known who he was from the day he was born. There were those who would take issue with that statement, but those people didn't know his mother and father. There wasn't an hour of his life that he didn't know about because his parents insisted he know everything. He always smiled when he got to this point in his reverie.

He knew he weighed fourteen whopping pounds when he was born and looked like he was already four months old. He knew that his parents fought over who got to hold him. And he was told that he was rocked in a chair from day one until he was three years old, at which point he'd announced he was no longer a baby and needed to be a big boy, and he wanted his *own* chair, which appeared within hours, thanks to his doting father. There had been a succession of rocking chairs as he grew. He was sitting, right now, this very second, in the last one.

The rocking chair was battered and worn, and was on its tenth, maybe even its twentieth, set of cushions, he couldn't remember. The chair was at odds with the rest of his plush office and a far cry from the kind of furnishings in the house he'd grown up in. Everything in this penthouse suite of rooms was elegant, as top-of-the-line as the decorator could make it. Ankle-deep carpeting, an array of built-ins, pricey paintings on the walls, soft, buttery furniture, and a view of Las Vegas that had no equal. The palatial suite had its own bathroom, where everything was oversize to accommodate him. He was almost ashamed to admit he never used anything but the towels. He did like the bidet, though. The suite was one massive perk arranged by the Nevada Gaming Commission to get him to sign on as their legal counsel. He'd argued over the Gaming Commission's contract, saying he wanted to be able to practice law with a few select clients and do some pro bono work, and he wouldn't budge. He'd actually walked away when they wouldn't cave in, but they caught up with him at the elevator and agreed to his demands, then threw in what they thought was the clunker, but to Cosmo it was the icing on the proverbial cake. He was to be on call to all the casino owners, who would pay him his six-hundred-dollar-an-hour fee for whatever work he did for them plus a year-end bonus. The only stipulation was that his private clients and the casino owners not interfere with the commission's work. It was a solid-gold deal that worked for everyone.

Twenty-three years later he had so much money, he didn't know what to do with it, so he let other people manage it, people who made even more money for him.

In the beginning, when the money started flowing in, he moved his parents to a mansion, got them live-in help, and bought them fancy cars all without asking them first. That lasted one whole week before they moved out in the middle of the night and went back to their little house in the desert, where they had lived out their lives. He still owned that house, and it was where he himself lived. He'd updated it and was snug as a bug in a rug.

Cosmo chuckled when he thought of the other perk he'd negotiated: acquiring the entire floor below his suite of offices. He'd been disappointed that he hadn't had to go to the mat on that one. The "powers that be" gave in meekly, and he rented it out for outrageous sums of money, which he, in turn, donated to his favorite charities.

Cosmo looked at Mickey again and saw that it was almost six o'clock, which meant it was almost nine o'clock back East. He looked forward to calling Elizabeth and talking for an hour or so. God, how he loved that woman.

Mickey told him he had fifteen more minutes to reflect before he headed home. Thinking about Elizabeth Fox made him smile. Never in his wildest dreams had he ever thought a woman like Elizabeth would fall in love with him. Or that he could love her as much as he'd loved his parents. It just boggled his mind.

Cosmo's smile widened when he remembered his parents sitting him down when he turned six and was about to go off to school. They told him how he was different and how the other children were going to react to him. He'd listened, but he hadn't understood the cruelty of children; he learned quickly. It hadn't gotten any better as he aged, but by the time he went off to college, he didn't give a shit what anyone said about him. He accepted that he was big and that his feet were like canoes and that he was ugly, with outrigger ears and a flat slab for a face, and that he had to have specially made clothes and shoes and a bed that would accommodate his body. He was comfortable in his own skin and made a life for himself.

And then along came Elizabeth Fox, or as she was known in legal circles, the Silver Fox. At first he couldn't believe she loved him, or as she put it, *"I don't just love you, Cosmo, I love every inch of you."* And she meant it. He was so light-headed with that declaration, he'd almost passed out. She'd laughed, a glorious, tinkling sound that made him shiver all the way to his toes. Then she'd sat him down and told him everything she was involved in.

"You can walk away from me right now, Cosmo, and I will understand. If we stay together, you will know I'm breaking the law, and so will you. I'm giving you a choice."

Like there was a choice to be made. He'd signed on and never looked back. He was now a male member of that elite little group called the Vigilantes.

Cosmo looked over at Mickey and saw that it was time to fight the Vegas traffic and head for home. He looked around to see where his jacket was. Ah, just where he'd thrown it when he came back from lunch, half on one of the chairs and half-dangling on the floor. He was heaving himself out of his rocking chair when he heard the door to his secretary's office open and close. Mona Stevens, his secretary, always left at five o'clock on the dot because she had to pick up her son from day care. Mona had been one of his pro bono cases. A friend of a friend had asked him to help her out because her husband had taken off and left her and her son to fend for themselves. He'd hired her once he'd straightened out her problem and gotten her child support, and he paid her three times what other secretaries earned on the Strip. She was so grateful and loyal she would have brushed his teeth for him if he'd allowed it.

Cosmo opened the door to see a woman sitting primly on one of the chairs. She looked worried as well as uncomfortable. When the door opened she looked up, a deer caught in the headlights. "Can I help you?"

She was maybe in her mid-forties—he was never good at women's ages—well dressed, with a large leather bag at her feet. Her hair looked nice to his eye, and she wasn't slathered in makeup. All in all a pleasant-looking woman whose husband had probably gambled away their life savings and the house as well. He liked to think he was a good judge of character and always, no matter what, he waited to see a client's reaction to meeting him for the first time.

This lady, whoever she was, didn't flinch, didn't blink, didn't do anything other than ask, "Are you Mr. Cricket?"

"I am. I was just leaving. Do you have an appointment I forgot about?"

"No. I did call three different times but . . . no, I don't have an appointment. Should I make one and come back? If I do that, I might not . . ."

"I have time. Come on in," Cosmo said, stepping aside so the woman could enter. He knew little about women's fashions and wondered what she carried in the bag that was heavy enough to drag her shoulder downward. He wasn't even sure whether the bag should be called a handbag, a backpack, or a travel case. His mother always referred to her bag as her pocketbook. It was where she kept a fresh hanky with lace on it, a small change purse, a comb, and a tube of lipstick. This woman's bag looked like it contained a twenty-pound rock and maybe the hammer she'd used to dig it out. He felt pleased with his assessment when the bag landed next to the chair with a loud *thump*.

Cosmo made a second assessment. The woman didn't want to be there. But she was, and she'd called three times, and had hung up probably because she lost her nerve. For some reason women did that when their problems involved errant husbands. He reached into a drawer and pulled out a clean yellow legal pad and a pencil. He never used pens, just in case he had to erase something. His first rule was: never commit something to paper you don't want anyone else to see.

Pencil poised, Cosmo spoke, his tone gentle for such a big man. "We've established that I'm Cosmo Cricket, attorney-at-law. Who might you be?"

"Right now I'm Lily Flowers. Last week I was Crystal Clark. Before that Ann Marie Anders. And before that I was Caroline Summers. I don't care to tell you at this time what my real birth name is. I have"—she bent down to poke in the bag at her feet, her voice muffled as she fumbled around for what she wanted, finally finding a small envelope and spreading the contents out on Cosmo's pristine desk—"a passport in each name, a driver's license in the same name, along with a credit card that matches the picture ID on the driver's license. Each one of these identities has a bank account with minimal activity, rent receipts, and utility receipts. In different parts of the country. And a birth certificate," she said breathlessly.

Cosmo made no move to inspect the documents on his desk. "I assume you got these," he said, pointing to the lineup on his desk, "illegally."

"It depends on your definition of the word 'illegal.' That's me in every photo. Just a different hairdo, a little spirit gum here or there to alter the facial features, a little shoulder padding, but it is me."

"At the outset I say to all my clients, 'Tell me the truth, or I can't help you.' I'm sure you are aware of the confidentiality agreement between client and lawyer. If you aren't, what that means is I can never divulge anything you tell me to a third party. So whatever you say to me today, here in this room, I cannot tell another soul. Whatever your secrets are, they are safe with me. Having said that, I now need to ask you why you feel you need four identities other than your real one? What kind of trouble are you in?"

The woman of many names drew in a deep breath and let it out slowly. "Right now I am not in any trouble, but I will be very shortly. I'm here because . . . because . . . I want to know if there is any way I can head it off. What my options are, assuming I have any."

"Okay. But you have to tell me what type of trouble you think is headed your way."

Lily Flowers took another deep breath. "You don't know who I am, do you?"

Cosmo shook his head. "No, I don't recognize you. Should I? Have we met somewhere? Right now you appear to me to be a potential client in distress. Like I said, you have to tell me your problem; otherwise, I can't help you."

"I operate the Happy Day Camp for Boys and Girls in Pahrump. Until a month ago, our revenues exceeded those of Sheri's and the Chicken Ranch. Uh, that's according to my accountant."

Shit! Good judge of character, my ass. "Prostitution is legal in Pahrump, which is over sixty miles from Vegas. What's the problem? Did your girls fall short of the medical requirements?"

"No, nothing like that. I operate the cleanest, safest brothel in the state. My girls are the highest paid in the state. My problem is that some of my powerful, wealthy clients asked me to branch out for special occasions. They arranged all the details, a rustic atmosphere, right down to the summer camp theme I operate here. There was noth-

ing in my name. I made sure of that. My girls are inde-
pendent contractors and pay their taxes and everything that
goes with it. As you know, there is no state income tax
here in Nevada. I can give you an operations lesson later
on. Right now word has filtered down to me that I'm likely
to be arrested for my activities. Not here in Nevada but
back East."

Cosmo felt his stomach muscles tie themselves into a
knot. "Where back East?"

"The nation's capital. That's where all the action went
down for Happy Day Camp. The clients, or johns, if you
prefer, were all politicians. After the election a few months
ago, when our first female president was sworn in, things
went south with the opposition and quite a few of the current members of the new administration. They've been
trying to keep the lid on it all, but word leaked out. It always does.

"It wasn't all that long ago that the woman they called
the D.C. Madam supposedly killed herself. And just for
the record, I don't believe that for one minute, and neither
does anyone else who is in this business."

By then Cosmo felt like he had an army of ants squirm-
ing around in his stomach. "Why did you do it? You could
operate safely here. Why go to a place like D.C. of all
places?"

"Believe it or not, I didn't want to. I called a meeting of
my girls, laid it all out, and—like a fool—allowed them
to make the decision. I can understand how none of them
wanted to say no—the money the clients were offering
was outrageous. A few of the girls planned to retire when
they got back. We only did it twice. Once before the election and once again afterward. 'Celebrations,' for want of
a better word.

"The minute word came down to me, I closed Happy
Day Camp and sent the girls off to a safe place to await

instructions from me. I traded in Crystal Clark and went back to being Lily Flowers five days ago. I put a sign up that said Happy Day Camp was closed for heavy-duty plumbing repairs. This is the fifth day, and my phone has been ringing constantly. People are looking for me. That's why I'm Lily Flowers at the moment. I want to know if I should join my girls or stay and fight it out."

Cosmo twirled the pencil in his hand. He licked at his dry lips and bit down on his bottom lip. "What do *you* want to do?"

"Anything but go to jail. The johns get off scot-free, and the women go to jail. Tell me where the justice is in that? Will they extradite me back to D.C.?"

"Yes. And I am not licensed to practice law in the District of Columbia."

"I thought that's what you were going to say. Okay, that means I have to take off and hope for the best. But I want to leave something with you for safekeeping. I'll pay your retainer if you agree."

Cosmo watched as Crystal again started digging around in the oversize bag. She finally came up with book after book, and plopped them on the desk, one on top of the other. "My check registers, my little black books. My business cell phones, all my records. And here," she said, counting out bills from a stack of money in a brown envelope, "is your retainer. Do not let those books fall into the wrong hands. Will it be all right if I call you from time to time to see . . . you know . . . how things are going?"

"Look, Ms. Clark, I know quite a few very good attorneys in Washington, D.C. One in particular who is excellent. Any one of them can help you. You really should think about this before you make a rash decision."

"I did think about it on the way here. No way am I going to let them come after me. Let them go after the johns. Why should they get off with no penalties? Do you really want to pick up the paper some morning to read that I killed myself? That's what will happen if I go there and lawyer up. You didn't answer my question, Mr. Cricket. Will it be all right for me to call you from time to time, and will you keep all these records safe until such time as I want them back?"

Every bone, every nerve in Cosmo's body wanted to shout *no, no, no.* "Yes," was his response. "Will you be okay?"

The woman of many names laughed. At least Cosmo thought it was a laugh. "I'll be just fine. I knew this day might come, and I've prepared for it."

Cosmo watched as she gathered up all her identity papers and shoved them into the bag, which now sagged together on the sides, then plopped it on top of Cosmo's desk. "What about money?"

"It's offshore. I'm not stupid, Mr. Cricket. Like I said, I prepared for this day a long time ago. And those records," she said, pointing to the pile of black books and check registers teetering precariously on his desk, "are the originals. The phones are real, and I have no others. The duplicate books and records are in safe hands and being delivered to the intended recipients, that's as in plural, as we speak."

The woman of many names stood up. Cosmo thought she looked taller without the weight of the heavy bag on her shoulder. "Don't you think you should tell me who has the copies? Just in case." *Christ, how lame did that sound?*

The woman laughed. This time it was a delightful, wicked laugh. She winked at him and laughed again. She held up her index and middle finger in the sign of a *V* before she sashayed out of the office.

Was that a *V*? Damn straight it was a *V*. The only *V* he could relate to was the *V* in the word "Vigilante." It couldn't stand for "victory," given her circumstances.

It was Cosmo's turn to laugh, and laugh he did. He couldn't wait to get home to call Elizabeth. He opened the huge safe behind the minibar by pressing a button. He started to secure the woman's records when he noticed a piece of paper sticking out of the uppermost black book. Curious, he pulled it out and read a signed statement giving him permission to use the records as he saw fit to help bring the johns to justice. After he returned the paper to its place in the top book, he closed the safe and moved the minibar back into position. Waving to Mickey, Cosmo turned off the lights, locked the door, and departed. He was still laughing when he climbed into his Porsche for the long ride out to the desert. He hummed an old Fleetwood Mac ditty as he tooled along, marveling at what a small world it was.

Chapter 2

It wasn't your ordinary retirement party, with laughter and balloons and bubbly gushing out of a fountain. Judges for some reason thought their parties should be bland, boring, and sedate. Perhaps it had something to do with this judge's age, which was seventy-seven. Maybe Big Foot, as Judge Paul Leland was affectionately called in the cloakrooms, didn't know how to have fun. Although, given his current wife, who was thirty years his junior, one wouldn't have thought so. On the other hand, maybe the poor old dear was just worn-out, thanks to his social-climbing young consort.

Lizzie hated these command performances. Soggy canapés, less than satisfactory wine, not even champagne, and no music to speak of. She refused to acknowledge the violin player who circled the room doing his best to annoy people. She glanced down at her watch and wondered if it was late enough to make her excuses and head for home. Three hours of torture was her limit. It was coming up to ten o'clock, time for this party to end, for her at least. She looked around to see if anyone else was getting ready to leave. Maybe she could start a trend. She really wanted to get home so she could talk to Cosmo. All day she had looked forward to her glass of wine and the phone call.

After talking to him, she'd fall into bed with a smile on her face. God, how she loved the man with the funny name.

All eyes were on Lizzie as she made her way through the crowd to reach the judge, who was surrounded by a sea of white hair and bald heads, men and women as old as he. A little while ago she'd seen the young wife guzzling wine with a tall, buff lawyer who was married but cheated like crazy. All the younger lawyers clustered together at the far end of the room, the not-so-old judges at the other end of the room waiting to be excused or for a bomb to drop so they could leave. She was surprised no one had pulled the fire alarm to clear the room.

The sea of white moved in tandem as the geriatric crowd parted for Lizzie to move closer to Judge Leland. Every eye was on the black sheath she wore like a second skin, on the stiletto heels that allowed her to tower over the man she was congratulating. No one missed the outrageous five-carat diamond Cosmo had slipped on her finger three months ago and which sparkled on her left hand; nor did they miss the three-carat diamonds winking and glimmering in each ear under the bright fluorescent lights, another present from Cosmo. The untamed mane of silvery hair tumbling down her back and around her shoulders looked like spun silver.

And then she was in front of the judge, every ear tuned to the conversation. "I'm so sorry, Judge Leland, but I have to leave this enchanting party because I need to double-check a motion I want to file in the morning. I hope you have a wonderful retirement and don't miss all of us too much."

The judge's voice was raspy and yet frail-sounding when he said, "Ah, Miss Fox, I will sorely miss listening to your outstanding oratory in the courtroom. My wife always quizzed me on your fashionable attire when I got home. Thank you so much for coming this evening to help me celebrate my retirement. I'll look forward to reading about your courtroom dramas in the days to come, as opposed to witnessing them firsthand."

Lizzie laughed, that tinkling sound she was famous for. She bent down and, to the amazement of just about everyone in the room, kissed the judge soundly on the cheek. She smiled, and the room grew brighter as she waited for the sea of white heads to part once again. Two minutes later she was out of the room and headed for the checkroom to retrieve her cashmere coat. But maybe she needed to visit the restroom first.

Inside the elegant restroom, she met three colleagues she knew quite well. They were whispering among themselves. "Okay, ladies, it's safe to leave. I paved the way for all of us to call it a night," Lizzie said.

"There is a God," one of the lawyers said dramatically. "Lizzie, have you heard?"

"Heard what?" Lizzie asked curiously as she headed to the far stall.

The three women as one moved down the length of the vanity and all of them started talking at once.

Lizzie exited the stall and started to wash her hands. She had trouble keeping up with what she was hearing.

"Biggest scandal since . . . God, I don't know when." "Practically the whole damn cabinet . . . even some of the Secret Service . . . try the vice prez . . . jeez, what's this all going to do to Martine Connor's new administration?" "Congress and the Senate . . . more than you can shake a stick at."

Lizzie was about to weigh in with a dozen questions when the door opened and a gaggle of women entered the room. All conversation among the lawyers screeched to a halt. Lizzie rolled her eyes as she held the door for the others.

Lizzie retrieved her long white cashmere coat, slipped

into it, and almost ran to the exit. She handed the valet her ticket and waited for her brand-new Porsche to be brought to where she was standing. Her head buzzed with what she'd heard and what she hadn't heard. Imagination was a powerful thing.

Her car roared to a stop. For some reason, Porsches driven by anyone other than their owners always seemed to roar. Lizzie slipped a ten-dollar bill into the valet's hand and slid behind the wheel. The powerful car purred and growled to life as she raced down the circular road that would lead her to the main highway. Another scandal in Washington. What else was new? She didn't want to think about scandals, she wanted to think about Cosmo Cricket and the coming weekend when she would fly out to see him.

Five hours later, Lizzie rolled over on her lavender-scented sheets as she struggled to figure out what had woken her. The phone, of course. She squinted at the clock on the nightstand. The large red numerals said it was 2:59. No one called her at this hour unless it was a dire emergency. Her first thought was Cosmo, but she discarded that thought immediately. He'd said he was going straight to bed when they hung up from their call, and she had done the same thing. One of the Sisters? Surely nothing was happening on the mountain that couldn't wait till morning. The caller I.D. said PRIVATE CALLER. Did she even want to take the call? No. She rolled back over, sniffed her pillowcase, and settled down to go back to sleep when the phone rang again. *Damn*. She rolled back over and picked up the phone. "This better be really, really good because it's three o'clock in the morning, and I was sound asleep." Lizzie didn't care who was listening to her tirade.

"Lizzie, it's Martine Connor. I am sorry to wake you, truly I am, but I do not have a minute to myself these days. This is the only time I can call you. I need to talk to you, Lizzie."

"Madam President," Lizzie said, bolting upright and swinging her legs over the side of the bed at the same time. "Is this how we're going to chat from time to time? Is something wrong?"

"First things first, cut out that 'Madam President' stuff. You only have to call me Madam President if the press is around. No, we are not going to chat in the middle of the night. No, I take that back, yes, that's about the only time we can talk. I can't sleep in this job. I haven't had a good night's sleep since I moved into this damn place. I used to sleep like a baby and, yes, something is wrong. I'm surprised you haven't gotten wind of it all, even though they're trying to put a lid on it. You know whenever they do that, an explosion always follows."

Lizzie's mind raced as she made her way out to the kitchen to make coffee. She knew there would be no more sleep for her that night. She thought about the conversation in the lavatory with her colleagues at the Hay-Adams a little while ago.

"I think you need to be a little more precise, Martine. I did hear something tonight at Judge Leland's retirement party, but it was in the restroom. Lawyers talk, you know that. Nothing seemed out of the ordinary in the party room. I think I would have picked up on it. Every damn judge and lawyer in this town was there. Also, there were quite a few congressmen and senators present. Give it to me straight up. Martine, does anyone know you're calling me? Aren't there invisible eyes and ears on you?"

"I'm on that crazy phone you gave me. I carry it on me at all times. Yes, my dear, in my bra if I'm wearing clothes without pockets. I have it set on vibration mode. I'm also in bed. Alone. There are no eyes and ears here that I know of. There damn well better not be."

Lizzie poured her coffee, added cream, then rummaged in the fridge for something to munch on. She reached for some chicken legs her day lady had left on a platter of Southern-fried chicken along with a side bowl of potato salad. She poked at the other bowls and saw a salad and some fruit. With the phone cradled between her ear and her shoulder, she carried everything to the round wooden table. "Talk to me," she mumbled.

"It's that old devil sex. It's reared its ugly head in my administration. This is worse than the scandal that erupted before I took office. You remember the D.C. Madam, don't you?" Not bothering to wait for a reply, President Connor raced on. "This time around, half my staff attended the damn party. I'm told there were Secret Service there. I lost count of the federal judges and congressmen who attended the damn camp weekend. Not just once, but twice," Connor screeched. "They had such a good time, they did an encore after I was sworn in. And don't tell me 'boys will be boys.' I don't want to hear it. I think every politician in this damn town was involved in one way or another. Do you know how this makes me look?" Again she didn't bother to wait for a reply. "I have an administration of perverts. Say something, Lizzie."

Lizzie for some reason enjoyed hearing Martine venting. *Welcome to Washington* was what she wanted to say. Instead, Lizzie said, "I heard there were quite a few senators who . . . uh, went to camp, and I also heard several of your fancy-dancy ambassadors and a few of their friends were also in attendance." Lizzie licked at her fingers and reached for a second chicken leg. "I hope you aren't calling me to ask me to represent any of those perverts because the answer is *no,* Madam President. I have long believed that the johns should be the ones who are arrested and punished, not the working girls and madams. The men went to the summer, or winter, camp, whatever it was, of their own free will, and they were willing to pony up outrageous sums of money for the pleasure. No one twisted their arms. Then they walk off scot-free, and the women take the fall. What's wrong with this picture? No, Madam President, I can't help you."

"Lizzie, you have to help me. Not directly, I realize that. I want you to get in touch with the Vigilantes and ask for their help. I can't think of anything else. I guess you can see I'm desperate, or I wouldn't be calling you."

"Martine, *no!* They won't help you! You're already running a tab with the Vigilantes. You owe them a pardon that has not been forthcoming. I'm sure they're on the same page I am when it comes to the johns. If you weren't sitting in the office you won, you'd be on our page, too. You know that, Martine."

"Lizzie, I could go down the tubes with what's going on. I'll be the laughingstock of the free world. The first female president, and I have an administration whose members can't keep their pants zipped. This is going to be a circus. I have to try to do *something.*"

"Chop them all off at the knees right now. By them, I mean every man within spitting distance of what went on, those that attended that . . . uh, camp. Go back to all your short lists and work from there. Make everyone involved in the administration resign. Then move on. There's no way you can contain this. You have to know that, Martine. We both know the media will be on this like fleas on a dog. You have to be aggressive. Whatever you do, don't go giving speeches, or just slapping any of the 'boys' on the wrist, and don't try to hide anything. That's the best advice I can give you right at this precise moment." Lizzie attacked the potato salad, eating right out of the bowl. She couldn't believe this conversation. And she couldn't believe she was eating cold fried chicken and potato salad at three o'clock in the morning. She refilled her coffee cup.

"So, what you're saying is you won't help me, is that how I'm to read your response, Lizzie?"

Lizzie sighed. She'd been friends with the president for more years than she cared to remember. As women, they'd been through a lot during that time. Together they had been in the box, out of the box, and over the top of the box, always coming out the victors. "What kind of help are you asking for, Martine? If you're asking me to defend any of those Happy Campers, the answer is *no*. I'll tell you something else, I'd represent the madam *for free*. I think the Vigilantes will be of the same mind. Having said that, I must be dense because I don't know what it is you think either the Vigilantes or I can do."

"I know, I know, Lizzie. I'm out of my mind. To be honest, I didn't know who else to call. I guess I thought you would have a magic bullet of some kind. It just isn't time for the pardon yet. I'll keep my word, but I can't do it yet. Damn it, I just took office. I've never, ever broken my word, Lizzie, and you damn well know it. Christ, I'll probably be impeached within my first 180 days in office. Can you imagine what the guys on the other side of the aisle are going to do with this?"

Until then Martine Connor had sounded like an agitated old friend with a terrible problem, calling for help and advice. Suddenly, she was back to being the first female president of the United States.

"I'm sorry, Lizzie, for waking you and bombarding you with my problem. I understand where you are coming from. I'll deal with it some way, somehow. Go back to sleep, Lizzie. Good night."

Like she was really going to be able to go back to sleep. Lizzie wondered if she'd ever be able to sleep again. Right now all she wanted to do was call Cosmo. She looked at the clock. It was a little after midnight in Vegas, and Cosmo slept soundly. Morning would be time enough, as he was an early riser. Cosmo would talk her through her angst then—when he was bright and alert. Simply put, she didn't want to be responsible for Cosmo losing any sleep.

Lizzie wrapped the platter and bowls of food and put them back into the refrigerator. She couldn't believe she'd consumed the whole pot of coffee. She consoled herself with the fact that it was a small pot, with only four cups, and somehow the fourth cup always seemed to evaporate.

The kitchen clock over the doorway said it was 3:45. If she took a shower, dressed for the day, she could make a second pot of coffee and not feel guilty. She knew she would need the adrenaline rush coffee gave her when she called Big Pine Mountain. Lizzie looked around to make sure she was leaving her kitchen nice and tidy before she went back upstairs.

Maybe she should call Maggie Spritzer before she called Big Pine Mountain. Or better yet, maybe she should make two phone calls before she called Big Pine Mountain. Calling Jack Emery and Maggie Spritzer was the way to go, she thought. Both lived within a mile of her house, and maybe she could get a better fix on things if she agreed to meet them at one of their houses. She'd offer to bring the donuts and coffee. Now, that was a plan. She'd think it through while she showered. For some reason she did some of her best thinking while standing under a stream of hot water. A good long shower always left her with a clear head, and she usually came up with a solution before she got out to towel off.

She knew for a fact that Jack got up at five o'clock and was usually at Harry Wong's *dojo* to work out by six. Maggie liked to be in the office by six o'clock, six thirty at the latest.

Lizzie's mind raced as she ran through what she had scheduled for the day. She thought about what she could postpone, reschedule, or blow off totally. When she was satisfied in her own mind, she picked up the phone and called her secretary, knowing full well she wouldn't reach her. Lizzie left a voice mail and knew Sandy would take care of things the way Sandy always took care of her schedule the moment she opened the office.

Cosmo would have to wait.

Chapter 3

Lizzie couldn't believe her good luck when she found a parking space right in front of Jack Emery's house in Georgetown. And from the looks of things, Jack was up and moving around inside because the house was lit up from top to bottom. She looked to her left, three houses down, and could see that Maggie Spritzer was up and about, too, her house lit up just the way Jack's was.

Lizzie was out of her car a moment later, an enormous paper sackful of cinnamon buns and three huge cups of coffee in hand. She set down her purchases on the stoop, called Maggie, and said, "Jack's house. Now!" Then she rang Jack's doorbell.

Jack opened the door, took in the sack of sweets and the coffee. He looked at Lizzie, and said, "Oh, shit! What now? It's only quarter to six!"

"Leave the door open, Maggie is on the way," Lizzie said, heading toward Jack's kitchen, where she rummaged for a plate on which to set the buns. "Come on, Jack. You need to smile when you greet your guests. It's the only way to start the day. And, I brought breakfast! That alone should put a smile on your face." She was turning around to reach for a stack of napkins when Maggie breezed into the kitchen, her freckled face alight with questions. High heels in hand, she was in her stocking feet.

Maggie reached for a bun, rolled her eyes, and sat down. "Oooh, these are soooo good, and I need this right now. What's up?" she asked as she happily munched away.

"Honey, if you thought that little gig in Utah was Pulitzer material, wait till you hear what I have to tell you. Right now, right this minute, I can probably give you enough fodder for your paper for the entire year! Banner headlines for a solid month. You are absolutely going to love what I am about to tell you," Lizzie said, reaching for a bun she knew she didn't need. But she wanted it, and she never denied herself anything if she could help it. That was what life was all about in her opinion.

"What about me, Lizzie, am I going to love this?" Jack grumbled as he eyed the cinnamon buns and tried to exercise willpower. Finally, unable to resist the sugary treat, he snatched one and shoved it into his mouth. "I hate Starbucks coffee!"

"Oh, boo-hoo," Maggie said as she swigged at the strong coffee. "Tell us, Lizzie, all the little 'ifs,' 'ands,' and 'buts.' Don't leave anything out!"

"Guess who called me at three o'clock this morning?"

"Cosmo? He asked you to marry him!" Maggie said.

Lizzie shook her head. Maggie looked crestfallen, as did Lizzie.

"Charles? He's on his way back, and the girls are planning to flog him?" Jack suggested.

Lizzie shook her head again. "You'll never guess, so I'm going to tell you." She paused dramatically. "Martine Connor. *President* Martine Connor."

Jack's face lit up like a Christmas tree. "She's going to pardon the girls! She's coming through on her promise!"

"No! Not yet. She said she can't do it yet, but she will. I told her what the consequences would be if she reneged. No, she called asking for help. I turned her down on behalf of the Vigilantes because she's already running a tab with the Sisters. No freebies, ladies and gentlemen. I hope I wasn't out of line. I haven't even called the girls yet. I have to tell you, she made me a little angry."

"I don't think they'll fault you, I would have done the same thing," Maggie said as she bit into her third cinnamon bun. "The president made you *a little angry.* So what's the deal?"

"A scandal of mega proportions involving her brandnew administration. Actually, last night at Judge Leland's retirement party, I heard some lavatory gossip but wasn't able to follow through on it at the time. Then when I got home, Cosmo called, and, as luck would have it, he has a client who is tied to the scandal. He suggested that she consult one of the 'very good lawyers' he knows in D.C."

"Cosmo's in Vegas. How does that tie in to the president calling you in the middle of the night?" Jack asked as he contemplated a second cinnamon bun.

"What? What?" Maggie snarled.

Lizzie grinned. "It seems that our new president has an administration of perverts. It would also seem that a good many of them, like fifty or so, enrolled in the Happy Day Camp for some . . . unorthodox . . . uh . . . activities. It would appear that when Martine won the election, they, the perverts of the current administration, got carried away and had a little camp outing. Then they had another camp outing after Martine took the oath of office." She waited for a reaction, and when she saw only blank expressions, she said, "A brothel. Happy Day Camp is a brothel in Las Vegas. Actually, it's a little more than sixty miles from Vegas. As you know, prostitution is legal in Nevada in counties with fewer than 400,000 residents. However, when the madam was contacted to bring her dog-and-pony show to the nation's capital, she balked, but they, the perverts, convinced her and her girls that there would be no blowback. It appears they were wrong."

"Oh, shit!" Jack said.

"Wow! You were right, this is big stuff. Do you have names?" Maggie asked as she picked frosting from the remaining cinnamon bun. Jack slapped her hand away from it.

"I don't, but Cosmo does. The madam is on the run and she gave him her books, financial records, and cell phones for safekeeping. The administration is trying to contain the situation, but the other side of the aisle must have gotten downwind of it somehow, and they're going to blow it wide-open. I don't know when, but I have to assume very soon. She's going to end up being known as not only the first female president but, as Martine said, also she'll be the laughingstock of the free world. Actually, the whole world."

Maggie snorted. "They'll go after the madam, string her up, and the johns will lose face, their jobs, and go on with their lives. Half of them will probably end up as lobbyists or CEOs. That's how it usually works. Wait a damn minute here. Are you saying the president wants the Vigilantes to . . . cover for all those guys so they can keep their jobs and not embarrass her administration, meanwhile letting the madam get slammed into jail?"

"Yeah," Lizzie said.

"Well, damn, I think the girls will take this one on for free. But no way are they going to do what she wants, pardon or not. By 'books' do you mean Cosmo has the madam's little black books?" Maggie asked.

"Yes, and some of those clowns actually used their credit cards. The woman was no dummy, she made sure she got fingerprints of the whole bunch, and she's matched them up to the payments. The reason she's on the run is she was tipped off that this was going to go down. She didn't waste a minute. She sent her girls off to the far corners of the globe, and she's taken on a new identity. She also told Cosmo that copies of all the materials she gave him were on their way to the 'intended recipients'—and then she winked at him and gave him the *V* sign! So Cosmo thinks she might mean the Vigilantes! How she would know where to find the girls I have no clue. However, there is every possibility she knows Rena Gold. You remember Rena, who helped us with that little caper at the World Bank and then again in Vegas when things went sour there last year? After all, it is Vegas. Anything goes in Vegas, we all know that."

"What is the objective?" Jack asked in a jittery-sounding voice.

"What, Jack, are you so dense you can't figure it out?" Maggie asked as she drained the last of her coffee. "The madam wants the johns to be punished. It's as obvious as the nose on your face. She's the one who, in the end, will hang by her toenails. She'll be rotting in jail, and the politicians will be dining at the Jockey Club. Eventually they will all weasel their way back into some political arena. Think back to the D.C. Madam. She ended up dead, and you know there were some who said she did not take her own life. Did even one thing happen to her clients? I think not. Every single one of them is going on with his life, and she's dead. *D-E-A-D,* Jack."

"Cosmo said his client made mention of that, and those on her side of the fence said they do not believe she took her own life. But right now the D.C. Madam is not our problem. So, Jack, to answer your question, Cosmo's client wants the johns to be brought up on charges, and she wants jail time for them. Or, she wants them . . . *taken care of.* She has no intention of going to jail herself. She provided a service, the johns paid. That's her bottom line."

"And as women you agree?" Jack asked tightly.

"Well, yeah," Maggie drawled. "Guys who think they're above the law need to get brought down a peg or two. If

justice was doled out equally, I'm sure the madam, whoever she is, would take her punishment like any woman
would. Favoritism will not work in a case like this."

"And you don't think losing a job, maybe his family,
and his reputation is enough punishment for the john?"

Maggie got up, reached for the last cinnamon bun, and
smashed it in Jack's face. "Does that answer your question?" she snarled.

"You're vicious," Jack snarled in return as he licked at
the frosting smeared across his lips. He then dunked his
head under the kitchen faucet and dried off with a length
of paper towels. "All I did was ask a question."

"Yeah, well, it was the wrong question," Maggie snarled
a second time.

Maggie turned to Lizzie, and said, "I'm on it. When
can you get me the names in the black books?"

"Hold on here, ladies. Isn't that violating the attorney-
client privilege?"

Lizzie smiled. Jack cringed. "She gave it up, Jack. We
have permission to run with this. Cosmo said she's one
tough lady, and she 'is not going to roll over and play
dead for a bunch of dick-dead men.' Those are her words,
in writing. She okayed, *in writing*, for Cosmo to do whatever he had to do."

"Okay, okay," Jack mumbled. "What's the plan? Just
so you know, if the girls jump on this, I'm not budging
without a plan. I know I'm speaking for Harry when I say
we need a plan."

Lizzie and Maggie both nodded. "I think a meeting is
called for," Lizzie said. "I have plans to fly to Vegas this
weekend. If you all want to arrange a meeting on the mountain, I can attend via webcam. If there's any way I can
arrange for a meeting with our new client, I want to jump
on it. The only problem with that is that we have no way

to contact her. Cosmo said she's gone to ground and will call in from time to time. I'm thinking she's already out of the country since Cosmo said her money is offshore. That's where she'll head. Always follow the money. You know that's the first rule. Maggie?"

"Hey, I'm on it. The minute you get me those names, we'll start raising some hell. This city will tremble. I can see the headlines now!"

"Guess my work here is done, then," Lizzie said. "You'll bring Harry up-to-date, Jack?" Not bothering to wait for a response, she moved on to Maggie. "Stay in touch, and I'll call the mountain and clue everyone in. Still no word on Charles, I guess?"

Both Maggie and Jack shook their heads.

All three left Jack's house, and waited while Jack locked his door. Maggie headed toward her house, where her car was parked. Jack said his was parked on the next block and started to jog toward it before Lizzie could offer him a ride.

It was raining, a steady, heavy rain that would flood the roads in Georgetown within a few hours.

Lizzie slid into her Porsche and was at the end of the street before Jack reached his car. She gave a light tap on the horn. She could see Jack raise his hand to show he heard her good-bye.

Thirty minutes later, Jack breezed into Harry Wong's *dojo* just as his early-morning class was disbanding. He screwed up his face so Harry would know something was up before he decked him for being late. Harry Wong was a pain in his ass.

The love-hate relationship between Harry and Jack boiled up, as it always did.

"I hope you're going to tell me you have a raging case

of shingles and a huge boil on your ass, and that's why you're late."

"Sorry, my little buttered muffin, but the only thing I can complain about this morning is a hangnail. Listen, something has come up. Let's have some of that shitty green tea you think has miraculous powers, and I'll tell you all about it." Sensing a smart-ass comeback, Jack said, "Yoko said to tell you she loves you." Any time Jack wanted to bring Harry to his knees, he would throw Yoko into the mix. Yoko was the only person who could put the fear of God into one Harry Wong. Jack delighted in seeing his best friend in the whole world crumble at his feet.

"Eat shit, Jack. And I'm not afraid of Yoko. I love her," Harry blustered weakly.

"Tsk-tsk," Jack said, clucking his tongue. "Listen up, and don't say a damn word until I'm finished. Your reward at the end will be me telling you we're going to head for the mountain tomorrow afternoon. You ready, you miserable excuse for a human being?"

When Jack finished regaling the martial arts expert, Harry looked at him like he was crazy. "Tell me you're jerking my chain! Please, Jack."

"Nah, it's for real. I tried protesting, but the two of them," he said, referring to Lizzie and Maggie, "damn near castrated me right there in the kitchen. The knife block was close to Maggie. My blood ran cold, I can tell you that," Jack said dramatically.

Harry was so into blood and guts and dismemberment, especially when he thought it could be Jack's, that he actually looked mellow at the moment.

"You know the girls are going to be on this like white on rice."

"Yeah, I know," Harry mumbled. He slurped from his tiny cup of green tea as he waited for whatever else was going to tumble from Jack's lips.

"There's no plan. As yet," Jack added hastily.

"No plan!" Harry screeched.

"Easy, Harry. I'm not even sure the girls know about it yet. Lizzie is calling them. We're going up tomorrow so that means we'll be there to uh . . . uh . . . help with the plan. Read my lips, Harry. *We-will-have-a-plan!*"

"That's what you said the last time, Jack," Harry said ominously. "Your cockamamie plan was a truckload of pumpkins."

"It worked, didn't it?"

"Just shut the hell up, Jack. I need to think about this. I hate guys who can only get it by paying for it," Harry muttered as he paced. That is, Harry thought he was pacing, but he was actually stomping around in his bare feet, powerful feet that could kill a man with one little kick, one big toe placed in the wrong place. Harry was a killer. Jack was glad his "archenemy" was one of the good guys.

"You done thinking yet?" Jack demanded a minute later. In the blink of an eye he was on the floor, looking up at his wiry friend.

"Yeah. Serves you right. You know better than to talk to me when I'm thinking." Harry reached down for Jack's hand to pull him to his feet. And then Harry was on the floor, with Jack straddling his chest. "Say it!"

"Up yours! You're a wuss, Emery!"

They went at it for a good fifteen minutes until both men collapsed, with no real winner. Huffing and puffing, both of them got to their feet, their eyes wary until Jack roared, "Enough! That was my workout for the day."

Harry extended his hand. "Pretty good, Emery. In ten years, you might be almost as good as I am."

"My ass. It was a draw. You want to drive tomorrow or should I?"

"We'll make better time on my cycle. Your call."

"Whatever gets us there the quickest," Jack said.

"Then it's the Ducati," Harry said, all smiles and sunshine.

"You are a piece of work, Harry Wong."

"You know, Jack, you are absolutely right. I am. And you are one damn lucky son of a bitch to have me as a friend."

Jack knew there was no way he could ever win an argument with Harry, so he let it drop. "Listen, I have to get to court. How about calling Bert and filling him in? Ask him if he wants to go to the mountain with us. I'm not sure about Maggie or Ted. I'm thinking they're going to be rather busy in the next few days. You know how Maggie loves a good headline."

"Okay, I'll call Bert. You want some tea to go?"

"What? You gonna slip something in it so I fall asleep in court?" Jack asked in pretended outrage.

"Never happen."

"Yeah, yeah, yeah."

Chapter 4

If spring was about to announce itself or was just around the corner, as the newscasters phrased it, it wasn't evident on Big Pine Mountain. Six inches of new snow carpeted the compound and, while it was late in the afternoon, it was still light enough to see that fresh snow was cascading downward.

Inside the main building a monster fire roared in the huge fieldstone fireplace, and the scent of pinecones that had been used to start the fire wafted about the dining room.

Remnants of the early dinner remained on the table as Alexis Thorne poured fresh coffee into everyone's cup except Yoko's.

Nikki Quinn poked at the food on her plate, which had been barely touched. "I think this is probably one of the worst dinners I've ever eaten." Her comment wasn't said in anger. It was merely a statement of fact. No one, not even Isabelle, who had prepared dinner, took offense. "Cupcakes are not my dessert of choice," Nikki continued in the same flat voice.

"What do you call this?" Kathryn asked as she moved the mess around on her plate for a better look. It was a known fact that Kathryn had a reputation for eating anything that wasn't moving. "I've lost eight pounds since

Christmas, and these cupcakes taste like sawdust," she grumbled.

"It's called hash. You just throw everything in a pot and mix it up. Don't blame me for the cupcakes, blame Little Debbie. They were frozen," Isabelle said in a voice that was just as void and flat as Nikki's and Kathryn's.

Yoko sat quietly as she nibbled on a rice cake, a cup of tea in front of her. She stared at the food on her plate, and finally commented, "It looks like a pile of dog poop."

Myra stared into the flames, her back stiff and straight.

Annie looked down at her empty plate, wondering what all the fuss was about. Food was sustenance. As long as she didn't have to cook whatever it was they were eating, she never complained. Well, she decided, there was a first time for everything, and this was going to be one of them.

She stood up and banged the stout wooden table with her fist to gain everyone's attention. "Enough!" she roared in a voice that would have ricocheted over the mountain if the door had been open. "I've had it with all of you! And that includes you, Myra!"

Myra snapped to attention, wondering what was going on. She eyed Annie warily. "What now?" she asked wearily.

"What now? What now? Earth to Myra!" Annie bellowed. "Did you hear what I just said? In case you didn't, I said I had enough. Either you all pull it together, or, as soon as it stops snowing, I am out of here. I'll take my chances that Avery Snowden can smuggle me somewhere safe. You can all sit up here and rot, vegetate, fall off the mountain, I don't give a damn. I am not going to spend one more day up here listening to all of you moan and groan and complain.

"You are the worst offender, Myra. You, all by yourself, set the tone for these young women. Because you're miserable, they think they have to be miserable. You're all like a pack of wet-haired cats.

"Just because Charles isn't here doesn't mean it's the end of the world. Is he coming back? I don't know. But if he does, I think we should take a vote to see if we want him to stay. Is that *ever* going to happen? I have no idea. In the meantime, time does not stand still. We didn't do terribly bad out in Utah even though we didn't have a plan. That won't happen again. Yet we pulled it off. And hopefully, we learned from our mistakes."

"We have cabin fever. Winters up here are the pits," Kathryn said defensively.

"They weren't the pits when Charles was here," Myra said.

"Maybe they weren't the pits for you, but they were for the rest of us," Nikki said. "All we can do is read, watch TV, eat, and shovel snow. So, don't blow smoke in our direction. You need to let it go and join in. Otherwise, I'm going to follow Annie's lead, leave the mountain, and take my chances."

The others murmured agreement. Myra stood up and walked over to the fireplace, where she held out her hands for warmth even though the room was stifling hot. She knew Annie and the girls were right. It was time to move on without Charles. She turned around, and observed, "Annie and Nikki are right. I'm sorry, I really am. I just . . . It's hard to turn your back on a lifetime of love and devotion that . . . that wasn't returned. I think my pity party has just come to an end. I can't promise I won't have a relapse, and if I do, Annie, you get the first shot at pushing me off the mountain."

"Now that's the Myra I know and love," Annie said happily, clapping her hands. "Let's clean up this mess and get on with it. I have something to tell you all. And the reason I'm the one who is going to be doing the telling is because as usual I am the one who answered the damn phone. And, no, it is not about Charles, so don't even go there. What do you think of that?"

"What? What?" Myra and the girls chorused.

Annie crossed her arms over her chest as she looked pointedly at the dinner table. The women scurried to clear away the remains of the dinner no one but Annie had eaten. Only when Annie heard the hum of the dishwasher did she relax and sit down.

"Tell us," Yoko said.

"Weather permitting, even not permitting, we are due to have guests tomorrow evening. I'm not sure who all is coming but I know for sure Harry, Jack, and Bert will be here. I expect we'll know more later. Having said that, someone had better come up with a menu that three strapping men will like."

"What's going on? Are we going to be planning a mission? Does someone need our help?" Alexis asked, her dark eyes shining with excitement.

"Yes and yes. And it came through Mr. Cricket in Las Vegas, who more or less turned it over to Lizzie, who then got in touch with Maggie and Jack early this morning, at which point Jack brought Harry and Bert into it. I don't have too many details but Maggie said we are absolutely going to *LOVE* this mission."

"That's it? That's all she said? Come on, Annie, I know Maggie told you more than that," Nikki said.

Satisfied that she had everyone's attention, Annie leaned toward the table. "Well, she did say a *wee bit more.*"

Suddenly Myra was on her feet and standing behind Annie's chair. "And that *wee bit more* would be *what?*" she asked, wrapping her hands around Annie's throat.

"The new president wants our help because her brand-new administration is full of guys who like to hire hook-ers. Something about the Happy Day Camp outside Vegas, which is a brothel!" Annie gasped.

"Oh, good Lord," Myra said, making her way to her chair where she sat down with a loud *thump*.

"Madams and johns?" Kathryn asked, her eyes as big as saucers.

"Right down to camp counselors, and I will leave it to your imagination as to who those beautiful, long-legged 'counselors' were. The camp boys are members of the administration, congressmen, senators, a couple of ambassadors. Name it, and they all went to camp. Not once, but twice!" Annie said happily as she looked around at the shocked faces of her Sisters.

"How long have you known about this?" Myra asked ominously.

"Just never you mind, Myra Rutledge. You were so busy feeling sorry for yourself, you didn't deserve to know. Now that you're back among the living, it's okay for you to get the whole scoop," Annie said imperiously. "We need to start making a plan."

"What did you mean when you said the prez wants our help?" Nikki asked.

"Lizzie turned her down. Reminded her that she was running a debit where we're concerned. I'm not absolutely sure about this, but I think the president wanted us to help the Happy Campers. *The men!*" Annie said, her disgust apparent in her voice.

"When pigs fly," Kathryn snapped. "I vote *no* on that, but I'm willing to go after them. I guess the president's plan as it now stands would be to pin it on the madam and let the campers off the hook. *Not!*"

Nikki nervously tapped her fingers on the table, her brow furrowed. "If we don't help the president, what will that do to the pardon she promised?" she asked.

Annie shook her head. "I don't know. For her even to

ask is something I'm having trouble comprehending. From what Maggie said, Lizzie set her straight."

"I remember reading about the D.C. Madam last year," Yoko said. "She died not too long ago. There seemed to be a good deal of speculation that she might not have committed suicide, which was the story they put out there. I do not recall reading anything after that about her . . . uh . . . clients."

Kathryn scoffed. "Those creeps always walk away. The worst thing they have to deal with is their spouses. They don't care what their families have to go through. So they get divorces and move on to the next set of bimbos. What's wrong with this picture?"

"Does that mean the madam is going to be our client?" Myra asked.

"Noooo, Myra, I don't think so. I think this is a freebie on our part. I'm all for it if that's the way it turns out. We have more than enough of a balance in our trust account for a freebie," Annie said.

"Then who is the client?" Isabelle asked.

"No client. We're just going to avenge the madam and make the men pay. If the madam turns out to be Lizzie's client, she's in good hands. Why should the madam swing in the wind while those damn guys walk away with no jail time? The madam is the one who will get sentenced. Look, I'm not saying I approve of prostitution because I don't, even if it's legal in Nevada and is the oldest profession in the world. I think when we see the list, and I do believe there is a list of the madam's clients, we'll make the decision to do whatever we decide based on all the families that are involved, possibly ruined, by men who couldn't keep their pants zipped. Let's see a show of hands if you agree with me or not."

Every hand shot in the air.

"That makes it unanimous," Annie said happily.

"That's it! You don't know anything else?" asked Myra.

"No, I don't. I'm sure by tomorrow we'll know all we need to know. We can't do anything anyway until we have *the list*. For now, we need to clean up from dinner, then we have to shovel snow from the cable car to the door, so let's get the menu thing wrapped up. There will be no more stuff dumped in one pot and called 'hash.' We have a fully stocked freezer and larder. I want to see menus. Like *now!*"

The Sisters fell to it as they squabbled about what vegetable went with what meat and which wine was the one Charles would have served. It took an hour before everyone agreed to a week's worth of menus that passed with Annie's and Myra's approval.

"What's for dinner tomorrow with our guests?" Kathryn asked.

Nikki looked down at all the scribbling on her legal pad. "Leg of lamb, mint jelly, little potatoes, gravy, pearl onions with the last of our snap peas, butter biscuits, salad, and a peach cobbler. We have two wines, a red and a white, that will work. Before anyone can ask, I'm cooking tomorrow, and I am not cleaning up."

"I'll clean up," Kathryn said.

The others said they would pitch in.

The Sisters were unified once again. Annie realized that it felt good.

Annie nodded in Myra's direction. She was happy to see that Myra's eyes were clear and focused. Her expression clearly said that the two of them were back on track. Annie nodded to show she understood and accepted Myra's silent apology.

* * *

"Close the door, guys," Maggie said to her star reporter and lover, Ted Robinson, and her star photographer, Joe Espinosa.

As a rule Maggie did business with her door wide-open. Everyone on the floor knew that when the door was closed it was worth their lives even to speculate as to what was going on behind it.

"This must be important since it's quitting time," Ted said as he tried to gauge Maggie's mood.

"About as important as it gets. We have a live one this time. I can tell you what I know, but I can't give you names. Yet. Listen up."

Maggie was like a runaway horse until she wound down and looked at her two *primo* employees. "I know this is a second Pulitzer. I can feel it. I can smell it. Hell, I *own* it! So, make me a promise, guys."

Both men looked at Maggie, and solemnly intoned, "I promise," in unison. Maggie sighed, knowing in the end they would deliver because they were the best of the best.

"I hate to ask this, Maggie, but whose side are we on?" Ted asked.

Maggie stiffened and locked her gaze with Ted's. "Whose side do *you* think you're on, Ted?"

Ted looked at Espinosa. "Your side, boss, which—if I can read you correctly—is the madam's," Ted said, opting to take the high road.

"I knew that," Espinosa said airily. He already felt sorry for the men they were about to start tracking.

"Good choice. I want hard proof, two sources, every little thing on background on every one of those miserable creatures. If it ever comes to court, the madam will be represented by Lizzie, with Cosmo Cricket in the background, but that is not our concern right now. Are we clear on that?"

Ted and Espinosa both nodded, their faces serious as

they tried to imagine what was going to go down and how it was going to work out.

"I want sterling headlines. I want impeccable sources. I want material that deserves to be above the fold. I want people standing in line waiting to buy the paper, and I want special editions with one-of-a-kind reporting and dynamite pictures. I want my competitors to hate the hell out of me and both of you. We're number one, and I want to stay at number one! Tell me you're going to make it happen. I have people straining at the leash waiting for your answer. Oh, yes, a really nice bonus and a five-day vacation in Hawaii will be your reward. It's okay to call it a bribe, but I'm tossing it out there."

"We'll make it happen, Maggie," Ted said.

"Yeah," Espinosa said.

"You're still standing here! Move!"

"I thought we were going out to dinner," Ted grumbled.

"*I'm* going out to dinner. You're going to work. Go, already!"

Maggie knew her dinner was going to be a street vendor's hot dog, which she would eat on the run. She took the thought as a lucky omen. Hot dogs and scoops equaled a Pulitzer.

Chapter 5

Cosmo Cricket lumbered out to his state-of-the-art kitchen, where he made coffee. While he waited for it to drip through, he walked back down the hall to the front door to pick up the morning paper, which had been shoved through the mail slot. He carried it back to the kitchen, his thoughts on Lizzie Fox and her arrival later in the day. Right then, right that minute, right that second, that nanosecond, all he could think of was Elizabeth Fox and how good it was going to feel when she was snuggled in his arms. Whatever news the paper held was of absolutely no interest to him. That wasn't usually the case. Normally, he read it from cover to cover, line by line.

But Cosmo Cricket was a creature of habit, and his habit was to get up, brush his teeth, shower, shave, and have his first cup of coffee while he skimmed the headlines of the *Las Vegas Review-Journal* before he got down to serious reading.

Cosmo picked up a pair of reading glasses off the kitchen counter. It made him nuts that he had to wear the eye-cheaters, but when Elizabeth said he looked like a forbidding, crack-the-whip law professor, he bought a couple dozen pair and had them everywhere. He had three pairs in his briefcase, four or five pairs in the office, and a

pair in every room in his house, even in all three bathrooms.

Glasses in place, Cosmo checked the weather. Cool
and dry. He moved on to the horoscope section, read his
daily blurb and Elizabeth's, too. He smiled. Perfect. He'd
die before he would admit, even to Elizabeth, that he reli-
giously read his daily horoscope.

As he sipped coffee, which seemed exceptionally hot
that morning, he flipped the pages of the newspapers.
Iraq, Afghanistan, National Guard from somewhere going
someplace. Like he could do anything about it. A flood in
Florida from some kind of tropical storm that dropped
twenty inches of rain. Nothing he could do about that either except to stay home and out of Florida. A woman
was just getting out of jail even though her missing child
hadn't been found. What kind of mother was she for re-
fusing to tell what she knew, and what kind of authority
would let her out of jail to begin with? Some people didn't
deserve to have children. His own parents would have
turned the world upside down if he'd gone missing. A
crane collapse someplace in New York City. No injuries
this time around.

Cosmo turned the page, looked at the kitchen clock.
Seven o'clock. Ten o'clock in Washington, D.C. In six
hours Elizabeth would be at his side. He could hardly
wait. The big problem was, what was he going to do during the six-hour wait? He replenished his coffee and sat
back down. He almost turned the page until he realized
he hadn't yet scanned the page he was on. It was just a
small article and he almost missed it. He bolted upright,
his coffee forgotten as he read the short piece.

> Local woman, 44-year-old
> Lily Flowers, crashed her Honda
> Prelude on the Cajon Pass last

evening as she was leaving Las Vegas when the front tire of her car blew out. The air bag did not deploy, and authorities said Ms. Flowers was killed on impact when the Prelude struck a guardrail. The investigating state trooper said a hotel reservation in San Bernardino was found in the woman's wallet in the console of the car, which leads them to believe San Bernardino was her destination.

Motorists who stopped to render aid said the woman was not driving at an excessive rate of speed. The trooper said there were no signs of drug usage or alcohol involved. Authorities are currently searching for next of kin. Anyone with information concerning Ms. Flowers is asked to call the sheriff's office.

"Son of a bitch!" The words exploded out of Cosmo's mouth like bullets. Well, now he knew what he was going to be doing for the next six hours, since he knew for a fact that there was no next of kin to notify concerning Lily Flowers's untimely demise.

Suddenly Cosmo was like a caged lion as he stormed his way around the kitchen, the floor rumbling and creaking as he stomped about. Accident? Or a crash made to look like an accident?

Lily Flowers had struck him as a woman who had her stuff together in one sock, or rather one giant handbag.

Single-minded, with tunnel vision. Her only objective was to get away to a safe place as soon as possible. Which meant she had to have had a plan in place, which she had indeed verified. Some plan, since she was now dead. She would have had her car checked from top to bottom, down to the tires. He could almost guarantee it. She would have been traveling light, no baggage to speak of to drag her down and certainly nothing in her purse to incriminate her. She probably had a small suitcase or one carry bag. He didn't know all that much about women, but he assumed that Lily Flowers would buy whatever she needed when she got to the first leg of her destination, which apparently was San Bernardino. From San Bernardino it was anyone's guess where she had intended to go. Somewhere far from American shores was his first thought. He knew in his gut that Lily Flowers had been a woman with a long-range plan.

"Crap!"

Cosmo tried to remember what exactly it was that he had secured in his safe when Lily Flowers came to see him. He knew better than anyone that you always followed the money trail. He wondered what he would find when he got there. Nothing good, he was sure.

Cosmo spent another ten minutes tidying up the kitchen before he poured the last of his coffee into a traveling cup, grabbed his briefcase, and left for the office.

The minute Cosmo got there, he called his secretary into the office and rattled off a list of things she was to do ASAP. "Put everything on hold. This takes precedence. I want to know the name of the trooper, any witnesses, and where they took the body. Call a funeral home, make arrangements. At the moment, I'm thinking cremation." Cosmo blinked. Where did that decision come from? Didn't he want an autopsy? Then cremation? Or did he want a burial? What would he do with Lily Flowers's ashes? She had struck him as a person who would want to be scattered to the four winds. Nameless. He had no idea where that insight came from either. How could he make such an important decision based on the few minutes he'd spent in Lily's company? He realized he wasn't entirely comfortable with that decision, so he rescinded the last part of his instructions temporarily, pending further investigation.

Cosmo closed and locked his office door, but not before he told his secretary not to bother him and to cancel a meeting he'd scheduled for ten o'clock. "And don't put any calls through either until I open this door," was the parting shot over his shoulder.

Cosmo opened the safe and carried everything Lily Flowers had given him to his desk. Did he really think there would be a clue among the books and ledgers that would give him some indication as to who she really was and where she was going to start a new life? He convinced himself that she would go wherever her money was or at least in close proximity to it. Of course, she wasn't planning on ending up dead, so maybe she hadn't left any clues for him. He winced at the thought.

Cosmo sat down and started going through the pile of books. He was still at it at noon when his stomach started to rumble. He leaned back in his custom-crafted rocking chair, removed his glasses, and rubbed at his eyes. He was three checkbooks and one little black book down, and he hadn't even made a dent in what needed to be done. There were no brokerage statements, which surprised him. One thing he knew for certain was that Lily Flowers, or whoever she was, had been a hell of a businesswoman. Her business accounts tallied to the penny. Her personal checking accounts under all her various aliases also tallied. Expenditures, nothing more. Everything looked normal. She paid her bills on time. She ordinarily didn't use credit cards even though she had several. Every so often a charge would appear, along with a bill, just to keep the accounts activated. Apparel stores, drugstores, and, once in a while, she charged a restaurant tab. Every bill was current and up-to-date. A record of utilities being canceled under all her identities was stapled into a neat packet. Two apartment leases had been canceled and paid to date under the names of Crystal Clark and Ann Marie Anders. The two houses in the names of Lily Flowers and Caroline Summers were owned free and clear, the utilities cut off. Property taxes had been paid ahead for five years on both properties. Did she do all this herself or did she use an accounting firm?

Cosmo shook his head. The lady had it going on. She walked away, believing she'd tied up all her loose ends. But, she'd had the good sense to come to him and leave all her records. He wondered if she had a suspicion something would happen to her. That alone had to mean she trusted him as her lawyer to do whatever would have to be done if something did occur. And now she was dead.

Just how wealthy was Lily Flowers?

What was it his mother used to say in instances like this? Oh, yes. *"This is a fine kettle of fish."* His father would have said, *"Grab that bull by the horns and wrestle him to the ground."* What fish or a bull had to do with anything was beyond Cosmo's comprehension.

Cosmo reached for his glasses and went back to work. Over and over he mumbled, "Who were you, Lily Flowers?"

It was one o'clock, almost time to break for lunch, when he carried one stack of check registers and books back to the safe. When he returned to his desk he shifted the remaining pile of black leather books, and that's when he saw that what he'd thought was another book was actually a case with a laptop inside. "Ahhh," he said happily.

* * *

Twenty-four hundred miles away in the nation's capital, Jack Emery parked in front of Harry Wong's *dojo*. Harry and Bert were waiting for him at the curb, small duffel bags at their feet. One look at Harry told Jack the martial arts expert was pissed that they weren't taking his Ducati. "Forget it, Harry. Get your ass in here and enjoy the scenery. Obviously, three people cannot ride on one motorcycle. You just sit there and plot my death, that will give you something to do while Bert and I talk about normal things like women, baseball, women, money or our lack of it, women and women."

"Your mistake, Jack, was putting me in the backseat. All I have to do is lean forward, extend my index finger, and you are toast. Before Bert can lean over to try to help you, his head will explode. So, sit back, drive, and enjoy the ride," Harry snarled good-naturedly.

"Harry, you are one ugly, cantankerous, evil, did I mention ugly, ungrateful son of a bitch! I'm the brother you never had, the brother you love with all your heart and soul, the brother you would die for. Where is all this negativity coming from? I'm doing you a tremendous favor by driving you to the mountain so you can see the love of your life. You will arrive looking like the avenging saint that you are, not some bedraggled, homeless derelict riding a motorcycle. Women don't care if it's a Ducati or not. They only want you to smell nice, be well groomed, and not be barefooted. I'm saving you from disgrace. Please apologize for your bad behavior." Jack risked a glance in the rearview mirror. It looked like Harry was going into a trance. He wondered what it meant.

"I think he said for you to kiss his ass," Bert cackled.

"Some other time," Jack said.

"I do have a bit of gossip if anyone cares to hear about it," Bert said.

"Shame on you! Since when have we been reduced to listening to gossip?" Jack asked. "As the director of the FBI, you should be above such . . . such shenanigans. What? Don't leave anything out. Harry thrives on gossip."

"What is it?" Harry demanded, coming out of his trance. He had to admit he did love juicy gossip, especially if it involved someone he knew. More so if it was someone he disliked.

"Alexis and Joe Espinosa text each other all the time!" When there was no noticeable reaction to this information, Bert carried on. "And Isabelle is mooning over that guy she socked in the eye in Vegas last year. Maggie Spritzer told Ted who told Espinosa who then told me that Isabelle asked Maggie to ask her hacker friend Abner Tookus to try and get a handle on the guy who went to the Caymans. She even has a name, not that the schmuck would be using his real name. She even went so far as to ask Maggie if she could hire a private dick to track him down. What do you think of that?"

"If that's the best you can do, I'm dumping you out of this car right now. Harry and I know all that, don't we, bro? Well, to be honest here, we didn't know the part about Isabelle and the dick or Abner."

"Nobody likes a smart-ass," Bert said.

"I was hoping for like . . . you know, *news*. Are you telling me the FBI is suddenly buttoned-up? What's coming out of the rumor mill?"

At last they were down to male talk. "Shit like you wouldn't believe. The whole damn town is hunkering down. Big stuff going on, but no one is talking out loud. Lots and lots of whispers. Hell, I made seven trips to the White House this week. Ain't good, boys." Bert's voice dropped to a hushed whisper even though there was no one in the car to hear him but Jack and Harry. "I heard *in the White House* several staffers whispering, and since I have such

keen hearing, I didn't have to try too hard to listen. The
scuttlebutt is one of two things. The dumb-ass money seems
to be on the Vigilantes coming to town as per someone's
request and the smart money is on the Vigilantes coming
to town of their own accord, which means a red alert is
going out.

"And, are you ready for this? I've heard resignations
are flooding the president's office, but I can't confirm
who and why. If I did know and told you, I'd have to kill
you."

"That's pretty funny," Harry said from his perch in the
backseat. "I don't doubt for a minute that you could take
Jack on, but you'd be dead before you could lay a finger
on me."

Bert knew it was true, so he didn't belabor the point.

"So why were you at the White House seven times this
week?"

It took Bert so long to respond, Jack had to prod him.

"Something kind of strange. Seems there is this woman
in Las Vegas named Crystal Clark who runs a cathouse
out there. It's legal, as you know. The Las Vegas Field Office was getting ready to put a tail on her, but she up and
disappeared. My guy out there said she did it like magic.
One minute she was there, then poof, she was gone. The . . .
employees are all gone. Even the maintenance and
groundskeepers—gone, with the exception of one old
guy. He said he was paid through the end of the month,
and he didn't take money for no work. No trace whatso-
ever. Now, here's where it gets a little . . . *sticky*. Somehow or other Cosmo Cricket's name came up at the White
House."

Harry unbuckled his seat belt and leaned forward.
"Are you telling us this woman's disappearance is tied in
to our visit to the mountain and your visits to the White
House? Lizzie is not going to like Cricket's name coming

up on this coast, especially at the White House. Jesus, you aren't telling us Cricket was that woman's attorney, are you?"

Bert's silence was all the confirmation Harry and Jack needed.

"Buckle up, Harry," Jack told him. For once, Harry didn't argue. He leaned back, buckled up, and closed his eyes as he tried to make sense out of what Bert had just said.

Keeping his eyes on the road, Jack chewed on his lower lip. Ten minutes later he finally had his thoughts in some kind of order. "Did you warn Lizzie or Cricket?"

"Not yet. But I have to go to Vegas tomorrow. Don't worry, you two don't have to leave with me. You have the whole weekend. Lucky stiffs. I already made arrangements for a car to be left at the Shell station down the road from our drop-off point. In fact, it should be in place when we get there. I'm going to want to check that out before I go up the mountain."

"Can you keep a lid on the Vegas part, Bert?" Jack asked.

"I can try, but you know I can't really interfere. It's all got to look on the up-and-up. My guys out there are sharp. I mean like *razor-sharp*. They're all seasoned pros."

"C'mon, Bert, Vegas is buttoned-up, FBI or not. Cricket's got the inside track, and those people out there are not going to open up to anyone, not even the FBI."

"Yeah, I know," Bert growled. "That guy Cricket is something else."

Harry chirped up from the backseat. "Put him together with Lizzie, and you have a stick of dynamite with a lit fuse. As you well know, they are now *as one*."

"You just *had* to say that, didn't you, Harry?" Bert growled again.

"Forewarned is forearmed," Harry said smugly.

Jack took his eyes off the road for a second to look at Harry via the rearview mirror. His stomach crunched into a knot at his friend's serene expression. Harry was up to something, but Jack knew he'd never know what that something was until Harry wanted him to know.

"Maybe we need to get off all this serious shit and have a little sing-along," Jack said. "When we were kids, my mother made us sing so we'd shut up and not fight in the backseat. It never worked, though."

"Then why did you bring it up?" Harry murmured.

"To have something to say because you are scaring the shit out of me, that's why," Jack said. "What are you think-ing?"

"Nothing. My mind is a total blank. I'm traveling cos-mically to other parts of the universe, and the universe has no place for bullshit. Now, shut the hell up and drive."

"Yes, sir," Jack said, saluting smartly.

Bert hunkered down in his seat and clamped his lips shut.

For the next three hours no one said a word. When he couldn't take the silence any longer, Jack slipped an Eric Clapton CD into the player and, like Harry, transported himself someplace else until they arrived at their destina-tion at the Shell gas station.

Jack watched from the car as Bert checked out the dull gray Ford sitting at the far end of the station. He watched as Bert reached up under the left rear fender and with-drew a key in a metal magnetic box. He shoved it in the pocket of his jacket, then loped back to Jack's car.

"Aren't you going to park this buggy?" Bert asked. "I thought the plan was to park here and make our way to the base of the mountain."

"No. We're driving to the base. I know where to . . .

stash this buggy. It's too damn cold to hike from here to there. Get in. Harry, call Yoko and tell her to send the cable car down. By the time we get there all we have to do is step in and, voilà, we're among friends."

Harry was speaking into his cell before Jack could finish what he was saying.

A satisfied look could be seen on Harry's face. "Yoko said they have a ton of snow on the mountain. She said they are looking for three strong backs to man the shovels." He cackled at the expressions on Jack's and Bert's faces.

After they hid the car, Bert started grousing about how much he hated the cable car. "I don't like dangling thousands of feet in midair. In daylight, you feel like you have a fighting chance should something go wrong, but at times like this, you're at the night's mercy. Hell, we won't even know if something is wrong till it's all over. That's if we don't plummet down and aren't dead."

"Shut up, Bert. Nothing is going to happen. Don't jinx us," Jack said as he flapped his arms for warmth. "C'mon, let's go," he said, jogging in place.

Fifteen minutes later the three friends stepped from the cable car to a rousing welcome. Flashlights skittered about as the women waved them for additional illumination. A light snow was starting to fall.

Laughs, kisses, and hugs were the order of the day, with Isabelle announcing the late-dinner menu as they all trooped through the knee-high snow. They all stomped their feet on the wide plank porch, then removed their shoes and boots. All three men sniffed appreciatively as Annie held open the door.

Two hours later, when dinner was over, Myra and Annie offered to do the cleanup so the "young people" could go off and do whatever they were going to do.

"Think of it as a free night," Myra said. "We'll meet here for breakfast at six sharp since Bert has to leave."

"The youngsters," as Annie called the little group, bundled up, and, with a lot of laughing and shouting, ran outdoors into the new-falling snow.

Left alone, Annie and Myra looked at one another. "I think, Myra, the two of us should have a . . . little snort. I'm not saying we should get schnockered or anything like that. I'm just saying we should have a little libation. What say you?"

"I say *yes*," Myra replied, getting out two squat cut-crystal glasses that felt like they weighed a pound each. "Let's get right to it, Annie. Skip the ice, the club soda, or whatever you were going to dilute this fine liquor with. Fine whiskey should be consumed the way it comes out of the bottle."

Myra looked so adamant, Annie could feel her eyebrows shoot upward.

"This . . . uh, very fine whiskey is 100 proof. Are you sure, Myra? One glass of this very fine whiskey could very well land us on our very fine respective asses."

"And this concerns you, Annie?" Myra asked as she poured generously into the crystal tumblers.

Annie looked hard at the amber liquid that threatened to spill over the top of the tumbler. "Maybe we should clean up before we start to . . . uh . . . party."

"I'm thinking maybe we shouldn't. I hate cleaning up. You don't like it either, Annie. It's a messy job and a few hours later you have to do it all over again. I think we should requisition those hard plastic plates and throw-away utensils. Why aren't you sampling this fine liquor, Annie?" Myra asked as she took a long gulp from her glass.

Annie pretended not to see the tears rolling down Myra's cheeks.

"This is quite smooth," Annie gasped as she took a robust drink. "Do we have any cigarettes?"

"We don't smoke, Annie. Charles smokes once in a while, so there might be some in one of these drawers. I suppose we could smoke one if we didn't inhale. Smoking is not good for you. The surgeon general says so. Ah, here are some," Myra said as she triumphantly held up a crumpled package of cigarettes from one of the kitchen drawers. "Since we don't smoke, we won't know if they're stale or not. Fire up, Annie."

Annie marched into the dining room and returned with a lighter that was used to fire up the kindling in the fireplace. She clicked it on and almost set Myra's nose on fire.

"Whoa! The cigarette, Annie, not my nose."

Annie puffed furiously on the cigarette in her mouth. She wiggled it from side to side. "Did ya see that, Myra? I saw Clark Gable do that in a movie once. See if you can do it."

"First, fill 'er up," Myra said as she struggled to talk around the cigarette in her mouth. The cigarette fell on the floor. Myra bent down to pick it up. She looked at the glowing tip and stuck the other end back in her mouth. "I don't want to learn that trick. You know what else, Annie, I don't want to look at that messy dining room table." Gingerly, she lowered herself to the floor and stretched out her legs. "Now we don't have to look at the mess. And if we pass out from all this fine liquor, we won't have far to fall."

"That really makes a lot of sense, Myra. Sometimes you hit it just right. I wish you weren't so sad. Charles will come back at some point. You know that," Annie said as she waved the whiskey bottle back and forth.

"I don't care to discuss Charles. Now or ever. Are we clear on that, Annie?"

"Crystal, my dear friend, absolutely crystal."

Myra burst into tears.

Annie's solution was to refill her glass. "Sometimes you gotta do what you gotta do," she muttered to herself. A good drunk never hurt anyone as long as it didn't become a habit.

Chapter 6

Lizzie Fox looked down at her watch when her cell phone rang. She frowned until she realized she hadn't set her watch back to Vegas time. Cosmo looked at her, his eyes full of unasked questions. "There's only one person who calls me at three o'clock in the morning. I have to take this call, Cosmo."

The big man walked away to allow Lizzie to speak privately with her caller. He wasn't sure, but he rather thought Lizzie would confide in him unless it was a client's privileged conversation. He jammed his hands in his pockets as he paced around his living room, then into the den, which was lined with books and a huge 106-inch television set mounted on the wall. His enormous custom-crafted rocking chair, which matched the one in his office, beckoned him. He tried to remember how many times he'd slept the night through in that very chair. He finally gave up when he realized that more often than not it was where he slept. His day lady was forever chiding him for not sleeping in his bed.

Cosmo watched the digital numbers change on his watch. Whoever Lizzie was talking to was either very verbose, or he or she was trying to convince Lizzie of something. He wondered whether, if they ever got married, Lizzie would still answer calls in the middle of the night.

If they ever got married. Why hadn't his thought been, **when we get married?**

Cosmo closed his eyes. First he had to ask Elizabeth to marry him. He admitted to himself that he was afraid to pop the question for fear Elizabeth had had second thoughts and would say *no,* she just wanted to keep the relationship the way it was. Fear was such a terrible thing.

In the next room, Lizzie paced, too, as she listened. "No, Martine. I can't give up my life to help you. No. Why would you even think I would consider much less accept your offer to be your White House counsel? You can't buy me; you could pay me my weight in diamonds, and I would still tell you *no.* Do I have to remind you that you made the decision to live in that fishbowl? I just helped you achieve your goal because I believed in you, and you're my friend. I owe you nothing more." Lizzie listened, her eyes growing wide with shock. "No, Martine, you can't do that! I know you're desperate, but you cannot infringe on my life. I will not allow you to do that." She listened again. This time her jaw set into hard lines and her blue eyes sparked with anger. "Don't ever threaten me, Martine. If you do, you'll regret it. I don't give a good goddamn about your Secret Service or the FBI or the CIA or the IRS or any of those other stupid alphabet-soup organizations. I know people who will chop those people up and spit them out. I'm going to hang up now, Martine, before either one of us says something even stupider than what has already been said." Lizzie snapped the phone shut and ran into the living room, where Cosmo was waiting for her.

"If your phone rings, do not answer it! The president of the United States is going to be calling you to ask if you want to be White House counsel. Oh, my God, Cosmo, you don't want that job, do you?"

"Whoa! Whoa!" Cosmo said as he struggled out of the

rocker. "Were you just talking to the president of the United States? Why in the world would I want a job like that?"

"Yes, that's who I was talking to, and she's going to call you. The only time she can call is the middle of the night."

The words were no sooner out of Lizzie's mouth than Cosmo's phone rang. He pulled it out of his shirt pocket and looked at the unknown name and unknown number that showed on the screen.

"She'll leave a message if you don't answer," Lizzie hissed.

"Elizabeth, I do not have to return her call. I do not have to answer this phone either. It's that simple."

"She damn well threatened me. I won't tolerate that, Cosmo. Did you hear me? The president of these United States threatened me! Me! We're friends. I helped her get into office. I cannot believe she threatened me. She did. With the Secret Service, the IRS, and all those other crazy ABC organizations. I hung up on her! I did, Cosmo, I hung up on the president of the United States! I can't believe I did that." All the while she babbled on, Cosmo's phone kept ringing. It finally stopped.

Cosmo laughed. "Do you want me to throw away the phone? I will." Without waiting for Lizzie to respond, he walked over to the fireplace and tossed the cell phone into the flames. He was grinning from ear to ear at Lizzie's horrified expression. "Just for the record, I did not vote for Martine Connor."

Lizzie burst out laughing as she threw herself into Cosmo's arms. "I love you, do you know that? When are we going to get married?"

Stunned beyond belief, Cosmo blinked. Then he laughed until the house shook. "How about right now? I know a twenty-four-hour chapel." He held his breath waiting for Lizzie's response.

Lizzie's smile lit the room. "Hey, I'm ready. Put your shoes on, and let's go."

Cosmo blinked. "This isn't very romantic, Elizabeth. I wanted to ask you myself. I rehearsed, in front of the mirror, for hours, and I had it down pat. And then I chickened out because I convinced myself you would say *no.*"

"I know." Lizzie giggled. "That's why I asked you. So, are we doing it or not?"

Cosmo held out first one foot, then the other. "See! I have my shoes on. Should we stop for some flowers? I have the ring. You said a plain gold band. I got a plain gold band. Do ya want to see it?"

"Well, yeah, Cosmo. On second thought, no, not until you slip it on my finger. Will that work for you?"

"It absolutely works for me, Elizabeth. It absolutely does."

"Then what are we waiting for?" Lizzie asked, linking her arm with his. "I can't wait to become Mrs. Cosmo Cricket."

Cosmo thought he was going to black out. In the whole of his life, he'd never been this happy. "They give you a video," he said.

"No kidding! Can you order extras? I want to send one to everyone I know so all my friends can see how happy I am."

Cosmo walked straight into the front door.

Lizzie laughed so hard she doubled over. "Come along, my darling. I don't want you killing yourself before I get to say 'I do.' "

Cosmo walked out to his car in a daze. He didn't say a word when Lizzie said she would drive.

"Last chance to back out," Lizzie said as she slid behind the wheel.

"You must be kidding!"

Lizzie laughed all the way back to town.

* * *

Annie woke with a start. Groggy and hungover, she groaned loud enough to wake Myra, who had been sleeping propped up against the refrigerator. "Oh, my God!" she wailed.

"Myra, it's five thirty! Quick, we have to clean up this mess and get breakfast ready. I knew we should have cleaned it up last night. My head is killing me. And, we smell to high heaven. *You* drank all that whiskey?"

Myra pushed her glasses higher on her nose to peer at the empty bottle lying on the floor. "I think I had a little help. All right, all right! I have an idea. Just wrap the tablecloth around everything and dump it all outside the door. Load the dishwasher with the pots and pans, splash some water on your face and we're good to go. It will work, Annie, if you move your ass like right now. I'll make breakfast!"

"You can't cook, Myra. I'll do the cooking, you do the cleanup. Hurry!"

Between the two women, they soon had the dining room back to normal, the dishwasher humming, bacon on the grill, and toast ready to pop. Also, a bowl of frothy yellow foam was standing ready, the sideboard held a pitcher of juice, and the coffee urn was working at full capacity.

"What did we resolve last night?" Myra shouted.

"Not a damn thing," Annie shouted back. "I don't think we should do that again for a long time. My head feels like it's going to fly right off my shoulders. How do you feel, Myra?"

"Sick and sorry I listened to you, that's how I feel. It snowed again during the night. Looks like maybe another six inches," Myra said, peering out the dining room window. "We're snowed in again. Did anyone call us during the night? I can guarantee the girls didn't have their phones turned on. We really should check the phones," Myra said fretfully.

"Forget that *we* business, Myra. As you can see, I'm rather busy here." Spatula in hand, Annie slid the pile of bacon from the grill onto a serving platter. She waited another minute, then added the sausage patties Bert Navarro loved.

Myra made her way back to the kitchen, the encrypted phones in her hand. "Oh, oh! Maggie called five times. Lizzie called three times. I'm leaving them turned off until breakfast is over, and we have our heads on straight. God, Annie, how do people drink like that day after day? I hope we didn't rot out our livers."

"Myra, shut up! Look, we got drunk, we're paying for it this morning. We are never going to do it again, so just shut up. Whatever Maggie and Lizzie were calling about can wait. It's now five minutes to six. Try to look alive even if you don't feel like it. And, remember this, we are of an age where we do not have to explain ourselves to *anyone*."

Myra fingered her pearls with one hand as she tried to smooth down her wiry curls with the other. She shrugged. Sometimes Annie made perfect sense. Other times she was halfway to the moon.

"My dear, you are absolutely right," Myra said, placing a hand on Annie's shoulder.

"If I hurt your feelings, I'm sorry. This just hasn't been a good time for me lately. I promise to do better. It is what it is. I'm going to build up the fire unless there's something else you need me to do."

"I got it covered. Tend to the fire while I carry all this over to the sideboard. I think I hear the girls! We pulled it off, my dear. Age and determination wins out every time."

Myra smiled to herself as she tossed a huge log onto the dying embers. Flames shot up the chimney as the log caught and blazed to life. She returned to the kitchen to wash her hands before she joined Annie in the dining room.

The early dawn chased away the dark, velvety shadows of the night as the girls crossed the compound, the men behind them, to the main dining room for the early breakfast they'd all been ordered to attend.

The mountain was quiet with a blanket of over five new inches of snow that had fallen during the night. They grumbled among themselves but only because they'd all wanted to sleep in that morning.

On the porch they stomped the snow off their boots, then slid out of them and set them aside once they were indoors.

The blazing fire along with the aromas of fresh-brewed coffee and fried bacon put them all in a good mood as they lined up at the sideboard to fill their plates. No one made a comment about Myra and Annie looking less than fresh or that they were wearing the same clothes they'd worn the night before.

The conversation was light, bantering, as they talked of the snow and the spring that was slow in arriving.

Myra nibbled on dry toast and sipped at her coffee. She murmured something vague about going on a diet. Annie, on the other hand, gobbled down her own breakfast and went back for seconds. She kept up a running dialogue about planting marigolds that were guaranteed to give triple the amount of blooms if sulfur was added to the potting soil. No one was interested enough to comment.

Yoko and Isabelle cleared the table the moment everyone placed their napkins on it, the signal that the social aspect of the gathering was at an end per Charles's previous instructions. Old habits were hard to break.

"I only have forty minutes before I have to head down

the mountain," Bert said as he inched his chair closer to the table. "Having said that, let me bring you up-to-date on what I know personally. I was called to the White House seven times in as many days. The new administration at the moment is in total chaos. I had two closed-door meetings with the president, and may I say she serves a good cup of coffee. She's haggard, she's a nervous wreck and admitted it to me. Half of her appointees are probably going to be resigning, and if they haven't done so yet, their resignations are ready to be handed in. That old devil sex has reared its ugly head once again. Martine Connor wants the FBI, me in particular, to find the woman who enticed her people—that's how she put it to me, 'the woman who enticed my people'—and arrest her. She wants this all done quietly. The only problem is that the other side of the aisle has already gotten wind of it. If that is the case, I have no idea why they aren't exploiting it. The president gave me a list half a mile long of the men in her administration who participated in, as she put it, 'nefarious doings.' She really thinks we can keep it quiet and cover it up. I told her it was impossible but that I would do my best. Personally, I couldn't believe how naïve she is.

"When I was leaving, I stopped for a moment to speak with her secretary, and she jokingly said it would be nice if the Vigilantes showed up to pull some magic rabbits out of a few hats. The chief of staff, who was on the list, turned a little green but pretended to agree. It's not good. I'm on my way to Vegas and will check in with you sometime this evening after I get briefed by the Vegas office."

"Lizzie is in Las Vegas. Her trip is purely personal," Annie said. "But I'm sure if you need her for anything, she'll be glad to help out. She volunteered to meet with us via webcam, but we postponed that because of your late arrival."

"So what is this meeting all about?" Nikki asked.

The women seated around the table looked at one another. As one, they shrugged.

"I think we're waiting to hear from Maggie," Myra said. "She's going to be faxing us a list of names. Until we get that, there's nothing any of us can do. Exxxcc-ceeppt," she said, drawing out the word as long as she could, "figuring out what and how we're going to deal with those names. And, I do not think we should concern ourselves with Martine's promise of a pardon or allow that to influence whatever decisions we make. We can always deal with Martine Connor on our own terms when the time is right."

"Myra's right," Jack said as he repeated everything Maggie and Lizzie had said at their early-morning meeting the previous day.

"Yah, Myra!" Kathryn said. "That means I agree."

The others nodded to show they, too, agreed.

Annie's eyes sparkled. "I look forward to this . . . adventure. Until we have more information, you're all dismissed. I do believe the shovels are on the porch, and the snowblower is gassed and ready to be put to use. The dogs need a good run. Myra and I will prepare lunch, and we'll all meet again and work on our plan after lunch, providing Maggie or Lizzie gets us the information we need."

The women clustered around Bert, who was putting on his jacket. It was Kathryn who walked him out to the cable car that would take him to the bottom of the mountain and out of their lives for a little while. The others dispersed to do Annie's bidding. They talked in low tones that didn't carry back to where the two older women were standing.

"I don't think any of them noticed that we aren't . . . up to par," Annie said.

"If you think that, then you're a fool, Annie. They're

all sharp as tacks, and they noticed our . . . attire and whatever else they noticed. Only good manners prevented them from mentioning that they *know.*"

"You always manage to rain on my parade, Myra," Annie said cheerfully. "I am now going to take a shower, change my clothes, and I might even put on some makeup and perfume. You can do what you want, or you can sit in the corner and play with your pearls. After which I am going to check with Avery Snowden to see if he's answered any of the e-mails I sent him. Then, and only then, am I going to call Maggie and Lizzie. Do you have anything to say, dear?"

There were a hundred things Myra thought she could say at that particular moment, but she opted just to smile sweetly, and say, "I'll be along in a minute."

Alone, Myra walked over to the fireplace to poke at the log she'd tossed in earlier. It was burned half-through. Oak was such a hard wood and Charles had been adamant about using only oak when building a fire. Charles had been adamant about so many things. She dropped to her knees and added several smaller logs and poked them about so they would burn evenly. The heat of the fire burned her eyes, and tears rolled down her wrinkled cheeks. She swiped at them angrily. She turned when she felt a gentle hand on her shoulder. "Annie!"

"Myra, you have to let it go and accept whatever happens. Anger and hatred are such wasted emotions. I'm the living proof, Myra. So are you. I made a promise to myself to never allow myself to go to that awful emotional place ever again. I know you made that promise to yourself, too, but then you broke that promise. The girls need you, Myra. I need you. Harry, Jack, all the others, they need you, too. You've always been our rock. You can't crumble now. I want you to pull up your socks and get with the program here. I don't want you to *pretend* either.

I want you to give it your all. Your all, Myra, I won't accept anything less."

Myra reached out her hand to Annie, who pulled her to her feet. Myra laughed. "Leave it up to you to pull me up short. I'm glad I never pushed you off that mountain back in Spain. I'm okay, Annie. I have my bad moments from time to time. Unfortunately, you always seem to be there when I'm having one of them. I mean it. I am okay, and I'm on board one hundred percent. You can all count on me. Now, let's go take those showers and come back here to prepare lunch. I think we should make a huge pot of hot chocolate, too. After we check our e-mails."

Arm in arm, the two women bundled up and headed for the main building. They watched, indulgent smiles on their faces, as the youngsters shoveled and threw snowballs that Murphy and Grady tried to retrieve, only to find the snow crumbled to nothingness once they got the balls in their mouths.

"Wouldn't it be nice to be that young again, Annie?" Myra asked.

"Only if we knew then what we know now." Annie laughed.

"You do have a point, my friend. You really do." Myra smiled as she led the way up the steps and into the Big House. "There's a lot to be said for old age but at the moment I can't think of what it is. What's more, I hope I never remember what it is."

"You rock, Myra!"

Chapter 7

Maggie Spritzer gnawed on a nail that was already chewed to the nub. Chewing her nails was what Maggie considered her only fault. Other than her nail biting, she thought of herself as perfect. Perfect with one teeny-tiny flaw worked for her.

Just then she was watching Lizzie's list shoot out of the fax machine at forty pages a minute. She was tempted to snatch at the sheets but didn't want to get anything out of order. The last page held a message that said Lizzie was faxing fifty-six pages including the cover sheet. The date and time were penciled in on the top page along with Cosmo Cricket's fax number. But it was the P.S. on the cover sheet that popped Maggie's eyeballs:

"I got married at one o'clock this morning.
I am now Mrs. Cosmo Cricket."

Maggie stared at the cover sheet with unblinking intensity. Damn. The Silver Fox had finally taken the plunge. "Way to go, Lizzie," she chortled. She turned around and sent the cover letter via fax to Big Pine Mountain. She couldn't even begin to imagine the reaction the girls would have when they read the news. They'd be as happy for Lizzie as she was, but then they would wonder, just the way she was wondering, how the marriage would affect the current status of the Vigilantes.

Maggie walked over to the copy machine and ran off five copies of the entire list. One set went into the safe. The second set went into a file in the cabinet behind her chair. The third and fourth copies would go to Ted and Espinosa. The fifth copy was hers, which she would fax to the mountain as soon as she familiarized herself with it.

From time to time, as she thumbed through the pages, she would gasp aloud; at other times she would smirk. Stupid, foolish men! And the families involved would never be the same. *Where in the hell did Martine get these people? Favors owed?* Favors that could be granted in the future by those same stupid males? Quid pro quo?

You wash my hand, I'll wash yours. Which all boiled down to: it wasn't what you knew but who you knew. It all sucked, in Maggie's opinion.

What really boggled Maggie's mind were the sheets of fingerprints that accompanied the scheduled appointments and the paid-in-full charge slips and the handwritten receipts for cash payments. Whoever the madam was, she was one smart lady. She had definitely covered her ass all the way around, for all the good it was going to do her. Everyone knew the madam went to the slammer, and the clients walked away.

"Not this time!" she muttered, starting through the list again. She knew that by the time she flipped the last page, she would have memorized every pertinent fact. For some reason God had gifted, or cursed, her with a photographic memory.

Maggie started to think about a headline. How should she refer to the madam? She needed a name, a catchy name that would resonate with readers. Her back suddenly stiffened. Why wasn't the opposition running with this? There was no way they weren't in the loop about what was going on. Whispers had a way of becoming full-blown shouts in Washington. Why would they hold back? What was to be gained by keeping quiet?

Not wanting to wait another minute, Maggie carried the stack of papers over to the fax machine, fed them into the automatic feeder, and hit the number for the mountain, which she'd programmed in a year ago. It would take a while for all the copies to feed through, so she went out to the coffee machine. She carried back coffee, a bagel loaded with cream cheese, two jelly donuts, and a banana. She started to eat, her eyes never leaving the fax machine.

Maggie's mind raced as she chewed and swigged. Maybe the way to go was to run with a drawing of the madam since she had no name or photo of the woman. She could have an artist do a rendering of a rhinestone cowgirl with a Stetson, rhinestone-studded boots, and a whip in one hand. That would certainly be eye-popping and sure to grab readers' attention, not to mention that of the White House. Her mind continued to race as she tried to contemplate how long she could keep the story alive and at the same time double the paper's circulation. If the Vigilantes appeared, she thought ten days was a safe enough number to run with. *If. If. If. If.*

The second fax machine in her office, the one behind her chair, squealed to life. The reason it was behind her chair was that Maggie was lazy, and with it stationed there, all she had to do was slide her chair backward and tear out the fax, as opposed to walking across the office. If there was one thing Maggie Spritzer was big on, it was making things as easy for herself as possible. She was down to the banana by then and the last of her coffee. She scooted back the chair and reached for the fax. It was also from Lizzie. Poor thing, working on her honeymoon.

"Holy shit!"

"What? What?" Ted Robinson asked from the doorway, Espinosa in his wake.

"Martine Connor called Lizzie and offered her the job of White House counsel. At three o'clock this morning, midnight Vegas time. Lizzie turned her down. Then Connor called Cosmo Cricket, but he didn't take the call. He threw his cell phone in the fireplace. Lizzie and Cosmo got married early this morning. Say something, Ted."

Ted echoed Maggie's words. "Holy shit!"

Espinosa flapped his arms. "What's it all mean, Maggie? You know what I mean. If Lizzie turned her down, is that going to . . . complicate things?"

Maggie scrounged around her desk for something else to eat, but everything she'd carried in from the kitchen was gone except the banana peel. "Yeah, it's going to complicate things. How the president got wind of Cosmo Cricket is something I'd like to know. I'm setting up a conference call with Lizzie and the mountain for later this morning. I'll know more then. By the way, I had a text message from Bert a little while ago. He's heading for Vegas, and the Vegas office is hot on the trail of the madam, who seems to have dropped off the face of the earth. Ditto for the madam's employees. The working girls," she clarified for Espinosa, who looked puzzled. "Bert said he'll check in later in the day once he gets a handle on what's going on."

"What do you want us to do?" Ted asked.

Maggie picked up the copies of Lizzie's fax she'd made for Ted and Espinosa and handed them over. "I want a complete background on every one of those guys. I mean everything. If there's a way to protect the wives and kids, I want to know what it is. I don't give a good rat's ass about any of those men. Let's be clear on that. The first inkling that either one of you is siding with those dumbbells, your ass is grass. Tell me you both understand what I just said."

Ted and Espinosa said they understood.

"I want this by the end of the day. My day is going to end at midnight, so get going. Call in every two hours. And, while you're out there sniffing around, see what you can pick up from the other side. It's not normal for them to be so quiet on something like this. I could be wrong, but I'm thinking that without the madam and her girls, there's no case to be made. Legally, that is. After that, it's a 'she said, he said,' or whoever the hell said whatever in the first place. I haven't heard a thing about *pictures*. Or *video*. Keeping in mind that both can be doctored. There's got to be a rabbit in the hat somewhere—assuming we can even nail down the right hat—or this thing will die on the vine."

Freshly scrubbed and smelling like flowers, Annie looked little the worse for wear and much better than she had an hour ago. She was pounding on the computer keys as she watched papers shoot out of the fax machine to her left when Myra walked over to where Annie was busy working. Annie looked up, smiled, and said, "I swear, Myra, we both look like we've been steam cleaned." Myra laughed, the first genuine laugh Annie had heard from her in months. Ah, life was on an upswing.

"Any e-mails?" Myra asked casually.

"No, my dear, no mail from Charles. You realize one day Charles will just show up. There will be no explanations, and it will be what it is at that moment. At that time it will be up to you if you push him under a bus or not.

"I also want to give you back your role as CIC. I only stepped in because you were in England. I don't want you to ever think I was out to steal your thunder. We were floundering, and the girls were turning anxious, so I did what I thought you would do."

Myra laughed again. "Annie, you did a wonderful job. Being the Cat in Charge is not a wonderful job. You can have the title if you want it."

"I don't. It's all yours. I'm only at this computer because you are dumber than dumb when it comes to computers and cooking."

"There must be something I'm good at." Myra wrinkled her nose to show she was teasing.

"I'm sure we'll find out exactly what that is very soon. For now, take a look, a good look, at this list of johns. I want to know what you think. And, I'm still waiting for a response to the e-mail I sent Avery Snowden, Charles's second-in-command. He was invaluable to us in Utah."

"Oh, dear! Are you telling me all these men . . . all these men participated in . . . in that fiasco involving a summer camp?"

"Well, Myra, that's certainly a polite way of wording it. The answer is *yes*. It must have been a real"—Annie grappled with just the right word and finally came up with it—"*extravaganza!*"

"But what are we supposed to do? What do Lizzie and Maggie want us to do?"

"I think for the moment we're in a holding pattern. Until the authorities can come up with the madam or her working girls, there is no case. Which means we are not needed. That's just my opinion. Maggie has her ear to the ground. So far there are just whispers, nothing has been made public. All of this," Annie said, pointing to the papers in Myra's hand, "is sort of like being preemptive. So we can hit the ground running if need be."

"So we have to come up with a plan?"

"Good Lord, I hope so this time around. I for one do not like to fly blind. We didn't even have a semblance of a plan when we all left for Utah. But we made it work somehow. Jack will have you believe his truckload of pumpkins was the plan. He was delusional. We had no plan. I think if we all put our heads together and get everyone in place, we can do just as good a job as Charles did. What do you think, Myra?"

"We're women, aren't we? That means we can do whatever we set our minds to. If we need a plan, then we'll come up with one. I have to warn you, though, getting in and out of Washington makes me nervous. We've been pushing our luck. I don't want to be a pessimist, but I have to wonder how much longer our luck can hold."

"It will hold as long as we want it to, Myra. Careful planning, dedication to detail, and a positive attitude will see us through. We have excellent backup with Lizzie, Bert, Maggie, and the *Post*. Negativity will get us nowhere, so don't even go there."

Myra suddenly let out a yelp of surprise. "Annie, why didn't you tell me about this?"

"What?"

"This!" Myra said, waving papers under Annie's nose. "Lizzie got married! The president offered her the job of White House counsel, and Lizzie hung up on her. Then the president called Cosmo Cricket and he didn't take the call and threw his cell phone in the fire! Did you hear me? Our Lizzie got married! To Cosmo Cricket! Someone is going to send us a video or something so we can see the wedding. Oh, Annie, how sad this is. Lizzie got married without any of us there to wish her well."

Annie sat down with a *thump* as she scanned the papers Myra had just shoved into her hands. "How wonderful for Lizzie. I'm sure she realized we couldn't be there. Maybe she wanted privacy. I don't think we should be offended, Myra. As for the president, I'm sure that call was made to ensure Lizzie's silence. The same thing would apply to Cosmo Cricket. I wonder what that will mean for our pardon."

Myra's shoulders stiffened. "I think we can kiss that pardon good-bye."

"According to this e-mail, President Connor threatened Lizzie with the Secret Service, the IRS, and the FBI. As you well know, no one threatens our Lizzie."

"I can't see the president threatening Lizzie!" Myra said, her voice so shocked she was actually sputtering.

"Well, I can. The president will be a joke the world over. Lizzie is not an alarmist. If she said she was threatened, then she was threatened. The girls are not going to like this. Not one little bit."

"This can't be good, Annie."

"What was your first clue, Myra?" Annie snapped.

Myra flipped through the pages in her hands, her eyes popping at the names she was seeing. She shook her head from side to side, disgust written all over her features. "Men are such cads."

"*Cads?* The word you're looking for is 'pervert,' Myra. Those men have power, wealth, prestige, and with their eyes wide-open chose to throw it all away for a roll in the hay."

"But Ambassador Kierson? I sat on so many committees with his wife, Julia. She's a lovely person, and they have four wonderful children. I'm sure there are some grandchildren in the mix by now. Harvey was . . . so distinguished. But he was . . . is the consummate politician. I always thought he was a nice man. Poor Julia, I don't know how she will weather this if it gets out."

"So many families are going to be ruined," Annie said. "I guess I can understand why the administration wants to pin all this on the madam. If that does happen, it won't make it all go away. Those men are ruined if it gets out.

That's a given. I guess I'm not really understanding what it is we're supposed to do as the Vigilantes."

Myra fingered her pearls as she walked over to the window to stare out at the young people, who were industriously shoveling snow. "It's snowing again, Annie. Charles would know what it is we're expected to do."

"No, he wouldn't know, Myra. Right now, this minute, we have the same information he would have if he were here. He would know exactly what we know, no more, no less. I appreciate your loyalty but Charles did not know everything."

"Point taken, Annie. I think we should call Maggie and Lizzie to arrange a conference call before we . . . uh, mobilize. Oh, I forgot, it's already on the schedule. Maggie is going to set that all up. Now, the question is this: Do we play it close to the vest and do it like Charles did and then just announce our findings, or do we call everyone in and make a unanimous decision before we proceed? We need to vote on certain things. I for one do not want to venture into the nation's capital unless we have a solid plan. We also need to give some serious thought to the president and how . . . angry she is with Lizzie. She can retaliate, Myra. I don't know if we could withstand the kind of retaliation she'd unleash on us."

Myra slammed her fist on the table. "Did I just hear you say what you said? I'm glad the girls aren't here to have heard that. Shame on you, Annie."

Annie backpedaled slightly. "Myra, I'm trying to be realistic. Up till now, we've been extremely fortunate. We're good. I will give us that. Give some thought to what and who Martine Connor has at her disposal. Also, do not forget that *she knows about us*. She knows about the mountain. She is indebted to us. Maybe this is her way of getting out of that debt because she can't make the pardon happen."

"Like I could ever forget something like that. I have nightmares, Annie, where Martine Connor is concerned. Lizzie says Connor is a woman of her word. I believe that Lizzie believes she is. At the time Lizzie said it, she believed she could get us a pardon, but that was then and this is now. I personally do not feel so sure right now. Martine Connor is going to do whatever is good for her, and, if we were in her place, we'd do the same thing. Which means, Annie, we are going to need a Plan B in addition to a Plan A. I think it's time to call in the young people and forget about the snow, at least for now. I've come to the conclusion that shoveling snow is an exercise in futility. We need to get down to business in case we have to . . . bug out of here on a moment's notice."

"Where, oh, where is all this insight coming from all of a sudden?" Annie teased as she made her way to the door. She opened it and let out a shrill whistle.

The girls turned as Annie waved for them to come in. Shovels and brooms flew in all directions as the women rushed to beat Jack and Harry to the door.

While everyone removed their snow gear and boots, Annie threw several more logs on the fire. Myra was already pouring hot chocolate into big, heavy earthenware mugs. Tiny marshmallows dotted the top of the cocoa. Barbara had always wanted more marshmallows than chocolate. Nikki was just the opposite, she was satisfied with a sprinkling of the tiny sweets. A smile tugged at the corners of Myra's mouth. Barbara and Nikki had so loved playing in the snow, then coming indoors to curl up by the fire with their hot chocolate. Myra just knew that more than one girlish secret had been divulged between the two inseparable friends, secrets she was never privy to as they giggled and laughed. Such a sweet memory.

"You do remember!"

Myra whirled around, her back to Annie, her eyes on

the huge hearth and the blazing fire. If she closed her eyes, she could see ten-year-old Barbara and Nikki.

"Oh, dear girl, I do remember. I always wondered what girlish secrets had to be kept from your mother."

Myra's spirit daughter laughed. The laughter sounded young and girlish. *"The biggest secret was that we'd shaved our legs. We were so afraid you would find out. Every day we kept looking at our legs, willing what little hair we had to grow back."*

Myra smiled. She wanted to ask her spirit daughter about Charles, but she couldn't bring herself to utter the words. Instead she said, "We're more or less floundering a bit right now, darling girl. We have to come up with a plan."

"Trust Lizzie and Maggie, Mom. There's a storm brewing, and I don't mean the Mother Nature kind."

"Can you tell me more?" Myra murmured.

The laughter and stomping was winding down. Surely the others would pick up on her strange behavior.

"Later, Mom. The girls need you. Give Nikki a hug for me."

"I wish I could give you a hug, dear girl. I would give up my life if I could somehow make that happen. Do you still have Willie?" Myra asked, referring to Barbara's old teddy bear.

"In a manner of speaking. Mom, Charles is fine."

"I know that," Myra said through clenched teeth. "The fact that he's fine is what bothers me."

Myra's spirit daughter laughed, the sound tinkling across the room. Myra knew immediately that Barbara was gone. She turned, walked over to Nikki, and hugged her. Nikki understood immediately what had happened when Myra said, "Barbara said to hug you."

"Oh, hot chocolate with marshmallows!" Kathryn squealed.

"I brought the fixings with me when we came back to the Big House. I didn't want to fight my way through the snow again. Sit down, get warm, then we can all talk. Enjoy the chocolate. There's more if you want it," Annie said, setting the giant carafe on a folding table she'd set up near the hearth. "We'll be in the war room when you're ready to join us."

Thirty minutes later, the Sisters, Jack, and Harry were seated around the huge round oak table.

Myra stood up and held up her hand for silence. "Annie is about to set up a video conference call with Lizzie and Maggie. In the meantime, I made copies of the list of men involved in this . . . whatever *this* is. As you can see by the names, it is a very impressive list. I can certainly understand why *President* Connor is a little cranky right now. What I didn't expect her to do was threaten Lizzie. If she threatens Lizzie, that's the same as threatening the rest of us."

"Do you want to explain that a little more?" Kathryn asked.

"I would, dear, but Lizzie is the one to explain it better than I. I don't want to say something that isn't so. So often things get lost in the translation. For Lizzie to hang up on the president of the United States has to mean she's very angry. Lizzie is ever the diplomat. But Lizzie knows how to threaten, too."

Annie and the girls digested Myra's comments with sly looks among themselves. Jack and Harry sat quietly, soaking up what they were hearing like sponges. This was the first time both men had been allowed to sit in on what they called "mission control." It was Jack's fear that the women were so tuned in to Myra and Annie, they didn't realize he and Harry were there. Better to remain quiet and try to be invisible. A risky glance out of the corner of his eye told him that Harry looked like he was thinking the same thing.

"I can't believe the names on this list!" Then Nikki's tone turned fretful when she asked, "What are we supposed to do? Make all those men disappear? Punish them? I'm not getting it. What does the president expect us to do?"

"If this were a perfect world, and we all know it isn't, I'd say the president wants the Vigilantes to figure out a way to make this all go away and save her administration the global humiliation that is sure to follow," Myra said. "So far, everything is being kept quiet. Even Maggie is being extremely cautious as far as the *Post* is concerned. No one wants lawsuits. Especially in Washington, D.C. It will be a terrible mistake to have the White House and those that live and work there suddenly become our enemy."

"Well, Myra, off the top of my head, I have to say if that's what the president expects, someone needs to tell her that's above our pay grade. I didn't hear anyone mention money," Kathryn said coldly.

"Is it possible the president thinks if we contain this situation, those . . . men can remain in their positions, then slowly, one by one, resign over time?" Alexis asked. "They'll blame the opposition for starting those scurrilous rumors, and everyone saves face. I don't like that one little bit."

"Don't they need the madam to make a case?" Yoko asked. "Without her, all anyone has is rumor, no proof, unless the opposition has something we don't know about."

Annie walked over to the round table, the remote control in her hand. "I have Lizzie and Maggie ready to go. We're set up so we can all talk back and forth. I do hope I did this right. Charles showed me how to do it once, but I have to admit I wasn't really paying attention. Thank God for Maggie, who has pulled this all together. So bear with me here," Annie said as she pressed a bright-red button.

The huge plasma screen suddenly came to life. Annie pressed a green button, and the screen was split, with Lizzie on the left and Maggie on the right. It almost looked as though they were physically in the room with everyone else. Their voices were clear and free of static as each woman offered up a greeting.

The Sisters as one, Harry and Jack chiming in, yelled, "Congratulations!"

Grinning from ear to ear, Lizzie made a low, sweeping bow as she dangled her left hand, her plain gold wedding band winking in the artificial light.

The Sisters hooted and hollered, Jack and Harry stomped their feet, while Maggie clapped.

Lizzie held up both hands. "Thanks, ladies and gents. Now, I have news. And it ain't good."

Chapter 8

The sun was high in the sky when Cosmo Cricket served his brand-new wife her first honeymoon breakfast.

Sitting at the glass-topped table out on the deck, Lizzie de Silva Fox Cricket eyed the fantastic gourmet tray and swooned. "Oh, Cricket, it's everything I love! Besides you, of course," she added hastily.

Cosmo almost swooned. He loved the way Lizzie called him Cricket. She only called him Cosmo when she was being professional and wanting to talk business. His last name sounded so endearing when it rolled off her lips. He looked down at the tray, which was the size of half a tree and had to weigh at least twenty pounds. On it were bacon, fluffy yellow scrambled eggs, sausage patties, pancakes that looked light enough to fly, warm golden butter with the syrup mixed into it, and a separate plate with waffles topped with the most perfect blueberries Lizzie had ever seen. The coffee urn was polished silver and held twelve cups. A matching pitcher that held pure cream sat nestled next to a little silver pot of sugar cubes. In the center of the tray was a single white rose, Lizzie's favorite. Her smile rivaled the sun as Cosmo served her.

"You get to clean up," Cosmo said, shaking out the Irish linen napkin and placing it on her lap.

"For you, Cricket, anything," Lizzie said as she attacked the food on her plate.

Cosmo himself ate sparingly.

Between bites of food, they commiserated about how Lizzie ate like a truck driver and never gained an ounce and Cosmo ate like a bird and couldn't lose weight.

"More of you for me to love, Cricket. Oooh, these pancakes are to die for."

"My mother taught me how to cook in case I ever fell on hard times. She taught me how to sew, too. Not that I sew, but I do know how. I can even make buttonholes."

"That's so nice to know. I have some skirts that need to be hemmed."

They both knew Cosmo wouldn't be threading a needle anytime soon.

"What would you like to do today, Elizabeth?" Cosmo asked.

"Absolutely nothing. I could sit out here all day and just talk to you. Or we could go inside and watch old movies. Or, if you want to go into town, we could do that, and I could try my luck on the slot machines. Whatever you want to do is fine with me as long as you're sure you don't have to go to your office."

"We should talk about our honeymoon and squaring away our time. I want to take you on a trip around the world. Would that work for you, Elizabeth? I've been, but I had no one to share it with. I'd like to see the world through your eyes so we can enjoy it together."

Lizzie gasped. "Around the *whole* world? How long would that take?"

"About a year, give or take. I did it after my mother died. I couldn't seem to get it together and I thought . . . I don't know what I thought. My parents always said someday they were going to do it, but someday never came for them, so I did it. Late, I grant you, so I don't want to be late again.

If you don't want to do it, that's okay, we can put it on our vacation-slash-honeymoon list and do it when you feel ready. I have to tell you, it's a commitment like no other."

"Oh, Cricket, I do. I really do. When we clear up here, we can get our day planners out and a calendar and go from there. I'm getting excited just thinking about it."

"The trick is to travel light and purchase as you go along. I don't mean that the way it sounds. I didn't discard anything, I gave it away. It worked. I fully understand that women are different, so whatever works for you will work for me. I will gladly carry your bags."

Lizzie's jaw dropped. "Cricket, I know how to rough it. I backpacked through five countries with only a knapsack. I will admit I was a bit . . . uh . . . *gamey* from time to time. That makes one appreciate a long, hot shower, even if it's under a tree with a hose."

Cosmo burst out laughing. The whole deck rumbled at the sound. He felt so pleased with himself that he couldn't stop.

"What? What's so funny?"

"You!" Cosmo continued to laugh. "Look at you, you're the most beautiful woman in the world, and you dress like a movie star and model. I'm just having a hard time imagining you *roughing* it, as you put it."

Just for a second Lizzie looked indignant, but then she, too, laughed.

Cosmo's laughter died in his throat when he suddenly stood up and lumbered over to the stairway that led to the lawn. "Mona! What's wrong? What are you doing here?"

"Mr. Crickct, I know what you told me but I think this is important; otherwise, I wouldn't have come all the way out here. If it turns out I made a mistake, you can fire me," Cosmo's secretary said.

"What happened? Don't tell me someone managed to rip off one of the casinos. Please don't tell me that."

"I won't tell you any such thing because that didn't happen. A messenger of sorts came by the office about an hour ago. It was a young girl, maybe eighteen, if that. She said her brother was supposed to bring this package to you yesterday morning, but he had a car accident and was taken to the hospital. When they released him last night, his father took him home, and he was groggy, but he kept worrying about a package he had been paid to deliver. I signed for it and gave her twenty-five dollars out of petty cash. The family has no insurance. You know how I feel about things like that, Mr. Cricket. So, here is the package."

Cosmo reached for the manila envelope, thanked his secretary, and watched till she was out of the yard. It was only when he heard the sound of a car's engine that he walked over to Lizzie and dropped the envelope on the table. "I think I might know what this is, and I'm almost afraid to open it."

Lizzie didn't say anything, she just stared at the envelope. From past experience she knew that when a messenger hand-delivered something to a lawyer, it meant either impending trouble or bad trouble that was already lying on your doorstep. Obviously, Cosmo was of the same opinion.

Lizzie made a production of tossing the remains of the coffee in their cups over the railing of the deck before she refilled their cups. "Okay, Cosmo, now you can open it."

Cosmo immediately picked up on his name change. He nodded as he pushed back the little tabs under the tape. He used the butter knife on the table to slit the heavy yellow paper of the envelope.

Lizzie waited until Cosmo had scanned the papers in his hand. "Does it concern your deceased client, the madam?"

"Yes. It's a copy of her will and her power of attorney. Both are dated a week before she came to see me. These are the originals. I know the attorney who drew them up. Lily Flowers must have had . . . a premonition that things were not going to go as she planned. This, together with the paper I told you about earlier, gives me all the authority I need to go after whoever she wanted me to." He slid the legal papers across the table for Lizzie's observation and opinion.

Lizzie looked over the top of Cosmo's half-moon reading glasses, which she snagged out of his shirt pocket. "Sounds to me like Lily Flowers's car accident maybe wasn't a car accident after all. Uh-oh, did you see this, Cosmo?"

"What? Something in her will?"

"Look at the last page, Sweetie. Stapled there is a list with the names of her girls and the amount of money she gave each one of them to clear out of town. Cell phone numbers, too. She must have been frightened out of her wits to send you all of this," Lizzie said, rattling the papers in her hands. "I have to give her credit; she was thinking about her girls right up to the end."

Sweetie? She'd called him *Sweetie*. Cosmo decided he loved being called Sweetie. Just loved it. Even his own mother had never called him Sweetie. She'd called him Honey or My Darling Boy or something like that. "I guess we have our morning's work cut out for us."

Lizzie peered over the tops of the borrowed glasses, her eyes full of questions.

"We have to call her girls and apprise them of their employer's untimely death. And I need to make funeral arrangements for my client. This isn't much of a mini-honeymoon, now, is it?"

"I'm loving every minute of it. We're together, doing what we do best. Not to worry, Cricket, this is going to happen again and again. The next time it might be my crisis that interferes with our plans."

Lizzie had no sooner finished speaking than her cell phone rang. It was Annie, alerting her to Bert's imminent arrival and his plans. Cosmo watched his true love as her head bobbed up and down, agreeing to whatever was being said. He actually jumped in his chair when she snapped her cell phone shut.

Lizzie removed the glasses and handed them back to Cosmo. "This is what you need to do, and you need to do it *now*. Pull whatever strings you have and claim your client's body. Have her cremated immediately. Pay off whomever you have to pay off and do it handsomely. I'll call all the women on the list and put them on alert. I have a friend here, several, actually, who can help us if need be. Rena Gold, I told you all about her earlier, and her friend Little Fish."

Cosmo was already through the door leading to the kitchen. He grabbed his briefcase and was almost to the front door when he turned around. Lizzie knew he was on his way back to the deck because she could feel it shaking under her chair. She held up her face for his kiss before he stomped his way back to the front door. She heard the powerful sound of an engine and knew he'd drive like a bat out of hell to do what he needed to do.

Lizzie sighed deeply as she poured fresh coffee before going into the house for her own eye-cheaters. She settled the glasses over her nose, looked down at the list in front of her. Her first call was to someone named Brandy, aka Jo Ann Scythe. As Lizzie waited for the phone to be answered she wondered what she would do if Lily's girls were too frightened to answer. If there was no answer, should she leave a message or go on to the next young woman? She panicked for one brief moment as she tried to remember what name Lily Flowers used at the Happy Day Camp. It ricocheted through her brain just as she heard a cautious hello.

"Brandy! Uh . . . Miss Jo Ann Scythe? This is Elizabeth Fox. Crystal Clark retained my law partner several days ago. I don't know how to tell you this other than to come right out and say it. Miss Clark was involved in a terrible car accident. She was killed instantly. My partner, Cosmo Cricket, and I are trying to piece everything together and to do what Miss Clark wanted us to do. She gave her power of attorney to my partner. Obviously, she made provisions for you and your . . . colleagues. That's why I'm calling. I don't know where you are and I'm not sure I want you to tell me either."

"Crystal is dead! She was the most careful driver I ever met. We were supposed to meet . . . oh, God! Did you tell the others?"

"You are my first call. Listen to me. I want you to call all the other girls and tell them what happened. I want you all to go to . . . to your final destination, wherever that may be as soon as possible. It would be a good idea, if after all the calls are made, you get rid of your phones and buy new ones. Buy extra minute cards for the time being. Designate one of you to be the spokesperson to stay in touch with me. I'm sure you can see my number on your caller I.D. Do you understand everything I just said, Brandy?"

The voice was stronger but still sounded a little jittery. "I do understand. How much time do we have?"

"The FBI should be arriving in a few hours. Does that answer your question?" Not waiting for a reply she rushed on. "Are you all together? If so, you need to split up, and you also need to look ordinary and travel under your real names."

"Yes, we're all together. We're in Seattle. Crystal has a house here that she said no one knows about."

"They'll know about it sooner than you think. Clean up the house and leave. And I mean, inside and out, fingerprints, hair, leftover food, anything that could contain your DNA, the bag from the vacuum cleaner, and all—everything. Then ditch everything in a Dumpster somewhere way down the road. Can you do that?"

"Consider it done. This is serious, isn't it? Do you need to know our final destination?"

"No, not right now, and yes, this is about as serious as it can get. How are you fixed for money?"

"Crystal has a stash we can draw on. She said we'd be good for a solid year. After that we were on our own. We thought that was fair, so we went along with it. Will you . . . will you . . . take some flowers to the cemetery for us? Just sign the card 'Friends.'"

"We're having Miss Clark cremated. But I will buy some flowers. Hang up now and go wherever you have to go. Call me as soon as you're all safe."

"Crystal, even under stress, always had her wits about her. Whatever happened, I can tell you this, it was no accident. I'd stake my life on it. Good-bye, Miss Fox."

Lizzie licked at her lips, then bit down on the bottom one as she scanned the papers in front of her. There was no doubt in her mind that this was all going to be one gigantic mess.

She cleared the outdoor table and carried everything into the kitchen. She looked around in dismay. Cosmo must have used every pot and pan he owned to make breakfast. She shook her head like indulgent mothers do when their children create chaos. The end result had been more than satisfying, she thought, as she cleaned the kitchen and turned on the dishwasher. The remaining pots and pans she did by hand. Satisfied that the kitchen looked the way it had before Cosmo wrecked it, she headed to the second floor to shower and change.

Before she stepped into the monster shower that had nozzles shooting water out from every angle and could have accommodated an entire football team, Lizzie called Annie to report the latest. Then she called Cosmo, but he didn't pick up, so she left a message. She'd call Bert later, once she knew he was actually in Vegas and not still airborne.

An hour later, Lizzie was dressed for the day in a denim skirt with fringe at the hem. It showed off her glorious, long, tanned legs. She pulled on the white leather rhinestone boots Cosmo had given her and that she loved almost as much as Annie loved hers. A camisole went under the short denim bomber jacket. At the last minute she plucked a snow-white Stetson that Cosmo had had made just for her. She looked hot, and she knew it.

At the bottom of the steps she stopped short. "Now what?" she asked herself. She was saved from making a decision when her cell rang. It was Cosmo.

"I'm having a slight problem with the mortician."

"What kind of problem?" Lizzie asked.

Cosmo told her.

"Give me ten minutes."

Lizzie called Annie, who then called Avery Snowden, who then called Little Fish, who called the mortician.

Lizzie waited exactly eight minutes before she pressed her speed dial and said, "I'm on my way. Tell me where you are exactly. My GPS will do the rest."

"Okay, it's a go. How *did* you do that?" Cosmo asked.

"Someday, Sweetie, I'll tell you all my secrets, but not right now. How long before the . . . you know?"

"She's on her way. We can pick up the urn later today. You want to do lunch?" Cosmo asked, his voice sounding so weird Lizzie had a hard time believing it was him.

Chapter 9

Maggie Spritzer stared down at the text message she'd just received. Bert Navarro was asking her to send Ted Robinson to Vegas. "What's up with this?" she mumbled to herself. She shot off a one-word response: "Why?"

The answer was, "To make it look good, and he's a hell of an investigative reporter."

Well, half of that was true, Ted was the best of the best.

"Give me ten minutes to confirm," was her next message, at which point she called Annie and asked for permission to send the Gulfstream to Vegas.

Annie authorized it, and Maggie confirmed, noting details would follow. She then hit her speed dial and ordered Ted to the airport.

"Damn, Maggie, you have to stop doing this. Or else you need to buy a condo or something in Vegas. I'm getting to be a regular commuter."

"You love it, admit it. You also need to stop whining, it's not becoming for someone like you who is sooo manly and virile. Just go. Bert and Lizzie will fill you in when you get there. Tell Espinosa he's on his own, but I need to see him ASAP."

Maggie worked the *Post*'s BlackBerry at the speed of light. She never let any grass grow under her feet.

Twenty-four hundred miles away, Bert Navarro exited

McCarran International Airport. He looked around for
the Special Agent in Charge, who was to meet him. When
he didn't see anyone he recognized, his eyes narrowed to
slits, and his lips stretched to a thin, straight line. Heads
would roll for this dereliction of duty. He was about to
leap the barricade and head to the taxi stand when he felt
a hand on his shoulder.

"Sir!"

Bert whirled around, then offered his hand to the head
of the Las Vegas Field Office. "Nice to see you again,
Wright. Where's the car?"

"Right there, sir," the Special Agent in Charge said,
pointing to a four-door black sedan parked third in the
line of waiting cars at the curb. Bert grinned; a person
would have to be totally blind to miss the two FBI signs,
one in the rear window and the other under a windshield
wiper. He also noticed at the same time how the busy
travelers were going out of their way to avoid going anywhere near the dark sedan.

The minute the two of them were seated in the official
vehicle, Bert took charge. "Fill me in. Every detail."

The short, stubby agent winced. Sweat glistened on
his balding head. He was tempted to swipe at it but
thought better of the idea and kept his hands tight on the
wheel and his eyes on the road. "I don't know which is
worse, Vegas traffic or airport traffic. I literally have nothing, sir. My agents have not been able to come up with
anything. We scoured the . . . the Happy Day Camp. Everything was in order, clean, neat, and tidy. Fingerprints by
the hundreds, but that was a given. The actual living quarters of the employees was wiped down clean. Nothing we
could match up. The madam's quarters the same thing.
The really weird thing is no one has ever had a picture of
the madam. Nothing has surfaced. It's like she never ex-

isted. There wasn't so much as a chewing gum wrapper or stray paper clip to be found anywhere. The refrigerator was clean, empty, and disconnected. All the major appliances were disconnected. It was so . . . sterile, for want of a better word, that my first thought was the place was just waiting for a new tenant."

"And her car?"

"In the garage. Wiped down clean. Paid in full. The lady dropped off the face of the earth."

"That's impossible, Wright. We're the fucking FBI. You must have missed something. Don't try telling me some stupid woman is smarter than the FBI because I am not buying it." Bert knew he'd pay for that remark if any of the Vigilantes discovered that the words had come out of his mouth.

Wright's voice turned testy. "Sorry, sir, but for now that's the way it looks. We did manage to speak with the gardener, who tried to give a description of the madam to our in-house artist. We tried sweating him, but it was a no go. He said he only saw 'the boss,' as he called the madam, on a few occasions. He's an old guy, moves pretty slow, and his English is limited. Other than 'she was a pretty lady,' and 'all the ladies were beautiful,' that's all we got. The composite, in my opinion, isn't worth circulating because he kept saying, 'No, no, that's not the way she looks.' Dark hair, medium height, weight about 110. He said that the few times he saw her, she was wearing sunglasses, jeans, and a jacket. That's it."

Bert felt secretly pleased at what he was hearing. The Sisters would be even more pleased. He cleared his throat, and barked, "Did any of your fine agents think to query the help at the casinos?"

"Sir, that was the second thing we did after we checked the Happy Day Camp. They'd heard of her, but no one claimed to have ever met her, much less availed themselves of her services. It's a dry hole unless you have some ideas we haven't come up with."

"How'd she find out something was going down?"

"That's a very good question, and I don't have the answer. I know, Director, that you aren't happy with what I've been telling you, but we don't have a single, solitary thing to go on."

"What about the working girls? How many were there? Where did they go? Did they leave en masse or one by one? Every madam has a right-hand. Who was it? Someone had to make travel arrangements for all those people."

Wright clenched his teeth. His knuckles were white on the steering wheel. "We know all that, sir, but it's a blind alley all the way. I can truthfully say we left no stone unturned. The departure was planned in advance, and it was like a drill. They got the word and acted on it. My guess would be they left one by one in their own cars, left them somewhere, and took flights to wherever they were going."

"Money. Always follow the money. Did you talk to any of the other brothel owners? What are they saying?"

"They're saying nothing other than that Clark ran a very lucrative business, much to their chagrin. Her girls were top-of-the-line, very much in demand. In other words, cream of the crop. Those other places, no comparison. And, before you can ask, yeah, we swarmed in and sweated them all. Those people do not talk to law enforcement, and they are not afraid of the FBI. One cheeky woman told me we should hire the Vigilantes if we wanted to find the ladies from the Happy Day Camp. Sir, she actually said that, and all the other women hooted and hollered and agreed. I can tell you we all felt like shit."

"And well you should," Bert snarled. "So, what's your next move?"

"We were waiting for you to get here to tell us what you want to do. We have no leads, no witnesses. Translation, we have zip, nada."

"What about the cell phone records, the camp telephone logs, the passenger manifests from the airlines? The johns, or whatever the clients are called these days, for God's sake! Did anyone think to check the doctors and dentists in the area? If this was such an up-and-up deal, those women had to have medical checkups. Five will get you ten they all had their teeth capped at some point. I want reports. Not guesses."

"All in the works, we're waiting for reports."

"Bank records?"

"Nothing out of the ordinary. Bills. Paid on time. Accounts closed. The business for the most part is cash. They did accept credit cards, but, again, we have some records and are waiting for others. No one wants to leave a paper trail, and the Happy Day Camp did not accept checks. Not only is it a stone wall, it's a *high* stone wall. Sir, you know prostitution is legal in the state of Nevada in certain areas. Crystal Clark acted within the law."

"Until she took her dog-and-pony show to the nation's capital. By the way, where are we going, Special Agent Wright?"

"I thought you'd want to visit the Happy Day Camp. Vegas is pretty filled up, room-wise, but you're all set for your hotel although you can't check in until four."

Bert nodded. He had to shake this guy pretty soon so he could call Lizzie to see what was going on. He fished out his BlackBerry and saw a text from Maggie that said Ted Robinson was on his way and would land in four hours and meet up with him at the Elvis Chapel. The message went on to say that Ted had assured her that Bert would know where the Elvis Chapel was. For sure he had to shake Wright, and he needed some wheels. He checked to see if there were any other messages and was disappointed that Lizzie hadn't checked in. He felt a chill run up his arms.

Thirty silent minutes later, Special Agent in Charge Duncan Wright swerved onto a gravel road that wound through a dense line of overgrown shrubs and trees. At night, road lights that looked to be solar-powered and were almost flush with the gravel road would light the way for the Happy Day Camp clientele.

"Here it is!" Wright announced, bringing the sedan to a complete stop.

"Who do those cars belong to?" Bert asked.

"My agents," Wright responded.

"You have four agents guarding an empty building? Why? I hope I can understand your rationale for this; otherwise, you're going to be guarding that dam out there in the distance."

Wright flinched. "They're waiting for me to give them their orders. I wanted to wait to see what you wanted to do. My plan was to send two back to town to keep canvassing the casinos. Believe it or not, Director, men who frequent this type of establishment do not advertise . . . their needs. The gardener has been paid through the month, so he's still working. One of my men keeps talking to him, hoping something might surface, but we aren't hopeful. And there is always the possibility that a few customers who haven't gotten wind of what is going on might come out here for a little . . . exercise. Like I said, we're working with what we have."

It made sense, Bert thought, so there was no reason to rip this guy a new one. He nodded. "Okay, leave one agent. Take the CLOSED sign off the door. Have your man stay indoors, but not until I finish my own inspection. Send the other three agents back to town but leave me our car. You can go with them, Agent Wright."

"Yes, sir. If there's anything you want us to do, call. I'll be at the office waiting for all the reports to come in. I'll let you know as soon as we know something." Wright held out his hand, and Bert grasped it.

"Good work, Agent Wright," Bert said, deciding to be magnanimous. "We'll talk later." Without another word, Bert trotted over to the steps, bounded upward, and entered the log cabin structure.

Just in case the remaining agent decided to take a look through one of the windows, Bert walked through the building. Downstairs he marveled at the quality of the workmanship, the beautiful furniture that looked neither old nor sleazy, and the building's clean fragrance. The kitchen had stainless steel appliances and was spotless. The bathrooms exquisite. He took a moment to wonder where the money had come from to build and outfit such a structure. The revenues must have been astronomical. Even the grounds outside, what he saw of them, were exceptional, with every variety of desert plant there was. The place looked, at least from the outside, just like what the sign said it was: a camp.

Bert made his way up the polished staircase to the second floor. The bathrooms there were just as beautiful as the ones on the first floor, though the six bedrooms were a little more spartan, with just enough furniture to make the rooms appear comfortable. He looked down at the buffed and polished wide plank floor. The Special Agent in Charge was right—the place was immaculate. There wasn't so much as a speck of dust, a thread, a paper clip, or a bit of paper.

Bert sat down on the edge of the bed and whipped out his phone. A second later he was talking to Lizzie, who cut him so short his jaw dropped. He blinked, snapped the phone shut, shoved it in his pocket, and walked back downstairs and outside. He motioned to the agent, and said, "It's all yours. You stay indoors until you hear otherwise or you'll be relieved."

"Yes, sir," the young man said.

"Plug in the television set and get caught up on ESPN."

The agent grinned. Like he wouldn't have done that anyway. "Yes, sir."

Bert walked around the back to the twelve log cabins that dotted the landscape. While he was no authority on such matters, he assumed that the cabins were where business was conducted. He figured that if he checked out one, he could be fairly sure that the others would be the same.

It was beautiful, with a huge fieldstone fireplace, minikitchen, and a loft. Plank floors throughout, deep, comfortable furniture. Empty wine rack on the wall in the minikitchen. Exquisite bathroom. No towels, soap, or anything else of that sort. He ventured up the open-backed wide plank stairs to peer into the loft. Stunning.

Bert went back down the steps and meandered over to one of the deep, overstuffed chairs. He sat down, his gaze going in all directions. His mind raced. *Where did the money come from to build this place? How long did it take to clean it out? What's up with Lizzie? Will Ted come up with something once he gets here?* Bert was no fool, he realized that people clammed up when it came to the FBI. Reporters were notorious for getting ordinary people to talk, especially when they offered to pay for information, something the FBI reserved for its paid confidential informants.

With time on his hands, Bert walked back outside to look for the gardener. He found him in a neat two-room utility shed. He was standing over a wheelbarrow, mixing peat moss and something that smelled like manure. He looked up, his weather-beaten face curious but not alarmed. Bert spoke to him in Spanish, and he answered in kind.

An hour later, Bert realized that the local Bureau personnel were right, the man knew nothing, was withholding nothing. He was just who he said he was, the gardener, who had been paid through the month. Bert asked him what he would do when he left.

The man smiled, and said in English, "I retire. I let my wife wait on me."

"Good idea. Do you have a pension?"

"*Sí.*"

"Well, that's good. You can sleep late and sit in the sun. Where is the pension from?"

It was an innocent question, but the man's face crumpled. The gardener pointed to the main log cabin. He bit down on his lower lip.

Bert nodded. "It's okay, I don't care about that. I won't say anything."

It was all said in Spanish, and the old man nodded. Bert watched as the man walked back into the shed and came out with a metal box. He opened the lid and waited, the fear on his face a terrible thing to see. Bert looked down and mentally calculated, as he rifled through the money, that there was $50,000 in the box. He nodded and pointed to the shelf to indicate the man should put it back. He put his finger to his lips, a sign that in any language meant he wouldn't say anything. "Take it home and hide it. Don't leave it here." He pointed to the main building and to the extra car in the parking lot.

The old man nodded. "*Sí.*"

Bert held out his hand, and they shook.

They talked for a few more minutes. He found out the gardener had worked on the premises from the day the buildings were finished. Twelve years.

Bert offered up an airy wave before he walked back to his car. In his car he sent off a text message to Ted, telling him the first thing he needed to do was trace ownership of the Happy Day Camp and to try to find out where the money came from, since his own people were having such a hard time coming up with answers.

Lizzie held the bouquet of champagne-colored roses tightly in her hand. This was the first time she'd been anywhere near a crematorium, and she didn't know what the protocol was. Cosmo looked like he didn't either. The room they were told to wait in could have been a chapel, she wasn't sure, but the three rows of pews pretty much confirmed it in her mind. There were arrangements of silk flowers on pedestals around the small room. There were no holy water fonts or religious statues, but there were two beautiful stained-glass windows of white doves in flight against sky blue glass.

"I don't like this place, Cricket," Lizzie whispered.

Cosmo reached across to take her hand in his. "I know. I hope we did the right thing, Elizabeth. I don't want to regret having my client cremated."

Lizzie squeezed his hand. "From everything you told me about your meeting with Lily Flowers, and from what I read, this was the only answer. I think you did what Lily would have wanted. She spent her whole life being anonymous, and she died the same way. It won't take the FBI long to figure this all out. They plod along when they aren't steamrolling forward, but in the end they manage to figure it out. When they do, you either hand·over the ashes in the urn or we beat them to the punch and take them someplace and scatter them. Do you agree or disagree?"

Cosmo stared at the white doves on the window. His big head bobbed up and down. "I say we scatter the ashes in the desert. I don't know why I say this, but I think Lily Flowers would like that."

Thirty more minutes went by before a tall, stately gentleman walked into the room carrying a silver tray with a sealed ceramic urn nestled among fresh greenery. Lizzie had picked out the urn. It was cobalt blue, with a cluster of lilies on the front. The man, whose discreet name tag said he was Lionel Tynesdale, held out the silver tray. Cosmo's hands, which were bigger than catcher's mitts, reached for the urn. He didn't know if it was his imagination or not, but the urn felt *warm*.

"Is there anything else I can help you with today?"

Cosmo wanted to say, *"Christ Almighty, no."* Instead he just shook his head. He waited a moment, then said, "We're both clear on the details, are we not?"

"Absolutely, sir. Everything has been taken care of. You have absolutely nothing to be concerned about. My staff and I are used to interrogations; this is, after all, Las Vegas, Mr. Cricket."

The tray still in his hands, Tynesdale turned on his heel and left the room, Cosmo and Lizzie following him to the long, incense-scented hallway, then out to the foyer, which smelled the same way, to the front door. Once outside, both Cosmo and Lizzie took deep breaths, expelling the pent-up air in loud *swooshes* of sound. They literally ran to where Cosmo had parked his car.

Lizzie climbed in and leaned over to open the door for Cosmo, which meant she had to hold the urn in her lap. She thought it felt *warm*. She stifled the urge to scream. "This is not a pleasant experience, Cricket."

"Tell me about it," Cosmo said through clenched teeth. "Where to now, Elizabeth?"

"Hey, Cricket, this is your turf, I'm just a visitor. If I have to give you an opinion, it would be this . . . Let's go to wherever Lily Flowers can be one with the universe. We scatter the roses along with the ashes, send the little card from her friends into the air, say a prayer, and be on our way. I don't see . . . any other way . . . to . . . to send Ms. Flowers into eternity."

Cosmo looked so relieved, Lizzie smiled. "That'll work, Elizabeth. Then what?"

"Then we arrange to meet the director of the FBI and see what else is going on. I have to call Bert and apologize for cutting him so short. Since I don't, as of this moment, know what's going down with the local field office here in Vegas, I suggest we meet him at the Rabbit Hole. Now, the question is this, Cricket, do we send Ms. Flowers into eternity first or later, after our meeting with Bert? It's your call."

"I think that depends on how much you want him actually to know and see. Always remember, Elizabeth, he is the director of the Federal Bureau of Investigation. If you can honestly answer that his first loyalty is to the Vigilantes and us, then we can do it later or we can do it within the next fifteen minutes."

"I don't have to think about it. His first loyalty is to the Vigilantes, namely Kathryn, but also to the rest of us. We need him, Cricket, to keep us informed when his people here in Vegas start unearthing whatever they unearth. That's how we stay ahead of the game. I think we should uh . . . do the deed . . . then tell him about it afterward if it comes up in conversation."

" '*If it comes up in conversation?*' Is that what you said? Is he the kind of guy who is just going to suddenly say, 'Hey, did you guys scatter some madam's ashes out in the desert?'?"

In spite of herself, Lizzie laughed. The urn she was holding clutched between her thighs jiggled. She sobered immediately. "Let's just do it, Cosmo."

Cosmo. Cosmo meant Lizzie was down to business. He nodded, the car picking up speed.

Ten minutes later, Cosmo turned onto a cutoff road and sailed up a winding, rutted lane, sagebrush and scrub lining both sides. The air was hot and dry when the car finally came to a stop. "We have to walk the rest of the way, it's not far."

Lizzie climbed out, the urn clutched tightly in her hands. Cosmo followed, the flowers and the little white card in his hands.

When they finally reached a small plateau that looked down on the desert, Lizzie looked down at the urn. "This is right, but it's so wrong, Cricket. We're strangers to Ms. Flowers. I know you met her that one time, but we're really strangers. It's sad and it's wrong. She died alone. We're sending her off alone. We need to find out who she was. I for one want to know."

"That's not going to happen, Elizabeth. For whatever her reasons, Lily Flowers, or whoever she was, wanted no ties to her real past. We have to respect her wishes and let it go at that." A second later Cosmo had his pocketknife in his hands as he cut the seal covering the top of the urn. Both Cosmo and Lizzie blinked and looked at one another. "I . . . I didn't expect the ashes to be in a plastic bag with a twist tie, did you, Elizabeth?" Lizzie swallowed hard and shook her head.

"Which way is the wind blowing? We don't want to be downwind when . . . when you release the ashes."

Cosmo whirled around one way, then the other way. His jaw grim, his huge body rigid, he reached for the plastic bag and released the plastic tie. He took a few steps forward, checked the slight breeze again, and then tossed the contents of the bag into the air, making sure he had a firm hold on the corners of the bag. They both watched the beige-gray ashes sail upward and disappear into the air. Lizzie bowed her head and offered up a prayer before she walked over to the edge of the little plateau where she stripped the petals from the roses and let them loose in the wind. "From your friends, Lily Flowers. *Requiescat in pace.*"

When Lizzie turned around, she saw Cosmo on his knees digging a hole in the sand big enough to bury the urn and the plastic bag. She turned back to where she'd been standing. She hoped when she died that someone who cared about her would be there to say good-bye. A tear trickled down her cheek. She brushed at it. Life sometimes was just too sad for words.

Chapter 10

The eatery-slash-diner also known as the Rabbit Hole was in downtown Las Vegas, a dingy place where no one paid attention to the customers who entered the establishment. The Hole was owned by a man named Peter Rabbit to the chagrin of his wife, Petra. Peter Rabbit had been a boxer before he was knocked silly in the ring. His wife did all the cooking, and Peter sat at the counter and talked to customers.

To say the Rabbit Hole was dismal would be an understatement. It had cracked linoleum on the floor, the tables listed, and there were chunks of cardboard under the legs to hold them steady. The vinyl on the chairs was covered with strips of gray electrical tape. The areas of the vinyl visible between the applications of tape might once have been turquoise. Dark green pull-down shades graced the windows. There were nine tables in all plus a long counter that could hold eleven people, twelve if Peter Rabbit wasn't sitting on one of the frayed stools talking to anyone who would listen.

The Rabbit Hole had four things on the menu: Beef stew, chicken noodle soup that was loaded with actual chicken, fresh hot bread, and honest-to-God homemade apple pie that was served with ice cream, whether you wanted it or not. All three wanted it.

Introductions made, Lizzie sat back, an amused expression on her face as the two men sized each other up. Whatever they were seeing appeared to be spot-on because both men grinned and shook hands. A lively discussion on the Rabbit Hole's food followed, with Cosmo telling Bert how much Lizzie could eat at one sitting.

The minute they finished their lunch and the scrumptious, honest-to-God-homemade apple pie with ice cream, the trio got down to business over steaming cups of coffee. Lizzie took the initiative. "What are your people telling you, Bert?"

Bert leaned in closer to the table, his voice low, "Nothing, Lizzie. It's a dry hole. The madam fell off the face of the earth. They're not going to be happy about this back home. 'Home' meaning Washington."

It was an impossible feat for Cosmo to lean into the table, but he did try. "Why is that?" he asked. "No madam, no employees, no case, would be my way of thinking. But then I'm just a corporate lawyer making sure the casinos stay on the straight and narrow, although in many ways, we operate the same way you guys do."

"You would think that normally, but when the high muckety-mucks in Alphabet City come front and center, they start looking for someone else to blame. We're all adults here, we all know how it works. The madam takes the fall, and so do her girls. The clients, or johns, depending on what you want to call them, hide under their rocks for a while, then surface again at some point, and everyone kisses and makes up. Everything is more or less forgotten, except by the clients' families, who are the ones who have to deal with the fallout from the whole mess. The ladies sit in the slammer and grow old wondering what the hell went wrong. Look, I'm no prude, no one is ever going to stop prostitution, and, no, I don't approve of it, but that's me. The Bureau frowns heavily on it, as does our current administration. If it were a fair horse race, I wouldn't even be here, and by fair I mean *everyone* goes on trial.

"The Vegas madam knows how the system works, so she split. Can't say I blame her either. The Sisters are raring to go the minute someone gives them the word." Bert finished off the coffee in his cup, leaned back in his chair, and was astounded to see a short, fat little man filling his coffee cup. He nodded his thanks. "Your turn," he said to Lizzie.

Lizzie opted to take the high road for the moment. "What would be the ideal solution where the FBI is concerned? Finding the madam or not finding her? What happens if she's never found?"

"Then a manhunt like you've never seen will begin. There are some big names back there in D.C. You also have a president who wants someone's blood for trying to drain hers. The lady is on a roll. More than anything, she's concerned about her reputation around the world, and well she should be. The potshots they've been taking at her since she assumed office are nothing to what you'll see if this blows wide-open. It is my job to make sure it doesn't blow wide-open. Does that answer your question?"

"What if she's dead?"

"Dead? She can't be dead! Who the hell in their right mind would believe drivel like that? No one in Washington would believe it, and I sure as hell wouldn't want to be the person who tells Washington she's dead. But, the johns would heave a sigh of relief, assuming she left no telltale evidence behind. That's just too ludicrous for words because there is always evidence. Those pesky little black books brothels seem so fond of keeping."

Lizzie stayed on the high road. She gave an airy wave of her hand. "You're probably right, Bert, it is ludicrous, but you have to admit, if nothing ever comes to light, it could mean she's dead somewhere under an alias. Or, what if she fakes her death and goes on about her life and is never seen again?"

Bert leaned in toward the table again. "It doesn't sound like you have too much faith in the FBI. We are slow sometimes, but slow translates to thorough, and in the end, we always get our man, or, in this case, woman. Do you know something I don't know, Lizzie? If you do, now's the time to tell me."

"Bert! Bert! I just got here, and I got married yesterday. Technically, I'm on my honeymoon. What could I possibly know on such short notice? You've known for weeks that I was taking a long holiday, and by long I mean four days. I didn't even hear you congratulate me." She sniffed indignantly to show what she thought of that statement.

Bert almost jumped out of his chair. "You got married!" He jerked his head in Cosmo's direction. "To Cosmo?"

"Yeah," Lizzie drawled as she flashed her brand-new wedding ring.

"Lizzie, that's great! Really great! Congratulations! Do the girls know?" Bert turned to Cosmo and held out his hand. "You got yourself a hell of a woman there, Cosmo."

Cosmo grinned from ear to ear. His first congratulatory handshake. He liked the feeling.

Bert sat back in his chair again and stared at the newly married couple. He knew in his gut he'd just been snookered by a real pro. Just for a second, he allowed himself to be envious and wished it was Kathryn and he sitting there in the Rabbit Hole. He knew that Kathryn would have had some of everything on the menu, had seconds, and bragged about it for days. She did love to eat.

Lizzie continued to wave her hand for Bert's benefit. "Cosmo is taking me around the world as soon as we can clear our schedules. An around-the-world honeymoon. It's just too wonderful for words, don't you think, Bert?"

"I think it's great. What's that going to take, a year, a little more?"

"Give or take," Lizzie said airily.

Suddenly, as if some silent alarm went off in the room saying it was okay to *really* get down to business, Bert said, "Okay, cut the bullshit and give it to me straight."

Lizzie drew in a deep breath. "She's dead, Bert. An accident on the Cajon Pass. We know she was headed for San Bernardino because there was a hotel reservation in her wallet in the console of her car. She was Cosmo's client. She got her girls out to safety. I don't think she was your everyday, run-of-the-mill madam. She provided for her workers, she was fair and paid decent wages. She saw to their medical and dental, and ran a top-notch brothel, not that I know much about such things, but that's what we've heard and read."

Bert's mind raced. How was he going to play this with the Bureau? "Where's the body?"

Lizzie looked at Cosmo, who shrugged. "If you take the temperature into consideration and the winds, which are about ten to fifteen knots, I'd say parts of her are still over land and some out there over water."

"Son of a bitch! You fried her?"

"That's such an indelicate phrase, Bert. But, yes, she was cremated. There was no next of kin. Cosmo was her lawyer, and he did, with my help, what his client wanted done," Lizzie said, stretching the truth a tad.

Bert, in his frenzy, started to crack his knuckles. The sound was so loud, the other diners looked over to see what he was doing. "No one is going to believe that story."

Lizzie sighed. "I always did say that truth is stranger than fiction. It's the truth, Bert. Ah, there is one little thing, though. The madam's girls don't think it was an accident. Cosmo and I agree with the girls, but we're just lawyers. The case is closed and labeled an accident. Front tire exploded, and she was killed on impact. Not even one inch of space on page thirty-four. Check it out yourself. That's if you want to make it public."

"What's the name on the death certificate?" Bert snapped.

"Lily Flowers," Cosmo snapped back.

"An alias, of course?"

"Yes, one of several. She operated the Happy Day Camp under the name of Crystal Clark. That's how she was known in these parts. When she left my office, she was Lily Flowers. That's all I can tell you, the rest is covered by attorney-client privilege."

Lizzie leaned forward. She was suddenly a different person. Her eyes were cold and bright, and she was in legal mode. "Are you going to let it play out, or are you going to let it wither and die on the vine, Bert?"

"You just put me between a rock and a hard place. I need some think time. My Special Agent in Charge out here is a bulldog. He'll sniff it out sooner or later. If I shut it all down, I'm going to have to answer to the lady in the White House. She wants that woman brought to justice. If I can't deliver, the stink remains on her administration." Bert looked over at Cosmo, and asked, "Who else knows you're the attorney of record?"

"The madam's working girls, the local police, the ME, and the people at the crematorium."

"Where are the . . . working girls?"

Lizzie shook her head. "They could be anywhere. The short answer is, I do not know."

"Don't know or won't tell me?" Bert snarled.

Lizzie ignored the director's sudden anger because she knew it wasn't directed at her but at the circumstances. "I don't know."

"Are the girls on the mountain privy to all this?"

"Oh, yeah," Lizzie drawled.

"Maggie Spritzer?"

Lizzie laughed, the sound like a musical bell. "Let's just say she has ten days' worth of headlines ready to go." Lizzie looked down at the platinum watch on her wrist. "You better get moving, Bert. You're supposed to be meeting Ted at the Elvis Chapel in thirty-five minutes. With Vegas traffic, it will take you that long to get there. Maggie text messaged me a few minutes ago. Ted was thirty minutes out, so the flight is right on schedule."

"And you're going to be doing . . . what?" Bert asked as he slapped some bills down on the table. "Consider this your honeymoon lunch on the Bureau." He grinned to show there were no hard feelings concerning the show-and-tell they'd just gone through.

Lizzie reached across the table to take Cosmo's big hand in hers. She made silly moon eyes at him that left him weak in the knees. "Silly boy, we're going to continue with our honeymoon just as if there were no interruptions."

Bert wondered how in the hell it was possible to take a dead body that had just been cremated, scatter it to the four winds, then get on with a honeymoon. He decided it wouldn't be wise to ask that particular question. Instead, he stood up, bent down to kiss Lizzie's cheek, then shook Cosmo's hand, and left.

"I thought that went rather well, don't you, Cricket?"

"Which part?"

Lizzie laughed as she stood up to leave the restaurant. "Come along, Sweetie, I have some wonderful plans for the two of us. Do you like chocolate lick-off cream?"

Cosmo's canoe-sized feet stumbled, and he almost went down on his knees. Somehow or other he managed to croak that he "loved chocolate lick-off cream."

Lizzie laughed all the way to the car.

When Bert pulled up to the curb outside the Elvis Chapel, he saw Ted sitting on the far curb punching away at his BlackBerry. Strains of "Love Me Tender" wafted across the street. The record sounded scratchy and tinny, but if there were any newlyweds, they probably couldn't have cared less. A spray of water from the sprinkler system shot high in the air, missing Ted by a scant few inches. He appeared oblivious. Bert blew the horn, Ted looked up, then finished his message to Maggie before he loped over to the car.

"What's up, Mr. Director?"

"All kinds of shit, Mr. Reporter. Any news?"

"Maggie's working it. The girls on the mountain are waiting for orders. They're in their mission-control stage, trying to come up with a plan. Jack and Harry are leaving in the morning. That's it on my end unless you haven't heard about the nuptials that took place here in Vegas."

"I heard. I just had a late lunch with the newly married couple. Do you know anything about the madam?"

"Only that she's dead and one with the universe. Where have you been, Navarro?"

"Shooting marbles with Elvis. I just got here myself. What's the game plan?"

"I wish I knew. I'm waiting to hear. Maggie gave me some instructions, and you want me to check out where the funds came from to build the Happy Day Camp. That's my agenda at the moment, pure and simple. If you don't mind my asking, how are you going to handle all this with the Bureau guys here in Vegas? This is just a guess on my part, but I would think you are going to have to be extra careful and watch who you're seen with. Since the madam is officially deceased, doesn't this more or less end the investigation? If that's not the case, then I'm not getting it."

"That makes two of us. The bottom line is that no one is supposed to know the madam is deceased. She died under an alias. Right this second, I don't know where that leaves us."

"I'll tell you where it leaves everyone, especially the Vigilantes. Now they have a clear shot at going after those jerks back in D.C. Poor bastards, they don't know what's coming at them," Ted said cheerfully.

Bert took his eyes off the road for a mere second to stare at his gleeful passenger. Reporters had to be one of a kind. He made a mental note to call Elias Cummings, his mentor and the man he'd replaced as director of the FBI, as soon as he dropped Ted off at his hotel. Then, he was going to head for the nearest bar, order a drink, call Kathryn, Jack, and Harry, then order another drink or three. Eventually he would get shit-faced enough that he could make some sense out of what he was going to do and how he was going to do it. He grimaced to himself. Like that was going to happen. The last time he was shit-faced he'd been in college, and he'd sworn never to go that way again. He was strictly a one-beer kind of guy.

Chapter 11

"Young love is a wonderful thing, isn't it, Myra?" Annie whispered as she stapled the reports Maggie Spritzer had just sent her. She continued to whisper. "I don't think we're supposed to know this—not that it's exactly a secret," she added hastily, "but I think Alexis and Joseph Espinosa have a *thing* going on. That means they're communicating."

"And your point is?" Myra asked, distributing the reports around the table.

"Well, if it's true, it's a good thing. I guess. That means only Isabelle is left unattached with no one in her life but you and me. And you don't even really count, Myra, because Charles will come back at some point. Lizzie got married. Nellie got married. Maggie has Ted Robinson. I know I'm not young anymore, so why would somebody even be interested in me? So, it's just Isabelle and me who are . . . manless, for want of a better term. I'm not sure I like the feeling. It's like no one wants us. How sad is that?"

Myra stopped what she was doing and stared at her old friend to see if she was serious or just being cranky. She decided Annie was serious. She struggled for just the right words to take the stricken look off Annie's face. "Annie, it's not like you're out there in the social scene, where you can make contact with the opposite sex. We're cloistered here on the mountain, with few if any visitors. And do I have to remind you of that gentleman in Las Vegas named Little Fish who wanted you so bad he could taste it? You flirted with him, and he flirted back. Never mind that you almost shot him to death; he overlooked that little caper. I know you have his telephone number, so why don't you just call him on the secure phone? Or, text him. The girls taught you how to text message."

Annie perked up and raised her eyebrows. "Do you think, Myra, that it could be that simple?"

Myra didn't know if it was that simple or not, but she said, "I do."

"I'll give it some thought. Something else is bothering me, Myra. Do you realize how many new . . . members we have? I know I came on the scene late, but in the beginning there were just seven women plus Charles. No one knew our secrets. Think about how many people now know about us. I have bad dreams where we're all concerned." Annie got agitated all over again. "There's Lizzie, Jack, Maggie, Ted, Joseph, Harry, Bert, Cosmo Cricket, Elias Cummings, Nellie Easter, Pearl Barnes, Paula Woodley, Rena Gold, Little Fish, and of course Avery and all those other people who are on Charles's payroll. And for God's sake, let's not forget the president of the United States, who just threatened Lizzie and Cosmo. We've become a regular little army here."

"How else can we operate safely, Annie?" Not for the world would she admit to Annie that she had the same fears and the same reason for countless sleepless nights.

"I don't know, Myra, I'm just saying that I'm worried. I don't think any of them will turn on us, but it does make me nervous that so many people know our business and how we operate, not to mention knowing people who know other people so they can get in touch with us. Did I say that right? If not, you know what I'm talking about."

Myra tried for a soothing tone but didn't succeed because now Annie had piled worries on top of her own private worry because what she said made too much sense. "I do know what you're talking about, but, except for Avery, none of the outsiders know where we are, Annie."

"The president knows! She stopped by for a little visit, or were you asleep when that happened? She *knows,* Myra. She promised us a pardon that has not come through. Now she's angry with Lizzie and Cosmo as well. We could be asleep in our beds, and, boom, this mountain could be surrounded by Black Hawk helicopters and we'd . . . we'd just disappear. The world would simply think the Vigilantes had retired."

Myra fingered the pearls around her neck. Annie was making even more sense than before. "How did we go from romance to Black Hawk helicopters?"

"Because aside from feeling left out, I can't sleep. That's why we're discussing helicopters. If I'm going to be miserable and worried, so are you. You're the one who brought me here and promised me all kinds of rainbows."

Myra huffed and puffed as she almost strangled herself with her pearls. "I did no such thing, Annie. I saved your life is what I did. You were sitting there watching the Weather Channel dressed like some guru twenty-four/seven. I gave you back your life."

Annie's eyes filled. "Yes, you did, Myra. I'm sorry. It's not myself so much that I'm worried about, it's the girls. Maybe I'm just horny."

Myra started to sputter and then laughed so hard her sides ached. "That's a wee bit more than I needed to know, Annie."

Both women were startled when the front door blew

open and the girls trooped over to the war room where all business was conducted.

"It's raining!" Kathryn announced. "By tonight I think all the snow will be gone and we'll be left with a giant mud puddle."

"We might have to slide down the mountain." Yoko laughed.

Nikki walked over to the huge fireplace and added a few logs, poked at them, then warmed her hands, her back to the others. She wasn't sure, but she thought she saw Barbara dancing in the flames. She blinked, and the vision was gone. She turned to the others and grinned. Real or not, Nikki knew Barbara was nearby, at least in spirit. Barbara wouldn't let anything go wrong. "Let's see what we're up against this time, girls."

Across the country, Ted Robinson swigged coffee from a Styrofoam cup as he drove down the boulevard. Five o'clock in the morning, and there was as much traffic as if it was rush hour, whatever the hell rush hour time was in Vegas, assuming there even was one. He grunted something obscene because even a fool knew rush hour was twenty-four hours a day in most urban areas. He was meeting for donuts and coffee with a reporter he'd made contact with on his last visit to Nevada. He had no great hopes of learning anything he couldn't find out on his own, but he was never one to miss any bets because of laziness on his part only to regret it later. He hated going through land records but, that's what he was going to do as soon as the building that housed them opened—assuming Lancaster turned out to be a dry hole when it came to information.

Ted rolled into the parking lot of Krispy Kreme, parked, walked into the shop, and ordered a dozen jelly donuts to go and four coffees. Two extra as refills. Toby Lancaster was a tubby man who didn't believe in exercise and loved sweets to the exclusion of all else. He was a good reporter, though. Ted had figured that out when he first met him. The rotund little guy had sharp eyes, a sharp wit, and he hated what he called "Vegas's bullshit machine," which never stopped.

Ted paid for his purchases and used his shoulder to open the heavy plate glass door just in time to see Lancaster roar into a parking space in his battered Toyota, which obviously needed a new muffler.

The two reporters shook hands and settled themselves in Ted's rental car. Ted waited patiently for Toby to inhale four donuts before he even spoke.

"What are you up to on my turf this time around, Robinson?" Toby asked as he adjusted his wire-rimmed glasses more firmly on his nose. "It's pretty damn early even here in Vegas."

"I need to find out who paid for the property and construction of the Happy Day Camp. The brothel out there in Podunk or wherever the hell it is. Do you know it?"

"Pahrump. Only by reputation. Pretty high-class. Top-of-the-line for such establishments. Waiting list of clients. That info came to me about a year ago, and nothing else has popped up since. If something was going on, I would have heard. I have snitches I keep on retainer just the way you guys do back East. Did you try checking online? Records are open to the public."

"Drew a blank. It's buried deep. Holding companies, shell companies, corporations. Ownership might not be U.S."

"Why do you want this information? What's in it for me, Robinson?"

"I'll share the byline. Can't hurt your résumé to see your name in the *Washington Post*. Did I say above the fold? I never write anything that doesn't go above the fold," Ted boasted.

"You're not telling me why. I need to know why, Robinson."

"Well, you'll need to know for a while longer, then. The minute my boss okays me telling you, the story is half yours. You have to take my word. Hey, man, didn't I just buy you donuts and coffee? I don't do that for just anyone," Ted said virtuously.

"You want to bribe me, you're gonna have to do more than buy me donuts and coffee. Try again."

"How much?"

"Nah, I was just jerking your chain to see if you were leveling with me. Forget the land records—if it's buried, it's buried. There's this guy out in the desert who has all this green grass. You gotta admire green grass in the desert. If anyone would know, it's him."

Something clicked in Ted's head. "You mean that crazy-ass mercenary who has his property laced with claymore mines? I heard about him when I was here the last time." He wisely omitted mentioning that Little Fish was a friend of the Vigilantes.

Lancaster screwed up his face into something that passed for disbelief. "You know Little Fish?"

"Yeah, you could say that. Sort of. Kind of. I know this lady who almost shot his dick off. Some mercenary." Ted guffawed.

Lancaster didn't laugh. "If that happened, Fish allowed it to happen. No one takes him. He's like an encyclopedia of our fair state. A one-man army. He's one guy you don't want to piss off. He's got a damn platoon of ex-something-or-others who watch his back. There's nothing he doesn't know about Las Vegas. There's only one problem: he doesn't see people. That means he doesn't talk to people either. He doesn't make appointments. No one I know has his phone number."

"You really think he might know something?" Ted asked.

Lancaster stuffed his seventh donut in his mouth. He frowned to show his second coffee cup was empty.

"You want more, get it yourself. I asked you a question," Ted snapped.

"Rumor has it the guy knows everything that goes on. Nothing gets past him. All I'm saying is he might know. *Might* know. Doesn't mean he's going to tell a reporter from back East what he knows, and, think about it, why should he? What's he going to get out of talking? *Not* talking is his stock-in-trade. So what else can I help you with?"

"How do we get out there?"

"Wh . . . What?" Lancaster sputtered. "You want me to take you out there? I-don't-think-so, Robinson. Are you forgetting the part about the claymores booby-trapping the guy's property?"

"Yeah, yeah, I know. I don't remember asking you to go with me. Well, okay, maybe I did, but I wasn't serious. Reporters are not supposed to be *wusses*. We're supposed to be intrepid. You need to be intrepid to work as a reporter in D.C. You'd never make it back East."

"Yeah, well, if that guy shoots your ass off, don't call me. And, just for the record, you couldn't pay me to go east and work and live in that fishbowl you swim around in. I'm going back home to bed. Listen, Robinson, that guy Fish is for real, okay? Call me if you make it back alive. I'll do whatever I can. I'll nose around when I wake up."

"Yeah, okay, but I need directions to this Fish. Hey, wait a minute, do most people know about Fish? I'm asking because the FBI is here. What are the chances of someone talking about him to the feds?"

Lancaster scratched at the stubble on his chubby cheeks. "You didn't say anything about the FBI. I have to draw a line if the fibbies are in on this. Those guys kick ass and take names later. I don't want them kicking mine for a maybe byline. So, my answer would be *not likely*. But what the hell do I know? Fish minds his own business, so there's no reason for the fibs to check him out. But maybe they're as intrepid as you are," he said slyly. "If so, watch your back."

"Lancaster, the directions!"

"Oh, yeah. Okay, this is what you do." He rattled off a full paragraph of twists and turns, then said, "Just type it into your GPS and you're good to go."

"I-knew-that," Ted muttered as he slid behind the wheel. Before he turned the key in the ignition he sent off a text to Maggie that said he was going into the uncharted territory of a former mercenary—some guy named Fish— whose property was booby-trapped with claymore mines, and if she didn't hear from him in two hours, it meant he was dead. Hoping for some sympathy or further instructions, he was disappointed when she returned the text that simply said:

I hope your will is updated.

What Ted didn't know was that Maggie did flinch at the text. So she called Annie, who then had a legitimate reason to get in touch with one Little Fish, who sounded delighted to hear from her. Delight went to ecstatic when she explained what she wanted.

Chapter 12

Annie used the excuse that she was going to go out to the kitchen to make fresh coffee while the girls looked through the profiles she and Myra had stapled together for their viewing benefit.

In the kitchen, she did prepare the coffeepot, then pulled out her special phone. She scrolled down till she found the number she wanted. She drew her lips inward as she tried to calm her jumpy nerves. She was acting like some giddy teenager instead of the sixty-year-old woman she was. She released her bottom lip, then bit down on it as she sucked in her breath a second time before she pushed the button that would connect her to the man known as Little Fish.

"Articulate," came the response.

"What kind of greeting is that, Mr. Fish?" Annie sputtered.

"The kind of greeting one gets when their name doesn't come up on my caller I.D. I haven't heard from you in so long I thought you forgot about me, young lady."

Young lady. All riiiight. They were on the same page. "I . . . uh . . . I've been rather busy lately. I find myself in need of a favor, Mr. Fish."

"Ask and you shall receive, young lady."

Annie almost swooned as she watched the water drip into the coffeepot.

"There's a young man, a reporter, who . . . uh, works for me, in a manner of speaking. He would like to converse with you. I'd appreciate it if you would share your extensive knowledge with him."

"You would, eh? What's in it for me, young lady? Are you trying to butter me up? Do you think I'm so easy that when a pretty lady asks me to do something, I'll do it?"

"Well, yes. That's the short answer." *Pretty lady. Oh, be still my heart.* "By the way, my people are still working on our . . . little business deal to buy the Babylon. My people tell me your people are a little slow out of the gate. I hope you aren't going to tell me you ran out of money."

"Does Fort Knox run out of money? My people are just being thorough. My money is nesting in escrow along with yours, dear lady. I'd love to continue this conversation, but I see a rather strange-looking man sitting out on the road in front of my house.

"Why don't we arrange a time for me to call you when we can *really* talk? A *personal* conversation. Is there a specific time that works for you, young lady?"

Annie's knees threatened to buckle. A personal conversation. What would Kathryn and Nikki say to such a question? They'd probably tell her to play hard to get. Well, she didn't want to play hard to get. She wanted to be *available*. Who cared what Nikki and Kathryn would say?

"Why don't we say after dinner my time. Before dinner for you. I have to go now, the girls are waiting for me." Annie snapped the phone shut and slid it into her pocket. She wondered if her legs would hold her upright if she stood. This had to be her little secret. She could go into the bathroom after dinner to wait for the call. She had to keep the phone call a secret, or the others would tease her unmercifully. Yes, she knew how to keep a secret. When she was satisfied that her legs would indeed hold her upright, Annie barreled through the doorway and out to the war room, where she bellowed, "Girls, you are never going to believe this!" Only teenagers kept secrets. She was no fool. She needed *advice*. Big-time.

Ted clambered out of his rental car and looked over the terrain. It was mind-boggling that he was seeing lush green grass in the middle of nowhere, with desert all around. Living in Washington, he didn't see too much grass, and never an expanse like he was seeing now. Little patches of lawn didn't cut it. He wondered what it would feel like to tramp over the green blades in his bare feet. He looked down at his shoes.

"Don't even think about running through my grass, young man. It's to look at, to lust over, to dream about. It is not to walk on. Even I do not walk on it."

"Then what good is it? How can you enjoy such a spectacle if you don't walk on it? I thought grass was sturdy," Ted grumbled, as his mind raced to a vision of himself and Maggie having sex amid the lush greenery.

"That won't work either, young man," Fish said, knowing what was on Ted's mind. Everyone wanted to have sex on his grass. If anyone was going to christen his meadow, it would be him and no one else.

Jesus, was the guy a mind reader? Ted flushed. "Ted Robinson," Ted said, holding out his hand.

"Little Fish. People just call me Fish. I'm Indian. No point in telling you my real name because it isn't important. What brings you out here, and what do you want?"

"What? You're a mind reader and you want me to believe you don't know why I'm here? I want to pick your brain," Ted grumbled. "Is it true you have claymore mines all over this place?"

"I do. Does it bother you, Mr. Robinson?"

"Well, yeah. I don't want to get splattered to hell and back. If you love this grass so much, how come you're willing to blow it up?"

"You talk too much. Come along and walk right behind me."

Ted made sure he stepped only where he was told. When they reached the front door of the long, sprawling house, he heaved a sigh of relief.

Fish smiled to himself. No one but he and his people knew there were no mines. It was a rumor he himself had started years ago to keep lookie-loos and other unsavory people away from his property. Especially when he had to truck in water all the way from Arizona to keep his grass lush and healthy.

It was a man's house for sure, Ted thought as he looked around. Plank floors, wood all over the place, leather furniture, no feminine touches anywhere. Maggie would hate it with a passion. Indian rugs dotted the floors in some of the rooms, others hung from the walls. Ted decided he could definitely live in a place like this. But, if Maggie got her mitts on it, there would be ruffled curtains on the windows, gizmos, and knickknacks everywhere, not to mention silk plants and artificial trees.

"I'm a kitchen kind of guy. That means we'll sit out here at the table. You want coffee or soda pop? I have both. I make good coffee. Strong but good. Grind my own beans, and you have to use real cream. Not that artificial crap. Sit down, young fella, and tell me what you want to know."

Ted sat down in a wooden chair that he knew had to

weigh five hundred pounds. The round wooden table looked like it weighed half a ton and was made from old tree trunks. A bowl of bright red apples sat in the middle of the table. He stretched out his legs, and asked, "Who are you, Fish?"

"I'm the man who's making you coffee." And that was the end of that.

Ted stared at the man who was making him coffee. He was leathered and wrinkled, but his eyes were his most remarkable feature. They were summer blue, not faded like some older people's. He had plenty of hair that was iron gray and tended to curl around his ears. The fishing cap he'd taken off and squashed into his pocket was as old and as worn as the jeans and plaid shirt he was wearing. If Fish had more money than Fort Knox, as Lizzie had told Ted on his last trip, it sure didn't show in his attire. Ted knew there was a gun tucked into the back of Fish's waistband. Another was strapped to his ankle. Lizzie had told him that, too. An old guy who used to be a mercenary and who wasn't about to give up that exciting life. A rich, old mercenary, a rare commodity, Ted expected.

"Talk to me," Fish said.

"I was told that you know everything there is to know about Vegas. How come they call Wayne Newton 'Mr. Vegas' and not you?"

"Just lucky, I guess." Fish grinned.

Ted blinked at the startling white teeth that shone like beacons in the sun-darkened face. "Who put up the money for the Happy Day Camp out there in Podunk?"

Fish laughed. "Pahrump. Why do you want to know? It's not a good thing to lie to me. Not that you would, but I frown on people who try to get one over on me. You got here on sterling credentials, but that can change in the time it takes your heart to beat twice."

Ted mulled that over, and said, "Some big shit is going

down in the nation's capital. It involves the new administration. Seems the madam of the Happy Day Camp took her crew on the road and got herself in a spot of trouble. Then she did a disappearing act. The FBI is looking for her, and so is the current administration, along with some Secret Service types. And the Vigilantes are on it."

"Oh, well, then you don't have to worry about anything if the ladies are on it." Fish guffawed. "Those FBI types can't find the end of their noses, and the Secret Service isn't any better. Didn't you check the land records?"

"I did, but it's buried. I was hoping you might have heard who put the money up. It's a given that the lady didn't have those kinds of assets. Someone had to bankroll it, and that someone had to have some clout to bury it all so deep. The big question is *why?* Prostitution is legal here in Nevada. Who cares who bankrolled something like a brothel?"

"Is that what you think?"

"Well, yeah," Ted drawled, "that's what I think because I can't think any other way at the moment. I'm in the 'what, where, when, and why' business. I'm thinking that person has a lot to hide by burying it so deep. I can't believe the revenue from one brothel could bring in *that* much money that it all has to be kept secret. It has to be more than that. So what do you know?"

"That's going way back—twelve, maybe thirteen years at least. My memory isn't all that good of late. Seems to me it was some group that put up the money."

Ted managed to look disgusted. "My ass, you don't know. I was told you know *everything*. Are you telling me that's a lie, or one of those myths, like your claymore mines? Five will get you ten you don't have one mine out there in your yard. Let's cut the bullshit, it was a simple question. If you can't answer it, then I'll be on my way.

My boss pays me by the hour, and she's hell on wheels when it comes to wasting time without gleaning useful information."

Little Fish let out a loud laugh and slapped at his thigh. "I like that. Short and to the point. Time is money, that kind of thing." He poured two cups of coffee and handed one to Ted. "Bring your coffee and let's see what we can come up with. On one condition, now."

Ted stopped in his tracks. "And that would be . . . what?"

"That you tell the ladies I was helpful. I'm inclined to think I let things develop into a bit of a mess the last time we ran into one another. I'd like to clear that up."

Ted's eyebrows shot up to his hairline. "Are you asking me to put in a good word with the Vigilantes? Is that what you're asking?"

"That's what I'm asking, young fella."

"What makes you think those ladies are going to listen to me?"

"You're here, aren't you?" Fish cackled.

Ted shrugged. The man had a point. "Okay, I'll do it."

Fish smacked his hands as he led Ted into a room that looked like it belonged at the Kennedy Space Center. All Ted could do was gawk and gasp for breath. He was so astounded at the array of computers, screens, and other equipment he sloshed his coffee all over his pants leg. Fish pretended not to notice his faux pas.

"What in the name of God is all this?" Ted asked as he waved his arm about, spilling even more coffee down his legs. He barely noticed or felt the heat of the hot coffee on his leg.

"This," Fish said, "is how I know *everything*."

Ted knew that Maggie was absolutely going to love all this. He could hardly wait to get back outside so he could text her. He knew if he tried right then, Fish would break his fingers. He watched in awe as Fish settled himself on a stool in front of one of the computers. He tapped away, then scooted to another computer until he'd made the rounds of the entire room. Paper literally flew out of a line of fax machines. Ted had to force himself to stand still in the little area Fish had pointed to, just far enough away so Ted couldn't see the various passwords he was typing into all the computers.

In the blink of an eye, all the screens suddenly went blank. Fish rolled across the room to the fax machines and started gathering up all the papers. "What are you going to do with this information, kid?"

Kid? "I don't think my boss is going to sit on it, if that's what you mean. We work for a newspaper. My job is to write stories, articles, gather news. My boss's job is to publish that news. We both know who owns that newspaper, so take your best guess. That's a hell of a lot of paper you're holding in your hands."

"So it is. You want a name, right?"

"Yeah. You want to tell me who it is? Why couldn't you just tell me instead of taking up thirty minutes of my time and printing out all that stuff? Aren't you into the environment and saving all those trees? You're holding at least three trees right there in your hands."

"If I just rattled off a name, where is your second source? Don't you need *proof?*"

Silly me, Ted thought. *This guy is one step ahead of me all the way.* "Yeah, I need proof."

Fish waved a piece of paper under Ted's nose. Ted looked at the name, felt suddenly light-headed. "Oh, shit!"

"That pretty much sums it up, young fella. You want some more coffee, seeing as how you spilled most of yours? Maybe this time we should put a little jolt of something in it to bring back your color. You're looking a bit pasty right now."

"Yeah. Yeah, a little jolt would be good right now."

"One jolt coming up." The old man cackled as he led the way back to the kitchen.

Chapter 13

It was late in the day, almost everyone was gone, even Maggie's secretary. Espinosa had just dropped off a ton of papers, profiles of just about every politico in the Connor administration. Maggie eyed the pile with a jaundiced eye. Then she looked over at a red folder labeled SENATORS and a yellow folder labeled CONGRESSMEN. Her reading for the evening. Oh, joy!

The big problem was, did she really want to lug this mountain of paperwork home, then lug it back in the morning? Maybe what she should do was go out to get something to eat or order something in and stay to work her way through the profiles to see what she actually had to work with. After five minutes of serious thought, take-out food and staying at the office won out. She hadn't had Chinese in two days, Italian in three days, a mishmash of every junk food known to man yesterday. Maybe ribs and some fries. She heard her arteries snapping shut at the thought. The deli around the corner was open till ten. She could order a vegetable salad, a fruit salad, some chocolate cake, a slice of apple pie, a loaded baked potato, and some hot garlic bread. That should tide her over till she got home and could eat some *real* food. Then she remembered her larder was bare. She needed to give some serious thought to hiring someone to do her shopping and maybe even preparing some meals once in a while. She made a mental note to call Alexis, as she used to be a personal shopper when she got out of prison. Alexis would know how all that worked.

Maggie was about to pick up the phone to call the deli when she saw a shadow pass her window and move toward her door. There stood Lizzie Fox Cricket in the flesh.

As always, Maggie moaned that even on her best day she could never come anywhere near to looking like the Silver Fox. Just hours ago Lizzie had been a newlywed in Las Vegas. Now, here she was looking like she'd just stepped out of a bandbox. Her makeup was so flawless, it looked like she wasn't wearing any. Her silvery hair actually glistened under the fluorescent lights. She was dressed in a dove-gray suit with an emerald tank top underneath that just barely peeked through the neckline of the jacket, but even a glimpse complemented the emerald earrings dangling from Lizzie's ears. Maggie knew she could retire on what those babies cost. Gray ostrich-skin shoes and bag completed the picture. "The lady in silver" was how Maggie later described Lizzie to Ted.

Maggie grinned now and bolted off the chair to run to Lizzie and hug her. "I can't believe you got married! What are you doing here? Something's wrong, right? Oh, Lizzie, I am so happy for you!"

"I came to take you to a late dinner. I already called Jack and Harry. They're going to meet us at Squire's Pub. Grab your purse and jacket, and let's go or we'll be late, and, yes, something is wrong. I'd rather tell all of you at the same time."

Squire's Pub! Hmmm. Carnivorous by nature, all Maggie could think of was the five-pound Porterhouse the pub was known for, a fully loaded baked potato, a few beers, and maybe a salad, with chocolate thunder cake for des-

sert. Something was always wrong, so why get her panties
in a wad until she heard whatever it was that had brought
Lizzie back to D.C. in the middle of her honeymoon?

The Squire's Pub was exactly what the name implied, a
British saloon. It had been closed for almost a year while
the new owners renovated what was perfectly fine before the
renovations began. The only difference to the eye was that
the brass was a little brighter, and the prints on the wall
were different—mostly celebrities rather than the old pictures of hunting dogs and polo ponies. The sawdust on the
floors was fresh, and there was no stale smell of beer or
ale. All in all a pleasant place after the rush hour crowd of
federal workers departed for the suburbs.

Jack and Harry were already in a back booth, their
old-time favorite, which had been re-covered in a deep
burgundy leather. The tables were long and shellacked to
a high gloss. The guys made an attempt to stand up, but
Lizzie waved them back down. Both women slid in opposite Jack and Harry. A waiter in a ruffled white shirt,
knickers, and leggings bore down on the table. Jack
pointed to the pitcher of beer, which was almost empty.
Another pitcher and two more glasses appeared as if by
magic. Jack poured generously into the frosty mugs.
Harry made the toast to Mrs. Cosmo Cricket. They clinked
glasses, and Lizzie's face went all soft and melting. Jack
nodded and winked at her. Love was a wondrous thing.

They waited another minute before they gave their
order: steaks and loaded baked potatoes all around, garden salad, dressing on the side, garlic bread, heavy on the
garlic, and double chocolate thunder cake and coffee for
dessert.

"Okay, Miz Cricket, what's up?" Jack asked, as soon
as the waiter scurried off with their order.

Harry was left to stare at the leggings, a bemused expression on his face. He shook his head when he couldn't

figure out why a grown man would put up with an outfit like the waiter was wearing, and he said so.

"House rules, Harry. I guess waiters dress this way in the pubs in England, or the current owner thinks that's how waiters dress across the pond. Don't worry about it. Just for the record, female waitresses are called barmaids, and they wear aprons with ruffles. End of story. Okay, Lizzie, you're on."

Lizzie looked first at Maggie, and said, "I'm sorry I'm the one with the news. Ted got it, but I warned him not to call or text it to you. I just thought it would be safer if you were all told in person. Ted went out to see Little Fish. He not only got the information we need verbally, but he also got hard proof in writing. All kinds of sources, Maggie, so you will be in the clear.

"And"—Lizzie paused to take a swig of her beer— "the madam is dead. She had a car accident several days ago on the Cajon Pass. So far, Cosmo, Ted, Bert, and I are the only ones who know that the person identified as Lily Flowers, the name the deceased was using when she died, was the madam. Cosmo had her cremated, and we ... what we did was scatter her ashes in the desert. No one, not even Cosmo, knows her real name. She had various aliases along with credentials that backed up each identity. Yesterday morning, Cosmo received a packet sent by messenger. It was Ms. Flowers's will, and she gave Cosmo her power of attorney, which was over and above the authorization she had already given him to go after the johns. That's why he went ahead and had her cremated."

"What's it all mean?" Harry asked.

Then Jack and Maggie also bombarded Lizzie with questions that she didn't have answers for.

"So where does all this leave us?" Maggie asked. "No body, no Vegas madam, no case? What?"

"Flowers's girls are safe and sound for the moment. Financially, they're sound, and I doubt they will be returning to Vegas anytime soon, if ever. They're too afraid. They don't think it was an accident. Cosmo and I don't think it was an accident either. But the troopers who investigated the incident are convinced that it was. A tire blew. At this moment, I don't know which way Bert is leaning. He's got a crackerjack agent out there who, according to him, is like a bulldog. The agent might sniff this all out eventually, but then again, maybe not. The madam had a well-thought-out plan, and she acted on it. But, she did end up dead."

"But, Lizzie, where does that leave us? Do we have a mission, or don't we? If the madam is dead, doesn't that leave the Washington bad boys off the hook?"

"I don't know. Like I said, our little group is the only one who knows she's dead. They'll keep looking for her. In the meantime, it would be my guess that politics goes on as usual until something more concrete comes up. I'm going to go up to the mountain tomorrow morning."

"So, what's the big news that had to be delivered in person?" Maggie asked.

Lizzie shot Maggie a warning glance when two waiters approached with their food. Maggie almost salivated at the array of meat on her plate. A five-pound Porterhouse steak was right up her alley.

They all ate with gusto, chatting about nothing and everything. Maggie wanted to know what Lizzie had worn to her wedding. Jack asked if Cosmo had been nervous, and Harry wanted to know if Elvis had sung at the ceremony. Lizzie got all soft and dewy-eyed again as she recounted her nuptials in detail.

When the dishes were cleared away and coffee served, Lizzie dug around in her briefcase and drew out a thick sheaf of papers. "Just turn to the last page, and you'll see who the madam's financial backer was."

Jack's eyes popped.

Harry's jaw dropped.

Maggie blinked, and said, "Hot damn!"

Lizzie leaned back in her chair, her thoughts a couple thousand miles away as she wondered what her brand-new husband was doing. She hoped he was sitting in one of his beloved rocking chairs thinking about her the way she was thinking about him.

The truth was, Cosmo Cricket was talking about Lizzie to Bert Navarro over drinks at the Babylon casino. Neutral ground, so to speak, was the way he had explained it to Bert when Cosmo called him at Lizzie's insistence before she left.

It started out being an easy conversation because Bert adored Lizzie, and Cosmo loved her. They talked about his new bride for a while with Bert regaling Cosmo with some of Lizzie's spectacular courtroom victories. Cosmo's chest puffed out with pride.

"I have to be honest with you, Cosmo. Lizzie was the kind of woman I thought would never marry because she loves her career so much. Consider yourself one lucky son of a bitch. How's that gonna work, you here and her there?"

"We've worked it out for now, but for the long run it's still a work in progress. I've never met Kathryn Lucas, but I feel like I know her because Lizzie talks about her all the time. Good luck."

"Well, it's not going to go anywhere unless the president gives them a pardon. It eats at me but there's not much I can do about it. For now all I can do is help in whatever way the women want. Which brings me to my next question. What's up with your deceased client? You going to lie low on it, pretend you don't know who she is, attorney-client privilege and all that? If they find out who she really is, some of these boys might want to charge you with obstruction of justice."

Cosmo laughed. Bert winced. "You're the boss, Bert. Have you given any thought to derailing the investigation? You have that power."

"There's power, and then there's power. But, to answer your question, it's all I have been thinking about. I have to let it play out for a few more days. To yank it now will look suspicious. I'm on it." Bert started to dig in his pocket for his wallet but Cosmo held up his hand. "It's on the house. Just a little perk."

"Damn, Cricket, I need to think about moving out here. My ass is whipped right now, so if it's all the same to you, I think I'll call it a night."

"How about if you wait just a minute. I see someone headed our way that you might want to meet. One of the new soon-to-be-owners of this fine establishment we're sitting in. Name's Little Fish."

"Who's the other owner? Bet this baby went for some serious bucks."

Cosmo laughed, the chair he was sitting on shaking with his mirth. "Annie de Silva is going to be the other owner. Lizzie and I handled the details. Old Homer decided he wanted more time to play with his grandkids, and his own kids wouldn't have anything to do with him while he owned this place. Ergo, it went up for sale."

"Jesus, she owns the *Post* and now this. How much money does that woman have?"

"Now, mind you, I don't know this for a fact, but I'd say she might have a tad more than Little Fish. High rollers, the two of them."

The grizzled Little Fish stopped at their table and held out his hand to Cosmo. "Nice seeing you again, Counselor. You here on business or just taking in the sights?"

"Fish, I'd like you to meet a friend of mine, Bert Navarro, director of the FBI."

Fish studied the director for a full minute before he extended his hand. "Mighty nice to meet you, young fella. That makes two young ones I met today. Must be my lucky day."

"Sit down and have a drink, Fish. Haven't seen you in town for a while. What brings you here at"—Cosmo looked at his watch—"the witching hour?"

"Checking out my investment, as is my right. I am a bit thirsty. I think I'll have a glass of chocolate milk and maybe some peanut-butter cookies."

"This is a bar, Fish. I'm not sure . . ."

Fish snapped his fingers, and a slinky blonde wearing slut shoes made her way to the table. "Fish, honey, long time no see. Bet you want a glass of chocolate milk and four peanut-butter cookies, right?"

"That would be so nice, Elaine. The kids doing okay? What about that bum husband of yours?"

"Tommy is at Duke and made the dean's list. Pammy will graduate law school in a few months. And Sasha got accepted to NYU for the fall semester. As to that bum I was dumb enough to marry, the last thing I heard was he was panhandling out on the Strip. I don't know if that's true or not. Couldn't have made it without you, Fish. I'll just fetch your milk and cookies now."

"Nice lady," Fish said once she'd left. "Waitressing is hard work. Kids needed a little help is all. We don't need to talk about this."

Cosmo smiled. He turned to Bert, and said, "Fish has sent just about every needy kid in this town to college. Listen, I have to head out to the desert, time to go home since my new bride might be calling to wish me a good night's sleep. I wouldn't want to miss that call. Nice seeing you again, Fish. By the way, thanks for talking with Ted Robinson. I owe you one for that."

The waitress was back with Fish's chocolate milk and cookies. Fish tried to give her a folded bill, but she waved off his hand. "No! We have a deal. You help my kids, and I help you. I'm doing okay. As long as I can pay my bills, eat, and buy a new pair of shoes every so often, I'm good." She leaned over and gave the old man a soft kiss on the cheek. Only Bert saw the hundred-dollar bill going into the pocket of her skimpy apron.

"Let's talk, Mr. Director of the FBI."

Chapter 14

In a daze, the foursome walked out of Squire's Pub and stood at the curb so Jack could smoke a cigarette. He smoked these days only when he was rattled and at that moment he was so damn rattled he couldn't think straight. He puffed furiously on his cigarette as he ran Lizzie's news over and over in his mind. He could hardly wait to get home to call Nikki and get her spin on the news. Shit! Nikki didn't know the news because Lizzie was taking that news to the mountain in the morning. They were all under strict orders not to discuss anything on their cells even though they were encrypted. He supposed it made sense in some cockamamie way, but he couldn't figure out what it was. Encryption meant encryption. What was the point in having it if it didn't work? Not that Lizzie said it didn't work, she was just being cautious. So, he'd call Nikki and talk about other things. His heart kicked up an extra beat at the thought.

"You done damaging your lungs, Jack?" Harry shouted.

"Not yet," Jack shouted back. "It's not like you have anywhere special to go, Harry. You don't have anyone to tuck in. You sleep on a damn mat, so you don't have any covers or pillows to fluff up. What the hell is your problem?"

"You're my problem. I told you to quit smoking. Now you're going to stink up my motorcycle. I hate you, Jack."

"I smoke two cigarettes a day, and I am not going to stink up that death machine you fly around on. Stop acting like my mother," Jack snapped, then backpedaled slightly, his tone changing because he knew Harry was more than capable of going over a speed bump and dumping him off the Ducati. "Okay, okay, I promise to quit.

"One of these days," he added, mumbling under his breath. He tossed his cigarette on the ground, stepped on it, then—under Harry's watchful eye—because Harry was hell on wheels when it came to littering, stuck the remains of the cigarette in his pocket.

Erroneously thinking he'd won that round, Harry clapped Jack on the back and motioned to the Ducati parked at the curb. Everyone hugged, then separated. Lizzie going one way, Maggie going the other way back to the *Post*. Harry bounded over to the cycle, pulled on his helmet, and fired up the engine. Jack hopped on the back, pulled on his own helmet, and off they went, the wind and drizzle that started to fall hitting them full in the face.

Fifteen minutes later, Harry roared into the back of his *dojo* and secured his cycle with a length of chain that looked like it came off the anchor of the USS *Constitution*. He opened all of the seven locks on the back door and stood aside for Jack to enter.

"I should start keeping half my wardrobe here. But first you have to update this place. Jesus, Harry, are you *ever* going to open your mail?" Jack asked, pointing to a cardboard box big enough to hold a television set. Harry had a thing about getting mail and the possibility of bad news. Since he had no family to write him, and no one had it in for him, Jack couldn't understand his paranoia. "You really should update this place. The mats stink, and the floors sag. The windows are drafty, and I don't think there's any insulation anywhere. The kitchen, or that place where you make that shitty tea, could stand an overhaul. Isabelle is an architect, so I bet she could work you up something, for free, Harry, and you could put this place on the map. And then I wouldn't be ashamed to leave my belongings here."

"I've been thinking about it, believe it or not. You want a beer, Jack?"

Jack blinked. "Yeah, sure, one for the road. Are you jerking my chain, or are you really thinking about it?"

"Yeah, I am. I even talked it over with Yoko. I own this building free and clear. But, you're right, it needs work, and the longer I put it off, the worse it's going to get. I need a new heating unit, too." He looked over at the huge box of unopened mail. "I'm going to get to that, too. I guess it's the fact that I'll have to move out while the work is being done. In this business, you snooze, you lose."

"Get off it, Harry. You just hate change. Your people will follow you wherever you go. I know damn well the cops will let you use their gym, and so will the fibs out at Quantico. The kiddies will go to the Y if you make arrangements. Just do it, for God's sake, then put it behind you." Jack's tone turned sly. "You need to give Isabelle free rein to redo that rattrap you live in upstairs. Let her pretty it up for Yoko. Make it what she wants. You know, curtains and a big mirror with lots of lights. Some fancy carpets that hug your ankles, that kind of thing. Yoko has good taste, like Nikki and the others. You suck when it comes to décor, Harry. You really have to do something about that mail, though. I bet those census people are going to come after you for not filling out their form."

"Eat shit, Jack. What census form?"

Jack smirked. He loved one-upping Harry.

"The one where they want to know how many people occupy this building, etc., etc. If you don't fill it out, they come and haul your ass off to jail." Seeing the look on Harry's face, Jack warmed up to his story. "They don't give you any warning either. They just swoop in, and they swoop you out. In handcuffs, for the whole world to see. It's beyond humiliating. Even Lizzie won't take on the census police. I know that because Nikki is a lawyer, and she told me no lawyer wants to take them on. Even though you're a U.S. citizen, you are still a foreigner to those census police. What's Yoko going to think about *that?*"

"I hate you more than I did before, Jack." Harry eyed the box of mail, then gave it a kick. The box, which had to weigh at least twenty pounds if not more, sailed across the room. All with one flick of Harry's big toe.

"See you tomorrow, Harry. That was some news Lizzie had, huh?" Jack grabbed his garment bag and his duffel. "Hey, if those census police come after you, call me. I think I read somewhere that they give you one call." Jack was already in the alley behind the *dojo* when Harry shouted to him.

"What can you do that Lizzie can't do?"

Did I hear right? Had the great Harry Wong, the number two martial arts expert in the world, actually asked me a question that implied he might avail himself of my legal expertise? Nah, I must have heard wrong. He called back over his shoulder, and said, "I can say 'I told you so'!" Jack laughed himself silly as he locked his car doors, gunned the engine, and backed out of the narrow alleyway. He laughed all the way home because he loved Harry as if he were his own brother.

While Jack was driving home, Big Pine Mountain was bustling with activity even though it was close to midnight. When the girls were on a roll, they rolled.

"Where did Annie go?" Myra asked as she poured hot chocolate into heavy mugs.

"She went over to the Big House for an extra sweater. She said she feels like she's coming down with a cold," Yoko said.

Myra sniffed. "Annie never gets a cold. She's forever taking vitamin C and those Airborne tablets to ward off germs. And she never feels cold either." Myra lowered her voice to a whisper. "I think she's up to something."

"And you're just figuring that out, Myra?" Nikki teased. "I think, and this is just my opinion, but I think she's been in contact with one Little Fish. I think she has the hots for him. I also think he has the hots for her."

Myra's fingers went to the pearls on her neck.

"But, if I was a betting woman, I'd bet when she comes back here, with her sweater, she's all smiles. And she won't be wearing the sweater either. The sweater is a prop." Nikki giggled.

"Oh, dear. Well, if it makes her happy to speak with that cantankerous curmudgeon, let her do it," Myra said.

"Love is in the air." Isabelle laughed.

"It's getting late, girls. Let's finish up here so we can go to bed. We want to be fresh and alert tomorrow when Lizzie gets here, and I want us to have a game plan that will work for all of us," Myra said.

Kathryn leaned across the table, her hands flat. Her expression looked fierce. "I have a question. Maybe it's not actually a question but more of a statement. Have any of you given any thought to Annie and Little Fish buying that casino from Homer Winters? I realize I'm no business major or financial guru, but don't you think it's a little strange, aside from the cost? When Annie bought the *Post,* we all understood that because it helped us. Maggie took it over and made it work. Again, for us. Ted Robinson and Joe Espinosa are now on board. Flash-forward to the Babylon casino. Why? Annie certainly doesn't need the money. So, it comes back to why?

"Am I the only one who is wondering what that means to all of us? Are we going to be relocating to Vegas? With Charles out of the picture, at least for the moment, I suppose it would make sense. I say when Annie gets back, we grill her. If she's buying it as an investment . . . then I'll not mention it again. Right now it just doesn't make sense to me. And, ask yourself, if I'm right, how could we be *safe* in Las Vegas?"

The other Sisters looked at one another, and, as one, they shrugged to show they knew nothing more than Kathryn did; but now that she'd brought it to their attention, they needed to discuss the situation.

Myra caressed the pearls at her neck. "You make it sound like Charles has abandoned us for good, and we have to find an alternative . . . I'm not sure I understand what you're all worried about."

"Oh, Myra, no, we aren't saying Charles will never come back," Alexis said. "I think he will, I just don't know when. This hiatus, for want of a better word, has to be dealt with by us right now. I personally don't want to relocate, especially for someplace as visible as Las Vegas. We're safe here, so why put that safety in jeopardy? I think it's just a business deal."

"Alexis, we aren't exactly safe right now. The current administration, the president in particular, and some members of the Secret Service know *exactly* where we are. They could fly overhead and pick us off like clay pigeons," Kathryn said. "With everything Lizzie has said to date about her and the president, and the fact that she cut her honeymoon short to come up here has to mean something. Maybe we *should* give some thought to relocating. At least we need to be open to the possibility and prepare to leave at a moment's notice. First thing in the morning, we need to contact Avery Snowden and apprise him of our current situation. Do we all agree?"

"We're making decisions here without Annie," Yoko pointed out.

"Did I hear my name mentioned?" Annie asked, slamming the door behind her. "In case anyone is interested, it stopped raining, but the wind is horrendous. I think we might lose a few trees at some point. What were you talking about?" They all noticed she was carrying a bulky sweater.

"You did, dear heart," Myra said. "We were discussing you and Mr. Fish buying the Babylon casino from Homer Winters. The girls, me included, are wondering if we might have to leave the mountain and possibly relocate to the desert. What did Mr. Fish have to say, Annie?"

Annie flushed a bright pink. "What makes you think I was talking to Little Fish?"

"Because you look guilty," Kathryn said.

Annie bit down on her lower lip. "I guess I'm not very good at subterfuge, am I?" Without bothering to wait for a reply Annie pushed on. "So, yes, I called him, and we talked. He said that he spoke to Ted Robinson and to Lizzie, but he wouldn't discuss what they talked about over the phone. He doesn't trust all that high-tech stuff. He's a boots-on-the-ground kind of person and does everything the old-fashioned way. He did say that he could keep us all safe if we ever want to venture to Vegas. Actually, he said he and his people could keep us safe. He said he's worried about us, me in particular. There, I said it. Now, are you all happy that I'm embarrassed?" She tossed the bulky sweater onto an empty chair, then eyed it malevolently like it was the sweater's fault that she was in the position she suddenly found herself in.

"Uh-huh," Myra said. "Serves you right for trying to hide something from us."

"All right, Myra. I lost my head there for a minute. I spoke to Fish just . . . just because I wanted to see if he was really interested in me as a person or because we are doing a business deal. I know the way I wanted it to go, but I didn't want to be humiliated in front of all of you in case I was wrong."

"Wow, Annie! We would have found a way to go out to Vegas and kill him if he was trifling with your affections. Didn't you know that?" Kathryn demanded.

Annie blanched, then she started to laugh. The others joined in at Annie's expense, even Myra, who wiped at her eyes. Finally, Annie managed to gasp, "I want this to be all about me."

The girls whooped.

"Absolutely it has to be all about you," Yoko said happily. "We can make that happen if you let us. How soon do you need our help in working out a plan for you?"

Annie gasped. "How soon? Good Lord, I don't know. I'm looking at this as . . . as *foreplay.*"

The girls whooped again.

"Foreplay, is it? Now you're getting it!" Nikki grinned.

"Enough, girls. We can work on Annie and her seduction later. We have issues to discuss, problems to solve, and plans to make," Myra said.

The women settled down in a nanosecond. They waited for Myra to speak.

Maggie Spritzer leaned back in her chair. Her eyes felt like they were full of grit. The heavy dinner she'd consumed hours ago was just a memory. She felt hungry. She tried to ignore her rumbling stomach. She closed her eyes for a moment as she tried to ignore her hunger and concentrate on the news Lizzie had shared with her, Jack, and Harry. Just hours ago, she'd had a plan. In her mind

she had ten days' worth of headlines. Now that was all
shot to hell with Lizzie's new information, and she had to
go down another road. It boggled the mind. Not that she
couldn't come up with bigger, bolder headlines; she could
but . . . But what? No buts. She was going to pack up and
go home and sleep in her own bed. She'd earned that
right. Tomorrow was another day. She'd be fresh and well
fed in the morning and ready to take on the world.

Thirty-five minutes later, the cab dropped Maggie off
at her door. Maggie paid him and climbed out of the cab.
She didn't know why, but she looked three doors down to
where Jack Emery lived and was surprised to see that
every light in the house was on. She frowned as she trotted down the street and up the steps to ring the doorbell.
It was twelve thirty.

Jack opened the door and didn't seem surprised to see
Maggie standing on his doorstep with her shoes in her
hands. "Come on in."

"Can't sleep, huh?"

"You got that right. I was just making some hot tea.
You want some?"

"Sure. You got anything to eat?"

"A deli rotisserie chicken. Help yourself."

Maggie helped herself. "How come you can't sleep,
Jack?"

"For the same reason you've been working all night
and are sitting here in my kitchen eating cold chicken.
How the hell is this going to end, Maggie?"

"Badly, Jack. People have to take responsibility for
their actions. There's a right way to do things and a wrong
way. You go after the bad guys and hope to hell you did it
right. I print the news to inform the reading public and try
to keep people honest. The *Post* is going to go with the
story. I have total control. What? Why are you looking at
me like that?" Maggie dropped the chicken leg she'd been

chewing onto a paper plate, then wiped her hands on a length of paper towel that Jack handed to her.

"I don't know. It doesn't feel right to me."

"Me either, Jack, but it's news. Big news! Actually, it's the biggest I ever came across. Don't even think about asking me to back off," Maggie snarled. No one told her how to run with a story, not even Ted. Certainly not Jack.

"I wasn't going to ask you to back off. But I think you need to talk to the girls. For Christ's sake, they don't even know what Lizzie just told us yet. Since no one knows but us, you can wait to print it for a few days—hell, for a week—unless something else crops up. Is something wrong with the chicken? There's still half of it left."

Maggie looked down at the exquisitely bronzed bird on the platter. Lemon pepper. She loved lemon pepper chicken. She wrapped the remainder of the chicken and put it back in the refrigerator. When she returned to take her seat at the table, she had a bottle of Yoo-hoo in hand.

"I'm full. It was good, just what I needed. You can drink the tea. Tea will keep you awake."

"You must have a tapeworm. I never saw anyone eat like you and not gain an ounce of weight," Jack grumbled. "Well?"

"It's all legit. Lizzie wouldn't have shared with us what she had if she were afraid of the content. It's for real, Jack, and, yes, I can hold off. That's not a problem. I just don't want to get scooped. This town leaks like a sieve; you know that as well as I do."

"Maggie, you make one mistake, and it's all over. I just want us all to be on the same page and everyone's ass covered nine ways to Sunday. They're going to go after you, you know that, right?"

"Oh, yeah," Maggie said, the light of battle in her eye. "They can try. I have the power of the written word. I have contacts at other papers. I can be global within seconds, you know that. You just have to prepare. I know how to do that, Jack. And before you can ask my opinion, let me voice it. There is no delicate way to put this other than to say the shit is going to hit the fan, and there is no way you can contain it. I, personally, do not feel sorry for any of the people involved, and that includes the president. My gut will tell me when to go with the story even if it doesn't fit your timetable. So, what's your opinion?"

Jack flapped his hands one way, then the other. "Actually, this may surprise you, but I agree with you. I'll do my best to watch your back, and so will Harry. When is Ted getting back?"

"He was supposed to come back with Lizzie, or Lizzie was supposed to come with him, but the Gulfstream needed some kind of servicing. He's airborne as we speak. He used the waiting time to do some more sniffing around. He said we'd talk in the morning, and that's good enough for me. I need to go home now. Call me if anything changes or if something goes down that I should know about."

Jack walked Maggie to the door and waited on the stoop until he saw her enter her house and the lights go on inside. He looked up and down the silent street with its sodium vapor lamps that had an aura around them. Across the street an elderly gentleman was walking a tiny dog that looked to weigh about two pounds. He knew the man's name was Thomas Ryder, and the dog's name was Priscilla. Ryder looked over at Jack and waved. Jack waved back. *Just another normal night in Georgetown? I wish,* Jack thought.

Chapter 15

Bert Navarro knew he couldn't stall any longer. It was time to show his face at the Las Vegas Field Office to exert his authority if need be. He looked at the clock on the dashboard of the Bureau car and winced. It was ten thirty AM. Kathryn or someone on the mountain should have called him already. His stomach muscles crunched into a hard knot.

Lizzie had texted him earlier in the morning saying she was on a six o'clock flight, and with the forty-minute drive to the base of the mountain from the airport, she would be on top of Big Pine Mountain no later than 10:30 EST unless the flight was late. By his watch, the girls were three hours late in calling. On the other hand, maybe the women had things to catch up on, girl things, before they got down to business. So, okay, two hours. Maybe they didn't think this was as important as he thought it was. The third possibility, since he was being so generous in giving them leeway, was they were having lunch, and Kathryn always said that the rule on the mountain was no business was ever discussed until after a meal, be it breakfast, lunch, or dinner. Despite these thoughts, his stomach muscles refused to relax.

"Screw it!" he mumbled as he pulled out of a Burger King parking lot.

Bert admitted to himself that he felt jittery, an alien feeling, something no good agent ever admitted to. Technically, he wasn't an agent anymore, he was the director of the FBI, which was even more reason not to admit to feeling jittery. Nothing good was going to happen that day, he could feel it in his bones.

The BlackBerry in his breast pocket chirped a cheery sound. He winced when he saw the caller was Cosmo Cricket and not Kathryn or one of the other girls on the mountain. He let loose with a mighty sigh as he tried to keep his eyes on the busy traffic and at the same time watch for the turnoff that would take him to the local field office.

The amenities took all of three seconds before Cosmo jumped right to the core of his call. "How do you want me to play this, Bert?"

"What are you talking about, Cosmo? I'm on my way to the office right now. I'll be there momentarily. Did something happen I don't know about?" Stupid question for the director of the FBI to be asking. He realized it the moment the words were out of his mouth.

"I have it on good authority that your people are on the way to see me sometime this morning. I think they found out about that little accident on the Cajon Pass. So I'm asking you how you want me to play this. I haven't heard from Elizabeth since she left this morning. She should be on the mountain by now. It's not like her to go silent. Have you heard anything?"

"No, not a word. I feel the same way you do at this moment. Okay, listen, Cosmo, I'm pulling into the parking lot. Let's do this. If I don't call you, give me ten minutes and call me again. Take my cues whatever they may be, and we'll go from there. We wing it."

Bert scrambled out of the car and made his way across

the lot to the field office. He walked in unannounced and proceeded down a short hallway to Duncan Wright's office. He stood in the doorway and waited for the Special Agent in Charge to end his telephone call. A moment later another agent shoved a cup of coffee in Bert's hand. Bureau hospitality at its finest.

Wright motioned to one of the three chairs in the room. Bert shook his head. He never sat with an agent. Elias Cummings had told him power came from those standing. "Talk to me," was all Bert said.

"I wish there was something to talk about, Director. Nothing really has changed since yesterday. It's a dry hole all around. But one of my guys has been running the accident chart and checking all the hospitals within a hundred-mile radius. He came up with an accident on the Cajon Pass that probably means absolutely nothing, but he's been checking it out. The profile of the victim could, I say *could*, match the woman we're looking for. Right age, according to her driver's license, but that's it. I just got off the phone with him. My guy has been talking with the troopers who investigated the accident. Tire blowout, driver killed on impact. Pretty cut-and-dried at first blush."

Bert could feel the fine hairs on the back of his neck prickle in alarm. "What? Don't make me pull it out of you. What happened after the first look?"

"My guy checked with the ME and was told that Cosmo Cricket claimed the body. The ME said there was no reason not to release the body. My guy was told there was no next of kin and that was why Cricket claimed the body. 'She was a client' is what Cricket told the ME. Digging even deeper, my guy was told Cricket had the body cremated and picked up the ashes of the deceased around four yesterday afternoon."

"And you want me to believe, because you believe,

that the accident victim on the Cajon Pass was possibly our madam. Is that what you're saying? That's a bit of a stretch, don't you think, Agent Wright?"

"No, Director, that's not what I'm saying. But, it is a possibility, a stretch, as you say. Since we have nothing else, we might as well check it out. Sometimes the most unlikely events turn into major events."

"What was the victim's name?" Bert pretended to look bored. If anything, he felt like he was going to jump out of his skin.

"Lily Flowers."

"And?" Bert asked through clenched teeth.

"And, she checks out. But, she's like some enigma. We can't find anyone who actually knows her. There's no one to verify she is Lily Flowers. By the same token, there is no reason to think the woman was traveling under an alias. I was planning on paying Cosmo Cricket a visit this morning. Since she was his client, he should be able to give us a description of her. There are no medical or dental records to compare. It's probably another dry hole, but it's all we have at the moment. I might be wasting manpower, but, like I said, it's all we have."

"Cricket isn't going to help you. Attorney-client privilege. Doesn't matter if the client is dead."

"Mr. Las Vegas himself," Agent Wright said, his tone flat. "If we try to put the squeeze on that guy, this town will shut down tight, but I want to give it a shot. He's the go-to guy. He's a legend around these parts. Having said that, I've never heard a bad word about him. All I've heard is he's a stand-up guy, and you don't mess with him."

Bert allowed himself a snort of disgust. "We're the fucking FBI. We mess with people; it's what we do. We're our own legend. A man of his stature will cooperate. This town won't want the entire resources of the Bureau swooping down on it." Bert hoped he sounded vicious enough to satisfy Wright.

"You aren't getting it, Director. We won't get a chance to *swoop* into town. They'll chop us off at the knees before that can happen. In these parts, FBI stands for 'Fools Bastards Idiots.' We tread lightly. People simply disappear. With people like Cricket and a crazy son of a bitch called Little Fish out there in the desert, we don't have a prayer, FBI or not. What I'm trying to say here is Vegas takes care of its own. And it's true what they say, 'What happens in Vegas stays in Vegas.' I'm just waiting for those damn Vigilantes to come back out here to make fools of us again. Just thinking about them makes my blood boil."

Bert wanted to say that one of the Vigilantes in particular made his blood boil, but he didn't. "Let's go see Mr. Cricket, Agent Wright."

The sharp-eyed agent stared at Bert, who held his gaze. "You want a rundown on Cricket before we head out? We can do it in the car, or do you plan on driving your own vehicle?"

"I'll follow behind you. I know all about Cosmo Cricket. Did you know he just got married? Actually, to a friend of mine. I missed the nuptials, but I did have a drink with him last night. He appeared to be a stand-up guy. Big man."

"Are you telling me some woman actually married that guy?" Agent Wright asked, his face registering disbelief.

"Well, yes, that's usually the way it works. Cricket's new wife is a high-profile lawyer back in D.C. Lizzie Fox. She's a personal friend."

"Jesus H. Christ! *She* married Cosmo Cricket! Why?"

Bert decided to add a little fuel to the fire. "Agent Wright, did you just fall off the turnip truck? Either they got married because they're in love, because usually that's the way it works, or it was a merger of legal minds and the two of them will own this town before long. Take your pick."

"Oh, shit!"

Then Bert added a little more fuel to the already raging inferno he'd just started. "Cricket told me the town is planning some big wingding to celebrate his marriage. They're actually going to shut down for six hours and it will be wall-to-wall parties. Stock options for gifts. Bonuses for gifts. Gifts, gifts, gifts! Lizzie Fox will be one happy bride. Women do love gifts!"

"Oh, shit!"

"You need to expand your vocabulary, Agent Wright. I'll follow behind you." Without another word, Bert turned on his heel and left the office, Wright trailing behind him.

Bert waited until the Special Agent in Charge peeled out ahead of him. He swung in right behind him and immediately pressed the number on his BlackBerry that would connect him with Cosmo Cricket. He didn't bother with a greeting. "We're on our way. Any word from the mountain?"

"I'm calling now, no one is responding. I'm sure nothing is wrong, the girls are probably weighing their options. Women, even the Vigilantes, have to talk things to death before they make a decision. Like I said, you know women."

Bert said, "Uh-huh," even though he didn't know if what Cricket was saying was true or not. For some crazy reason he thought Cricket knew less about women than he did. And what he *didn't* know about women would fill a bushel basket. Based solely on his size, Cricket would have ten bushel baskets of things he didn't know. What didn't he know about Kathryn? She was pretty outspoken. With Kathryn it was black or white. And she never beat a dead horse. Kathryn was all action. His face and neck grew warm at the thought of his new love.

Bert did his best to shift his thoughts to the problems at hand, but his mind stayed on the girls, Kathryn in particular. Why wasn't anyone calling him? What the hell was going on up there on the mountain?

Ten minutes later, Bert turned over his car to a valet and followed Agent Wright into the casino that housed Cosmo Cricket's offices. They rode up in the elevator in silence. When they exited, Bert looked around and marveled at the money that poured in and out of the very place he was standing in. He tried to stifle the grin he felt building. Lizzie had done all right for herself.

Cosmo's secretary smiled at both men, and said, "Mr. Cricket is expecting you. Go right on in."

"See! See! He *knew* we were coming. He *knows* everything. Before it happens," Agent Wright hissed out of the corner of his mouth.

Cosmo was standing next to the portable bar at the far corner of his luxurious office, which was bigger than the entire field office building. He turned and lumbered over to where the two men were standing inside the inner sanctum. "Gentlemen, please, come in. Can I offer you coffee, tea, or perhaps a light breakfast? I have a chef who can whip up whatever you're in the mood for." He motioned to the huge plate glass window, beyond which a table was set for four. A squat cut-crystal bowl held a dozen delicate pink roses. Both men declined his generous offer.

Bert held out his hand, then introduced Agent Wright.

The brief amenity over, Cosmo waved his hands, which were bigger than a grizzly's head, to show that the men should take a seat across from his desk. Cosmo walked around to his rocking chair and sat down. Bert thought the floor shook momentarily.

Cosmo took the initiative, and said, "I assume you are

here on business that you somehow think involves a client of mine who is now deceased."

Agent Wright bristled. Bert felt amused as Cricket leaned back in his rocker, a smile on his face.

Still bristling, Wright asked in a surly tone, "So you admit that Lily Flowers was a client of yours?"

"Agent Wright, why would you think I would deny it?"

"Because lawyers are big on denial from the git-go," the FBI man said in the same surly tone. "What can you tell us about her?"

"Why?" Cosmo asked.

"Because we think she might be part of an ongoing investigation."

"What investigation?" Cosmo asked.

"That's need to know, Counselor. Just answer the question."

"I don't answer questions about my clients until I know why you're asking them. Since you seem reluctant to inform me, I will assume it's because you don't have anything to go on in your investigation of the madam out there at the Happy Day Camp. Which brings me back to my original question, *why?*"

"Cut the crap, Cricket. I'm not in the mood to dance around on this. It was a legitimate question, so answer it."

"My response was a legitimate response. In fact, I answered the question for you as a show of good faith. By the way"—Cosmo pointed to a weird-looking machine on the corner of his massive desk—"this conversation is being recorded."

"What? That's illegal. You didn't . . ."

"I don't have to inform you of anything. I didn't invite you here. There's a sign right there by the machine and another one on the door saying all conversations are recorded unless otherwise stated. If you didn't see it, that's your problem, not mine. My employers insisted. If you don't like it, take it up with Judge Orenstein. Next question."

Agent Wright was beet red from the neck up. He looked at Bert, who was staring at a colorful painting on the wall behind Cosmo's desk.

"What can you tell us about Lily Flowers?"

"She was a client, and now she's deceased," was Cosmo's response.

"I know that. What I want to know is what you can tell us about her. We can't find any next of kin or anyone who knows her. The ME told us you claimed the body, then had it cremated. Why did you do that? I don't see that being part of attorney-client privilege."

"My client had no next of kin. I personally don't know if she had friends or not. No one claimed the body. Because she was my client, I claimed her and had her cremated and her ashes scattered. I felt it was the right thing to do. As my client's personal representative or executor of her will, I stepped up to the plate. End of story."

"You certainly didn't waste much time, did you?"

"I take great exception to that comment, Agent Wright. I don't think anyone, client or otherwise, should lie in a cold morgue in a drawer if someone is willing to make the final arrangements. Like I said, it was the right thing to do. If you feel I did something wrong, sue me. Or go before Judge Orenstein and take it up with her."

Bert switched his attention to another painting. It was obvious to him that Cosmo liked bright colors.

"What did she look like?"

"Who?"

"Will you cut the crap, Cricket? You know damn well who I'm talking about, Lily Flowers. I can haul your ass down to the office and sweat you there for seventy-two hours if I want to. Now answer the goddamn question and stop screwing around."

Cosmo leaned closer to his desk and folded his big hands as he stared at Agent Wright. "Make me."

Bert almost laughed out loud. He simply pointed to the weird-looking machine on Cosmo's desk. The movement was not lost on Agent Wright, who somehow managed to look properly chastised.

Bert took his turn. "Cosmo, is there anything you can tell us about Lily Flowers that won't breach the privilege attached?"

Cosmo smiled. "Not much. I only met her once, and it was after-hours. She didn't have an appointment and got here just as I was leaving. I don't think we spoke for more than an hour, if that long. She asked me to handle her affairs. I have her will and her power of attorney. She said she would get back to me to tell me precisely what she wanted me to do for her. She paid me a retainer, $5,000, to be exact, then she left. A day or so later I saw a notice in the paper about the accident. I followed up on it, and that's all I can tell you."

"Did you make a photocopy of the check?" Bert asked, knowing what the answer was going to be.

Cosmo laughed. A great, booming sound that ricocheted around the huge room. "This is Las Vegas, Director. Cash is king. Miss Flowers paid me in a single bundle of crisp hundred-dollar bills. There was a bank band around them, which led me to think human hands had never touched them. And, no, I did not photocopy the bills. My secretary deposited the money the following day. Alas, no fingerprints, if that's your next question."

Bert nodded. "Can you give us a description of your client?"

"I can do better than that. I can give you a video. It goes without saying there is no sound. And, no, you won't be able to get an expert to lip-read. My employers insist on little things like that. Would you like to see a picture of my client?"

Agent Wright almost fell off his chair in his excitement. Bert just leaned back and crossed his legs and waited while Cosmo fiddled and diddled with a remote. Cosmo pointed to a small screen that appeared suddenly over the bar. A second later they were all looking at Cosmo's late-evening client.

Agent Wright jumped up. "I want that!"

"I bet you do, but you aren't going to get it. Memorize it and have one of your in-house artists do a rendering. Look at it all you want, but it stays here."

"You're obstructing justice, Cricket," Agent Wright snarled.

"Bullshit! Are we done here? I have a meeting and a call coming in that I absolutely have to take." He might as well have said, *"Get the hell out of my office so I can deal with real business."*

Bert was up like a jack-in-the-box. "Then we'll leave you to it, Counselor."

Bert understood what was going on immediately when he saw Cosmo look down at the vibrating cell phone sitting on his desk—a call was coming in from the mountain. Now all he had to do was shake Agent Wright and either take his own call, which would likely come through any minute, or wait until Wright was out of the building so he could go back to Cricket's office. He decided to opt for the latter and when they reached the hallway Bert told Wright to go on ahead while he went to the restroom. His parting shot to his agent was, "FBI 101: you get more flies with honey than vinegar. I'll take it from here, Agent Wright."

If Agent Wright had had a tail, it would have been between his legs when he scurried ahead of the director.

What Bert didn't see as he turned right to trace his way to the men's room was that Agent Wright turned left, then doubled back. Nor did Bert see Wright when he came out of the restroom and headed back to Cosmo Cricket's office.

The moment Bert opened the door, Cosmo's secretary was off her chair and headed toward him. "Mr. Cricket is waiting for you, Director." In the blink of an eye, the door was locked, and she was back behind her desk. At Bert's questioning look, she said, "Your agent didn't leave. He's . . . lurking on the floor."

Lurking. So much for FBI stealth and having the upper hand. He shrugged because there was nothing else he could do. He pushed open the door to Cosmo's office and waved airily. Cosmo motioned for him to sit down.

Like he was really going to sit down. He was too jittery to sit. He was too jittery to stand still, too. So, he paced first one way, then the other, until Cosmo hung up the phone.

"Relax, Bert! That was Elizabeth. Seems there was a snafu at the airport when she landed. They were out of rental cars and one had to be brought to her from another agency. The translation is there was a two-hour delay. She also lost some time on the highway because of a tractor trailer accident. She is safe on the mountain as we speak, and the girls are going into the meeting now. That's the sum total of what I know at the moment."

"That's it?" Bert asked, as his stomach muscles clenched and unclenched.

"Well, Bert, if you want all the details, Elizabeth said she loves me and misses me. Did my secretary tell you Agent Wright stayed behind on the floor and saw you come back here?"

"She did. I would have done the same thing if I were in his position. He's a good agent. Top-notch, as a matter of fact. Look, I'm straddling the fence here. I have to be careful."

"Understood. I have a private elevator if you want to leave unannounced. You could go down one floor, come back up by the main elevator and come up behind him to show you weren't asleep at the switch. Will that work for you?"

Bert laughed. "Damn straight it will. Just for the record, were you really recording our conversation?"

"Yeah. Like I said, my people leave nothing to chance. Sorry, but it's beyond my control. You might want to give some thought to reining in your agent before things get out of hand. All the FBI needs to know is that Lily Flowers died in a tragic car accident and has nothing to do with any ongoing FBI investigation. If you don't do that, it's out of my hands."

"I'll take care of it. Where's the elevator?"

Cosmo heaved himself up and out of his rocking chair and walked him over to what Bert thought was a door to either a closet or possibly a bathroom. He watched as Cosmo pressed a button, and the door slid to the side. Bert knew the elevator had been constructed to fit Cosmo Cricket.

The two men shook hands. The door slid shut, and Bert pressed the button that would take him down one floor. When he stepped out, he looked around for an EXIT sign and climbed the steps to Cosmo's floor. He almost laughed out loud when he saw his agent hiding behind a huge, bushy ficus tree that reached almost to the ceiling. Bert crept up to his agent and tapped him on the shoulder. "You waiting for a bus, Agent Wright?"

Agent Wright whirled around and for one crazy moment Bert thought he was going to try to scale the tree. "What? How?"

"I guess you thought I didn't see you doubling back. Since when do my agents spy on their director?"

Speechless for the moment, Agent Wright just stared at Bert. "It's in my job description. I guess I failed the test."

"Yeah, Agent Wright, you failed the test. And you also wasted your time, my time, and Mr. Cricket's time. All because you had a wild hair up your ass. There's nothing here. Do we at least agree on that?"

Agent Wright drew himself up to his full height and stared at his boss. "I don't agree with you, Director. I do think something is here, and Cricket is stonewalling us."

Bert motioned for the Special Agent in Charge to follow him to the main elevator. "I'm going to give you two choices. One, I'm going to let you pursue this dry hole so that you can make an ass out of yourself, at which point I will have you transferred to the Mojave office, or, two, I'm going to give you a few hours to come to the realization that there is nothing here, and you close out this case because it's a dead end."

Going to the Mojave was a fate worse than death. Cosmo Cricket wasn't a dead end. Wright could feel it in his pores. There was something here, he just wasn't sure what it was. Twenty years as an agent had honed his instincts to a sharp point. And his instincts told him he was right.

The director was waiting for his response. Wright didn't have to squeeze his eyes shut to remember what it was like at the Mojave office. He'd been there twice when a case demanded he track a trail that led him there. It was the end of the road for agents who had screwed up. "With all due respect, sir, I'd like to have a composite made up and a few days to show it around. If I come up dry, I'll lay it to rest."

It wasn't an unreasonable request, and there was no good reason for Bert to deny it. "Okay, you have forty-eight hours."

Agent Wright wanted to stomp his feet in frustration.

What the hell could he do in forty-eight hours? His facial features closed tight. He was so angry he couldn't speak, so he nodded.

"Good, we're on the same page. I'll meet you back at the office in an hour or so. I have a couple of stops I want to make. Don't even think about putting a tail on me, Agent Wright. I have to admit it took some guts to double back and spy on me, but it is still going in your file."

Agent Wright found his tongue. "Yes, sir." As he made his way through the revolving doors, he mumbled under his breath, "Fuck you and the horse you rode in on."

Bert grinned as he waited for the valet to fetch his car. He knew exactly what Agent Wright was muttering under his breath because he would have muttered the same thing.

Chapter 16

The moment the cable car slid into its nest on the platform, the Sisters ran outside to welcome Lizzie de Silva Fox Cricket. The greetings were loud and cheerful, the hugs bone-crushing. And then came the grumbling about missing the big event, to which Lizzie just smiled and smiled.

Annie herded them all to the dining room, where a festive table was set, the decorations homemade but made with love. In the center of the table a three-tier wedding cake that listed slightly to the side welcomed the new bride. Tears rolled down Lizzie's cheeks as another round of hugs and congratulations were bestowed on her.

"Pineapple-coconut, your favorite," Annie, the baker of the cake chortled. "Coconut frosting."

"Oh, girls, it's exquisite! I wasn't expecting anything like this. I didn't have a wedding cake! This is so wonderful! Thank you, thank you, thank you. Somehow, this makes it all the more official. I need to take a picture of this cake so I can send it on to Cosmo. I bet you all don't know Cosmo can cook! He can! And he uses every pot, pan, and bowl he owns just to make scrambled eggs. He's a better cook than I am." More tears dripped down Lizzie's cheeks. A moment later a picture of Annie's slightly crooked cake was on its way to Cosmo.

"We didn't have an opportunity to shop for a wedding gift. So, we all talked it over and agreed that we want you to have a ten percent interest in the Babylon. That's our gift to you and Cosmo," Annie said.

"Oh, my God!" was all Lizzie could say.

"Since you're handling the legal end of things, make sure you work that in. Little Fish is quite happy with the deal, by the way. Now it's time to eat this wonderful cake. Myra made fresh coffee, and it's just waiting to be poured. Lizzie, you get to cut the cake. Give me your phone, and I'll take a picture so you can send it on to Cosmo," Annie said as she reached for Lizzie's cell.

More pictures were taken and sent to Cosmo, the cake cut, the coffee poured. The Sisters babbled happily as they devoured the confection.

"You have to take some of this wonderful cake with you and put it under your pillow tonight," Myra said. "All your dreams will come true."

"No, you're supposed to put it in the freezer and save it for next year on your anniversary," Nikki said wistfully.

In the end it was decided that Lizzie would take two pieces, one for under her pillow and one for the freezer.

"Okay, girls, it's time to get down to business. When I leave here my plan is to head back to Vegas after I make one more stop," Lizzie said.

Isabelle and Alexis cleared the table. Yoko was making more coffee as Lizzie hauled her briefcase up and onto the table.

"Listen up, girls!"

"We're listening, Lizzie. Tell us what's going on. We need to know what's expected of us," Nikki said.

"Some of this you know, but let me give it all to you in order. We all know what went down before and after the election. As far as we know, the other side of the aisle is either not sure or simply can't confirm that the dastardly deed did indeed happen. And while it is being whispered about, the media are not running with it. Martine Connor is trying to contain it and went so far as to try and bribe me to be her White House counsel. I turned her down. She implored me to intercede with the Vigilantes on her behalf. She was quite clear on what she wanted, which was for you to find the madam and pin this on her so her people could skate free. She really believed that fiasco wouldn't get out, and her administration would remain unscathed.

"You all have the list I sent to you. Maggie forwarded the profiles of the men in question and I was astounded. I told her you wouldn't take it on because you would be on the madam's side. Not because you condone prostitution but because the law will let the madam's clients get off with a slap on the wrist, and the madam will do hard time. For some reason Martine could not, would not, accept that. She threatened me with the IRS and every other agency in Washington. I have to tell you that annoyed me a little.

"Here is the ironic part. Cosmo was leaving the office a few days ago around six when a woman appeared and wanted to hire him. It was the madam, Crystal Clark, but she was going under the name Lily Flowers when she hired him. She said she was going to get railroaded and had prepared for that eventuality. Cosmo said she would have stayed and taken the heat if her clients got the same treatment she got, but she was realistic enough to know that wasn't going to happen. She turned all her books, all her records, over to him for safekeeping. Included with the material was an authorization for him to go after the johns. She paid him a cash retainer of $5,000. Then two days later, a messenger delivered a package that contained her will and her power of attorney.

"The lady made sure she got her working girls to

safety. I actually spoke to one of them, and they're all set for a full year. I don't know where they are, I just know they're safe for the moment, probably out of the country. The madam told Cosmo she was leaving and would be in touch.

"You would not believe the thoroughness of this woman. She didn't miss a trick. She had other identities with backgrounds that are impeccable. I can't imagine living like that, but she did it. She refused to tell Cosmo what her real name was. She had a ton of money socked away. The Happy Day Camp is very high-end. Millions went into the construction and maintenance. She didn't take in the kind of money to build such a place. When she moved to Vegas from wherever she was before, all of a sudden the land was bought, and the building went up. No one knew, and she didn't tell Cosmo who her benefactor was, and, trust me, there was a benefactor.

"The following day, when Cosmo was reading the morning paper he saw, I think it was on page thirty-four, that a woman named Lily Flowers was killed in a car accident. It's on the books as an accident, a tire blowout, she hit something and died on impact. The working girl I spoke to said she and the others did not believe it was an accident because Lily would have had her car checked from top to bottom since she was leaving. They said she never left anything to chance. But, like I said, the police report lists it as an accidental death.

"With no next of kin and no friends to claim the body, Cosmo claimed it and had Ms. Flowers cremated. We scattered the ashes in the desert yesterday. Are you all following me here? Any questions?"

"If the madam is dead, that's the end of it, right? Or am I missing something here?" Nikki asked.

"On the surface one would naturally make that assumption. It depends on all of you. A woman is dead. We have to decide if she would still be alive if not for the rumor mill. She was alerted by someone soon enough to make her getaway, but we don't know who that someone was.

"The way things stand now, Washington is just in the whispering mode. Will it go to full audio anytime soon? I don't know. As we all know, the FBI is involved. Bert's main guy at the Las Vegas Field Office, Special Agent in Charge Wright, along with his fellow agents, have come up dry until early this morning, when they paid Cosmo a visit. One of Wright's men hit on the accident that killed the madam. Because Cosmo claimed the body, they pounced on him. There's nothing we can do about that, it's Bert's show out there."

"Then there's nothing for us to do," Myra said.

"Where's the rabbit in the hat, Lizzie?" Kathryn demanded.

"The rabbit is the madam's backer. The man who put the money up for the Happy Day Camp. The man who got a cut of the madam's profits. The man who had a long-standing affair with the madam. The man who arranged that dog-and-pony show in D.C."

The Sisters all leaned closer to the table.

"Who is it, do we know?" Annie asked.

The name rolled off Lizzie's lips like liquid silk. "Hunter Pryce."

The Sisters sat in stunned silence, all of them speechless.

It was Kathryn who finally managed to gasp, "The vice president of the United States?"

"The one and only," came Lizzie's response.

"Hard proof?" Nikki asked.

"Solid gold. Two sources," Lizzie said.

"But . . . but the media and Martine herself finally admitted she was *seeing* Mr. Pryce. She said they had a relationship, and Mr. Pryce confirmed it. The media had a field day with that information when it got out," Myra said as she fingered the pearls at her neck. "Good Lord, what does this all mean? The vice president!"

"It certainly doesn't mean anything good, that's for sure," Lizzie said.

"It explains the president's reason for wanting us to take on the madam and not the clients," Nikki said, her voice ringing with anger. "We were such fools, we put her in office! She promised us a pardon!"

The others weighed in, their outrage as strong as Nikki's.

"Where does all of this leave us, Lizzie? Do we keep quiet? Do we go after Hunter Pryce and the others?" Myra demanded.

"That's why I'm here, Myra. I didn't want to trust that the vp's name is going to get out. Cosmo knows. Maggie knows and so do Jack, Harry, and Bert. You're the last to know, and I apologize for that, but it had to be this way. But to answer your question, now that you know everything I know, the decision has to be yours. Always remember, a woman is dead. We don't know if it was foul play and we may never know that. So think hard before you come to a final decision."

"It will ruin Martine Connor. The first female president, and she goes down in a sex scandal. She'll either resign or be impeached and convicted. You can always count on that old devil sex to rear its ugly head at the most inopportune times," Annie grumbled.

"*Unless* we step in and take him out and keep the rest quiet. Or, we could also take out a couple of those senators as well as Ambassador Kierson at the same time," Kathryn said.

"Maggie told me a while back, maybe a month or so ago, that the political gossip in D.C. was that the prez was still *seeing* the vice prez. I thought that came to a screeching halt when they were sworn in in January," Nikki said.

"If anyone would know, it's Maggie. She's up on all things political, especially the gossip end of it. Big mistake on Martine's part if it is true. I'm having a hard time believing she'd be that stupid for a roll in the hay. I think that was just political fodder for the gossip columnists," Lizzie said.

"Hunter Pryce was such a good pick for vice president. He's got charisma, he's still young, has all his hair, a killer smile, and all that money he inherited from his railroad-tycoon granddaddy. He's probably more politically savvy than Martine on her best day."

"He was the perfect choice," Isabelle said. "Unless . . . unless, she really did break it off somewhere along the way, and he blackmailed her. Don't look at me like that, it is a very good possibility because Connor is not a stupid woman. She had to have seen the handwriting on the wall. Yeah, yeah, I bet that's what happened."

The Sisters looked doubtful, but as they started to spin it, they all came to the same conclusion: Isabelle was probably right.

"Now it makes sense," Annie said. "The president contacted Lizzie to get us to intervene. If we took out all the party campers, then no one would be looking at Hunter Pryce unless one of his buddies gave him up. Pin it all on the madam or kill her off, and Pryce is free and clear. Oh, that is so terrible I don't even want to think about it. That poor Flowers woman. I wonder if she was still in love with him. I bet he's the one who tipped her off. If so, that just makes it all the more terrible."

Yoko turned to the others, her body rigid, her eyes sparking dangerously. "We all know how much money is involved in this kind of thing. Just remember back to my father and what was going on when we went after him. Maybe Lily Flowers, or whatever her name really was or is, was coerced into doing what she did. We should keep our minds open where that is concerned. Some women will go to extreme lengths and do anything for the man they love."

Her Sisters nodded in agreement.

"I've got to get moving, as much as I don't want to, girls. I told you I have one stop to make before I take the red-eye back to Vegas. It's a long drive to the White House from here. I tried to get a ticket, but both flights were sold out. So, I have to drive."

"Just like that, you're going to the White House?" Annie gasped.

Lizzie's eyes twinkled. "I am going to call ahead, as I don't have an appointment. Since nothing exciting is going on in the world, there is every chance Martine will fit me into her busy schedule. What do you want me to tell her?"

Myra looked around the table at Annie and the girls. "Everybody has a vote."

Twenty minutes later, just as Lizzie was slipping into her gorgeous white cashmere coat, Annie said, "We'll do it. We'll come up with a plan, but you have to get back to us with a time frame. The minute you do that, we'll be ready to act."

Lizzie was halfway to the cable car when Yoko sprinted after her with a plastic container. "Your wedding cake!"

Lizzie's smile made the early-afternoon light that much brighter as she accepted the container and pressed the button that would take her to the foot of the mountain. "I might need an act of Congress to get this through security."

"You're going to the right place to make that happen," Yoko shouted, her voice carrying on the wind.

Lizzie's tinkling laugh ricocheted across the mountain.

Back inside, the women gathered up their jackets as they prepared to go to the war room to work out the details of the impending mission.

Rather than go to her own house, Lizzie headed for Jack Emery's the minute she hit Washington. Jack had promised to be home by the time she got there when she'd called him from the road. Her second call had been to Maggie, who said she had some kind of mess to clear up and would get there as soon as she could. The rest of her driving time was spent talking to Cosmo about everything and nothing and telling him all about the wedding cake she had to put under her pillow. She finally ended the call when Cosmo said his last client of the day had arrived, but not before she told him about the Sisters' spectacular wedding gift. "I'll see you in time for an early breakfast on your time, my darling."

Ninety minutes later, Lizzie managed to find a parking space directly in front of Jack's house. She was surprised to see Jack standing in the open doorway waiting for her. He waved.

Good host that he was, Jack had takeout on the kitchen table. Lizzie waved it off and told him to go ahead and eat while she talked. Jack was finished with his chow mein and crunchy noodles by the time Lizzie brought him up-to-date.

Jack was about to attack one of the deep-fried sugar donuts the Pagoda Restaurant was known for when Lizzie dropped the vice president's name. "I'm speechless, Lizzie. How the hell could that woman be so stupid?"

Lizzie shrugged. "Sometimes love is blind, Jack. As the girls pointed out to me, some women will go to any lengths and do anything to keep the men they're in love with. The girls were talking about the Vegas madam at the time, but it would appear it also seems that the president is cut from the same mold. I hate it, Jack. Listen, I have to call her right now, try to wangle a meeting with her, then get to the airport to catch the red-eye back to Vegas."

"Anything I can do?"

"You're the first person I'd call if there was. Shhh," she said, putting her finger to her lips as she pressed the digits of Martine Connor's private number. She shrugged for Jack's benefit to show she didn't think the president would actually answer the phone. Her silvery eyebrows shot upward when she heard Connor's voice.

"It's Lizzie, Madam President. I'm calling to ask if I can take you up on your offer of a girl-to-girl visit. I have to tell you I'm on the red-eye back to Vegas so if you have some free time about now, I can be there in fifteen minutes. Did I say it's crucial that we talk, Madam President?" Lizzie drummed her fingers on the table. The waiting was unnerving.

"I'll have one of my agents meet you at the West Wing gate, and he'll bring you to my quarters. This will be so nice, an old friend dropping by to stay in touch. I miss that. It's a nice evening, perhaps we could take a stroll through the Rose Garden."

"That would be very nice. I'll see you in fifteen minutes, Madam President. Good-bye."

"Jesus, just like that the president agreed to see you!"

"That's because she wants something, and she thinks I can help her. Don't be impressed, okay?" Lizzie belted her coat and gathered up her purse and briefcase. "If Maggie shows up, fill her in. She pretty much knows everything, but there are a few blanks. Tell her to call the mountain and talk to the girls."

"Lizzie, what are you . . . are you sure . . . ?"

"Jack, I'm going to lay it out for her. That's all I can do."

"Good luck. And congratulations again. Be happy, Lizzie. I mean that."

"I know you do, Jack. Before you know it, I'll be the one congratulating you and Nikki. Believe that, okay?"

"Sure." Jack hugged her so tight she growled but with delight.

"I'll call the minute I'm away from the White House."

"Be careful, Lizzie."

"Always, Jack. Always."

Jack watched from the open door until her taillights were just tiny specks in the distance. He closed and locked the door, his gut churning. He should call Harry while he waited to see if Maggie was going to show up. Or, maybe he should just call Maggie to see what time she would be knocking on his door. If it was much later, he could hop in the car and drive over to Harry's *dojo*. When Maggie didn't answer her cell, and the call to Harry went straight to voice mail, Jack went back into the house and ate all six of the sugary donuts. He washed them down with a bottle of rice beer.

Chapter 17

The Sisters were four hours into the planning stages of their mission, and the war room gave testament to that fact. File folders and stray papers were everywhere, some in midair. Murphy and Grady gracefully gave up their positions at Kathryn's and Alexis's feet and sauntered over to the doorway to get out of the way of the blizzard of paper that seemed to be sailing in every direction. However, they remained alert to these strange goings-on.

Myra looked around in dismay. "Now that we've created this mess, what have we come up with that will enable us to take on the vp and his cohorts?"

"We know a little more now than we did before we started," Annie said cheerfully. "What I don't understand is how Hunter Pryce got through the vetting process with nothing coming to light other than his romance with Martine Connor."

"Puh-leeze!" Nikki said. "The media wanted another Camelot, and Connor and Pryce were Jack and Jackie. The country was in dire need of some good news. First female president. Would the president marry the vice president? The country couldn't wait to find out. The photo ops were out of this world. Maggie doubled her circulation for months with all those photos. And then, bam, nothing!"

"None of us were able to track Pryce, and if it wasn't for Little Fish, we would still be back at square one. The good news is Pryce thinks he's safe. We're going to puncture his little bubble of security as soon as Lizzie gets back to us," Kathryn said.

"What if the president doesn't confide in Lizzie, what happens then?" Yoko asked.

Annie made a very unladylike sound. "Girls, do you really think Lizzie will leave the White House empty-handed? Actually, she isn't going to be holding anything in her hands. She's going there to . . . to inform the president of the current situation. The Lizzie I know will leave the White House with exactly what she wants, in this case permission to sock it to Hunter Pryce."

Myra looked dubious as she started to separate and stack the scattered papers on the table. "Let's all be clear on our temporary plan. Lizzie will ask Martine Connor for the personal e-mail addresses of the men in question as well as their personal cell phone numbers. I don't see the president withholding that information. Once Lizzie tells Martine everything there is to tell about Hunter Pryce, assuming, of course, that Martine doesn't already know, she won't have a choice. Once we have that information, we will make contact with the men and arrange a meeting, at which point we will do what we have to do."

"I contacted Avery Snowden earlier," Annie said. "He said he would have his people briefed and ready to go the moment we get back to him." Annie looked down at the Mickey Mouse watch on her wrist, and said, "That was six hours ago, so he should have a plan in place by now."

"Bert called in and said the FBI sketch artist had completed the picture of Lily Flowers, and the networks are flooding the airwaves. It went out over the Net at the same time," Nikki said. "Since there are no actual pictures of Crystal Clark, the artist could only work with what he had by way of descriptions that were sketchy at best. Bert said there is no resemblance between Ms. Flowers and the sketch. If nothing goes awry, Bert should be pulling the plug in less than thirty-six hours, possibly sooner."

"What exactly does that mean to us?" Alexis asked.

Annie did one of those *tsk-tsk* things with her tongue. "It means the madam is answering to a higher authority, and we don't need to concern ourselves with her. We're going to go after her clients to even up the score for her. According to Lizzie, Cosmo said Lily Flowers would have turned herself in if she were guaranteed to be treated legally the same way the clients were treated. She was willing to take her punishment. But it didn't work out that way, they went gunning for her. I for one want to know if Pryce is the one who tipped her off so she could take it on the lam."

"Who else could it have been?" Kathryn asked. "You don't think for one minute he trusted her to keep quiet where he was concerned, regardless of her feelings for him? The man is in a rather exalted position right now and could at some point in the future be our next president if anything were to happen to Martine Connor. The first one who talks and shares is the one who gets to cut a deal. When you're looking at prison time, it pays to try to cut one. Bottom line, he was covering his own butt, not hers. He just did what he felt he had to do. By the way, has anyone given any thought to the possibility this was a plan by the vp all along to destroy Martine Connor so he could step up to the presidency? He had everything buried so deep that it didn't come to light when he was vetted. Another thing, do we know what Pryce's net worth is?"

"Three hundred and eighty million plus railroad stock and a whole bunch of real estate," Isabelle said.

"He's got a yacht and a fleet of antique cars. I think you could safely say the guy is solvent," Nikki said.

"Not shabby, Kathryn! What a brilliant deduction!" Annie chortled. "Think about it, girls! It does make sense. But would he risk killing Lily Flowers, or was her demise just a tragic accident? We should find out where he was at the time Ms. Flowers met with her accident. Even though it's unlikely he would have done the deed himself."

"Maybe it was all a ruse, the part about his alerting her and getting her out of town to someplace where she couldn't be found. She would have thought . . . God knows what the poor woman thought, but she was getting out of town. I suppose she trusted the man," Myra said.

Kathryn rifled through some loose papers in front of her. "Pryce's relationship with the madam happened before he became involved in politics and way before he met Martine Connor. This is just my opinion, but I'd say his rich life was boring, so he was looking to go outside the box and do something that would kick up his adrenaline. Maybe he's a sex junkie. Then he had to turn his life around and get squeaky clean so he could withstand the vetting process." Kathryn shuffled more papers. "It doesn't look like Pryce ever held a real job. I would surmise his spare time was spent clipping coupons and showing up at ribbon-cutting ceremonies. Maybe the soirees he arranged before and after the election were his swan song, so to speak. You know, one last fling on the seedy side of life. He knew he could count on the madam to keep quiet."

Annie, who was an avid reader of all things printed, announced, "I read somewhere that Pryce is a great economist. And he's up-to-the-minute on foreign affairs. Connor said she had to do some serious arm twisting to get him to agree to run with her on the ticket. I think that was just political spin. The party wanted him badly, and until this cropped up, he'd been working tirelessly for the administration. Pryce is not the kind of vice president who will just attend funerals for foreign heads of state and otherwise take a backseat. I think he's got both feet into global warming, too. At least that's what the media are saying. About two weeks ago he was on some Sunday talk show, and he said he absolutely refuses to discuss his private life. The talk show host let him off the hook and went on to other things. The media likes the guy."

"Well," said Nikki, "now we have a reason for him wanting to get rid of the madam, thanks to Kathryn for opening our eyes to that possibility. If Kathryn is right, and he has his sights on the presidency via the back door, he needs to make sure nothing comes back to bite him. I think he thinks he's got it covered. We should be doing everything possible to find out if the madam truly had a freak accident or if she was murdered."

"We aren't going to go there, dear," Myra said. "Bert will take care of that end of things. If Kathryn is right, and I think she well might be, our job now is to take care of the men involved and at the same time protect the president and the administration. We can't fault her for their deeds."

The Sisters turned when they heard the familiar pinging sound that meant there was an in-coming e-mail.

Nikki got up and raced to the bank of computers. "It's from Bert. He wants us to send him a letter on White House stationery telling him to cease and desist in the case of the Vegas madam!"

"How are we going to do that since we don't have any White House stationery?" Alexis grumbled.

"Well, Lizzie is in the right place to get that particular piece of paper, now, isn't she?" Kathryn asked.

"I'll text her right now," Annie said.

The Sisters waited to see if there would be a return text. There wasn't.

"I'm sure Lizzie is occupied at the moment. I doubt she'll leave the White House without checking her text messages. Lizzie is very thorough, as we all know."

"I don't get it," Nikki said. "Why does Bert want a letter like that? Everyone knows the White House can't tell the FBI what to do. It's the FBI that puts the fear of God into the White House."

Kathryn turned defensive. "I'm sure Bert knows what he's doing. He's out there in Vegas and can see and get a feel for what is going on. He wouldn't ask for something like that if he thought it would backfire in any way. The buck stops with him. By that I mean if his guy—what's his name?—oh, yeah, Duncan Wright, wants to kick up a fuss, which it sounds like he does, and is making waves, that may be why Bert wants it. Then there's that other agent that Bert likes, John Clawson. Clawson is not a hothead like Wright is."

Seeing the blank expressions on her Sisters' faces, Kathryn said, "I'm just saying that Charles always encouraged us to say whatever was on our mind, no matter how weird or bizarre it sounded."

"I'm all for pillow talk," Nikki quipped.

Kathryn's face turned bright pink. And then she laughed. "One does come up for air from time to time, and one has to talk of . . . of other things."

Annie looked confused. "Explain that," she said fretfully.

"Annieeeee!" Myra, her own face flushed, said, "Use your imagination."

It was Annie's turn to flush the same rosy hue as Kathryn.

The girls were relentless as they pelted each other with scrunched-up paper balls and shouted romantic instructions for Annie's benefit. If nothing else, it was a release of the mounting tension in the room.

* * *

President Martine Connor could hardly contain herself as she waited in the hallway. She peered through the French doors as one of her Secret Service agents escorted Lizzie to the impromptu meeting.

Lizzie's first thought after she went through her security check was how drawn and haggard her friend looked. She thought she saw a few more gray hairs at Martine's temples. The president was dressed casually in jeans and a pullover sweatshirt, with a logo of the presidential seal over her heart. Not that fashion counted after hours. The two women hugged and then linked arms as they walked away, the agent far enough behind that he couldn't hear their whispered conversation.

"So this is where you hang out, huh?" Lizzie grinned. "Pretty impressive, Madam President."

"It's a nice place to visit, but I don't think you'd like living here, Lizzie. I don't think I've ever been so lonely in my entire life. In my other life, I at least had a life back then. Here, I'm a virtual prisoner. Sometimes I have this crazy desire to get in my car and go to the drugstore. I won't bore you with what I would have to go through to do that. Enough about me. You absolutely *glow,* Lizzie. You must be very happy."

"I've never been happier, Madam President. You said something about showing me the Rose Garden . . ."

"Yes, yes, just let me scoot upstairs to get a shawl. I'll be right back."

Lizzie took that moment to pull out her cell phone, which was vibrating. She looked down at the message and started after the president. "Madam President, can you wait a minute? I was wondering if you would . . ." Lizzie mouthed the rest of what she was going to say just as one of the president's detail sauntered up to see if there was a problem.

Martine waved him off as she sprinted down the hall and around the corner. Lizzie stood still and smiled at the agent. She was still smiling when Martine returned, wearing a soft pink shawl.

"We're going out to the Rose Garden, Agent Roberts. I would appreciate some privacy."

The agent inclined his head slightly to show he understood. It was also clear that he would be within shouting distance but would give his boss the privacy she'd requested.

Five minutes later they were walking through the garden. "You didn't come here to walk through the Rose Garden, Lizzie. Give it to me straight."

Lizzie didn't mince any words, she gave it to her straight. "The Vegas madam is dead. It's on the books as an accident. I know better, and the FBI knows better, but it's going to be put to sleep as an accident. Your people are not off the hook. In fact the hook has grown to encompass something that could take down your presidency."

Lizzie could feel President Connor shiver underneath the pale pink shawl. Lizzie wondered if Martine knew what was coming. Suddenly, Lizzie felt sorry for her friend and reached out an arm to wrap around the shivering woman's shoulders. "I'm sorry to have to tell you this, but I know in my gut you'd rather hear it from me than read about it in the papers or on the news.

"Hunter Pryce is the devil in the woodwork. He's the one who put up the money for the Happy Day Camp in Vegas. He and the madam were . . . I'm not sure what they were exactly, but whatever it was had longevity. Someone alerted the madam that things were going to go down. On the face of it, you'd think he cared enough to get her safely out of the way, but then she had an accident and now she's dead.

"Take that one step further, and ask yourself: if it all got out, wouldn't you, too, be dead in the water, so to speak? Who then steps into your place? Hunter Pryce, that's who. He thought he had it all buried really deep, but we found it." Lizzie decided to stretch the truth a little, and said, "You can thank the Vigilantes."

Lizzie thought her walking companion was stiff as a board.

"Are you sure, Lizzie?"

Lizzie hated the deep hurt she heard in the president's voice. "I wouldn't be here if I wasn't sure. The smartest thing you could have done was dump Pryce before you asked him to be your vp."

"I didn't dump him. He dumped me, Lizzie. I was crushed. I actually thought about withdrawing from the race, but I couldn't bring myself to do it. You have no idea how much I loved that man, Lizzie. I was like a lovesick puppy where he was concerned. When my people came to me to put him on the short list, I wanted to die. I really did. Do you have any idea how hard it was for me to pretend it was all my idea? I never thought he would accept, but he did. I haven't had a personal conversation with him since the night he told me we needed to go our separate ways because he didn't want to live in a fishbowl. To my credit, Lizzie, I didn't cry, I didn't scold, and I didn't beg. I held up my damn head and walked away."

As she talked, Martine Connor opened her shawl and handed Lizzie two sheets of White House stationery and another folded piece of paper with cell phone numbers and e-mail addresses. Lizzie deftly slid them under her coat.

"There are two pieces in case you make a mistake, and I don't want to know what you're going to do with them. We should go back, it's cold out here. Just tell me one thing, are the Vigilantes going to help me or not?"

"They are. You can sleep easy tonight, Madam President. But, that means you are now two for two. Do we understand each other?"

"We do, Lizzie. But you're wrong about my sleeping. Was that really Hunter's plan?" Lizzie's silence confirmed all the president needed to know.

Martine Connor stopped and turned to face Lizzie. The wind picked up, with hard little gusts that were like clenched fists beating at them. The thin sliver of the moon seemed to wink at them before the dark cloud cover sailed across the dark sky.

"You're a good friend, Lizzie. I'm sorry about being so . . . pushy with you. Listen, let me make it up to you. Can I host a luncheon or shower for you here at the White House? It would make a wonderful memory, and you deserve it. Don't give me an answer right now, talk it over with your husband and let me know."

"Talk it over with your husband." How wonderful the words sounded. "I'll do that, Madam President. You okay with all I've told you?" Lizzie jammed her hands into the pockets of her coat just as her cell vibrated. She withdrew it and stared down at the text Annie had just sent her. She looked up at the president, and said, "I need to do something, Madam President. Like first thing in the morning. I can arrange for the *Post* to report it the minute I get in my car, but you have to okay it. Now, listen carefully."

The president listened intently. "No, I'm not okay with it, but, I'll survive. Uh . . . thank the . . . girls for me." She slowly nodded. "I'll follow your orders, and you do what you have to do. I'm not even going to ask any questions, Lizzie."

The two women hugged each other. Martine whispered something in Lizzie's ear, but with the gusty wind, Lizzie didn't know what she'd said. A moment later the president of the United States walked through the French doors. Lizzie waved. She thought she saw tears rolling down her friend's cheeks before she disappeared from sight.

"This way, miss," the agent said as he walked Lizzie to the West Wing gate, then to her car. "Have a nice evening, ma'am."

"Yes, I will. You, too. Take good care of her, Agent Roberts. She's a wonderful person."

"Yes, ma'am, I will."

Chapter 18

It was almost midnight, the witching hour, as Annie put it, when they had wrapped up their last meeting of the day. Tidy to the point of obsessiveness, Annie insisted the work area be cleared and all reports and files stacked neatly for the next round of decision making the following morning.

Myra fiddled with her pearls as she fixed her gaze on Annie. "Thailand, Annie?"

Annie stopped what she was doing, and said, "Myra, you need to broaden your horizons and step outside the box. But, to answer your question, yes, Thailand."

"Broaden my horizons? Is that what you said? Do I have to remind you that you were sitting on top of that damn mountain wearing a caftan and watching the Weather Channel for *ten years* before I brought you here?"

Whoa. The girls stepped back and watched the two older women as they went at it. They loved it when the two of them argued, then hugged and made up.

"How could I forget? You remind me every day of my life. I love you for doing it. I thank you for doing it. You told me I needed to get a life, and I did. I think it's time *YOU* got a life. You're no fun anymore, Myra. No fun at all."

Myra drew in her breath, then let it out in a long, hissing sound. "I think I'm a little too old to be having fun. So are you, my friend."

Annie sniffed. "You're never too old to have fun. Never, ever. One needs to laugh either at something or at oneself. I bet if I tickled you, you wouldn't even laugh. That means you're a stiff, Myra. And you need to get rid of those damn pearls that you think of as your lifeline. You need some colored beads to ward off evil spirits, and I know just where to get them—eBay!" she said triumphantly. "They're featuring chains with circles on them. Joan Rivers has a lovely selection. I saw it on the Shopper's Channel. They're cheaper on eBay, though. And they have matching earrings. They were really lovely."

"All of a sudden you're an authority on everything including me?"

"Well, someone has to be. All you do is poop on everyone's parade. I was thinking of getting an eye lift if Mr. Snowden can find a way for me to get it done so I don't get . . . uh, caught. We could probably get a discount if we both do it. What do you say, Myra? Or we could get our bums lifted. Maybe at the same time. They sag, you know. Our bums, that is. Well, our eyelids are drooping, too. Hell, everything droops. We could go in for a complete overhaul. You could certainly use a little slicing and dicing, Myra."

Whoa.

The girls backed up another step as they listened and watched the verbal exchange going on between Myra and Annie.

Myra squared her shoulders, dropped her hands from worrying her pearls, and said sweetly, "And is this all because of someone named Little Fish?"

"Damn straight it is, Myra, but I'm also considering it for myself. I'm just glad I got to this place in time and still have my wits about me. What's wrong with doing a little improving of one's self? Nothing, that's what. Now, are you with me or not?"

Myra looked like she was going to go for her pearls again but changed her mind at the last second. "I think I'd like to think about it before I make a commitment."

"You rock, Myra, you really do. We owe it to ourselves to look the best we can. I don't mind getting old, I just don't want to *look* old."

Myra nodded as if she completely understood. "Order me some of those chains, Annie. I'm suddenly thinking pearls are passé these days, order some for yourself and the girls. My treat. Are they gold or silver?"

"Either/or. Why don't we get one of each?"

"Good thinking," Myra said. "By the way, give me that report on Thailand so I can read it before I fall asleep."

One of the girls sighed. So loud that both Myra and Annie asked, "What?"

"Not a thing," Yoko said as she gathered up her own files and folders.

Annie was smiling and waving her arms about. "Breakfast at seven. We reconvene here in the war room at eight thirty to wind up our details."

They all said good night and went their separate ways. Annie walked over to the dining hall and readied the coffeemaker for the morning. She reached into a bin and brought out a bag of oranges she was going to put through the juicer for fresh juice. She turned when she saw Myra standing in the doorway. "I thought you were tired and wanted to go to bed."

Myra perched on one of the stools, the one Charles usually sat on. "I guess I am a . . . stiff. I envy you, Annie, you just roll along and take it as it comes. I wish I could be more like you."

Annie sliced into an orange. Out of the corner of her eye she saw that Myra wasn't wearing her pearls.

"Myra, did you ever think maybe for just a minute or two that I am trying to catch up on the ten years I lost on that mountain? I think that's what I'm doing. I have so many regrets, my friend. I know you do, too. We can't live in the past, we tried that, and it didn't work. Too many people need our help. We have the funds to help those people, so we should feel good about that. I'm so glad you and Charles came to the mountain that day and saved me. I truly, truly am. Now I have to give back for my good fortune. Tell me you understand."

"I do, Annie, I do. Maybe we should get our ears pierced to see how we handle that before we decide to get all that slicing and dicing. Two holes in each ear. That's so dramatic."

Annie burst out laughing. "Baby steps? That will work, Myra. As long as you're sitting there, you might as well help slice these oranges."

"I thought you'd never ask," Myra said, reaching for the knife.

The juice machine whirred to life. The moment it stopped, Annie turned to Myra, and said, "I wasn't serious about the slicing and dicing."

Myra laughed. "I know that, Annie."

Annie huffed and puffed. "How did you know?"

"Because at our age *a little* slicing and dicing won't work. I'm all for the ear piercing, though. Another thing, do you really think for one minute that Little Fish is worrying about not looking like George Clooney?" Myra laughed so hard she almost sliced two fingers off.

Annie held up her hand. "How do you feel about doing something outrageous?"

Myra whacked through an orange. "How outrageous?"

"As long as we're getting our ears pierced, let's take it a step further and get our belly buttons pierced. We could get a really big diamond. Or we could get one of those belly chains with a diamond in the middle. A chastity belt. Kind of. Sort of. What do you think, Myra?" Annie asked fretfully.

Myra whacked another orange. "How long have you been thinking about this, Annie?"

"Five minutes."

"Hmmm, five minutes? Okay, let's do it. Do you think it will hurt?"

"How the hell would I know that? It's the price we'll have to pay. Three carats at the very least. Do you agree?"

"Absolutely. I'm kind of excited. You're right, it is outrageous. I never thought I would do something so . . . so . . . decadent."

The juicer whirred again. "See, Myra, we're having fun. Now we have something to look forward to. Piercings! Who knew?" Annie cackled gleefully. "Wait a minute. How about if we go for something really out of the box, over the top, totally, totally outrageous?"

Myra looked dubious, but at the gleeful look in Annie's eyes, she said, "Hit me."

Annie whispered in her ear.

Myra's jaw dropped and her eyes popped. "Oh, Annie!"

"Come on, Myra, you only go this way once, we have to make the most of it. I already went online to check it out."

Myra now looked beyond dubious. "Where . . . where . . . will we put it?"

"On our asses, where else? We don't want anyone to see it, so where else could we put it?"

Myra's voice rose in pitch as she said, "A tattoo seems so . . . tacky."

"That depends on one's point of view. Think of it as making a statement. Listen, Myra, this is all about us. Are you ready to step out of the box?"

"What kind of statement will we be making if it's on our asses?"

"We answer to no one, Myra. I think I'll get the scales of justice. What will you get?"

"A flower, a heart, maybe a rose?"

Annie ignored her friend's jittery-sounding voice.

"That's so last year, Myra. Go big! Remember, we're being outrageous. How about a smoking gun?"

"Dear God! Do I have to make a decision right now?"

"No, dear, not right now. For now it's enough that you committed to doing it. I'm so proud of you, Myra."

Myra looked around the kitchen. She squared her shoulders and decided at that precise moment she was proud of herself, too.

Neither of them noticed Nikki loitering just outside the door to the kitchen.

"Now that we're on a roll, how about if we order those chains?"

Annie covered the pitcher of orange juice and set it in the refrigerator while Myra cleaned off the counter. Annie washed the juicer and Myra dried it.

"We're a team, Myra," Annie said, linking her arm with Myra. "Let's take on eBay. We might be able to give Nellie a run for her money. She's addicted to the Shopper's Channel. We can hit their Web site while we're at it. Isn't the Internet a wonderful thing? You can shop in the middle of the night in your jammies if you want. Life is just so good, isn't it, Myra?"

"It is, Annie, it is."

Jack Emery woke with a pounding headache. He looked toward the window and saw that it was going to be another gray day, with rain that wasn't needed. As he walked sluggishly toward the shower, he wished he hadn't eaten the rack of spareribs Harry had fixed last night. He'd eaten more than Maggie, something he didn't think was possible.

He gulped down a handful of aspirin before he stepped into the shower. He thought his head was going to explode right off his neck when the steaming hot water hit him. He danced around under the spray when he turned the nozzle to COLD. He cursed a whole new language before he turned it back to the HOT setting.

Ten minutes later he was shaved and dressed when his doorbell rang. He galloped down the steps. He peered through the peephole to see Maggie standing on his doorstep.

"What?" he growled. "You just left here a few hours ago. You better not be trying to bond with me this early in the morning. What?" he growled again. "There are no more spareribs. You took the leftovers."

"Well, aren't you the little bucket of sunshine this morning? I'll settle for a cup of coffee. I brought the morning paper for your perusal."

"I have a really bad headache, Maggie. What's it say?" Jack filled the coffeepot with water from the tap, then added the coffee grounds. He got a container of half-and-half out of the refrigerator and set it in the center of the table along with a small bowlful of sugar cubes and sweeteners. "Well, what does the paper say?"

"It says that POTUS, or the President of the United States, has invited Main Street America to a dinner at the White House. POTUS invited eleven families from the Kalorama area. One whole street. The street where Karl Woodley, the ex–national security advisor, and his wife, Paula, used to live."

"And you think I need to know this . . . why? Of all places, why that one? The girls were almost caught out there not too long ago." Jack massaged his temples, which were still pounding like a jackhammer. He felt like banging his head against the wall to drive away the pain, but if he did that, he'd probably crack his skull.

"Because, Jack, that's where the action is going to go down. No one would ever think they'd go back to the scene of an old crime. They'd think the Vigilantes are too smart to do something like that. It was the girls' idea. Lizzie set it up with POTUS and it's on. I reported it for the reading public and, at the same time, did a bit of a recap, reminding that same reading public that POTUS's advisors and the DNC pushed to have Hunter Pryce put on the ticket. I also reminded the reading public that POTUS wanted Chandler Maddox as her running mate, not Hunter Pryce, because she didn't want the voters to think she was picking Pryce because of their prior romantic relationship. The DNC somehow convinced her to go with Pryce. That's why I kept running those editorials every day reminding everyone that she really wanted Chandler Maddox. I even ran an in-depth interview Ted did with Maddox. Trust me, we got our licks in. The purpose of this morning's edition is so when the dark stuff hits the fan, it won't splatter in Connor's direction. We have to keep her on our side, Jack, so she gives the girls the pardon she promised. She's two for two now. Are you getting it now?"

Jack mumbled something that sounded like *yes*. "What's the plan?" he asked as he poured coffee into two bright-red mugs. One of the mugs said "Jack" and one said "Nikki" in fancy white script with tiny snowflakes all over the mugs, a gift to Jack one Christmas from Nellie Easter.

"I'm waiting to hear. At the moment there are a lot of loose ends that have to be tied up. Lizzie is working on it, and so is Bert. The girls are doing what they do best, planning and plotting. I'd really like to stay and chat, but I want to get to the office to see how this front page is going to play out. You should put a vinegar rag on your forehead, and it will make your headache go away."

Jack just gawked at her.

"It's an old-timey remedy, but it kind of works. Of course, you'll smell like vinegar, but what the heck, your headache will be gone."

"Go, already, and leave me to my misery," Jack bellowed.

When the door closed behind Maggie, Jack rummaged in the pantry to see if he had any vinegar. He didn't. He felt relieved when he gathered up his briefcase and keys.

Standing on the doorstep with no umbrella, Jack cursed again in the new language he'd come up with in the shower. "Screw it," he muttered as he ran to his car, which was parked a block away.

Just as he settled himself in the car his cell phone rang. Nikki. Suddenly he felt like singing. *Singing in the rain, would that be too clichéd or what?* he thought.

Chapter 19

Bert Navarro climbed out of his car and headed toward the building housing the field office. He chewed on his lower lip, knowing he was walking into a hornets' nest. Not that he was worried, but he hated confrontations with his men.

Special Agent in Charge Duncan Wright and Special Agent John Clawson were busy on their respective computers. A newbie named Chuck Symon was sticking colored pins on a wall map. All three Special Agents snapped to attention when Bert walked into the office.

"Let's hear it," Bert said, not bothering with amenities. "It's been over twenty-four hours since you sent out the artist's sketch. What's the feedback?"

"Sorry, sir, nothing worth a hill of beans. Every loony tune within a fifty-mile radius has called in. Nothing," he said again succinctly.

Bert was tempted to say something cutting, but Wright looked too miserable. "Don't beat yourself up, Agent Wright. You gave it a shot."

Agent Wright nodded. "A fax came in for you early this morning, Director." He plucked it off his desk and handed it to Bert. "Begging your pardon, Director, but since when, and I know I asked this before but I'm asking again, since when does the White House interfere with FBI business?"

Bert scanned the White House communiqué and shrugged. It didn't get any better than the White House telling one to cease and desist—even though the message was a fake.

"Elias Cummings, my predecessor, developed a good rapport with the past administration, and it's carried over to this presidency. It's called sharing and not withholding information that the White House deems important. Obviously, they are on top of what's going on. In the end it's my decision; but, like Director Cummings, I want to keep relations open and aboveboard with 1600 Pennsylvania Avenue—even though I'm not exactly keen on the whole deal. One learns to pick one's battles, Special Agent Wright."

"I'm getting it, Director, but it doesn't mean I have to like it. So, we file it away as a case closed?"

Bert grinned. "That's what it means. I see you're a fast learner, Wright." He looked over at John Clawson, whose gaze was disconcerting. Bert had always prided himself on being able to read people, and Clawson wasn't buying the whole drill, for some reason, but he was too good of an agent to go up against Bert or the White House. Bert felt a chill run up the back of his neck.

He opened his briefcase and was about to slip the directive from the White House into it when Agent Clawson asked, "Shouldn't we have a copy for our files here?"

Clawson had his answer when Bert snapped his briefcase shut. "File a detailed report to my office, Agent Wright. List every lead that has come in and every call that came in once the artist's sketch went public. I'll be in touch. I'll call when I get to the airport to let you know where I parked the car." Hands were shaken, then Bert was outside. He heaved a sigh of relief.

Once Bert settled himself behind the wheel and turned on the engine, he ran the short meeting over and over in his mind until he was sure there would be no repercussions from it. Since the buck stopped with him, he now felt confident enough to shift gears and pull out into traffic. He keyed in Cosmo Cricket's office phone number and settled back, his eyes on the road, the Bluetooth headset secure in his ear allowing him to talk and keep his hands on the wheel. "I'm on my way to your office. Please wait for me." He ended the call, then shifted his thoughts to a neutral zone so he could travel mentally to Big Pine Mountain and Kathryn Lucas.

Forty minutes later, Cosmo Cricket greeted Bert at the door to his office, Lizzie Fox at his side.

Bert grinned. "Case closed on the Vegas madam. I'm taking a seven o'clock flight back to D.C. I just stopped by to see if I could take you both to a very late lunch or a very early dinner."

Cosmo looked adoringly at his new wife and smiled. "She's the boss."

Lizzie, to Bert's eye, looked so happy he thought she was going to burst out singing. She nodded. "That would be nice, Bert. We accept."

Cosmo beamed his pleasure. "Just let me shut down and we'll be good to go. My secretary had to leave early for a parent-teacher conference after school hours. I won't be long."

Lizzie motioned for Bert to take a seat in one of the soft, buttery leather chairs. She looked at him questioningly, but she didn't say anything.

"Under control, Lizzie. You look happy."

Lizzie leaned forward. "I've never been happier, Bert. Never. I don't want to go back to D.C. I guess I don't have to tell you how that is. The pardons will come, I just don't know when. This latest incident makes the president even more indebted to the Vigilantes. She's a woman of her word. But patience is not something any of us is known for. I just want you to know that."

The phone in Cosmo's office rang three times before it was picked up. Whoever it was, Lizzie knew Cosmo would cut the call short. She continued to expound on Martine Connor's capabilities. Suddenly, Lizzie frowned as she looked toward Cosmo's private office. Bert sat up straighter, alert to the change in the tone he was hearing coming from the inner office, even though neither he nor Lizzie could distinguish the words. Lizzie got up and made her way to the doorway, Bert on her heels. They both stared at Cosmo, who looked to be in a state of shock. They were just in time to see him set the phone back into its base.

Cosmo cleared his throat. "That was . . . that was the Vegas madam, Lily Flowers."

Lizzie blinked.

Bert's jaw dropped.

"She's alive," Cosmo said.

Lizzie, who was never at a loss for words, couldn't think of a thing to say. Bert seemed to be suffering from the same problem.

"I cremated someone who wasn't Lily Flowers."

Lizzie rushed to her husband. "Cosmo, you didn't know. Don't blame yourself for that. Did Ms. Flowers say who it was? What happened?"

Cosmo's eyes glazed over. He threw his hands in the air to show he was having trouble trying to understand what was going on. "Miss Flowers, who is now Caroline Summers, said that the night she left, she stopped on the Strip to say good-bye to an old friend. When she came back out of the building, her car was gone. She had her purse with her, but she'd left one of those folding wallets with her

Lily Flowers's driver's license, insurance card, and the car registration with about twenty dollars in the console, along with a copy of the receipt for a hotel reservation in San Bernardino. It goes without saying she was suddenly suspicious, so she had her friend rent her a car under the friend's name, and she drove to where she was going, and, no, she didn't tell me where that was, and took a plane to where she is now, and I don't know that location either. She said she just today logged onto the Internet and read the obituary for Lily Flowers. She called to tell me she was alive, well, and safe. She also said she had had the car checked from top to bottom and even had the tires rotated and checked before she set out for her trip."

Bert finally found his tongue. "The case is closed officially."

"Who was driving Ms. Flowers's car that night?" Lizzie asked. "Was it planned, or was 'Lily Flowers' just at the wrong place at the wrong time? Whom did *we* cremate, Cosmo?"

"And I just violated my attorney-client privilege by divulging it all in the presence of the director of the Federal Bureau of Investigation."

Bert waved his hands in dismissal. "Case closed, remember? Pay me a dollar and my lips are sealed."

Cosmo's hand moved so fast Lizzie and Bert both thought it was magic. Bert pocketed the dollar and grinned. He stretched out his hand, and the two men shook on it.

"So, Cosmo, do we think the madam was set up? If we go with that theory, it doesn't make sense. No one knew she was going to make a stop on the Strip that night. So, was the tire tampered with? Was it just a car heist? I'm having a little trouble with the idea that a woman who matches Lily Flowers's description heists a car, then heads, we think, to where Ms. Flowers was going to go. None of it makes sense," Lizzie said.

"Maybe someone did something to the tire so that when it was driven at a higher speed, it would blow. It's been known to happen," Bert said. "Maybe Flowers was the intended victim but things got derailed when her car was stolen. The case is closed, 'terrible car crash' is the final word by the locals. Can't argue with the locals. I can see you're going to beat yourself up over this, Cosmo. Don't. No one claimed the body. The victim had no prints on file. No dental or medical records, no ID on the body or in the vehicle, other than Lily Flowers's billfold in the console. The woman would have stayed at the morgue for two weeks, then the State of Nevada would have buried her in a potter's field as a Jane Doe."

"I think there was some kind of plan being implemented either by Hunter Pryce or someone he hired," Lizzie said. "It was dark. Perhaps the person who stole the car resembled Ms. Flowers. Or, the car's tires were tampered with earlier, and the person responsible just sat back and waited, knowing sooner or later there would be an accident. It's the best I can come up with."

"The case is officially closed by the locals and now by the FBI. It's time to move on. There's nothing we can do at this point unless the Vigilantes come up with something when they take over. The case can be reopened at any time. As you know we call it a 'cold case' if and when we go back to take a second look."

"This is going to haunt me," Cosmo said.

"All the cases haunt me to varying degrees. You learn to shelve it and compartmentalize. And, no, it doesn't get better, it seems to get worse because the bad guys keep coming up with new shit to terrorize us. Just when you think you have a lock on an MO, they throw you a curve. You deal with it the best way you can and hope you win a few along the way. The ones you don't win go on the shelf. That's the way it is, Cosmo. Welcome to our world."

"Come on, Cricket, we're going out to eat. We are not going to talk shop, and we are not going to moan and groan about would haves, should haves, could haves. Besides, the FBI is picking up the tab."

Lizzie's laugh tinkled around the office as Cosmo turned off his computer and the lights. Being the last one out, he locked the door and followed his dinner companions to the elevator. He felt lower than a snake's belly when he stepped into the elevator. *Maybe Bert was right. Maybe.*

Jack Emery walked out of the courthouse. He broke into a full sprint to get to the lot where his car was parked. By the time he got to his car, he was soaked to the skin. Only then did he realize that the headache, which had plagued him all day, was gone. It was already late, 4:50, according to his watch and the clock in the car. No point in going back to the office. He could go in a half hour early in the morning and do what he had to do. He debated all of two minutes as to whether he should go home or stop at Harry's *dojo.* For some reason he always felt better when he was with good old Harry. Someday he was going to take the time to try to figure it out. He kept a change of casual clothes in his locker there, so that was another reason to stop by. The *dojo* was a good place to play catch-up on the day's events. For all he knew, all kinds of things that he wasn't privy to might have gone on while he was in court.

With the rush hour traffic and the rain, it took fifty minutes to get to Harry's place. He swung into the narrow alley that led to one of the four parking spots allotted to the *dojo.* The small lot was empty except for Harry's motorcycle with its plastic cover. Harry babied his wheels the way a mother protected a newborn.

Jack was drenched to the skin a second time even though he ran at the speed of light to the back door of the *dojo*. He fished around in his wet pocket for the key Harry had given him a long time ago. To his knowledge, he was the only one other than Harry who had a key. He remembered how honored he'd felt at the time, how choked up he was. Then Harry had called him a shithead, and the warm, cozy feeling was gone. Harry was never comfortable when other people said nice things to him or about him. Jack knew if Harry ever needed an organ transplant, he'd be first in line to donate one of his, assuming he had two of whatever Harry needed.

Jack opened the door. His jaw dropped, then he squeezed his eyes shut, blinked, and blinked again. His voice was so shocked, he couldn't believe it was his own when he said, "Harry! Is that you? Holy shit, talk to me, Harry! Who died?" he asked desperately.

"Eat shit, Jack. It's me. You know it's me."

"Harry! You're wearing a suit! You don't own a suit! And it's an Armani!"

"No one died. I bought it. I have a personal shopper at Nordstrom who picked it out. What do you think? He said this is a power tie. Is it a power tie, Jack? The shirt is raw silk."

"Hell, yes! Raw silk? What the hell is raw silk? I think you're lying to me. Someone must have died. How much did that outfit cost?"

"I told you, no one died. It cost . . . none of your damn business. Why do you care anyway?"

"I care because . . . because I care. Are you planning on getting married? What's with the fancy duds! By the way, you planning on wearing that getup on your motorcycle?"

Harry was already ripping at his power tie and raw silk

shirt. "Not that it's any of your business, but next week I have an appointment at the bank to apply for a loan to remodel this place. You happy now that you know my business?"

"Yeah. Put me down for a character reference. I'll do you proud, buddy. I bet you could use Maggie, too. And Judge Easter and Elias Cummings. See what a ray of sunshine I am on this miserable, wet day? Anything else going on?"

Harry's voice was muffled as he undressed behind a rice paper screen. It sounded to Jack like he said that nothing was going on.

"I see you didn't get around to opening this box of mail. Guess you were too busy shopping." Jack guffawed. "Let's call Maggie and have her and the *Post* buy us some dinner. If anything went on today, she'll have the latest. We'll go in my car, though. And we need umbrellas."

Harry walked around from behind the screen. "You plan on wearing those wet clothes or what?"

"Nah, you just took my breath away in all of those fancy duds. Whatever is wrong with me? I bet you could pose for *GQ.* I feel the need to tell you that your suit calls for *shoes,* not open-toed sandals. No one will give you a loan if you don't wear shoes. Shoes, Harry!"

"I have shoes, Jack. Look! Nine hundred bucks. Bally shoes."

Jack pulled on a sweatshirt that said GEORGETOWN on the back. "Did you try them on, Harry?"

"No. The guy just picked them out."

"You never wear shoes, Harry. That means you are going to get blisters if they don't fit right, and I don't give a shit how much you paid for them. You have to wear socks, too. How much did that personal shopper charge you?"

Harry had an ugly look on his face when he looked

down at the shoes in the box he was holding. "Nothing, the service was free. They hand-delivered it. That was free, too."

"My ass, it's free. Nothing in this life is free. They build that service into the cost of what you buy. You could have hired me, and I would have gotten you the same thing. Okay, I'm ready. Are you calling Maggie, or am I?"

The ugly look was still on Harry's face when he closed the shoe box and threw it across the room. "You call."

Not liking the look on Harry's face, Jack yanked out his cell phone and keyed in Maggie's cell phone number.

"She said okay. Squire's Pub. She's buying. Hey, Harry, look at it this way, that suit will last you forever. If a funeral pops up, you're good to go. If you decide to marry Yoko, you got a classy suit unless she wants you to wear a tux, at which point you'll have to find a personal renter."

"You are just too stupid for me to admit I know you," Harry said as they walked out. "I'm going to sit in the backseat so no one will see me with you."

"Oh, get over yourself. Put your ass in the car and shut up. I have a funny feeling in my stomach that something happened today, or else something is going to happen."

"I hate it when you get those feelings, Jack."

"You can't hate it more than I do, Harry." Jack turned on the ignition, then the windshield wipers, but he didn't shift gears. Harry looked at him expectantly.

"I need to tell you something, Harry. I don't want to, but . . . I need to say it out loud to . . . *someone*."

"What? Are you saying I'm good enough to tell or not good enough to tell? Or am I the only one you would consider telling whatever the hell that is eating you?" Harry asked, his tone surly.

Jack pondered the question as the wipers slashed back and forth across the windshield. "Yes. No. Hell, I don't know. Will you just listen?"

"Yeah, sure." Harry turned sideways, as did Jack, so they were facing each other.

"Look, maybe it's more of a confession. Don't say anything, just let me spit this out since I'm finally getting up the nerve to say it out loud. I can't tell you how relieved I was when I heard the Vegas madam was dead. No, don't misunderstand. I don't mean I wanted her dead, I just wanted her *gone*. Because if Lizzie represented her, that would mean I'd have to prosecute. Lizzie is the best of the best. She's a legend in her own time. Me and every prosecutor in the office . . . We're afraid of her. The minute she walks into a courtroom, she fucking *owns* the place. None of us have ever won a case she defended. One time I . . . Christ, I can't believe I'm telling you this, but one time I actually, honest-to-God faked a ruptured appendix to get out of a case she was defending. The case was then assigned to Josh Maddox. That was seven years ago, and the guy has never spoken to me since. He lost. Lizzie not only chewed him up, she spit him out. I love Lizzie like a sister, and I know she feels the same way about me, but when she gets in the courtroom, she's like no one you've ever seen. We aren't brother and sister then. They don't come any better than Lizzie. Yeah, I'm jealous."

Harry cocked his head to the side and looked at Jack. "So, let me get this straight. You're saying Lizzie can out-lawyer you? You, Jack Emery, you of the silver tongue, you who knows everything? You're afraid of a lady lawyer."

Jack looked uncomfortable. "Yeah, Harry, that's what I'm saying."

Harry unbuckled his seat belt, got out of the car, then opened the back door, climbed in, and buckled up.

Jack turned around. "Why are you sitting back there?"

"You dumb shit, now I definitely don't want anyone to see me with you."

Jack's shoulders slumped. He shifted gears and started to back out of the small lot. His foot slammed on the brake when he felt a hand on his shoulder. A firm but gentle hand. A comforting hand. Harry's cockamamie way of saying he understood and it was okay.

Chapter 20

Myra clicked off her cell phone and turned to Annie and the girls. "That was Maggie, and she had a startling piece of information to share with us." Seeing that she had everyone's attention, she continued. "Cosmo Cricket received a phone call a while ago from the Vegas madam, one Crystal Clark. She is alive, safe, and well, and supposedly out of the country. She told Cosmo she logged on to the Internet, and, I would assume, the Nevada papers online, and read about her own demise in a car accident. It seems she stopped to say good-bye to a friend before she left Vegas and while she was visiting with the friend her car was stolen. The friend rented a car for her under the friend's name and Ms. Flowers, as we know her, continued with her journey to the safe place where she is now residing.

"Bert was there in the office with Lizzie when the call came through. He stopped only to tell them he was closing the case at the request of the White House. Lizzie called Maggie to give her a phone number for one of Crystal Clark's . . . working girls, and then said her work is done and she's going on a short honeymoon with her new husband.

"Bert will take a seven o'clock flight back to D.C.

Maggie is meeting up with Jack and Harry as we speak to share this new news. I find this all beyond bizarre."

"What does it mean, Myra—is our mission off or on?" Isabelle asked.

"The mission is on. We were never concerning ourselves with the madam, only her clients. I guess the question is, are we clear on everything? Should we go over it one more time before we leave the mountain?"

The Sisters looked at one another and shrugged.

"It won't hurt to go over it one more time," Alexis said.

Annie stepped forward. "From the moment we arrive at our target area, our window of time is two hours and thirty minutes. That time is carved in stone via Lizzie and POTUS. Don't confuse our thirty minutes of prep time with the actual mission time.

"As we speak a heavy-duty Dumpster is being delivered to Paula Woodley's house. Within the next hour, even though it is night, a delivery of roof shingles is also being delivered. Earlier in the afternoon a tree truck arrived. The tree people left their truck with the cherry picker and wood chipper. Around five thirty a FOR SALE sign was posted in Paula's front yard, with an extender that says there will be a two-and-a-half-hour open house tomorrow. And all the renovations and price reductions will be discussed at that time in order to boost the sale of the house. Those neighbors who haven't seen the Dumpster, the sign, the tree truck, and the shingles will see them first thing tomorrow morning."

Myra looked down at her notes. "Four, possibly five, White House cars will be picking up the neighbors for the Middle America Main Street luncheon that President Connor is hosting. It's been played up big on the news all day today. The pickup is scheduled for eleven o'clock. A half-hour ride to the White House will get the neighbors there at eleven thirty, give or take a few minutes. There will be a photo op with POTUS that will take anywhere from thirty to forty-five minutes. Possibly an hour. Then a two-hour lunch, with a short speech by President Connor, some more handshaking, a little personal conversation, then the neighbors will be taken back to their homes, each of them carrying a personal White House memento signed by the president. Hopefully, if all goes well, we'll be in and out by then and on our way back to the mountain."

"An open house and all those fake home repairs! We might have boxed ourselves into a real mess," Nikki said. "Our . . . uh . . . guests might be a little shy about being seen at that house with so much activity going on."

"But they'll be afraid not to show," Alexis said. "Are we still going to do half and half?"

"Yes," Kathryn said. "Half will come through the kitchen and half will come through the front door. It's going to be interesting to see how many show up. We'll round them all up and work out of that huge family room. The boys will be watching our backs. Ted and Espinosa will just be themselves, human interest in the neighborhood that got picked to be the first of many to be invited to Main Street luncheons at the White House."

"And where will Avery Snowden's people be?" Yoko asked.

"Inside in one of the bedrooms. Supposedly they're the tree and roof people," Nikki said.

Their orders understood, everyone left the room.

Ahead of the girls, Myra and Annie huddled, whispering to each other.

"They're up to something," Kathryn said as she pointed to Annie and Myra and whispered to Nikki, "I can feel it."

"I know," Nikki whispered in return.

Kathryn leaned closer to Nikki so her voice wouldn't carry. "Do you really think the vice president is going to be able to ditch his security detail and come to Kalorama under his own power?"

"Yeah, I do. If we're right—that this was his plan all along to destroy Martine Connor—he'll be there. Being a heartbeat away from becoming the president is all the impetus he needs to meet up with the madam to try and keep her quiet. He hasn't, at least I don't think he has, considered that the other campers are going to be in attendance. He's toast," Nikki said.

"Do you think he knows the real madam is still alive?"

"No, Kathryn, I don't think he does. Isn't he going to be surprised? At this time yesterday, he thought he was just a hair away from having Martine Connor stepping aside. I would guess that he thinks he's ready to step right into her shoes without missing a beat. Well, maybe not today literally but as soon as he can leak or anonymously call the media and mention names, and then the tsunami begins."

"Mr. Snowden is on board?" Yoko asked.

"He's one of the uh . . . roofers," Annie said. "Jack and Harry, properly attired, will be Realtors and will be driving a van with a fictitious logo on the side. Ted and Joe Espinosa will be just who they are, *Post* reporter and photographer. Keeping the reading public informed."

"What if people show up for the open house?" Kathryn asked.

"I don't see that happening, but if it does, Mr. Snowden's people will divert them."

"I don't know if I am one hundred percent comfortable using Paula Woodley's house a second time. In my opinion, that's just inviting trouble," Isabelle said.

"I can see why you would think that, but nothing will happen," Kathryn said. "No one will expect us to return to the same place a second time. We can't allow ourselves to think along those lines. It's too late to have second thoughts. We're on, so to speak."

"And the johns, or the clients, whatever you want to call them—what if they don't show?" Nikki asked.

"That is also being taken care of as we speak. Just about now Maggie should be," Annie said, looking down at her watch, "calling Miss Brandy, who will then have the other working girls call all of their clients, thanks to Martine Connor giving Lizzie the Happy Campers' personal cell phone numbers. Lizzie even gave me the president's private cell in case something goes awry. That was so generous of her. Each of Lily's girls will explain about the real estate open house, mentioning the roofing people to prove to them they're serious about a meeting. They're going to tell the campers to show up or they'll go to the media. A diversion as well as a command performance for their safety and security, so to speak. I think we can be certain attendance will be a hundred percent."

"And the vp's arrival? That might prove a little tricky," Kathryn said.

"Maggie is making that particular call herself. Not as Maggie Spritzer, of course, but as Crystal Clark's very good friend," Myra said.

The Sisters looked at one another, then shrugged as one.

"Then I guess we're good to go," Nikki said.

"I hear the cable car," Yoko said. She strained to see out the window. "It's two of Mr. Snowden's men."

"With everything going at breakneck speed, I guess I forgot to tell you I had Avery send two of his people to see to the dogs and to guard the mountain while we're away. I do believe they are the same two who took care of the mountain and the dogs when we left for Utah," Annie said briskly. "Alexis, you have your Red Bag?"

"I'm good to go, *Mom.*"

Annie laughed. She absolutely loved it when the girls called her that.

The Sisters trooped out to the cable car. The two men saluted smartly as they strode past the departing women. Murphy and Grady, knowing the drill, turned and followed the two men. Myra held open the gate to the cable car while Annie and the girls stepped inside.

A minibus with lettering that said it belonged to the Northeastern Fellowship Federation, which didn't exist, would be at the bottom of the mountain. It would carry the women to Washington, with Kathryn doing the driving.

"We should get to D.C. about two in the morning," Yoko said. "We park, we sleep till the sun comes up, then we ride around and hope we don't get caught until it's time to go to Paula Woodley's house. Do I have that right?"

Annie and Myra listened indulgently to the girls' grumbling as the cable car descended. Neither Myra nor Annie liked the idea of sleeping on the bus either, but kept their opinions to themselves.

"You do have it right, dear," Myra said cheerfully as she hopped into the bus and took her seat.

"I'm excited," Annie said just as cheerfully as she climbed in beside Myra.

The Sisters settled back for the long ride to the nation's capital.

The dead-end street that included the Woodley house was alive with activity. When Jack and Harry rolled up in a white van that said ADNOLINI REAL ESTATE on the side, they saw Ted and Espinosa leaning against a dark blue sedan that belonged to the *Post*. A huge green-and-white sign that said PRESS could be seen on the dashboard. Press tags hung on chains around their necks. Both were dressed casually, in creased khakis and button-down shirts, the sleeves rolled up. Both wore boat shoes and had back-packs. They looked bored out of their minds, but the truth was, they were more alert than they'd ever been on a stakeout.

Jack felt silly when he reached into the back of the van and came out with a bundle of balloons he quickly tied to the OPEN HOUSE sign on the front lawn. He looked up at the man poised in the cherry picker, who was pretending to inspect the limbs of a monster maple tree that was misty green with leaves not yet in full growth. As Jack headed for the front door he risked a glance at the Dumpster sitting at the far side of the property. He wasn't sure, but he thought he knew what was going to go into it.

Ted whistled sharply.

Jack looked up and brought his wrist up to his mouth. "Talk to me, Ted."

"Caravan two-and-a-half blocks out. Five vehicles, I'm told. Maggie is sitting on the corner three streets over. I'm seeing people walking out their doors now. Snowden has six men in the house. They entered through the back door. Except for the guy in the cherry picker. He makes seven."

Jack pretended to fiddle with the lockbox attached to the Woodley front door. "Where are the girls?"

"They were cruising Independence Avenue and should be here in about fifteen minutes, according to Maggie. No sign of the other guests, but it's still early. So far it's lookin' good, Jack."

Jack stepped aside to allow Harry to enter the house first. "Yeah, right, it always looks good at first, then the shit hits the fan. Tell me the truth, Harry, if you were one of those johns, would you show up here?"

"Hell, no, Jack. I would have split a long time ago at the first whisper."

"And just left your family behind?"

"No, I would have sent them off somewhere. Would you show up?"

"No. And if I did and saw that mess outside I would probably wet my pants, turn tail, and run. Politicians are a whole other breed so it's a crapshoot. I don't see the vp showing up either. It's almost impossible to shake those Secret Service guys."

"How desperate all those guys are will determine whether they show or not. Yoko said they will be here. All of them. Maybe the girls know something they didn't share with us."

"Emery, nice seeing you again," Avery Snowden said from the kitchen doorway. He offered up a crisp salute that Jack envied. "We're on target, Emery. Your people aren't going to screw this up, are they?"

Jack wanted to kick his ass to the moon, but he just shook his head. Snowden, after all, was responsible for the removal, be it trees or bodies.

Snowden was dressed in what Jack recognized as tree-removal gear, a harness with clanking chains and boots with spikes in their soles. He was carrying the boots. Though Jack knew nothing about tree removal gear, he thought that Snowden looked the part.

"Ted?"

"The caravan is turning the corner now. Oh, man, the lead driver is pissed with all the commotion on the street. He's getting out. He looks like Secret Service to me. The other drivers are getting out, too. The lead driver is heading for your doorway. Jesus, Jack, get the hell out of sight. Espinosa is snapping away. The residents are lining up to get in the cars. Oh, shit, Maggie says the Federation bus is down at the bottom of the hill. She's waving them off."

Jack and Harry ducked into the hallway bathroom as

Snowden tripped and clanked his way to the front door. He opened it with a flourish. "Yeah, who are you?" Without waiting for a response he said, "The open house don't start till one."

The man standing in the doorway whipped out a folder with a badge.

"Yeah, I got one of those, too. What?"

"You have to move that truck out there."

"No, I don't gotta move that truck. I got a permit to be here. What's your problem? You have a whole goddamn road out there, a circle in the bargain, and you want me to believe you can't drive your car out of here! Where'd you get your driver's license—Walmart? I don't have a key, hotshot. My driver went out to bring back lunch, and he has the key." Snowden peered out the door, and said, "Back up. Use REVERSE, and you'll go backward. Now, get out of my face, I have a job to do, and you're interfering with that job."

Inside the bathroom, Jack muttered, "Oh, shit!"

Snowden wasn't finished. "Hey you, Mr. Reporter, and you with the camera, take this picture, will ya?"

Espinosa whirled around and managed to capture the ugly look on the Secret Service agent's face, his fist raised, his badge clearly visible.

The homeowners started climbing into the cars that had pulled up as two of the agents posing as drivers made their way to the Woodley doorway. Ted held out his digital recorder and captured the lively dialogue that ensued as Espinosa clicked away.

"Give me that goddamn camera," one of the agents snarled.

"Make me," Ted said, dancing out of the way.

Harry stepped out of the bathroom and walked to the front door. He managed to wiggle his way between Snowden and the agents. He took his time looking from one to the other before he reached up and out. The agents dropped to the ground. Harry shook his head from side to side. "I hate it when these guys try to interfere with free enterprise."

Espinosa stepped forward for a better shot of the "sleeping" agents. The two remaining agents rushed forward as the homeowners piled out of the cars, the better to see what was going on.

"Hands up, you're all under arrest!" one of the agents shouted.

"Why?" Harry asked. He sounded like he was asking if it was going to rain. He eyed the drawn guns and smiled. "You want to put those back where they belong, or do you want me to take them away from you?"

"On the ground and spread 'em."

Harry dropped to a half crouch, and, quicker than lightning, his hands up, the fingers splayed, hit both men in the crotch. They dropped instantly.

"Now what?" Jack asked from the doorway. "Oh, oh, here come the homeowners, and they don't look happy. Their ride to the White House just went to sleep. Harry, Harry, what am I going to do with you? I hope you have a solution to this little mess."

Harry looked over at the Dumpster and shrugged. "Snowden, get your men out here so they can drive those irate people to the White House. Make sure they use their sirens and blue lights. Ted said they're in the trunk, and, no, I don't know how he knows that."

Ted rushed forward with Espinosa, who announced that he wanted pictures of all the homeowners for the *Post,* along with names and which house they lived in.

One of them, a lady with blue hair and sharp eyes, wanted to know what was going on and why their drivers were on the ground. "Who is that foreigner?" she then demanded indignantly.

"The Russian?" Ted asked, feigning surprise. "This all has to do with White House security and you are not supposed to ask questions."

"He wasn't Russian, he was Oriental," the blue-haired lady protested.

"No, ma'am, he's not Oriental, he's Russian and his name is Vladimir Rusky," Ted said. "Trust me, we have his picture on file at the *Post*."

"Well, he looked Oriental to me." The woman sniffed. She looked to her neighbors, who had heard the exchange and who now all agreed the man in question was Russian.

Back across the street, Avery Snowden was venting. "Emery, this was not in the plan. I'm being reminded of a truckload of pumpkins right now." He whistled sharply, two blasts, and his men appeared dressed in the same gear that their leader wore.

"Change of plan, men. You will be driving all these dressed-up people to the White House. You will then return here with the vehicles. Move!"

The homeowners scrambled back across the street and climbed into their assigned cars. The moment the last vehicle backed down the street, Snowden, Jack, and Emery prepared to deposit the agents in the Dumpster.

"How long are they going to be out, Wong?" Snowden asked, his tone clearly saying he didn't care one way or another.

"We need two hours, Harry," Jack said.

"In that case, I can grant your wish." Harry leaned over first one agent and then another as he touched a spot behind each man's ear. "Done!"

"Espinosa, just get the guys' backs. We don't want any frontal shots of our people."

"What, you think I'm stupid? We're thirteen minutes behind schedule, Ted."

"I know, I know. Here comes the bus."

When the Federation bus backed into the driveway, the Vigilantes piled out and raced into the house. "We're running late, Jack. Is everything under control?"

"Depends on what you mean by 'control.'" He quickly briefed the girls, then stood back to see what they would do. They burst out laughing as Yoko pinched Harry's cheeks, and cooed, "You're the man, Harry." Then she kissed him until his teeth rattled.

Alexis opened her Red Bag and started pulling things out. Jack, Harry, and Snowden marveled at how well the women worked together. The TV was on, the videos in place. Hypodermic needles were laid out in a neat row on the coffee table along with vials of clear white liquid. The clock on the mantel ticked off the minutes.

Outside, next to the Dumpster, Ted cupped his hands under Espinosa's foot so that he could get a leg up to shoot the contents.

"It's not pretty, Ted."

"Maggie's gonna love it. You know what she would love even more, Espinosa?"

"I'll flip you for it, Ted. Heads!"

Ted flipped the coin in his hand. "Okay, but how the hell am I going to get out?"

"Pile them up and climb out."

"Smart-ass."

"Think bonus on top of bonus. Five will get you ten Maggie will reward you tonight."

"This thing stinks," Ted said as he rifled through the agents' pockets. He laid all the badges out in a neat row. He clicked away with great abandon. "Ask Maggie if she wants the badges. What about the guns?"

A minute passed, then another. "She said take them all."

"I'm gonna need a sack or something."

"Take off your shirt. Like I carry a sack around with me."

All Espinosa could hear were grunts coming from inside the Dumpster as Ted piled the agents one on top of the other. And then Ted was over the top and on the ground. He quickly dumped the IDs and the guns into the trunk of his car.

"Maggie said good work."

Ted slipped into his shirt and buttoned it. "Okay, we're outta here. We're driving one street over and returning on foot through the backyards. Let's go!"

"We could go to jail for this," Espinosa said fretfully.

"Nah. We have powerful friends, Joe. Hey, this is just a guess on my part, but I think somehow, some way, those IDs and the guns will find their way back to the White House."

"They got a look at Harry, Ted."

"Harry who? I was standing right there, I didn't see anyone named Harry. Did you, Joe? Those homeowners were all wearing glasses. I convinced them the guy was Russian. Like I said, what good is having powerful friends if they can't come to your aid from time to time?"

Espinosa brought his phone to his ear. "Lots of traffic coming this way. Six cars at the bottom of the hill. Stay alert. More stragglers farther back."

Ted relayed the message to Jack as soon as Espinosa clicked his phone closed. The two men sprinted toward the backyard, which would lead them to the Woodley yard and the back door.

"They're on the way," Ted said breathlessly.

Chapter 21

Maggie Spritzer was busier than a queen bee in a hive and loving every minute of it as she scanned the road with a powerful set of binoculars, a gift from her predecessor. She was text messaging Ted with her left hand while using her hands-free cell phone to talk to Lizzie. Her mind raced as she ran through the possibilities. So much to do and so little time. She ended her call to Lizzie, saying she was on top of it and would take care of the matter. Then she punched in Ted's number. She just knew she would have raccoon eyes when she finally laid the binoculars to rest, that was how tightly she'd had them pressed to her eyes.

"Listen up, the parade has started. I can guarantee there was a run on baseball caps and wraparound sunglasses in every store in the District today. Five more minutes, and your guests should be at your doorstep. Oh, shit, oh, shit, oh, shit! Guess who just whizzed past me? That guy you hate from the *News*. The squirrelly one. What's his name? Oh, yeah, Zack Tyson. This is not good, Ted. Traffic is picking up. I count eight. And I think this is the vp bringing up the rear. He's in a maroon Saab. Yep, it's him. Two more behind him. Ooops, traffic light! I see three bringing up the rear. You all set, Ted? Ted? Talk to me. Tyson should be hitting the Woodleys' street about *now!*"

Inside Paula Woodley's house, chaos reigned. Ted relayed Maggie's news to the group assembled in the kitchen. In the blink of an eye, Harry had one of Snowden's men stripped down to his underwear. In the next blink of an eye, he was dressed in the man's tree gear and out the front door, hitching up the too-long pants as he went.

As a group, they all rushed to the huge bay window in the living room just in time to see Harry approach the reporter. A second later the *News* reporter was on his shoulder, after which he joined the other guests in the Dumpster, and Harry was back inside dusting his hands dramatically.

"Before you can ask, Jack, he'll wake up the same time the others do."

"Oooh, Harry, I saw that. It was masterful," Yoko said, nibbling on his ear as Harry stripped down again, to everyone's delight, especially Yoko's.

Harry blushed. He was glad he was wearing his new Calvin Klein underwear.

"This was not in the plan, Emery," Snowden growled.

Jack shrugged. "You know what they say about the best-laid plans of mice and men, Avery. We're all intact, and it worked."

The Vigilantes clapped their hands in approval.

Outside, the man in the cherry picker looked down as the first guest arrived. "Back door, mister." He continued to give cheerful directions with airy waves of his hand as guest after guest parked and walked up the driveway. He smirked to himself when he saw that none of the guests looked up, the billed caps so low on their faces they almost touched their respective noses.

Snowden talked into his sleeve. "Make sure no one

blocks the driveway, the Federation bus has to get out of here in one piece. Over and out."

Over and out, my ass, Jack thought as he took up his position in the dining room behind the swinging door. Only Myra and Annie were in the kitchen to welcome the guests, then herd them into the great room. He looked over at Harry. "I could have sworn you were a boxer kind of guy. Calvin is cutting them kind of skimpy these days, doncha think?"

Harry offered up his favorite expression where Jack was concerned. "Eat shit, Jack."

It looked to Jack like Harry was about to tweak his fingers in his direction, so he danced away, but not before he got in the last word. "Bite me, big guy!"

In spite of himself, Harry laughed. The little discourse was nothing more than a stress reliever and both men knew it.

The two heard the front door open, then close. Both knew it would be Nikki and Kathryn who would greet the vice president.

"Game's on, boys and girls. Take your positions," Snowden said. He snapped off a sloppy salute in everyone's direction, one that no one returned.

Jack just rolled his eyes before he flipped him the bird. Harry laughed again.

Snowden went to the front of the house, where he checked something with Nikki and Kathryn, then, after Kathryn took her position by the front door, held a whispered conversation with Nikki.

When they were finished, Kathryn looked over to Nikki and raised her eyebrows to ask, *"What's up?"*

Nikki shook her head, and mouthed, *"Later."*

In the kitchen, Myra and Annie stared at the politicians "cluttering up Paula Woodley's kitchen," as Annie later put it. The politicos all started talking at once, blustering, threatening, as they shook their fists at the two women. It was Ambassador Kierson who looked closely at Myra, then reached out to grasp the kitchen counter for support.

"I see you recognize me, Harvey. The next question I suppose is, do you recognize me as Myra Rutledge, your wife's old friend, or do you recognize me as a member of the Vigilantes? I guess this is a trite question, but does Julia know you're here?"

The junior senator from New York said, "Oh, sweet Jesus!"

"Hats and sunglasses off, gentlemen. Such pathetic disguises," Annie said. "And to think you people make decisions for the country. *"NOW!"* she roared, when none of the men made a move to do as instructed. Ball caps and sunglasses flew in all directions just as Ted and Espinosa entered the kitchen.

"Say 'sex' six times real fast." Espinosa grinned as he clicked away.

No one did.

"Someone really should say something," Myra said. "Unless you want me to do all the talking. You might feel better if you get it off your chests."

When she still had no takers, she motioned the men forward. Ted led them to the great room where the other Sisters waited.

"Son of a bitch!" a fat congressman from Nebraska bellowed. "What's going on here? You're the Vigilantes!"

Nikki pretended to look puzzled. "Congressman, what was your first clue? What gave us away?" Not bothering to wait for a response, she said, "Sit down and put your hands behind your backs. Girls, you know what to do."

A senator from Delaware and a congressman from New Jersey tried to make a run for it, but Harry wagged his finger at them. He then waved that same finger to a spot where the two men should sit. Without being told, they put their hands behind their backs. Yoko slipped on the FlexiCuffs.

All eyes were on the hypodermic needles and the vials on the coffee table.

"Do any of you know why you're here?" Kathryn asked. "Well, speaking strictly for myself, I can certainly understand your reticence. Having said that, let me clear it up for you. You all participated in a rather unsavory event, not once but twice. You also placed the president of the United States in a very untenable situation. So untenable, she could be forced out of office. We're," she said, motioning to the Vigilantes, "all thinking it's maybe because she's a woman just like Crystal Clark is a woman. And while you all like to use and abuse women, you don't really like the commander in chief or the woman who arranged the unsavory events you all participated in. The way things are going, or the way you all thought they would go, is that the president would bow out gracefully so as not to besmirch the presidency. Miss Clark would go on trial, and end up in jail. And the worst thing that would happen to the lot of you is a slap on the wrist, a few days of bad publicity, and you'd all go about your lives not caring that your families were damaged, possibly beyond repair. Everyone nod if this is all true."

An aging congressman from Alabama started to cry. "What are you going to do to us?" he sniveled into the shoulder of his shirt.

"That depends on your answers. Here's the question," Yoko said. "First one who gets it right gets to go home. Was my fellow Sister right in her summary of what went down? Was that the game plan? And, most important of all, who was the person who arranged the campout? We want a name."

Ted was text messaging Maggie so fast, his fingers were a blur on the small keypad. Espinosa was sending off his pictures at the speed of light.

The handcuffed men all started to talk at once. The moment the door to the great room opened, a sharp, shrill whistle ricocheted around the room. Standing in the doorway was the vice president.

"That's him! That's the son of a bitch!" Ambassador Kierson shouted. "It was all his idea. He had a thing with the madam. It went way back. Ask him. He'll probably lie like the devil he is, but I damn well taped him the day he came to my office. Can I go now?"

"Do you have to use the bathroom?" Alexis asked.

"No! Well, that's the only place you can go. For now."

The Alabama congressman was sobbing steadily by then.

The vice president, his hands cuffed behind him, blustered. "If you would all just use your brains and shut up, we can square this away, and we can all go home. Lying, Ambassador Kierson, will get you nowhere."

Jack gave the vice president a shove that sent him skidding across the room. He landed between the Alabama congressman and the senator from Delaware. Both men struggled to move away from him.

Annie walked to the center of the room, Myra at her side. "Allow me to introduce ourselves, gentlemen. We," she said, waving her arm around, "are the Vigilantes. These other gentlemen are our . . . helpers. If you like the word 'enforcers,' we can go with that. It makes no never mind to us. Now, we have you dead to rights. Ms. Crystal Clark was a very thorough lady. She had all your fingerprints, including yours, Mr. Vice President. The lady kept impeccable records. And pictures. Fantastic videos. We have them all. As you may have noticed, we're women. We do not like, not even one little bit, what you all tried to do to the president and Ms. Clark. Having said that, we are now going to show you a video. Don't blush like that, gentlemen, you aren't in this particular video, but I'd wager to guess you will be, sooner rather than later. Look alert, gentlemen, I don't want you to miss anything. Kathryn, show these fine men where they're going."

The film that appeared on the monster screen was crystal clear in HD. The colors were vibrant, the foliage lush and thick as the photographer panned the area where the documentary had been filmed. The voice-over sounded British. Then the camera homed in on a large, ramshackle building. Here, the lush foliage and vibrant colors were gone. Everything looked drab and brown. There were no crystal pools, no fruit trees or flowers to be seen. There were no cars, only mule-drawn carts.

> "This place," the voice said, "is a male brothel, one of many in Thailand. This is where the dregs of society come to end their days. There is little in the way of food. When the males aren't working, they are permitted to roam the streets to beg for coins and extra food. Here in this land, no one runs away, they always come back to this building or one just like it. Because . . . there is nowhere else to go."

The screen turned black. The silence in the room was total, so total, the click of the remote being turned off sounded like a thunderclap.

Then the room came alive with sound as the men struggled to their feet, their faces masks of horror and disbelief.

"You can't do this!" cried Ambassador Kierson. "Hunter, stop this goddamn crap and tell these people the truth. Do you hear me, you piece of scum? I'm not going to end my days in some . . . male brothel in—Jesus Christ—Thailand! These women can make that happen. Will you look at them? Look at their faces; they look goddamn gleeful. Tell them what they want to know."

Hunter Pryce looked sick. He licked at his lips. "Let's make a deal; you let me go, and I'll tell you everything you want to know." He jerked his head in the direction of the others, and said, "They were all for it. They wanted the risk, the thrill, and they were willing to pay for it. Yes, I made promises to them. I would have kept them, too. So, do we have a deal or not?"

The women pretended to confer.

Annie stepped forward. "Well, you are the vice president. I guess we have to treat you a *little* differently from these other offenders. Okay, we have a deal. Now answer this question. Did you love Crystal Clark?"

"Yes."

"What about Martine Connor? Did you start up your affair with her to advance your career? I guess I want to know if you loved her or if you used her."

"She was pleasant enough, but, no, I didn't love her, and, yes, she was part of my plan."

Annie snapped her fingers. Alexis rummaged in her Red Bag and came up with a small notebook and pen. She handed them to Annie, who waited until Pryce's cuffs were removed. "Now write exactly what I tell you. Make it clear and legible. If you don't screw up, you can go."

The only sound that could be heard was the scratch of the pen on paper as Annie dictated the words. Once or twice Pryce looked up at Annie, then at the other Vigilantes, with raised eyebrows and a smirk on his face. When he was finished he handed the notebook to Annie and turned to go. Alexis replaced the pad and pen in the Red Bag.

"I said you could go, I didn't say where," Annie said, as Jack and Harry forcibly held the vice president for a new set of FlexiCuffs.

"Time for our shots, gentlemen. You can't travel to a new country without your shots. Which ones, Annie?" Myra asked.

"They each get two." Annie giggled as she picked up two syringes and went to work.

Jack and Harry had their work cut out for them as the men tried to fight the needles coming their way.

"Tsk-tsk, politicians shouldn't talk that way," Jack said as Annie jabbed the congressman from New Jersey. "What are your constituents going to say when they see this on the evening news?"

"Audio is perfect, Jack," Ted said. "The networks will bleep it out, but what the hell, the viewing public is pretty astute at deciphering what isn't said."

"Who's watching the time?" Nikki shouted.

"Me," Yoko said. "We're okay."

"Who's moving the cars?" Kathryn shouted.

"The guy in the cherry picker. He's been moving them around the corner for the past fifteen minutes," Isabelle shouted in return.

Snowden and his men, who had just returned from the White House, entered the room and immediately surrounded the politicians, guns drawn.

Jack couldn't resist asking Snowden what the plan was.

"We march them one by one to the Dumpster, where they can join those cruds from the Secret Service."

"What if they yell or scream or shout at the top of their lungs? People are going to hear them."

"Wong! Front and center. Do that thing you do with your finger. Then my men will dump them in the Dumpster. Can you do that?"

"What's in it for me?" Harry teased, knowing Jack was loving every minute of the countdown.

"A bullet if you don't. And don't for one minute think you can snatch a bullet out of thin air."

"Well, the truth is, Snowden, I can do that, but it takes energy, so I'll just do what you can't do, and I'm telling Charles what you said the next time I see him."

"Smart-ass."

"Street's clear except for the Secret Service cars. There's no sign of the truck that's supposed to haul the Dumpster away," Jack said.

Snowden listened to the voice in his Bluetooth headset and then barked an order. "He's one street over. The rest of you move those cars up on people's lawns. Move! Move! Do I have to do everything?"

"God forbid," Jack muttered.

"Dammit to hell, Emery, I'm the extraction team. This other shit is not my forte. Do your part, and everyone will be happy. Come on, Espinosa, how the hell many pictures do you need?"

"I'm done. You are free to go."

"Time?" Nikki shouted.

"Fifteen minutes. We're still good," Yoko responded.

"Is everything packed?" Annie asked.

"We're good to go, Mom," Yoko said.

Annie grinned from ear to ear. The Vigilantes headed for the door.

"I have an idea," Myra said.

When Myra had an idea everyone stopped to listen. Myra talked. Then the Vigilantes started to laugh. Ted and Harry turned white, then red, then they clung to each other in panic.

Yoko made loud kissing sounds directed at Harry. Nikki blew Jack a kiss, then raced after Yoko and the others.

"Tell me they aren't going to do what they said they're going to do?"

"I wish I could, Harry, but I can't. How we have to look at this is that there are photo ops, and then there are photo ops. This is *the* photo op of the year! We need to clear out of here right now. We can see it and hear about it tonight at my place. C'mon, we need to call Lizzie and Maggie. We did good, Harry, and I saw something I never thought I'd ever live to see."

Harry fell right into that. "What's that?"

"Your underwear!" Jack took off at a dead run and was behind the wheel before Harry could get to him. Both men laughed all the way to the *Post,* where Maggie was waiting for them.

Ted and Espinosa were waiting outside the gates of the West Wing when the residents of Kalorama exited the White House grounds. Espinosa snapped busily as the guests preened and held up their White House souvenirs, their gazes sweeping the area for their ride back to their homes.

"Change of plans, ladies and gentlemen. It seems the Dumpster at the Woodley house got stuck in the middle of the road somehow and your drivers are unable to move their vehicles. Not to worry," Ted said cheerfully. "We have a ride for you with some very interesting people who want to meet you. All aboard," he cackled, as the men and women trooped onto the bus.

Kathryn hit the gas pedal the moment the last passenger was seated and buckled in.

The Vigilantes stood up and bowed. "We're taking you home, ladies and gentlemen, and we're also apologizing for the inconvenience."

"Are you really . . . ?"

"Oh, this is soooo exciting. So much better than that syrupy lunch we had to endure. And these tacky mementos, what can I say? I wouldn't want to go there again. Well, maybe at Christmastime. Is that Russian man still in the neighborhood? I can't believe the Vigilantes are chauffeuring us to our homes." Then the blue-haired lady turned around to converse with her excited neighbors, who were all babbling at the same time about how boring the White House was and how devilishly exciting the ride home was.

"Can you tell us what happened on our little street?" a shy older man with thick glasses asked. "I suspected something was up. That house is just a haven for bad things to go on. I'm not saying you did a bad thing. You probably did something that made something else right, isn't that so?"

"You could say that," Annie said.

"If you need any new recruits, can we volunteer?" a sprightly seventysomething queried. "We're as old as you two," she said, pointing to Myra and Annie.

That shut Annie up, who then whispered in Myra's ear, "Did you hear that? We absolutely have to get those tattoos now."

"You're right. We don't look like them, do we, Annie?" Myra asked fretfully.

"Not yet we don't," Annie said grimly. "I'm thinking that tattoos will take care of . . . whatever."

Nikki stood up. "You ladies and gentlemen aren't going to rat us out, are you? Tomorrow you can talk all you want, but first we have to get safely away."

"What can we do to help you, dear?" a man in his sixties asked. "My daughter Millie is never going to believe this."

"Just let us get you safely home and promise to keep

this secret until tomorrow morning is the best you can do for us. Now, who wants a picture with the famous Vigilantes?"

Espinosa clicked and clicked until he thought he would go out of his mind. He promised to send pictures to everyone. Ted copied down names and addresses as the passengers chatted and gurgled about the "dry-as-dust White House and the food that should have been a buffet where one could pick and choose instead of that thick sauce stuff and baby carrots that were no bigger than your little finger." Yada, yada, yada. "And the president wasn't even wearing a tiara or any jewelry that amounted to anything. She just looked plain. Plain is not good." Yada, yada, yada.

Kathryn yelled, "Hold on," as she took the curve at a very wide angle that would lead her to Evergreen Terrace. She parked the bus in the Woodley driveway and waited for all the neighbors to climb out.

Another round of pictures was called for. Espinosa gritted his teeth but complied.

"Do you have any idea how late you are?" Snowden bellowed. "You screwed up my plan."

"Where's our ride out of here?" Kathryn bellowed in return.

"You're looking at it, lady. Get in the Dumpster. The sleeve talkers are still sleeping it off in their cars. They're going to wake up in ten minutes, if Wong is right. Now, get the hell in and let's go."

"What about the Federation bus?" asked Espinosa.

"I'm driving it out. Come on, ladies, you can chitchat later. You and you, you're coming with me," Snowden said, pointing to Annie and Myra.

"Why?" they both squeaked in unison.

"Because I said so, that's why. Move your fannies back in the bus."

Snowden waited for Yoko, who was the last one into the Dumpster, then he waved his hand at the driver of the truck, who would haul the Dumpster to a safe place.

The residents of Evergreen Terrace clapped their hands, stomped their feet, and offered up a rousing send-off as the huge truck and Dumpster lumbered down the street and around the corner.

Myra and Annie waved frantically, blowing kisses, which were returned with gusto by the seniors.

"Where are we going, Mr. Snowden?" Annie asked.

"To a tattoo parlor I know in Chevy Chase. I took the liberty of bringing you a catalog of designs. And don't ask how I knew. If I told you, then I'd have to kill you. So just sit back and enjoy the ride, ladies."

"Oh, Myra, that makes it official. *We're doing it!*"

"Think of it as, we're making a statement!" Myra said, getting into it. "I'm excited, Annie."

Annie laughed and almost fell out of her seat. "Me too, Myra. Me too."

Epilogue

It was a beautiful day on Big Pine Mountain. The sun was golden and warm, the heady scent of the pines wafting through the open windows. The beauty of the day matched the Sisters' good mood as they assembled in the war room to go over the mission details. The fact that they were safe and back on the mountain proved they had been successful. They were waiting now for Nikki to print out copies of the online morning papers, especially the *Post*.

Even though Maggie had called and told them what to expect, there was nothing like seeing it in black and white. Nikki pressed the PRINT button, and seven copies spewed out of the printer. She stapled them and handed them out to her Sisters.

Smiles. Laughter. Raised eyebrows. More laughter, then a round of high fives.

"Washington will never be the same," Isabelle said.

"An invitation was issued to Bert to visit the White House," Kathryn said.

"The seniors in Kalorama are like rock stars. They're all going on the morning talk shows. There's talk of a book offer." Nikki laughed.

"Listen to this," Alexis said. "One of the seniors said they were disappointed in the Secret Service, who left them high and dry, and they were just grateful that the Vigilantes came to their aid at the White House and got them safely home. Lovely, ladies, just lovely. She went on to say someone needed to pay attention to the Russian who was so deadly. 'At first I thought he was Oriental, but I soon realized he was Mother Russia's favorite son, and he was right here in Kalorama. Everyone knows Churchill said Russians were Orientals with their shirts tucked in.' She said the ride home was more exciting than the lunch at the White House."

"I didn't know Churchill said that," Annie said.

"I bet Charles would have known it," Myra said.

"Jack and Harry are boxing up the Secret Service agents' weapons and badges, and they will be delivered to the White House today by special messenger. In other words, one of Harry the Russian's people," Yoko snickered.

"And we now have the package that was sent to Lizzie's office that was delivered to Maggie, who gave it to Ted to give to us," Nikki said. "Copies of all the madam's records. The letter inside said she didn't know how to get the materials to us, but she remembered that Lizzie was our attorney when we were arrested. Just goes to show you what a small world it really is. Anyway, we have it all. And now the world knows we have it all, thanks to Maggie. I imagine the White House is doing a little shivering and shuddering. And according to Lizzie, the madam is a world away with her girls, and everyone is safe."

"That's a good thing," Annie said. "It will keep them on their toes where the Vigilantes are concerned."

"Everyone is yelping for new task forces to be set up to catch us. We're making Alphabet City the laughing-stock of the planet," Kathryn said. "Those pictures of the Secret Service agents sleeping it off inside the Dumpster flashed around the world faster than you could imagine.

YouTube has already had over 3 million hits. There are a lot of agents who are going back to the Farm for additional training. The FBI has announced a major shakeup," she added with a giggle in her voice.

"And no one can figure out why the Vigilantes went back to Evergreen Terrace. We're being touted as bold and brazen, with no regard for the law," Alexis said. "The flip side of that is the seniors on Paula's street are painting us as wonderful, beautiful, and they say we should have an 800 number for people to call us for help. Polls on the street say we're the number one topic of conversation worldwide. Damn, I feel so important."

The women did another round of high fives.

"We have to decide when we're going to send the president the note we had the vice president write for us. Getting it will make her day and make her more in debt to us," Annie said. "I have her personal cell phone number and her personal e-mail, thanks to Lizzie. I think around lunchtime would be good. That way she and her administration will have had a few hours to digest the morning's headlines. And the absence of key members of the House and the Senate has been noted by the media. The vice president's resignation and sudden disappearance are front and center this morning, but the FBI, the CIA, and the Secret Service are on it."

Another round of high fives.

"Any other loose ends?" Myra asked.

Annie and the girls looked at one another.

Isabelle spoke up. "All but two families affected left the area to avoid the fallout, thanks to Avery Snowden and his offer of a free ninety-day vacation. The Alabama congressman's wife said hell, no, she wasn't leaving. She wants to see what else that devil she was married to had done. The wife of the senator from Delaware said she was staying and hoping for a book offer. She and the senator have no children, so she isn't worried about the fallout, and her friends and neighbors are making her a celebrity."

"Harry got a new suit! An Armani. Jack said he looks like a mogul," Yoko chirped.

"Lizzie is on her way to Tahiti on the first leg of her honeymoon as we speak," Myra said. "Cosmo is going to take her around the world later in the year, when they can clear their schedules. Lizzie is now seriously looking at accepting Martine Connor's offer to be White House counsel on her return."

"And the financial cost of this mission?" Annie asked.

"We're in the black," Nikki reported. "To pay for all those ninety-day vacations I helped myself to some of Hunter Pryce's money. Snowden's people have been paid. I sent the rest of Pryce's money offshore. Oh, I did keep a little for us to pay for all those gold and silver chains Annie is ordering for us and . . . another $500 that neither Annie nor Myra will tell me what they need it for," she said, a fleeting smile coming and going so quickly that anyone who blinked would have missed it.

Annie and Myra shared a glance, smug expressions on their faces.

"If there are no more loose ends, no more business to conduct, I suggest we adjourn," Myra said.

The girls scattered to the outdoors to work on the compound. It was time to plant some flowers, clear away the debris, and share a few secrets.

"My God, I thought they would never leave. Hurry, Myra, before I explode."

Myra was right on Annie's heels as they headed to the kitchen, where Annie went to the ice maker and quickly made two ice packs. She handed one to Myra and sat down on the other one.

Myra slid to the floor, the ice pack on her fanny. "Dear God, this feels better than an orgasm," she sighed.

"Oh, Myra, don't get carried away. Next week this will just be a sore memory. Do you think we should invest in *ink?*"

"I don't see why not. Maybe we could invest Hunter Pryce's money in ink and keep our own funds intact. You know, in case *ink* doesn't take off."

"Myra, Myra, you really rock!"

If you enjoyed *Razor Sharp*,
don't miss the next two exciting novels
in Fern Michaels's Sisterhood series!

Turn the page for special previews of

VANISHING ACT and DEADLY DEALS,

Zebra paperbacks on sale in January 2010 and
April 2010.

VANISHING ACT

Prologue

Five Years Earlier

It was a beautiful restaurant, beautifully decorated with well-dressed diners, discreet service, and ambience that had no equal. It was the kind of restaurant where there were no prices on the parchment menus because if you had to ask the price, you didn't belong in The Palm—or so said the owner. Not the Palm Restaurant in New York. This was the Palm restaurant in Atlanta, Georgia. On Peachtree Road. A hundred-year-old eatery passed down through multiple generations of the same family. When people talked about this particular restaurant, they always managed to mention *Gone With the Wind* in the same breath.

Plain and simple, it was a place to be seen. Not necessarily heard.

Not that the young couple wanted to be seen. Or heard, for that matter. They didn't. They were there because they were celebrating the possibility of a business venture, and what better place than the Palm? Years from now, no one would remember that the couple had been there drinking priceless wine, eating gourmet food served on the finest china, and drinking superb champagne from exquisite crystal flutes.

The woman was striking, the kind of woman men turned to for a second look, the kind of woman other women looked at and sighed, wishing they looked more like her.

She was a Wharton graduate. Her professors had given her glowing recommendations, assuring all and sundry that she would go far in the world of finance. She believed them implicitly.

The young man looked athletic, the boy next door, clear complexion, sandy hair. Tall, at six-two, a hundred and eighty pounds. He, too, was a Wharton graduate. He also dressed well—and women stared openly; men took a quick look and turned away, vowing to do something about their receding hairlines and paunches.

They looked like the perfect couple, but they weren't really a couple in the true sense of the word. Partners was more like it, but in time they would drift together, not out of passion but out of need.

The man was fearless.

The woman was a worrier.

They were not compatible.

The only real thing they shared was their mutual greed.

The woman held her champagne flute aloft and smiled. The man clinked his flute against hers and liked the sound. A clear *ping* of crystal.

"So, is it a deal or not?" the woman asked.

"It has flaws."

"Every plan has flaws. Flaws can be corrected," the woman said.

"That's true. I'm inclined to go along with it. But I think I need some reassurance."

The woman set down her glass and reached over for her clutch bag. It was small and glittery and gold in color. She opened it. There was only one thing in the small bag. She withdrew the little packet and slid it across the table.

The man blinked, then blinked again as he looked inside the dark blue covers. At first he thought he was looking at a small stack of passports. What he was really looking at was a pile of old-fashioned bankbooks. Something in his brain clicked as he calculated the last stamped numbers. He pushed the little stack back toward the woman. She, in turn, redeposited the bankbooks in their nest inside the clutch bag.

"Well?"

"There's over one million dollars on those books."

"And I did it all myself. Imagine what we could do together. In five years, we could have a hundred times that amount of money. Offshore, of course. You look nervous," the woman said.

The man sipped his champagne. "Only a fool wouldn't be nervous. I'm not a fool. What you're saying is that you require my organizational skills to continue, is that it?"

She hated to admit it, but she said, "Yes, that's what I'm saying."

The man remained silent long enough that the woman had to prod him. "It's risky," he said.

"Everything in life involves risk," she said, finishing her champagne.

The waiter approached the table and poured more. She nodded her thanks.

The man raised his glass, smiled, and clinked it against hers. "All right . . . partner."

"There is one thing," the woman added. The man's eyebrows lifted. "This is a five-year project, not one day longer. We need to agree on that right now. On December thirty-first, five years from now, our assets are divided equally. You go your way, I go my way. If you don't agree to it, there's no reason for us to stay here to eat the meal we ordered. I'll leave now, and you can pay the check."

"Why five years?"

"Because that's my timeline, my deadline."

The man shrugged. "Okay. Should we shake hands or something?"

The woman reached into the pocket of her suit jacket

and withdrew a tape recorder that was no bigger than a credit card. She smiled. "It's on record. We don't need to shake hands. Oh, look, here comes our food!"

An hour later, just as they were finishing their meal, the man asked, "Aren't you forgetting something?"

The woman twirled a strand of her hair as she stared across the table at the man she'd agreed to partner with. Her eyes narrowed slightly. "I don't think so." She let go of the hair between her fingers and started to crunch up her napkin and gather up her purse.

"What about the . . . ?"

The woman froze in position. "Do not go there. I presented the deal to you, and you accepted it. There are no other perks. That's another way of saying what's mine is mine. Not yours."

The man wasn't about to give up. "But—"

"There are no buts. Any other operations I have going on are solely mine. I mentioned them only to show you that the possibilities are endless." She was fast losing patience with her dinner companion. "Well?"

The man still wasn't about to give up. "Can we address this at some later point?"

"No. This is the end of it." She could tell by the man's expression that it was not the end of it. She sighed. Greed was the most powerful motivator in the world. She was on her feet and walking toward the door. *Like I'll really share my little gold mine with someone like him.*

Chapter 1

The Present

The day was hot and sultry, the sun blistering in the bright-blue cloudless sky. Even the birds that usually chirped a greeting when the Sisters appeared poolside seemed to have gone for cover in the cool, tall pines on Big Pine Mountain.

"I can't believe this heat! It's only July, and we're on a mountain!" Alexis said as she fanned herself with the book she'd been reading. "It's a good thing we aren't on a mission. We'd disintegrate."

Nikki stood up, a glorious nymph in a simple, one-piece pearl-white swimsuit, and headed for the diving board. "Don't even say the word *mission*, Alexis. We're on hiatus. My brain has gone to sleep," she shouted over her shoulder.

The Sisters watched Nikki as she danced her way to the end of the diving board. She bounced up, then hit the water, barely making a ripple. A perfect dive that would have been the envy of any Olympic diver who might have seen it.

After Nikki—a glorious bronzed creature—surfaced, she swam to the far side of the pool, climbed out, and walked back to the chair that sat under a monster outdoor umbrella. She immediately started to lather on an SPF 35 sunblock.

Yoko appeared out of nowhere carrying a huge tray, with plastic cups and a frosty pitcher of lemonade.

"What's for dinner?" Kathryn asked.

"Whatever it is, it better be slap-down delicious," Annie warned.

"Then you better get on the stick, my dear, since it is your turn to cook," Myra said with a straight face.

The wind taken out of her sails, Annie got up and headed toward the main building. "Don't you all be talking about my sagging ass while I'm gone," she tossed back.

"Don't worry, dear, when it gets down to your knees it will be time enough to talk about your derriere."

The Sisters giggled as Annie flipped her friend the bird and continued her march to the kitchen.

"Slap-down delicious! I wonder what she'll whip up," Isabelle said.

"Weenies on the grill. Wanna bet? And she'll talk the whole time about how slap-down delicious they are," Yoko said, laughing. "We had weenies twice last week. I hate it when Annie cooks. A very nice shrimp stir-fry with jasmine rice would be nice."

"With a light, fluffy lemon pie or maybe a pineapple cake for dessert," Kathryn said.

"I'd settle for a corned beef on rye with a ton of mustard," Nikki said.

"Well, none of that is going to happen unless we get up, go to the kitchen, and toss those weenies I know she's going to make down the garbage disposal," Alexis said.

"We could go in and help," Myra said hesitantly.

"We could, couldn't we," Nikki said, making no move to get up.

No one else moved, either.

No one said a word.

Because it was suddenly so silent, the Sisters were able to hear the gears of the cable car as it descended the mountain. Suddenly realizing that the cable car was going *down,* the Sisters looked at one another.

They moved then as one, racing to the main building, where the gun cabinet was located. Within seconds, Nikki had it opened and was handing each Sister her weapon. In bathing suits and bare feet, they ran out of the building, across the compound, and stopped only when Annie shouted for them to wait as she flew down the steps, gun in hand and a string of hot dogs dangling around her neck.

"Jack's in court," Nikki said. "I just talked to him at lunchtime."

"Harry's at Quantico," Yoko said.

"Bert is at the White House having lunch with the president," Kathryn said.

Alexis and Isabelle looked at one another and shrugged before Alexis finally said, "Joe Espinosa is on assignment in Baltimore."

"Lizzie?" Annie asked.

"She's in Las Vegas. She checked in early this morning," Myra said.

"Nellie and Elias went to New Jersey to see Elias's new grandchild," Isabelle said.

"Then some stranger is on his or her way up the mountain," Annie, the best shot of them all, said. "Wait a minute, what about Maggie?"

"She and Ted went to Nantucket for a long weekend," Nikki volunteered.

"Then it has to be someone who knows us, knows about the cable car, and knows about the switch at the bottom of the mountain," Myra said. "Maybe we should stop the car halfway up until we decide who it is."

"But if someone knows about the car and managed to

get it to the bottom, they know about the safety switch inside," Kathryn said. "We should cut the power! As you can see, the dogs aren't real happy. Otherwise, they'd have gobbled those weenies, and Annie would be flat on the ground."

The Sisters looked down at the two dogs belonging to Kathryn and Alexis, then to Annie and her necklace of hot dogs. As the two dogs pranced on and off the platform that housed the cable car when it was inactive, they snarled and pawed the ground.

"C'mon, c'mon, someone make a decision here," Kathryn hissed. "The car is coming up. Now, goddamn it!"

"Wait two minutes and cut the power," Myra said calmly.

Kathryn raced to the platform, her index finger on the master switch. "Tell me when, Myra."

Myra looked down at the oversize watch on her wrist with the glow-in-the-dark numbers. One hundred and seventeen seconds later, she said, *"Now!"*

The dogs went silent, running to their mistresses and panting as though to say, *What now?*

The Sisters looked at one another.

"I suppose we can hold out longer than the person in the cable car. We need to make a decision here," Nikki said.

Annie waved her gun. "Unless there are seven people in that cable car, I'd say we outnumber our visitors."

"Feds? CIA?" Alexis demanded.

Myra shook her head. "Bert would have let us know if anyone at the Bureau was looking at us. I was thinking more like Secret Service, but even that's a bit of a stretch. It is entirely possible some hunter, some stranger, stumbled over the hidden switch and is just exploring for a look-see."

Annie made an unladylike sound. "If you believe that,

Myra, I am going to strangle you with this string of hot dogs."

"At least then we wouldn't have to eat them," Myra quipped.

For the first time, the two dogs seemed to get the scent of the wieners wrapped around Annie's neck. As she broke off some of the weenies and handed them out, she was suddenly their new best friend.

"How long are we going to stand here in the boiling sun?" Yoko asked as she swiped at her forehead with the inside of her arm. "I say we let the car come all the way up but stop it before it hits the pad. Let the passenger swing over the side of the mountain. We'll still be in control."

Myra thought about that for a moment before she looked at Annie and nodded. Kathryn flicked the switch that turned the power back on. They all held their breath as the cable car started upward, the gears protesting at the status change.

Myra looked down at the dogs quivering at her knees. Their ears were flat against their heads, the fur on the nape of their necks standing straight up and bristling, their tails between their legs. A trifecta that could only mean trouble.

Up high, a fluffy cloud bank sailed past, momentarily blotting out the orange ball of the sun. Someone sighed.

Annie looked at her fellow Sisters and liked what she was seeing. Then she looked at their hands. Steady as rocks. She took a moment to wonder how loud the sound would be this high on the mountain if all seven guns went off at the same time. Pretty damn loud, she decided.

Myra licked her lips. "Turn off the power now, Kathryn."

Kathryn turned the switch. The sound of the cable car's grinding gears screeched so loud that the dogs howled. The Sisters rushed to the platform and peered over the side. But all they could see was the top of the cable car and the grille on the side. The identity of the occupant was still in doubt.

"How about if we announce ourselves?" Annie whispered. The others looked at her, their eyes questioning. "You know, a shot across the bow, so to speak. In this case, I think I can shave it pretty close to the grille. If you like, I can shoot off the lock. Of course, if I do that, the person inside *could* fall out. Not that we care, but we should take a vote!"

Knowing what a crack shot Annie was, the Sisters as one decided it was a no-brainer. "Do it, dear. We don't need to vote," Myra said.

Annie did it. Sparks flew, and the roar of outrage that erupted from inside the cable car made the Sisters step back and blink.

"Charles!" they shouted in unison.

One look at Myra's expression kept the guns in their hands steady as Kathryn turned the power switch back on. They all watched with narrowed eyes as the car slid into its nest, the door swinging wildly back and forth.

Chapter 2

Charles Martin stood rooted to the floor of the cable car. He dropped his duffel bag and raised his hands as he eyed his welcoming committee with a jaundiced eye. Whatever he had been expecting, this definitely wasn't it. He couldn't remember the last time he'd seen so much exposed bronzed, oiled skin. Nor had seven women ever gotten the drop on him. One part of him was pleased to see that the guns were steady even though they were aimed at every part of his body. He knew Annie could blow his head off in the blink of an eye. Myra would aim for his knee and hit the pine tree fifty feet away. The others would hit their marks, and he'd wind up dead as a doornail. Then they'd bundle him up and toss him off the mountain. *Cheerfully* toss him off the mountain.

He knew they were all waiting for him to say something. Anything that would make this little scenario easier. For them. Not for him. He hated the look he was seeing on Myra's face.

Murphy and Grady pawed the ground but stayed near the Sisters. They could not understand these strange goings-on. Charles was the guy who had slipped them bacon, fed them twice a day, and even gave them root beer on special occasions. And he was always good for a belly rub before going to bed. He had a good throwing arm, too, and would throw sticks for them to retrieve for hours on end. They whimpered in unison, hoping for a kind word. They whimpered even louder when nothing of the kind happened.

Charles had known this little reunion wasn't going to be easy, but he didn't think it was going to be quite so devastating. He cleared his throat. "The way I see it, ladies, is this. I have two choices here. Three, actually. One, I can pick up my bag and leave and apologize for this unexpected visit. Two, I can pick up my bag and go to my quarters, and we'll pick up where we left off. Three, you can riddle my body with bullets and toss me over the mountain. Decide, ladies. I'm very tired right now and in no mood to remain in limbo."

Annie risked a glance at Myra, who seemed to be in a trance. "An explanation would go a long way in helping us make our decision."

"As much as I would like to provide one, Annie, I'm afraid that I can't. Do you know you have a string of frankfurters hanging around your neck?"

Annie ignored the question. "Can't or won't?" she snapped.

"Both!" Charles snapped in return.

"You think you can just waltz back to this mountain and pick up where you left off with no explanations? You left us flat, to fend for ourselves," Kathryn screeched, her voice carrying over the mountain. "Your conduct is . . . was . . . unacceptable regardless of the circumstances. We deserved more, Charles," she continued to screech. Murphy reared up and pawed at his mistress's leg. "I don't think so!"

"You want us to trust you, but you don't trust us? That's not how it works, Charles," Nikki said, frost dripping from her words. "Kathryn is right—your behavior is unacceptable."

"My situation is different from yours, Nikki. I have to answer to Her Majesty. In the past, you only had to answer to me. If I could, I would answer all your questions. Unfortunately, I am duty-bound to say nothing."

Myra squared her shoulders and leveled the gun in her hand. "NTK, is that it? If there is no trust on both sides, then it doesn't work. I think I'm speaking for the Sisterhood when I say need-to-know doesn't work for us."

Charles looked at his ladylove and noticed that she wasn't wearing her pearls. Chains with circles draped her neck. Annie was wearing the same set of chains. He didn't like this new look. Myra wasn't Myra without her beloved heirloom pearls. He realized at that moment that things had indeed changed here on the mountain since he'd left.

Isabelle stepped forward. "We found out the hard way that we don't *need* you. Back in the day, we may have *wanted* you because you made it easier with your meticulous planning. We managed two missions. And even though we bumbled our way through them, we are standing here in front of you, guns drawn. On you! There is no reason to assume we cannot bumble our way through more missions. Actually, *Charlie,* we're getting rather adept at meticulous planning."

"You used my people. *My people,* ladies," Charles said quietly.

"*Your people* are mercenaries, Charles. Mercenaries go where the money is. We have the money. I rest my case," Alexis replied.

Charles took his time as he looked from one to the other, then down at his bag. Without another word, he picked up his bag and turned around to flick the power switch that would connect the power to the cable car. All he had to do was get in and then hit a second switch that would send the cable car to the bottom of the mountain. "Then I guess there's nothing more to say. Good-bye, ladies."

Yoko stepped forward, but not before she clicked the

safety on her gun. Her hand dropped to her side. "I haven't spoken yet, Charles. I would like you to stay," she said softly.

Charles turned back to face the women. He smiled, and his tone matched Yoko's when he said, "I appreciate your vote, but I can't stay unless it's unanimous."

The women watched in horror as Charles pressed the main switch, not realizing he had just turned the power off. Then he sat down inside on the little bench so he could hold the door closed. When he realized his mistake, he stretched out a long arm to hit the power switch. He was going, leaving them again. Murphy and Grady howled. A lone tear rolled down Myra's cheek.

"Mom, don't let him go. If he goes, he will NEVER come back. You have to take Charles on faith. You know that. Pride, Mummie, is a terrible thing. Hurry, Mummie, hurry!"

Myra whirled around as she tried to reconcile what she was hearing from her spirit daughter and at the same time saw Charles reaching for the switch that would activate the cable car and take him to the bottom of the mountain. She literally leaped past the two dogs and pulled Charles's hand away from the switch. "We want you to stay, Charles."

The collective sigh behind her told Myra all she needed to know. The girls wanted Charles to stay but were willing to send him packing, thinking it was what she wanted. When she stepped back, she felt Annie's arm go around her shoulder. It felt so comforting that she wanted to close her eyes and go to sleep.

"Will you get rid of those weenies, already? Charles will be preparing dinner this evening," was all Myra could think of to say.

Annie laughed as she peeled the string of weenies from around her neck and handed them all out to the dogs, who were waiting politely for the rest of their unorthodox early dinner.

Charles stepped out of the cable car and started to walk toward the main building, the girls following behind. Yoko was the last in line, her head down.

"Honey, I admire your courage," Annie said to her.

"I'm sorry, Yoko. I should have been the one to speak up to tell Charles to stay," Myra said. "It's refreshing to see you have the courage of your convictions. I don't know what we all thought we were trying to prove back there," she went on, waving her hand behind her, "other than to make Charles sweat and punish him in some way. It's my fault entirely. The others thought I wanted to send Charles packing, and they went along with it."

"We need Charles," Yoko said softly.

"Yes, we do," Annie said forcefully.

"I agree," Myra said. "But we are going to have a few new rules this time around."

"Do you believe Charles is not allowed to talk about whatever it was that went on over there by orders of Her Majesty, or was he pulling our legs?" Annie asked fretfully.

"Charles never lies. Rather than tell a lie, he simply says nothing. The fact that he even offered up the explanation makes it all ring true. Whatever went on over there, we are never going to know about it, so we had better get used to the idea," Myra said.

"Does that mean you are moving back into the main house, Myra?" Annie asked.

"It means no such thing. I'm more than comfortable right where I am, in the room next to yours. That's not to say I won't be . . . uh . . . moving back at some point in the future. Then again, I may never move back in. I'm not that same person who followed Charles to England."

"I see that," Annie said, with a twinkle in her eye.

"I see that, too," Yoko added, giggling.

"I wonder what's for dinner," Myra said as she linked one arm with Annie and the other with Yoko.

"Barbara told me to do it," Myra whispered to Annie.

"I know, dear. I actually heard her this time."

"Oh, Annie, did you really?"

"Absolutely," Annie lied with a straight face.

Up ahead, Charles closed the door loudly behind him and walked through the main building that he and Myra had shared for so long. He stopped, dropped his duffel bag, and looked around. He struggled to figure out what was different but couldn't quite hone in on what it was. Everything was neat and tidy. There were fresh flowers in a vase on the coffee table. There was no sign of dust. The windows sparkled.

Charles picked up his duffel bag and walked into the war room. Again, it was neat and tidy. The computers were on; the clocks were working. No sign of disarray anywhere. He flinched at the emptiness. He continued his journey down the hall to the suite he shared with Myra. And that's when he knew what was different. Myra had moved her things out of the suite. He tossed his oversize duffel on the bed and hurried to the closet. All he could see were empty hangers. There were no shoes on the floor. No boxes on the overhead shelf. His eyes burning, he stepped into the huge closet and saw his own clothing at the far end, all enclosed in garment bags. When he'd left, his things had been hanging loosely on hangers. Someone, probably Myra, not knowing when or if he would return, had hung them in zippered garment bags. His shoes were in boxes instead of on their usual shoe trees. He swiped at his eyes before he looked over at the dresser where Myra kept the jewelry box in which she put her pearls every night. The box was gone, the dresser bare, save his own hairbrush and his own small box for cuff links. His things were now encased in a plastic bag. He bit down on his lower lip as he made his way to the bathroom.

It was a large bathroom, the kind any woman would love, and Myra had loved this bathroom, with its built-in Jacuzzi and the shower with seventeen different heads that shot out steaming-hot water from all angles. The vanity held only his things on the right side, again encased in plastic bags. The left side, Myra's side, was bare as a bone. He opened the linen closet to see a stack of hunter green towels that were enclosed in a zippered bag. Myra's fluffy yellow towels were gone, as were all her sundries. Only his remained, encased in plastic. Suddenly he had a hate on for plastic.

His eyes still burning, Charles walked back into the bedroom, and this time he noticed that the comforter on the bed was different. When he'd left, there had been a green and yellow appliquéd tulip spread with matching pillows. Now a darkish green and brown comforter was on the bed, and there were no matching pillows. It looked depressing. He realized then how alone he was. He hated the feeling. He swiped at his eyes again. Sometimes life just wasn't fair. He wondered if it would ever be fair again.

Charles stripped down and headed back to the shower, where he stood under the seventeen needle-spray jets and let them pound the tension out of his body.

Forty minutes later, he was dressed, freshly shaved, and on his way to the kitchen, where he was expected to prepare a gourmet meal, the last thing in the world he wanted to do. A smile tugged at the corners of his mouth when he remembered the string of frankfurters hanging around Annie's neck. Obviously, the girls had been eating things that were quick and easy.

A check of the larder and the Deepfreeze gave the lie to that. Someone had ordered and stocked everything just as he'd done. He took a minute to go to the back door that would allow him to see the garden, which—he knew— would be a disaster. He blinked at the neat, tidy rows of plants. The pole beans were tied neatly, as were the tomato plants. Shiny green peppers in need of picking peered up at him. He just knew there were at least a hundred zucchini under the trailing vines. Cucumbers were deep green and plentiful. The broccoli looked wonderful. He knew it would be tender and savory. Thanks to Yoko and her green thumb.

So his girls had managed nicely without him. He had to admit it hurt to know they had not only survived but prospered. Which then brought up a nasty thought. Did he subconsciously want them to have failed without him? The fact that he even thought such a terrible thing bothered him. Knowing and hearing Isabelle say aloud that they didn't *need* him even though they *wanted* him was almost impossible to accept, but it was a sad reality, and he had no choice but to deal with it. He told himself he just needed patience. Well, his time in England had certainly not instilled patience in him.

As Charles checked out the vegetable bin and the freezer, his thoughts raced. If there was some way he could explain to Myra and the others, he'd do it in a heartbeat. But Her Majesty had looked him in the eye and made him swear never to divulge what had gone on during his stay in England. He'd promised, and he would die before he would break that promise.

The best he could hope for now was that time would heal all the wounds he'd created. Women, he knew, were, for the most part, forgiving creatures. He corrected that thought. Most women, with the exception of Myra, possibly Annie, too, were forgiving creatures. The only word that came to mind was *endurance*.

And endure he would.

Shifting his thoughts to the matter at hand, he finally decided on his menu—or, rather, his peace offering. He would prepare Shrimp Étouffée. A crisp summer salad from the garden, some of the pole beans in a light, savory garlic-butter sauce, homemade biscuits with soft honey butter. Myra loved his Chinese Almond Rice, so he would prepare that, too, and hope she understood he was making it just for her. For dessert he would make Rice Pudding with Raspberry Sauce and, of course, pots and pots of coffee. He dusted his hands together, satisfied that in the midst of all the turmoil in his mind, he could think of other things.

Charles licked his lips, crossed his fingers for luck, and started to prepare his homecoming dinner.

DEADLY DEALS

Prologue

It looked like a cozy building, and it was . . . in the spring and summer. Ivy covered the brick walls, and flower beds abounded, all tended by the new manager of the Quinn Law Firm, a twelve-member, all-female firm, as everyone was quick to point out. In whispered tones, of course. Previously owned by one Nikki Quinn, one of the infamous Vigilantes.

In the fall and winter, the three-story brick building in Georgetown took on another appearance. Usually smoke could be seen wafting up through the chimney from the fireplace in the spacious lobby. A wreath of colorful leaves adorned the stark white door.

The Monday after Thanksgiving, the building underwent another transformation. A fragrant evergreen wreath with a huge red satin bow almost as wide as the door arrived from a grateful client in Oregon. Inside, the fire blazed; the birch logs, from another grateful client somewhere in the state of Washington, arrived like clockwork the day before Thanksgiving.

It was a low-key firm. All the lawyers were friends, each of them helping the others. There was no shortage of clients, but that hadn't always been the case. At one point the firm had struggled to keep its head above water, but that all changed when the Vigilantes were captured and then escaped. The media had a field day as they splashed the news that the Quinn Law Firm's owner was one of the notorious women. Within twenty-four hours, there were waiting lines of women—some men, too—forming up outside to be represented by the now-prestigious, outrageous, famous law firm.

Nancy Barnes, the firm's business manager, was new to the firm but not that new. She'd replaced her aunt Maddy, who had retired to stop and smell the roses a year after the Vigilantes had gone on the run. She knew the firm inside and out, having worked there summers and holidays for as long as she could remember. She herself was a paralegal but had found out that management was more to her liking. She had a wonderful rapport with the lawyers and clients. At Christmas time alone she had to have a friend come by with a pickup truck to take all her presents home: gifts from the lawyers, gifts from all the grateful clients.

Nancy Barnes loved her job.

On the first day of October, Nancy was huffing and puffing as she struggled with an oversize pumpkin that she somehow managed to get into the lobby after she opened the door and turned off the alarm without dropping the pumpkin. She knew by the end of the week there would be about twenty more pumpkins around her scarecrow-and-hay arrangement, all brought in by the lawyers themselves, along with the paralegals and the secretaries.

Cozy. A feel-good place to come to when in trouble.

Nancy looked up to see a young woman coming through the door. Her first thought was that she looked like a deer caught in the headlights. Fragile. Scared. But there was a spark of something she couldn't quite define. Yet.

Nancy Barnes was a chunky young woman who wore sensible shoes. She had curly hair, *unruly* curly hair, and a bridge of freckles danced across her nose and rosy cheeks.

She wore granny glasses and always had two or three pencils stuck behind her ears or in her hair. It was her smile that put new clients at ease, or maybe it was her first words of greeting, no one was ever quite sure. "Good morning. What can I do to help you?"

"I'm Rachel Dawson, and I need to talk to a lawyer as soon as possible. I don't have an appointment. I'm sorry. I just . . . What I did was . . . My husband doesn't know I'm here. I can't afford to be here." The woman flapped her arms and then said, "But here I am."

"I'll tell you what, walk around here to where I am, and then I'll get us both some coffee, and you and I can talk. What that means is after you tell me your problem, I'll decide who it is that would work best with you. We have donuts, too."

Rachel Dawson tried her best to smile but couldn't bring it off. Nancy could see she was fighting back her tears.

Settled at her desk with coffee Rachel Dawson wasn't going to drink, she said gently, "Tell me what you're comfortable telling me so all of us here can help you. I want you to think of this firm as your extended family. Everyone here works for the client, and it doesn't matter which attorney is assigned to you. Do you understand that?"

"I can't afford to be here. My husband is going to be upset when he finds out I . . ."

"Let's not talk about payment right now. But for the record, we do quite a bit of pro bono work. I'm usually the one who makes that particular decision, so we aren't going to worry about whether you qualify or not right now. Tell me how we can help you."

Rachel Dawson fooled Nancy. Before she spoke she gulped at her coffee and drained the cup. "I can't have children. It's me, not my husband. I had every test in the book. I'm thirty-seven. My husband is thirty-eight. We both have very good jobs, but right now I'm on a leave of absence. We were so desperate to have a child, but the wait was so long, and going outside the country didn't work for us. A friend of a friend told us about a lawyer who arranged adoptions. We went to see him a year or so ago, and in the end what we did . . . what my husband did was donate his sperm to a surrogate. It was all legal. We paid the lawyer one hundred thousand dollars. I don't know how much of that went to the surrogate. We paid all of her medical expenses. I even drove her to the doctors when she had to go. She was a student at George Washington University. We bought her clothes, food, paid her rent. She gave birth to twins, a boy and a girl. We were overjoyed. I can't tell you how giddy we were. We went into panic mode the day we found out. We had to redo the house—you know, make room for two babies instead of one.

"I guess I should tell you we had to borrow forty thousand dollars from our parents. Call us foolish, but we've been saving for a college fund even though we had no children. We hoped that we would eventually be blessed. We're savers, Miss Barnes."

Nancy watched Rachel peer into her cup. She seemed surprised that it was empty. Without thinking, Nancy reached for the cup and went to the kitchen for a refill.

"We were so happy. It was like suddenly our life was now complete. We didn't sleep. We sat up and watched the twins sleep. I guess all new parents do that. My husband took leave, too, for a month, so I could get things working. We couldn't afford a nanny, and our parents helped out. We literally thought we'd died and gone to heaven."

Rachel reached for the coffee and again drained the full cup. She set it down precisely in the spot it had been in. Nancy waited, knowing the worst was about to be revealed. She wasn't wrong.

"Then our world turned upside down. A letter came in

the mail from a lawyer saying his client, the surrogate mother, wanted the twins back. We thought about fighting it, but we had seen cases like this played out in the media, and the birth mother always got the children. Our parents offered to mortgage their houses. We were going to cash in our retirement funds and the college fund but were advised not to do that. My husband talked to several lawyers, and they basically told us to move on and put it behind us. I went to the lawyer we used to arrange the adoption. I called and called, and he didn't call back. I went to his office, and they wouldn't let me see him. I thought about going to the newspaper, but the truth was, I wasn't strong enough mentally or physically for that kind of onslaught. You'll find out sooner or later that I had a minibreakdown. That's what they called it, anyway."

Nancy looked down at the small recording machine she'd decided to use at the last second. As usual, she'd forgotten to mention it to this frail woman sitting in front of her. "Mrs. Dawson, I'm recording this conversation. I hope that's okay. I should have told you that before I turned it on."

"That's okay. Is there anything you can do for me and Tom?"

Nancy's mind raced. Was there? "I'm going to turn this off for a few moments. Then I'm going to get you some more coffee. I have to make a few phone calls. Will that be okay? I think I know just the person to help you."

"Truly? You do? Oh my God, I'll do anything. Anything at all if you help me."

"Which lawyer did you go to to arrange the adoption?"

"Baron Bell."

"Baron Bell?" The name shot out of Nancy's mouth like a bullet. "Baron Bell refused to see and talk to you after . . . after . . . ?"

"Yes, Baron Bell. He seemed like such a nice man.

He's always in the papers, and he's an advocate of everything. Everyone Tom talked to backed away when he told them it was Mr. Bell who arranged the adoption."

"Who was the surrogate mother?"

"Her name was Donna Davis."

Nancy ran to the kitchen, refilled Rachel's coffee cup, and then walked down the hall to an empty office and called her aunt Maddy. "I don't know what to do with her, Maddy. Nothing like this has ever come up before. I'll be honest, I don't think any of our lawyers here at the firm will agree to go up against someone like Baron Bell on what could become a high-profile case like this one. Talk to me, Maddy."

Nancy listened. She reached for a pad and pencil and scribbled furiously. "Maddy, are you going to do what I think you're going to do?"

"Can you think of anyone better?"

Nancy smiled. "Actually, I can't. Wouldn't it be wonderful if . . . Rachel could get her babies back for Christmas?"

"It's the time for miracles. I'll do what I can. Keep me in the loop, honey."

"Will do, Maddy."

Back in the office, Nancy sat down and reached for a small pad. As she wrote down Lizzie Fox's name, address, and phone number on a slip of paper, Rachel Dawson kept on talking. "I think this is some kind of baby ring. Tom says I'm out of my mind, but on my really bad days I would go to the park and just sit. I talked to a lot of nannies and young mothers. One of the mothers looked at me when I told her what had happened and told me about someone else the same thing happened to. I have her name right here in my purse. I even went to talk to the adoptive parents, and they're in the same position Tom and I are in. They used Baron Bell, too. Their surrogate is a student at Georgetown. Is there any way, any way at all, that we could get our babies back for Christmas? We had such plans. Our first family Christmas." Rachel burst into tears.

"Rachel, I can't answer that, but the person I want you to go see is just the right lawyer for you. Trust me when I tell you she could take on Baron Bell with her hands tied behind her back and blindfolded. If anyone can help you, it's Lizzie Fox."

Rachel Dawson bolted upright. Her tears stopped in midflow. "She's the lawyer that . . . She was . . . the Vigilantes' attorney."

Nancy stared across the table, her gaze steady and direct. "Yes," she said softly.

"Oh! Oh! When should I go to see her?"

Nancy's phone rang. She picked it up and listened. All she said was, "Thanks, Maddy."

Nancy looked at Rachel. "Right now. You can walk to Lizzie's office from here." Nancy was out of her chair and around the desk. She put her arms around the woman's thin shoulders. "Just tell Lizzie everything you told me. Be sure to give her the other surrogate's name. By the way, is your surrogate still living wherever she was living before the birth of the twins?"

"She is. I . . . I would park down the street hoping to get a glimpse of the twins. They never seem to leave the apartment. I guess she has a babysitter while she goes to class. I was so obsessed. I don't know how to thank you. Will Ms. Fox work on a payment plan for us? Do you know?"

"You'll work something out. I wouldn't worry about that right now. Just go and talk to her, and I wish you all the luck in the world."

Nancy waited until Rachel Dawson was through the door and out of sight before she walked back to her office. She called her aunt, and they talked for ten long minutes. Nancy was smiling when she hung up the phone. Then she laughed out loud. "Rachel, honey, you are in such good hands," she murmured under her breath.

Chapter 1

1600 Pennyslvania Avenue. The most famous address in the world.

Lizzie tried her best not to gawk like a starstruck tourist at the magnificent Christmas decorations as she trailed behind the Secret Service agent escorting her to President Connor's private quarters. She was here for lunch and so much more.

President Connor herself opened the door and literally dragged Lizzie inside with a whispered, "I'll take it from here, Agent Goodwin."

As soon as the door was closed, she turned to her friend and burst out, "God, Lizzie, I am so glad to see you! I mean I'm *really* glad!"

"Me, too, Madam President." And she *was* glad; she and President Connor had a history. Then they wrapped their arms around each other in a bone-crushing hug, strange for two such elegant women.

President Connor laughed. "Stop with that president stuff. In here we're Lizzie and Marti. I *need* you to call me by name, Lizzie. I don't want to forget who I really am. Can we do that?" She sounded so anxious, Lizzie nodded.

Lizzie looked around. "Pretty fancy digs, Marti. This is my first time in the White House. I'm impressed. The Christmas decorations are beautiful."

"If you have the time, I'll give you the tour after lunch. Right now I want you all to myself. I can't thank you enough for accepting my invitation. You look so happy, Lizzie."

Lizzie smiled as she was shown to a deep off-white chair that would have held her and Cosmo. She watched as the president sat down across from her and then kicked off her shoes. Lizzie did the same thing, and then they giggled like two schoolgirls. "There are no words to tell you how happy I am, Marti. I wish I could say the same for you. You look like you have the weight of the world on your shoulders."

Martine Connor forced a smile she was far from feeling. "I *do* have the weight of the world on my shoulders. See how bowed they are? And before you can ask, the world slowed down for some reason this week to allow me time for this luncheon."

"You want to talk about it, or is it all NTK? Your approval ratings are in the 70 percent area, so you must be doing something right."

Martine shrugged. "I had a hard time getting used to every second of my time being budgeted. Sometimes bathroom breaks are a luxury. There's always a crisis brewing somewhere that has to be dealt with. You know me, I'm cool under fire. It's when I get up here that I lose it."

Lizzie blinked. "This was what you wanted, Marti."

Martine brushed at the soft bangs falling over her forehead. "Yes, and if it wasn't for you . . . and . . . your friends, I wouldn't be here. I know that, Lizzie. It's with me every second of every day. That's why you're here, isn't it? That's why you accepted my job offer, right? You're here to spell it out to me. Again."

Lizzie stared at her old friend. She gave a slight nod. "Six months. Pro bono. I walk away unless the job proves to be something beyond my expectations. I have to admit I was surprised you agreed to my terms."

Martine burst out laughing. "Oh, Lizzie, I wish you could have seen the expressions on all *their* faces when I listed your demands. I thought the lot of them would choke to death. Nine to five! Every weekend off. Pro bono. I realize one hundred sixty-eight thousand dollars is a lot of money, and yet it isn't much money to live on here in the District, what with rent, travel back to one's home state, taxes, everyday expenses, and the maintenance of two residences. It's hard to raise a family and keep up two residences all for the sake of doing one's duty. When I told them you weren't interested in adding the White House to your resume, because yours was impressive enough without it, several of them had to be resuscitated. It's safe to say your fame has preceded you. Actually, Lizzie, you're a legend in your own time, and I for one am honored to be called your friend. How does your new husband feel about you taking on the job?"

Lizzie leaned forward. "You know what, Marti? My husband is that rare breed of man who only wants to see me happy. If all it takes is his approval, he's all for it. We take turns traveling on the weekends. You need to give him a huge slice of credit for helping get you to where you're sitting right now." Lizzie looked around and then lowered her voice. "Is this place bugged? Are you recording me?"

"Lizzie!"

The president's outrage was so total, Lizzie relaxed. "What I was going to say was my husband numbers among his friends some of the most powerful, some of the most respected, some of the richest people in the world, and those he doesn't know personally, he has access to via those same friends that are in his Rolodex. You should see his Rolodex, Marti. I think it's safe to say your own cannot compare."

"What are you trying to tell me, Lizzie?" There was an edge to the president's voice that did not go unnoticed by Lizzie.

"Nothing, Marti. I was simply commenting on your question about my husband."

"Point taken. Oh, look, our lunch is ready. It's one of the perks here. I hope you enjoy it." The president nodded to the waiter to show he could leave. "I know you don't like to eat heavy at lunch, and most days I don't have time for lunch. We're having sesame-crusted salmon, grilled asparagus, and a garden salad."

It looked delicious, but Lizzie wasn't hungry. She lifted her glass of ice tea and clinked it against Martine's. "Here's to a thankful Thanksgiving and a Merry Christmas, Madam President."

"And the same to you, Lizzie." The bite was still in Martine's voice, Lizzie noticed. Well, she hadn't invited herself here. She was the invitee. She smiled as she mashed the salmon on her plate. Martine was cutting her asparagus into tiny pieces. Lizzie couldn't help but wonder if the president was going to eat it or was just playing with her food the same way she was.

"Does my office have a window, Marti?"

Marti offered up a genuine smile this time. "It was one of your requirements, so, yes, your office has a window. You did say you would be willing to negotiate the second half of the year. Is that still on the table?"

Lizzie mashed the salmon some more. "Yes, but no promises. So, tell me now, who do I have to watch out for?"

"Everyone, would be my guess. You've been Googled so much since we made the announcement I'm surprised the site didn't shut down. You're the next thing to Public

Enemy Number One at 1600 Pennsylvania Avenue. My chief of staff understands that you are to have direct access to me 24/7. Of course he went ballistic, but we're on the same page now. Everyone is replaceable. He understands that, too."

"Guess you aren't going to eat that asparagus. You must have a hundred little pieces on your plate."

"You always were perceptive, Lizzie. I'm listening when you're ready to talk."

"My friends are very unhappy, Marti. I thought you would have gotten the message when your Secret Service agents were thrown into a Dumpster, and then their weapons and badges were sent back to you."

Martine started to mash at her salmon the way Lizzie had. "We're going to have to put all this food in the disposal so the kitchen doesn't get their knickers in a knot. I did get the message. I wasn't amused. We had to do some fancy dancing to explain all of that."

"I bet you did. My friends weren't amused, either. You have six months to keep your promise."

"I can't believe you're giving the president of this country an ultimatum! And if for some reason I can't deliver on the promise in the allotted time, then what?" the president asked in the same frosty tone.

Lizzie smiled. "Marti, I might be many things, but I'm not clairvoyant."

"What? Are you seriously warning me that the Vigilantes can penetrate the White House? Is that what you're telling me? Are you telling me they're smart enough to outwit the best of the best? It's simply not possible. What are they going to do, hold a gun to my head and make me sign a pardon, and then we're all going to disappear in a puff of smoke?" Lizzie was pleased at the look of pure horror on the president's face.

Lizzie continued to smile. "I said no such thing. That's

your interpretation. Although the ladies did take on the Secret Service and came out on top. And if I remember correctly, that little neighborhood White House luncheon you sponsored didn't go over so well, either. Your guests were more impressed with their ride home compliments of the Vigilantes than they were with your luncheon, the photo op, and their souvenirs."

Martine Connor got up and carried the two luncheon plates to the sink. She scraped the plates and turned on the garbage disposal. Lizzie listened to the loud clunking noise and then a shrieking, grinding sound. "The plumbing leaves a lot to be desired," Martine said.

"You could call a plumber," Lizzie volunteered.

"It doesn't work that way here. In the real world, yes. I can't even describe to you what it's like living here. I can't step out and go to the drugstore to get shampoo. If I want to do that I have to notify the Service a month in advance. Then they have to empty out the store so I can shop. I can't go to a bookstore. I can't drive a car. I can't use my credit cards or carry money. If they ever found out or find out I have that phone, they'll probably pack me off to Outer Mongolia.

"You know what I miss, Lizzie? I miss going out to the mailbox for my mail. I miss all those catalogs I used to get by the pound. I always looked forward to Sunday afternoon, when I'd browse through them and order something. You know what else? I made potato pancakes one day. They came up here on the run and said I was stinking up the White House and not to do it again. They fucking told me I can't make potato pancakes! It was the onion I put into it. I'm not excusing my language, either."

For all of a minute, Lizzie almost felt sorry for her old friend. Almost. Then she burst out laughing. "Remember that old saying, be careful what you wish for, because you just might get it. You wished for this, we made it happen for you at the eleventh hour, and now you have to live with it. And you have to honor your debt. That's the bottom line."

"God, Lizzie, how cold you sound. That's the real reason you agreed to sign on, isn't it? You're here to protect your friends, and if it means taking me down, you'll help them do it, right?" Lizzie just smiled.

"Goddamnit, Lizzie, say something."

"Where I come from, Marti, and where you've been, a person is only as good as their word. I really should be going. I've taken up enough of your time today."

Martine Connor turned to stop her furious pacing. Lizzie thought she looked great in a honey-colored suit with a copper-colored blouse underneath her suit jacket, which was open. Her haircut was stylish, and the feathery bangs falling over her forehead were new, too, since the last time she'd seen her. She looked presidential.

"But we haven't had dessert, and I was going to give you the tour. Lizzie, I'm sorry. I'll find a way, I promise you. Please, I need you to believe me."

"It's not me you have to convince, Marti. I'll pass on your message. Six months. Not one day, not one hour, not one second longer. I'll report in on January second. I hope you have a wonderful holiday. Are you staying here or going somewhere?"

"Camp David. I plan to sleep through the holidays. Do you want to hear something really sad? I don't have a single soul I can invite to spend the holidays with me. Well, that's not quite true. I had several people I was going to invite, but the Service said when they vetted them they were unsuitable. *Unsuitable!* That's what they said. I'm whining, and I didn't want to do that. I apologize."

Lizzie stepped forward and wrapped her arms around the president. She squeezed hard. "Six months, Marti," she whispered. "Now, how do I get out of here? Is that guy with the 'football' still outside the door? Oh, one last thing—watch out for Baron Bell."

Martine grimaced. "You mean the marine with the nuclear codes? Yes, he's out there. You just walk past him, it's that simple. One of my agents will take you home."

Lizzie stared at her old friend. She could feel her eyes start to burn at what she was seeing on her old friend's face. She lowered her voice to a bare whisper and said, "I wouldn't want to be you for all the gold in Fort Knox."

Martine Connor shed her personal persona, and in the blink of an eye she was the President of the United States the moment the door opened. "Thank you for that observation, and thank you for coming, Lizzie. I enjoyed our luncheon. I hope we can do it again soon. Happy Holidays to you and *yours*."

"Don't eat too much turkey, Madam President." Lizzie flinched at the sound of the door closing behind her. She straightened her shoulders and walked alongside the agent escorting her to a black limousine, where another agent waited to drive her back to her home.

Lizzie kept her eyes closed all the way home, her mind racing as she sifted, collated, and made mental notes.

The moment Lizzie was inside her cozy little home, she shed her lavender suit and donned a pair of jeans and a fleecy, warm shirt. She had the crazy urge all of a sudden to make potato pancakes. But first she had to check things at her office, call her husband, and then call the mountain. Maybe she should call the mountain first. Or maybe she should wait, think about her visit some more, and make the potato pancakes first. Multitasking, so to speak.

Before she did anything, though, she was going to make herself a pot of strong black coffee to get her adrenaline going at full speed. While the coffee was dripping,

Lizzie fiddled with her CD player and then slipped in one of Cosmo's favorite CD's. Frank Sinatra's mellow voice filled her kitchen. She immediately felt the tenseness leave her shoulders. Then she made herself a sandwich, the kind of sandwich Cosmo raised his eyebrows over but later admitted was tasty. Swiss cheese, lettuce, fire-roasted peppers, and one slice of salami. That mess she'd mangled back at the White House couldn't come close to the sandwich she was devouring. There wasn't a crumb to be seen when she finished.

Lizzie moved then at lightning speed. She called the mountain; then she called Jack Emery and then her office. She had two calls left to make when she poured her coffee. The first call was to Nikki's old law office, where she asked more questions than she answered. She had one call to go before she could call her husband. With business taken care of she could talk for hours if he had the time. At the crack of dawn she'd be winging her way to Vegas to spend Thanksgiving and the rest of the holidays with her husband. A radiant smile lit her features.

Lizzie was huffing and puffing when she opened the doors of the fireplace, placed the logs just so, and then threw in a pile of birch kindling. The fire blazed instantly. She then moved a pile of silky red cushions near the hearth so she could curl up and be comfortable.

One more trip to the kitchen to replenish her coffee. She was walking through the dining room when retired judge Nellie Easter picked up the phone. "Lizzie, Judge. Several things. I want to wish you and Elias a wonderful Thanksgiving and a Merry Christmas. I'm leaving in the morning for Las Vegas." They made small talk for a few minutes, with Lizzie asking about Elias's new grandbaby and his other children before she got down to the real reason for her phone call.

"Nellie, tell me everything you know about Baron Bell. And ask Elias if he knows anything. Better yet, use the speaker phone if he's agreeable."

"Baron was always a gentleman in court. He fights to win for his clients. He and I belong to five or six of the same organizations. He's been Man of the Year for so many years I've lost count. He used to do a lot of pro bono work. Lovely wife, kind of timid, stays in his shadow. Two grown children. One is a doctor at Georgetown, and one is a public defender in Georgia. Several grandchildren that he dotes on. No matter the cause, you can count on him for a donation, and he gives his time willingly to any worthy cause. He plays Santa every year for some children's group—it always makes the paper. He always arrives in a sleigh with his helpers, be it on wheels or with horses pulling the sleigh, and he does it at his own expense. It's usually quite an event. As far as I know, I never heard a hint of any kind of scandal. He's quite wealthy, and, as you know, there are always a few who will take a swipe at you for that. Elias said there's a file on him at the Bureau, but nothing bad is in it. There are those who are the recipients of his generosity who think he's the Messiah. Why are you asking, Lizzie?"

"No one is *that* perfect, Nellie. What's his flaw?"

"If you believe his court record and his PR, then he is *that* perfect. Why? What happened to make you ask these questions? Did I also mention he has a pass to the White House? That means he's invited to *everything*. So he's on your radar, eh?"

"A little under it, but he's there. Do me a favor, Nellie—ask around, see if there's anything of interest there. Then call the mountain and share it with them. Are you going to spend Christmas on the mountain or just Thanksgiving?"

"We are. We're coming back Sunday night but will return the following weekend. Elias said his family is heading for a warmer climate. We both like the cold, and both of us are looking forward to spending the holidays with old friends. I'm sorry you won't be joining us."

Lizzie laughed. "Thanks, Nellie, and one more time, Happy Holidays!" She sighed happily. Now she could curl up and talk till she fell asleep. Business was taken care of. She'd packed before she left for the White House and was ready to go as soon as she rolled out of bed in the morning. Damn, she forgot to call Maggie at the *Post*. A minute later she had Maggie on the phone. She spoke quick and fast as she explained about her meeting with Rachel Dawson. "There's something there, Maggie, I could feel it. It isn't good, either. I'll be working on her case while I'm in Vegas." Her final words were, "The window of time is going to be short, Maggie. Make it work if you can. See you when I see you."

Life was good, Lizzie thought as she settled into her nest of colorful cushions.

Across town, Maggie flipped open her Rolodex and then looked at the clock. Four o'clock. She punched in the numbers and waited for Abner Tookus to pick up. He did on the fourth ring. "I thought you said you were taking my name out of your Rolodex" was all the computer hacker said by way of a greeting.

"I lied. Just the way you lied to me about working for Big Blue, and even then you lied some more, saying you were going on a honeymoon. You snookered me, Abby. I want my pound of flesh."

"Call someone who's fat and can afford to lose a pound or two. I don't have any to spare. I'm working. That means I have no time to do anything for you."

"You better find the time, and this one is for free. F-r-e-e!

That job you have, the one that is paying you in eight figures? That's all compliments of me. I can take it away just like . . . that," Maggie said, snapping her fingers.

"Go ahead, take it away," Tookus blustered. "I hate nine to five. I hate wearing a suit and tie. You want to fall back and regroup and call me again like in twenty years?"

"Nah! I'm going to come over to those plushy digs where you work and rip the skin right off your face. What I can't decide is should I do it before or after I sic the Vigilantes on you. Now, if you're really nice to me I'm going to forget you challenged me. Truce?"

"Truce. What do you want?"

Maggie's voice turned syrupy sweet. "Not all that much. I want everything there is to get on one Baron Bell. I want it from the moment he came into being in his mother's womb until this very minute, and then I want hourly updates."

"You gotta be kidding me, Maggie. Mr. Squeaky Clean himself! Mr. Man of the Year! Mr. Personal Buddy of every power broker in Washington! That guy is the Easter Bunny, the Tooth Fairy, and Santa Claus all rolled into one. He is beloved and cherished beyond belief. What'd the son of a bitch do to put him on your radar screen?"

"Just never you mind, Abner. At the moment Baron Bell is *under* my radar but rising to the top. That's all you need to know. I want this by nine o'clock tomorrow morning. I do not care if you sleep or eat, is that clear? If you're one minute late, you will find yourself skinless. Nice talking to you, sweetie."

Maggie let loose with a deep sigh. She had no doubts at all that Abner would come through for her. But would he have anything worthwhile her friends on the mountain could use? Well, she was the master of spin, if she did say so herself.

Time to get ready to close up shop and head for the

mountain with the others. She could hardly wait to sit down to a Thanksgiving dinner with all the trimmings prepared by Charles. She smacked her lips in anticipation.

At least she wouldn't be going empty-handed. Abby's file would be her gift to the host. She laughed as she envisioned Charles's expression when she handed it over.

Chapter 2

It was Thanksgiving eve, and the compound on Big Pine Mountain was quiet. The reason for the quietness was the late hour and the fact that snow had been falling for the past nine hours. A giant white blanket covered the mountaintop, making it picture-postcard perfect.

Charles Martin prowled the confines of his command center, his thoughts all over the map as he stared down at the paperwork Maggie Spritzer had brought with her earlier in the day. With the investigation his own people had done, he felt like he had a solid basis to move forward when the guests left on Sunday and they got down to the mission at hand. He walked out of the command center, slipped on a heavy mackinaw, and opened the front door. A blast of early winter air rushed through the room. He smiled at the high drifts of snow on the porch. He stood under the overhang and fired up his pipe. The smoke from the cherry tobacco in his pipe and the heady scent from the evergreens was an intoxicating mixture. He loved it. Loved seeing the steady snowfall, knowing all his chicks inside were safe and sound. For now.

Tomorrow they would all sit down to a huge dinner he would begin preparing in just a few short hours. They would all pray and give thanks for so many things. He hoped his voice didn't falter when he offered up his own anks. He thought about his son he'd never gotten a chance to know as he puffed on his pipe. He knew if he let the tears flow they'd freeze on his lashes. He shook his head to clear his thoughts. It wasn't that he was banishing all thoughts of Geoffrey, more that it was unbearable to think about his son the traitor.

Charles listened to the silence around him. He wondered what it would be like to live in a world as silent as the one he was standing in. To never hear the sounds of laughter, never hear the wind rustling in the trees, never hear the birds chirping early in the morning. *That* was a bearable thought. He shifted his mental gears to the work at hand. Not that dinner was work; he could prepare a Thanksgiving feast with his eyes closed. What he couldn't do with his eyes closed was figure out what was going on with Baron Bell. Or with his eyes open, for that matter. He whirled around when he sensed a presence. "Myra! What are you doing up at this hour?"

"I'm up because the bed got cold. Why are you standing out here, Charles?"

"The world looks so clean and pure right now. It's so perfect I just want it to be like this forever, but that's a foolish wish on my part."

Myra reached out and nestled her hand within his. "It is beautiful. The snow came early this year. I'm ready to get married now, Charles. I thought maybe on New Year's Day. I'd like Nellie to marry us. Say something *now*, Charles, because I don't think I will get the nerve again to make this commitment."

"But you didn't ask me. You made an announcement. I'm supposed to get down on my knee and *ask you*."

"Well, what are you waiting for?" Myra asked.

Charles dropped to one knee and reached for Myra's hand. "Myra, will you marry me on New Year's Day? If you say yes, I promise to love and honor you into eternity."

"My answer is yes, Charles. Will you make the announcement at dinner?"

"If that's what you want, then, yes, it will give me great pleasure to announce our betrothal. You just made me the happiest man in the world." Charles moved his arm and wrapped it around his beloved's shoulders. "What made you pick this moment in time, if you don't mind my asking?"

"Well, Charles, we aren't getting any younger. In fact, we're getting older by the day. If that isn't enough of an answer, I realized I don't like cold beds. And you're right—this moment, right now, this instant, is so perfect it just seemed like the right time.

"I'm going to have Annie stand up for me. Who will you choose, Charles, to be your best man?"

"Elias. You don't think the boys will be upset, do you?"

"No more than the girls will be upset with me choosing Annie."

"I don't have a ring for you, Myra."

Myra laughed. "The ring isn't important. Just ask Elias for one of his cigar bands. That will do nicely."

Charles held his bride to be. "My life is now complete, Myra. I think we should go inside before we both freeze to death out here, and then there won't be a wedding at all."

"I think you might be right. Come along, my darling, I'll help you get started with your Thanksgiving dinner."

Charles pretended horror. "My dear, you are worthless in the kitchen. But you can watch me. Let's have an early breakfast. You can brown the buns and make the coffee and squeeze the juice. We received a box of Baby Bell oranges with our food order yesterday. Wait till you see them. Each one is more perfect than the last, and to think you can only get them at this particular time of year. Amazing."

Myra linked arms with Charles. "I'm going to learn to cook, Charles. I've been watching the Food Network." Charles laughed all the way across the compound as he half dragged Myra through the deep snow.

Thanksgiving dinner was everything everyone hoped it would be. Good friends breaking bread together and giving thanks together. Chef Charles accepted the accolades heaped on him with a gracious smile. Conversation was light, at times bantering, but always in good taste. Even Murphy and Grady whooped their thanks at the heaping plates Charles set out for them, but instead of turkey they had roast chicken.

Jack passed on the pumpkin pie by saying he was allergic and went with the pecan pie. The others hooted with laughter at the remembrance of the truckload of pumpkins back in Utah. One and all agreed that it seemed like a lifetime ago.

Coffee and brandy was served in the living room in front of a blazing fire that Elias and Bert maintained. Outside the snow continued to fall. Soft music, golden oldies that no one objected to, played softly.

Even though there were football games on the big screen via satellite, no one opted to watch them. All were content to sit and revel in the peaceful atmosphere with good friends.

When Charles walked into the living room carrying a huge silver tray with two bottles of champagne, they all knew something interesting was about to happen. Myra, at his side, held an identical silver tray with exquisite cut-glass wine flutes.

Nikki looked over at Jack and winked. The heirloom crystal flutes had appeared months ago, brought to the mountain by Nellie from Myra's farmhouse. This, whatever this was, must really be important. Feeling a nudge to her shoulder, Nikki turned and wasn't surprised when she heard a whisper in her ear.

"This is Mummie's big day, Nik. She's finally going to do it."

"About time," Nikki said under her breath. She risked a glance around the room, but no one seemed to be paying attention to the fact that Barbara's spirit was in attendance.

Charles uncorked the first bottle of champagne. They all watched the cork sail upward and then spiral down to land at Myra's feet. The second cork went upward, spiraled down, and settled at Charles's feet. The little group clapped their hands.

"Nice going, Barb," Nikki mumbled.

"You should see what I can do when I put my mind to it," the spirit giggled. *"Shh, here it comes."*

Charles cleared his throat. "I have an announcement to make. I've asked Myra to marry me, and she finally said yes. I asked her on bended knee in the snow at four-thirty this morning on the front porch. I hope you're all as happy for us as we are for ourselves. So, let's drink a toast to this happy couple."

Nikki wasn't sure, but she thought she saw her spirit sister settle herself between her mother and father. Then again, maybe it was the smoke that suddenly billowed out of the fireplace before it was sucked back in and then straight up the chimney. "Nice going, Barb."

"Thanks, Nik. Give them both an earthly hug for me, okay?"

"You got it!" Nikki untangled herself and got to her feet to accept her flute of champagne. To Charles and

Myra, she whispered, "I have orders to give you both an *earthly* hug. One earthly hug coming up." She wrapped her arms around Charles and Myra without spilling a drop of champagne.

"She was here, wasn't she?" Myra whispered.

"Oh, yeah, she was here." Nikki smiled. "She approves."

"I felt her right beside me," Charles murmured.

"She was between us, wasn't she, Nikki?"

"Smack dab in the middle. I am so happy for you both."

The little group started to sing "For He's a Jolly Good Fellow," and then they switched to "She's a Jolly Good Lady." All off-key, but no one cared.

Cushions and blankets appeared out of nowhere as the happy guests sprawled wherever there was room. No one noticed until later that Annie and Isabelle had left the living room and returned to the building where they lived.

"I saw how unhappy you were, Isabelle. I know how you feel. I pretty much felt like a third wheel myself. Suddenly everyone became a couple. Don't get me wrong, that's a good thing. I don't think anyone will miss us, at least not for a little while, and even then they'll think we ate too much and are taking a nap. Everyone has a partner but you and me. I think we should do something about that, and I think we should do it *right now!*"

"And that would be . . . what?" Isabelle asked tentatively.

What indeed. "Well, you did tell me and the others on one or more occasions that you thought that guy in the Vegas casino was pretty hot. For a while after we got back to the mountain, I thought you were pining for him. You said you looked right into his eyes and liked what you saw. You know the guy I'm talking about, the one you socked in the eye! You even remembered his name. Stu Franklin. He said if you ever take a vacation you'd be able to find him on the beach in the Caymans. You said if we were ever pardoned, that was the first place you were going. You even asked Charles to have his people run a profile on him, and if I'm not mistaken, you have it in your possession."

Isabelle sighed. "All true, but that was then and this is now. How do you suppose one would go about finding someone on the beach in the Caymans, someone who is hiding out from the law?"

Annie could feel herself getting into it. "*I know people, Isabelle,*" she said vaguely as her mind raced. "Listen, you're an architect. Draw me a picture of him from memory. Do it *now*."

Isabelle ran to her room and returned with a sketch pad. Her drawing pencil moved swiftly, with sure, deft strokes. Ten minutes later she held up Stu Franklin's likeness.

Annie stared at the picture. "Damn, girl, the man looks *hot!*"

"He was so hot, Annie, I felt like my eyebrows were on fire. How else do you think I was able to draw such a likeness? I wonder if he remembers me or his invitation. He probably has hundreds of beach bunnies running after him."

"Trust me, honey, he remembers you. He singled you out." Annie wondered if what she was saying was true. "You're beautiful, and he was helping *you*. He didn't have to do what he did that day. I think it's safe to say he meant every word he said."

Isabelle threw her hands in the air. "What good is this going to do for me except make me more sad that I'm alone?"

"Not for long. Come on, put your jacket and boots on, and let's go to the command center. I told you I know people."

Outside the snow was still falling. "Do you think it will ever stop, Annie?"

"Oh, who cares? You need to be thinking of crashing waves, white sand, sultry breezes, and that . . . that guy on the beach. I wonder if anyone told him he's safe from prosecution. See, that's your . . . your reason for calling when we finally locate him. Even a lame reason is better than no reason, because he probably already knows, but there's no way for you to know that he knows. Did that make sense?"

"Well, yes, in a cockamamie way."

They were in the command center, and Annie was standing at Charles's workstation. She took a deep breath, picked up one of Charles's special encrypted phones. She dialed a number from memory and waited. Isabelle watched her and knew in her gut that whatever Annie was up to, she was going to pull it off. She walked off, sensing that Annie didn't want her eavesdropping on her secret private conversation.

"So, do you know who this is?" Annie said to the person who answered the phone.

"Ah, Miss No Name. Just for the record, I'm wearing my magic decoder ring. That means our conversation is safe. Are you calling to wish me a Happy Thanksgiving?"

"Among other things. Are you keeping your eyes on my half of our business, *partner?*"

"24/7. Did you have your dinner yet?"

"I did, and it was wonderful. I need a favor, and I need it *now.*"

The voice on the other end of the line grumbled, "What is it with you women? You always want everything *now.* Since I'm three hours behind you, that means I have not had my dinner yet, and my now is not the same as you now with the time difference."

"Don't worry about it," Annie snapped. "You'll be eating turkey for a week anyway. I want you to find someone for me right away. You did say you were . . . well, what you said was you . . ."

"The term you're looking for is . . . connected. Which I am. All right, all right. What am I going to get out of this deal? *If* I decide your request is worthy of my expertise."

Annie swallowed hard. What would the girls say? What would Myra say? "Well, Mr. Fish, partner, you get *me*." Oh God, did she really say that? Obviously she did, because Fish was sputtering on the other end of the phone. Annie listened. "Oh, get over yourself, Mr. Fish. Admit it, you don't have a clue as to what to do with me. Not to worry—I'll show you." Oh God, did she say that, too? She blinked when she heard laughter on the other end. Annie listened again. "What do you mean when? It's not like I'm free to come and go as I please. When you least expect it, I'll be there." Annie groaned inwardly. She rather thought there was a song with lyrics like that. She felt her face flame.

"So, give me your fax number, and I'm going to send you a picture of the man I want you to find. Think in terms of *rewards* for a job well-done. The kind you never dreamed of, that's what kind." Annie squeezed her eyes shut, knowing she was going to have to powwow with the girls to come up with *rewards*. Her whole body felt so hot she wanted to run out naked in the snow. Fish was still sputtering on the other end of the line.

Annie slid the drawing into the fax machine and punched in the number Fish had managed to give her during his sputtering.

"How long is this going to take?" Annie asked. "Did I

so mention that I . . . we need the man's cell-phone number, and we want a guarantee that he will answer it when we call? You can do that, can't you, Fish?"

More garbled words.

"What? What? Are you saying you lied to me? You said you worked for some secret branch of the government no one ever heard of. You said you were a terrorist and a mercenary. I believed you, otherwise I wouldn't have called you. Oh, I cannot believe I tumbled to your silver tongue. You can just forget those rewards." She listened, her eyebrows shooting upward. "Well, that's more like it. The rewards are back on the table. Of course I'll wait for your call, where do you think I'm going to go? No, I'm not sending you a list of the rewards. Well, maybe I could send the first three." Annie made kissing sounds into the phone before she broke the connection.

"Isabelle!" Annie screeched at the top of her lungs.

"Oh, no, your source said he couldn't help. It's all right, Annie. You tried, and I appreciate it. I guess it just isn't meant to be."

"Shut up, Isabelle. It's in the bag. In a few hours you will be talking to Mr. Franklin. It's what I promised—to get the information for you."

"Oh, Annie, what did you promise? Are you saying you can't deliver on your promise?"

Annie told her. Isabelle blinked. Then she blinked again before she doubled over laughing. When she finally stopped laughing, she managed to gasp, "I think we can come up with a suitable list of rewards. We might even be able to come up with *instructions*. You do realize what the problem is, right?"

"Oh God, what could be worse?" Annie groaned.

Isabelle started to giggle and couldn't stop. "Following through," she finally managed to gasp.

Annie sat down with a thump. "What should I wear?"

"You aren't getting it, Annie. Zip."

"But . . ."

"A promise is a promise, Annie."

Annie rose to the occasion. "My dear, if you can make contact with Mr. Franklin, I can certainly honor my promise. *YIPPEEEEE!*"

Four hours later, eastern standard time, Annie's cell phone rang. She bolted upright from where she'd been dozing on the sofa. She gave Isabelle a shout to wake up where she, too, was dozing by the fire. "My phone is ringing. I think this call might be for you, honey."

Isabelle reached for the phone and said, "Hello, this is Isabelle."

"Well, Isabelle, this is Stu Franklin. There's this guy standing here with a gun to my head, and he's telling me to talk pretty to you. Not that anyone needs to tell me something like that. I'd appreciate it if you'd tell him he can leave us now so we can have a private conversation. I'm going to put him on the phone right now before he blows my head off."

Isabelle managed to squeak out, "Thank you for your help, sir. I appreciate you doing this for me on Thanksgiving. I hope I didn't take you away from your dinner." The voice on the other end of the phone mumbled something that sounded like he was glad he didn't have to kill anyone on Thanksgiving. Isabelle was so light-headed she had to sit down.

The voice was soft, cultured, intimate-sounding. "Somehow or other, Isabelle, I thought you would have gotten in touch with me in a more conventional way. But I admire your aggressiveness. I'm glad you called. Are you having a nice Thanksgiving?"

"I did . . . I am . . . I was until . . . Oh, never mind. I didn't spoil yours, did I?"

"No. I just had a hot dog with all the trimmings on the beach. Did you have the whole enchilada, meaning a turkey with all the trimmings?"

"I did. I love hot dogs with all the trimmings, too."

"I saw that picture you did of me. Pretty good. Are you an artist?"

"No, I'm an architect. I feel . . . I feel kind of foolish and pushy right now. Maybe someday I can explain what made me . . . What I mean is . . ."

"Just for the record, I would have gotten in touch, but I didn't know how. I was hoping you might take me up on my offer one of these days."

"That's kind of hard, but I'm working on it. We have two feet of snow where I am right now."

"It's sunny and eighty degrees where I am. There's not a ripple in the ocean, and it's sapphire blue. There aren't many people here right now, which is unusual. I guess the economy is as bad as they say it is."

"Has anyone told you that you're free from prosecution? If not, you can come and go as you please. We . . . we took care of that for you."

The silence on the other end of the phone lasted so long Isabelle had to say, "Are you still there?"

"I'm still here. No, I didn't know that. Well, this is a wonderful Thanksgiving, after all. But how do I know it's true?"

"Because I tracked you down to tell you. I don't lie. I think we might, I say might, be going to Washington soon."

"Is that an invitation? If it is, I accept."

"It is. If you give me your phone number, I can call you if it happens. You can call me anytime, but not on this number." She rattled off a number that Stu Franklin said he memorized.

"Let's talk, Isabelle. I want to know what happened that day at the casino. I want to know all about you."

And so Isabelle told him while Annie pretended to snore lightly on the couch.

If you love the Sisterhood series,
but are wanting a non-Sisterhood "fix" from Fern Michaels,
you are in luck!

Her next stand-alone novel will be
coming from Kensington in May 2010.

Turn the page for a special preview of

RETURN TO SENDER,

the wonderful new bestseller by Fern Michaels.

Prologue

January 13, 1989
Dalton, Georgia

Rosalind Townsend, whom everyone called Lin, held her newborn son tightly in her arms as the orderly wheeled her to the hospital's administration office. A nurse tried to take him from her so she could tend to the business of her release, but she refused to give him up.

After eighteen hours of agonizing labor without any medication, she'd delivered a healthy six-pound eight-ounce baby boy. She wasn't about to let him out of her sight.

She'd named him William Michael Townsend. A good, solid name. She would call him Will.

Like his father's, Will's hair was a deep black, so dark it appeared to be blue. Lin wasn't sure about his eyes at this point. She'd read in her baby book that a newborn's eye color wasn't true at birth. Nothing about him resembled her, as she was fair-haired with unusual silver-colored eyes and milk white skin.

She gazed down at the securely wrapped bundle in her arms and ran her thumb across his delicate cheek. Soft as silk. He yawned, revealing tender, pink gums. Lin smiled down at her son. No matter what her circumstances, she made a vow to herself: she would devote her life to caring for this precious little child.

Lin had spent the past seven months preparing for this

ay. During the day she worked at J & G Carpet Mills as a secretary. Five evenings a week and weekend mornings, she waited tables at Jack's Diner. Other than what it cost for rent, food, and utilities, Lin saved every cent she made. She had to be conservative, because it was just her and Will. She'd allowed herself a week off from both jobs so she could bond with her son, adjust to her new life as a mother. While she would've loved spending more time with her son, being the sole caregiver and provider made that impossible. She'd lucked out when Sally, a coworker at Jack's and a single mother to boot, had asked her if she would sit for her two-year-old daughter, Lizzie. In return, Sally would look after the baby on the days that she wasn't working. Lin had agreed because she had to. There were still the days to cover, but Sally gave her a list of reliable sitters she'd used in the past. Dear Sally. Only five years older than Lin but so much wiser to the ways of the world. They were fast becoming good friends. Sally was the complete opposite of Lin—tall, olive-skinned, with beautiful brown eyes that had a slight upward slant, giving her an Asian look. Lin had called three of the sitters: two high-school girls and one elderly woman. She would meet with them later in the week. Lin was sure that if Sally approved, she would as well.

Sadly, there would be no help from Will's father or her parents. Lin recalled her father's cruel words when he learned she was pregnant.

"May you burn in hell, you little harlot! You've disgraced my good name. Get out of my house. I don't ever want to lay eyes on you again or your bastard child!"

Lin had appealed to her mother in the hope she would intervene, but, as usual, her mother had cowered behind her father, accepting his word as law. Lin would never allow a man to intimidate her the way her father did her mother.

Never.

"Miss?"

Lin directed her attention back to the woman behind the administration desk. "Yes?"

"If you'll sign here and initial here." The woman slid a single sheet of paper across the desk.

Lin signed the paper, releasing the hospital from any liability. Since she had no health insurance and refused public assistance, she could only afford to stay in the hospital for twenty-four hours. She'd spend the next two years paying a hundred dollars a month until her debt was paid in full.

The woman behind the desk reached into a drawer and pulled out a thick envelope. "Here, take these. You might find them useful."

Lin took the envelope, peered inside. Coupons for diapers, formula, baby lotion, and anything else one might need. She gave the woman a wan smile. "Thank you."

"You're welcome."

Throughout her pregnancy, she had visited the local dollar store once a month. She'd purchased generic brands of baby items that were on the list of layette necessities she'd read about in the baby book given to her by her obstetrician. Lin didn't have extra money to spend on a homecoming outfit for the baby, so she'd gone to Goodwill and found a secondhand pale blue sweater set. She'd carefully hand washed it in Dreft detergent. Subsequently it had looked good as new. Someday, she swore to herself, her son wouldn't have to wear secondhand clothes.

The orderly wheeled her back to her room, where she dressed in the maternity clothes she'd worn when admitted to the hospital the day before. She ran her hand across her flat stomach. Now she would be able to wear the uniform Jack required, thus saving wear and tear on her few meager outfits. She gazed around the room to make sure she wasn't leaving anything behind. Had it only been

enty-four hours since the taxi had dropped her off at the
nergency room? It seemed like a week.

Lin carefully removed the sweater set she'd placed in
her overnight bag. With ease, she dressed her son, smiling at the results. Will looked like a little prince in his
blue outfit from Goodwill. Briefly, she thought of his father and their weeklong affair. What would his reaction
be when he saw his son for the first time? After months of
indecision, she'd finally written him another letter two
months ago, the first one since she had been on her own,
and mailed it to his parents' address in New York, the only
way she knew to contact him. She'd begged Nancy John-
son, a girl Will's father had introduced her to, for his phone
number as well, but the woman had been adamant about
not revealing more of her friend's personal life. She'd told
Lin that if Nicholas wanted her to have his phone number, he would have given it to her. The harsh words had
stung, but there was more at stake than her raw feelings.
She had a child to consider. She'd written a lengthy letter,
revealing her pregnancy, telling Nicholas he would be a
father shortly after the new year. Weeks passed without a
response. Then just last week she'd trudged to the mailbox only to find the letter she'd sent unopened and marked
RETURN TO SENDER.

What's one more rejection? she'd asked herself.

Her father hadn't accepted her, either. Her mother had
once told her that he'd always dreamed of having a son.
At the time, Lin had been terribly hurt, but as the years
passed, she learned to set those feelings aside. She'd been
the best daughter she knew how to be in hopes of gaining
some kind of approval, and maybe even a bit of love and
affection from both parents, but that was not to be. When
she told her parents about the decision to keep her baby,
they were mortified and humiliated. She'd been tossed out

of the only home she'd ever known with nothing more than the clothes on her back.

A soft, mewling sound jerked her out of the past. "It's okay, little one. I'm right here."

With the quilt that Irma, Jack's wife, had made for him, Lin gently wrapped Will in a snug bundle. It was below freezing outside. Lin had halfheartedly listened to the local weather report as it blared from the television mounted above her bed. An ice storm was predicted. Meteorologists said it could be the worst in north Georgia history. With only two small electric space heaters, her garage apartment would be freezing. How she wished she could take Will to her childhood home. While it wasn't filled with love, at least it would be warm.

But Lin recalled the torturous evenings of her childhood. She would rather die than subject her son to such a strict and oftentimes cruel upbringing. Every evening, as far back as she could remember, she'd had to pray while kneeling on the hardwood floor in the living room as her father read from the Bible.

A die-hard Southern Baptist who considered himself a man of God, her father had constructed a pulpit for himself in the center of the living room from which he would gaze down at her with disdain, as though she weren't good enough. Then, as if that weren't bad enough, he'd make her recite the names of all the books of the Bible in order. If she missed one, he would make her start from the beginning until she named them correctly. Once, when she was about seven or eight, she remembered spending an entire night on her knees praying. She'd prayed hard, her father watching her the entire time. Little did he know she'd been praying for his immediate death. Many times she'd wet herself while on her knees in prayer. Her father wouldn't allow her to change her clothes or bathe afterward.

"The devil lives inside you, girly! Taking a shower n't gonna cleanse your dirty soul!"

She'd winced the first time she'd heard those words. After a while, she became immune to his cruel words. She'd even gotten used to smelling like urine. The kids at school were relentless, calling her Miss Stinkypants. And she would do what she always did when she was hurting.

She prayed.

Every night that she knelt on that cold, hard floor, she prayed for her father's death. Not once in the seventeen years that she had lived in her father's house had he ever relented on this evening ritual. She had thick, ugly calluses on her knees to prove it.

When she left home, or rather when she was thrown out, she made a promise to herself: she would *never, ever* kneel again.

Freezing definitely held more appeal.

She checked the room one last time. One of the nurses waited to wheel her downstairs, where the hospital's courtesy van would take her and Will home.

In the lobby, the automatic doors opened, and a gush of icy air greeted her, smacking her in the face. She held Will close to her with one arm and carried her small suitcase with the other. The driver, an older black man, opened the door and reached for her bag. "You best hop inside, miss. This here cold ain't good for the young'un." He nodded at the bundle in her arms.

Shivering, Lin stepped carefully up into the van. Thankful for the warm air blowing from the heater's vents, she sat on the hard vinyl seat and realized she was still very sore from the delivery. Her breasts felt as though they would explode. She couldn't wait to get home to nurse Will. She'd only be able to do so for the week she was home. Then she'd have to resort to formula. She'd calculated the expense, and while it was very costly, she would manage. Unfortunately, she had no choice.

"Thank you," she said to the driver as she placed Will in the car seat beside her. When Lin had discovered she was pregnant, she'd been frightened, fearful of having inherited her parents' harsh and unloving manner. However, when Will was placed in her arms, the love she felt for him was the most natural thing in the world. Her worries had been for naught.

When mother and son were secure in their seats, the driver made his way through the parking lot. Waiting at the traffic light, he perused a stack of papers attached to a clipboard. "Tunnel Hill, ma'am?"

"Yes, just make a left on Lafayette, then take the second right." Lin hated having to take Will home to a one-room garage apartment. Someday they would have a home with a big yard with flowers, a white picket fence, and lots of trees for him to climb. Will would have a swing set, and she'd watch him play. Yes, she would see to it that Will had a good home, and, whatever it took, she would make sure he had an education.

Lin remembered her father telling her years before that it was foolish for women to go to college, a waste of money. He'd assured her then that he would not contribute to her education, so after she'd preenrolled at Dalton Junior College during her senior year of high school, she'd saved enough money for the first year.

Having spent three terrifying nights alone in a cheap motel after her father threw her out, she'd made her first adult decision. Instead of using the money for college, she'd paid three months' rent on an apartment. In retrospect, her father's attitude had worked out well since it forced her to save for her education. If not, there wouldn't even be a place for her to bring Will.

The driver parked in her landlady's driveway. She hurriedly removed Will from the car seat and took her bag from the driver. "Thank you. I appreciate the ride."

"Jus' doin' my job, miss. Now scoot on outta here. That ice storm's gonna hit real soon."

"Yes, I know. Thanks again for the ride."

Lin felt rather than saw the driver watching her as he slowly reversed down the long driveway. She didn't feel creepy at all, because she knew he was good and decent and just wanted to make sure she made it inside safely. A stranger cared more about her well-being than her own flesh and blood. Sad. But she smiled at her thoughts. She had the greatest gift ever, right here in her very own arms.

Holding Will tightly against her chest, she plodded down the long drive that led to the garage apartment. She felt for the key in her pocket, then stopped when she heard a whining noise. Putting her bag on the ground, she checked Will, but he was sound asleep. She heard the sound again.

"What the heck?" she said out loud.

On the side of the garage, at the bottom of the steep wooden steps that led to her apartment, Lin spotted a small dog and walked behind the steps where he hovered. Holding Will tightly, she held out her hand. Its brownish red fur matted with clumps of dirt, the ribs clearly visible, the poor dog looked scruffy and cold. He or she—she wasn't sure of the animal's gender—whined before standing on all fours, limping over to Lin, and licking her outstretched hand.

She laughed. "You sure know the way to a girl's heart."

"Woof, woof."

With the ice storm ready to hit, there was no way Lin could leave the poor dog outside. She fluffed the matted fur between its ears and decided that the dog was going inside with her.

"Scruffy, that's what I'm going to call you for now.

Come on, puppy. Follow me." The dog obeyed, stay
foot behind Lin as she made her way up the rickety s
while holding Will against her chest.

Unlocking the door, Lin stepped inside and droppe
her bag on the floor. Timidly, Scruffy waited to be invited
in. "Come on, Scruffy. You're staying here tonight. Something tells me we're going to get along just fine."

Two unwanted strays, Lin thought.

Scruffy scurried inside and sat patiently on the kitchen
floor. With Will still clutched to her chest, Lin grabbed a
plastic bowl from her single cupboard, filled it with water,
and placed it on the cracked olive green linoleum. She took
two hot dogs out of her minirefrigerator, broke them into
small pieces, and placed them on a saucer next to the
bowl of water. "This should tide you over for a bit. I've
got to feed the little guy now."

Scruffy looked at her with big, round eyes. Lin swore
she saw thankfulness in the dog's brown-eyed gaze.

With her son still clutched in her arms, Lin managed
to remove her jacket before loosening the blanket surrounding him. Making the necessary adjustments to her
clothing, Lin began to nurse her son. Reclining on the floral-
patterned sofa, she relaxed for the first time in a long time.
Her son was fed and content. She'd inherited an adorable
dog, however temporarily, and she was warm.

For a while, that would do. Someday their lives would
be different.

Lin stared at the sleeping infant in her arms. "I promise
you, little guy, you'll have the best life ever." Then, as an
afterthought, she added, "No matter what I have to do."

Chapter 1

Friday, August 31, 2007
New York University

Will's deep brown eyes sparkled with excitement, his enthusiasm contagious, as he and Lin left University Hall, a crowded dormitory for freshmen located at Union Square. If all went as planned, Will would reside in New York City for the next four years before moving on to graduate school to study at North Carolina State University College of Veterinary Medicine, one of the most prestigious veterinary institutions in the country.

"I just hate that you're so far away from home. And in New York City, no less," Lin said for the umpteenth time. "With all the remodeling and holiday parties going on at the restaurant, I doubt I'll be able to make the trip north for Thanksgiving. I don't want you to spend your holiday alone."

"Mom, I said I'd come home if I could. And I will. I promise," Will said. "Besides, I'm a big boy now. I just might like spending some time alone in this big city full of hot chicks."

Laughing, Lin replied, "I'm sure you would." She watched her son as they rode the elevator downstairs. Over x feet tall, with thick, raven black hair, Will was the spitting image of his father, or at least her memory of him.

Lin recalled all those years ago when she'd first met his father. She'd fallen head over heels in love while he'd been visiting a friend in Georgia. Briefly, Lin wondered if Will would follow in her footsteps or his father's. She prayed it wasn't the latter, though she had to admit she really didn't know how he'd turned out. But she didn't want her son to take after a man who denied his son's existence. Lin knew he was very wealthy, but that didn't mean he was a good man. Good men took care of their children, acknowledged them.

Three weeks after she'd brought Will home from the hospital, she'd sent his father a copy of their son's birth announcement along with a copy of the birth certificate. She'd shamelessly added a picture of herself just in case he'd forgotten their brief affair. Throughout the years, she had continued to send items marking Will's accomplishments, the milestones reached as he grew up. Photos of the first day of school; first lost tooth; then, as he aged, driver's license; first date; anything she thought a father would have been proud of. Again, all had come back, unopened and marked RETURN TO SENDER. After so many years of this, she should have learned, should have known that Will's father had no desire to acknowledge him. To this very day, she'd never told Will for fear it would affect him in a way that she wouldn't be able to handle. Recalling the hurt, then the anger each time she and her son were rejected, Lin tucked away the memories of the man she'd given herself to so many years ago, the man she'd loved, the man who had so callously discarded all traces of their romance and in so doing failed to acknowledge their son's existence. When Will had turned twelve, she'd told him his father had died in an accident. It had seemed enough at the time.

But as Jack, her former employer and substitute father always said, "The past is prologue, kiddo." And he was right. She'd put that part of her life behind her and moved forward.

The elevator doors swished open. The main floor was empty but for a few couples gathered in the corner speaking in hushed tones. Most of the parents were either visiting other dorms or preparing for the evening banquet. Will hadn't wanted to attend, but Lin insisted, telling him several of the college's alumni would be speaking. She'd teased him, saying he might be among them one day. He'd reluctantly agreed, but Lin knew that if he truly hadn't wanted to attend, he would have been more persistent.

She glanced at the exquisite diamond watch on her slender wrist, a gift from Jack and Irma the day she'd made her last payment on the diner she'd purchased from them eight years ago. "I'll meet you in the banquet hall at seven. Are you sure you don't want to come back to the hotel?"

Will cupped her elbow, guiding her toward the exit. "No. Actually, I think I might take a nap. Aaron doesn't arrive until tomorrow. It might be the last chance I have for some time alone. I want to take advantage of it."

Will and his dorm mate, Aaron Levy, had met through the Internet during the summer. Though they hadn't met in person, Will assured her they'd get along just fine. They were studying to become veterinarians and both shared an avid love of baseball.

"Better set your alarm," Lin suggested. Will slept like the dead.

"Good idea." He gave her a hug, then stepped back, his gaze suddenly full of concern. "You'll be okay on your own for a while?"

Lin patted her son's arm. "Of course I will. This is my first trip to the city. There are dozens of things to do. I doubt I'll have a minute to spare. Though I don't think I'll any sightseeing today, since I made an appointment to have my hair and nails done at the hotel spa."

Will laughed. "That's a first. You never do that kind of stuff. What gives?"

"It's not every day a mother sends her son off to college." She gently pushed him away. "Now go on with you, or there'll be no time to relax. I'll see you at seven."

Will waved. "Seven, then."

Lin gave him a thumbs-up sign, her signal to him that all was a go. She pushed the glass door open and stepped outside. The late-afternoon sun shone brightly through the oak trees, casting all sorts of irregular shapes and shadows on the sidewalk. The autumn air was cool and crisp. Lin walked down the sidewalk and breathed deeply, suddenly deliriously happy with the life she'd made for herself. She stopped for a moment, remembering all the struggles, the ups and downs, and how hard she'd worked to get to where she was. Abundant, fulfilled, completely comfortable with her life, she picked up her pace, feeling somewhat foolish and silly for her thoughts. She laughed, the sound seemingly odd since she was walking alone, no one to hear her. That was okay, too. Life was good. She was happy, Will's future appeared bright and exciting. The only dark spot in her life was her father. Her mother had died shortly after Lin had moved into Mrs. Turner's garage apartment. She'd had to read about it in the obituaries. Lin had called her father, asking how her mother had died. He told her she'd fallen down the basement steps. She suspected otherwise but knew it would be useless, possibly even dangerous to her and her unborn child, if she were to pry into the circumstances surrounding her mother's death. She'd tried to establish a relationship with her father on more than one occasion through the years, and each time he'd rebuffed her, telling her she was the devil's spawn. Her father now resided in Atlanta, in a very

upscale nursing home, at her expense. Lin was sur
pure meanness had launched him into early onset ⁄
heimer's.

Lin thought it was time for her to proceed at her ow.
leisurely pace, kick back, and totally relax for the first
time in a very, very long time.

Lin continued to ponder her life as she walked down
the sidewalk toward a line of waiting taxis. After ten
years of working at Jack's Diner, when she'd learned that
Jack and Irma were considering closing the place, she'd
come up with a plan. Though she'd skimped and saved
most of her life, for once she was about to splurge and do
something so out of character that Jack had thought she'd
taken temporary leave of her senses. She'd offered him a
fifty-thousand-dollar down payment, a cut of the profits,
and a promissory note on the balance if they would sell
her the diner. It took all of two minutes for Jack and Irma
to accept her offer. Since they'd never had children and
didn't think they'd have a chance in hell of selling the
diner given the local economy, closing the doors had
seemed their only option.

Lin laughed.

She'd worked her tail off day and night and most
weekends to attract a new clientele, a younger crowd with
money to burn. She'd applied for a liquor license and
changed the menu to healthier fare while still remaining
true to some of the comfort foods Jack's was known for,
such as his famous meat loaf and mashed potatoes. Within
a year, Jack's was booked every night of the week, and
weekends months in advance. From there, she started cater-
ing private parties. With so much success, she'd decided it
was time to add on to the diner. In addition to two large
private banquet rooms that would accommodate five hundred guests when combined, she added three moderately
sized private rooms for smaller groups. The remodeling

▎ ▎ ▎ its final stages when she'd left for New York the day ▎re. She'd left Sally, her dearest friend and manager, in ▎arge of last-minute details.

Lin quickened her pace as she saw that the line of taxis ▎at the end of the block had dwindled down to three. She waved her hand in the air to alert the cabbie. Yanking the yellow-orange door open, she slid inside, where the smell of stale smoke and fried onions filled her nostrils. She wrinkled her nose in disgust. "The Helmsley Park Lane." She'd always wanted to say that to a New York cab driver. Though it wasn't the most elite or expensive hotel in the city, it was one that had captured her imagination over the years. Its infamous owner, known far and wide by the well-deserved epithet the Queen of Mean, had been quite visible in the news media when Lin was younger, especially when she'd been tried and convicted for tax evasion, extortion, and mail fraud, and had died just over a week before.

Through blasts of horns, shouts from sidewalk vendors hawking their wares, and the occasional bicyclist weaving in and out of traffic, Lin enjoyed the scenery during the quick cab ride back to the hotel. New York was unlike any city in the world. Of course, she hadn't traveled outside the state of Georgia, so where this sudden knowledge came from, she hadn't a clue, but still she knew there was no other place like New York. It had its own unique *everything*, right down to the smell of the city.

The taxi stopped in front of the Helmsley. Lin handed the driver a twenty, telling him to keep the change. Hurrying, Lin practically floated through the turnstile doors as though she were on air. She felt like Cinderella, and the banquet would be her very own ball, with Will acting as her handsome prince. He would croak if he knew her thoughts. Nonetheless, she was excited about the evening ahead.

She dashed to the elevator doors with only se
spare. She'd lost track of time, and her salon appoir
was in five minutes. They'd asked her to wear a b
that buttoned in the front so she wouldn't mess up her .
do before the banquet. She punched the button to the for.
sixth floor, from which she had an unbelievable view o
the city and Central Park. Lin cringed when she thought
of the cost but remembered this was just a onetime treat,
and she was doing it in style.

She slid the keycard into the slot on the door and
pushed the door inward. Overcome by the sheer luxuri-
ousness, she simply stared at her surroundings, taking
them in. Lavender walls with white wainscoting, cream-
colored antique tables at either end of the lavender floral
sofa. The bedroom color scheme matched, though the
coverlet on her bed was a deep, royal purple. She raced
over to the large walk-in closet, grabbed a white button-
up blouse, and headed to the bathroom. This, too, was beyond opulent. All marble, a deep Jacuzzi tub, a shower
that could hold at least eight people, thick, soft, lavender
bath towels and bars of lilac soaps and bath beads placed
in crystal containers gave Lin such a feeling of luxury,
and it was such a novel feeling, she considered staying in
the room her entire trip. She laughed, then spoke out loud.
"Sally would really think I've lost my marbles." She'd
discussed her New York trip with her, and they'd made a
list of all the must-see places. If she returned empty-handed,
Sally would wring her neck. She'd bring her back something special.

They'd practically raised the kids together, and Sally
felt like the older sister she'd never had. And she'd bring
Elizabeth, Sally's daughter. something smart and sexy.
She'd opted to attend Emory University in Atlanta instead
of leaving the state as Will had. Sally told her she was
glad. Not only did she not have to pay out-of-state tuition,

e was able to come home on the weekends. She
graduate next year. Where had the time gone?

e hurried downstairs to the spa for her afternoon of
pering.

Three hours later, Lin returned to her room to dress for
ie banquet. The hairstylist had talked her into a pedicure
and a facial. After an afternoon of being catered to, she
felt like royalty. Of course, it all came at a price, one so
high she didn't dare give it another thought, or she'd have
such a case of the guilts that she'd ruin the evening for
herself and Will. No, she reminded herself again, this was
a once-in-a-lifetime trip. As she had explained to Will, it
wasn't every day that he went away to college. Besides,
she wanted to look her best at the banquet, knowing there
would be many well-to-do parents attending with their
children. No way did she want to cause Will any embarrass-
ment just because she was a small-town hick who ran a
diner. Her accomplishments might mean something in Dalton, but here in New York City she would just be seen as a
country bumpkin trying to keep up with the big-city folk,
even though her net worth these days could probably match
that of many of New York's movers and shakers.

Discarding her self-doubts, Lin took her dress out of
its garment bag. She'd ordered it from a Macy's catalogue
four months ago. She slid the black, long-sleeved silk
dress over her head, allowing it to swathe her slender
body. Lin looked at her reflection in the full-length mirror.
With all the skipped meals and extra work at the diner,
she'd lost weight since purchasing the dress. The curve-
hugging dress emphasized her tiny waist. She twirled
around in front of the mirror. *Not bad for an old woman,*
she thought.

"Shoot, I'm not *that* old." She cast another look in the
mirror and slipped her feet into her ruby red slingbacks

she'd been dying to wear since she'd purchased them years ago. Lin remembered buying them on a trip to Atlanta as a prize to celebrate her first million. On paper, of course, but still it was monumental to her, since she'd clawed her way to the top. It hadn't been all rainbows and lollipops, either.

Clipping on the garnet earrings Sally and Irma had given her for her thirtieth birthday, she returned to the mirror for one last look before heading downstairs.

Five-foot-three, maybe a hundred pounds soaking wet, Lin scrutinized her image. The stylist had flat-ironed her long blond hair, assuring her that it was the current style, and, no, she was not too old to wear her hair down. Her face had a rosy glow courtesy of Lancôme and a facial. The manicurist had given her a French manicure, telling her it, too, was "in vogue." After leaving the spa, she returned to her room with a few makeup tricks under her belt. Plus, her hairstylist had sashayed back and forth, showing her the fashionable way to strut her stuff so that she'd be noticed when making an entrance. While that was the last thing on her mind, she'd had a blast with the women, more than she cared to admit. Lin had confessed that she hadn't had time for such things as a girl, but she hadn't explained why.

She glanced at her watch. Six-fifteen. It was time for Cinderella to hail her carriage.

"Get off it!" If she continued thinking along those lines, she would have to commit herself.

Lin visualized her mental checklist. Purse, lipstick, wallet, cell phone, and keycard. All of a sudden her hands began to shake, and her stomach twisted in knots. It wasn't like she would be the only parent there. Unsure why she was so jittery, she shrugged her feelings aside, telling herself she simply wanted to make a good impression on 's professors and classmates. Plus, she wasn't on her n turf, and that in and of itself had the power to turn er insides to mush.

Instead of exiting through the turnstile doors, Lin allowed the doorman to open the door for her. Discreetly, she placed a twenty in his hand and hoped it was enough. Sally told her you had to tip everyone for everything in the city. Lin calculated she'd be broke in less than a year if she remained in New York.

"Thank you, ma'am," the elderly man said as he escorted her to a waiting taxi.

Okay, that was worth the twenty bucks. She would've hated to chase down a cab in the red heels.

The inside of the taxi was warm. Lin offered up a silent prayer of thanks that there were no strange odors permeating the closed-in space. She would hate to arrive at the banquet smelling like cigarettes and onions.

More blaring horns, shouts, and tires squealing could be heard. Lin enjoyed watching the throngs of people on the streets as the driver managed to weave through the traffic. Lord, she loved the hubbub, but she didn't think she could tolerate it on a daily basis.

Poor Will. She smiled. *Not* poor Will. After the slow pace of Dalton, he would welcome this. It was one of the many reasons he chose to attend NYU in the first place. He'd wanted a taste of the big city. Lin thought he was about to get his wish and then some.

Twenty minutes later, the cab stopped in front of the building where the banquet was being held. She offered up two twenties, telling the driver to keep the change.

"Do you want me to pick you up later?" the driver asked as he jumped out to open her door. Lin thought the tip must have been a tad too generous.

"Uh, I'm not sure. Do you have a card?" she asked.

He laughed. "No card, lady, but if you want ride, you gotta ask for it."

"Of course. Midnight. Be here at midnight." Now was starting to *sound* like Cinderella.

"Will do."

Her transportation taken care of, Lin stepped out into the cool night air.

A SPECIAL INTERVIEW WITH FERN MICHAELS

QUESTION: With so many novels of yours published—many of which are *New York Times* bestsellers—did you ever imagine you would have such a prolific and successful career as a writer? How did you first get started? What put you on the path to becoming an author?

FERN MICHAELS: Never in a million years did I imagine I would be where I am today. I think I knew someway, somehow, that I was going to write *something* someday in the fourth grade when I wrote a story about a tadpole and the teacher gave me a big red A. What put me on the path to writing years and years later was when my youngest son went off to kindergarten and my husband told me I had to get a job. Being a wife and mother did not qualify me to go into the outside workforce. Plus, and most important, I didn't have a car to get to and from work. So I thought I would try my hand at writing a book. It was that simple. What was even more amazing was that the storytelling came easy to me. Please note, I did not say the *writing* came easy—it was the storytelling part that worked for me.

QUESTION: *Razor Sharp* marks the fourteenth book in
~~sisterhood~~ series. When you started the series with
~~first seven books, did you ever think it would become~~
successful, and you'd still be writing about the Ladies
of Pinewood so many years later?

FERN MICHAELS: I've kept the series going because
so many fans wrote and asked me to continue. But even I
had withdrawal from the Sisterhood when I finished what
I thought was the last one with number seven [*Free Fall*]
and had a long break before finally starting to write *Hide
and Seek*. I lived with those characters during the first
seven books for so long they were part of me. The bottom
line was, those wonderful characters were not ready to
ride off into the sunset, and I made the decision to continue because there were so many more stories in my
head that needed to play out.

QUESTION: What is it about the characters in your Sisterhood novels that allows for you to connect so deeply with
readers, and how did you first conceive of these women on
your pages? Is there any thread of you in any of these
characters?

FERN MICHAELS: I have a lot of friends and meet a
lot of people, and as women do, we moan and groan
about injustices we see and experience along the way.
One would say, boy, if I could just get even in some small
way, or, somehow that guy/gal shouldn't be able to get
away with this or that! Then I would sit down and plot all
these different revenge theories that maybe would work
or maybe wouldn't, but since it is all fiction, these gals
could do whatever, and I could control the outcome. The
"sisters" all kept reminding me I was a storyteller. In the
end, I was convinced that the woman hadn't been born yet

who didn't want some sort of revenge in her life. ~~with~~ with it. The seven women of the Sisterhood and t~~he~~ characters that I developed along the way are comp~~osed~~ of those same friends, family, and to some extent som~~e of~~ my neighbors. Even the guys. Is there any thread of me ~~in~~ those characters? Oh yeah! In every single one.

QUESTION: To the disappointment of many fans, *Final Justice* was going to be the "second end" to the Sisterhood series. But to everyone's delight, the stories keep coming. When will you decide to end this successful series, and what have the reactions of your fans been?

FERN MICHAELS: To end the series after *Final Justice* was my original intention because twelve books is a lot in a series. But . . . remember now, I am a storyteller and I still have more stories swirling around in my head. When I sent off *Final Justice* to my publisher, I stood at the FedEx place holding the box and felt physically sick. I thought I was going to cry. It was like saying good-bye to a group of my best friends that I was never going to see again. I went home in such a funk I made a pot of coffee and drank it all . . . black. Then I was so wired up I didn't know what to do. When I don't know what to do, I write. I posted a letter to my readers on my website and let it run for ten days. I asked my readers if they wanted me to end the series. I got over three thousand replies. All but twenty-two wanted me to continue it. Of the twenty-two, eleven of them said no only because they thought I wouldn't write other books. But I assured them that I am still writing non-Sisterhood books, including *Mr. and Miss Anonymous*, the upcoming *Return To Sender*, and of course the Christmas novellas I do for Zebra's anthologies every year. You know what they say: it isn't over till the big lady sings.

ION: While many people know you through your
, not many people are aware of your charitable
, which includes buying bulletproof vests for police
s and creating day-care centers set up for the needs of
ngle mothers. You also created the Fern Michaels Foun-
dation, which grants scholarships to needy children. How
did you get involved in these projects, and why is philan-
thropy such an important part of your life?

FERN MICHAELS: When I was a kid my old Polish
grandmother said something to me that I didn't understand at the time but do understand now. She said when
God is good to you, you must give back. I do my best. A
day doesn't go by in my life that I don't thank God for all
he has done for me. How could I do less? I have a new
project right now, which is our local police department in
the town where I live. With the passing of my daughter
due to a heart condition way before her time several years
ago, I wanted to do something in her memory. So I made
sure every officer in the department had a defibrillator
and was trained to use it, a thermal-imaging camera, plus
every officer now has a taser, along with training and hiring a new police officer every year to help safeguard the
people in my little town.

QUESTION: With the publication of several books a
year, along with your ongoing charity work, how do you
manage to balance writing, home, family, and book events
with all this going on in your career and life?

FERN MICHAELS: I don't know how to answer that
other than to say I take it one day at a time, look at what the
day holds when I get up in the morning, and put things in
the order of importance. Somehow or other I manage to do
what has to be done, even if it takes me till bedtime. My

kids tell me I have grease on my sneakers, othe~~
wouldn't be able to do what I do. I love it.

QUESTION: Where do you draw your inspiration fro~~
Are there any specific people—friends, family member~~
etc.—that help provide the characters found in your novels?

FERN MICHAELS: Just everyday life. I think my brain
is on overdrive from eight in the morning till around midnight. I hear, I see, I smell, I think, and I write it down.
Sometimes it can be something really silly. Like the day I
was babysitting my grandson and he was watching car-
toons and it was Alvin and the Chipmunks and they were
shouting, "Finders keepers! Finders keepers!" I had been
struggling for a title on the book I was writing at the time.
You guessed it—turned out to be *Finders Keepers*.

QUESTION: Throughout all of the years you've been
writing and promoting your novels, what have been the
most rewarding and memorable experiences for you?

FERN MICHAELS: Oh my gosh, there are so many! I'm
going to give you two, but they are sad. A lady's daughter
e-mailed me and said her mother was dying, literally dying,
and had maybe a month to live if she was lucky. She had
read the first two books in the Kentucky series and wanted
to know how the third one ended because she wouldn't be
here when it came out. The third book was done and in
production, but it was months to go before it would be in
stores. I called my publisher, Kensington Publishing, and
somehow they found a way to get the advance galleys to
me to send to the daughter. The daughter e-mailed me
later and said every day she read to her mother and they
finished the book *in time*. The second incident was almost

..., but this lady was a friend of someone who had
...ancer and was in a hospice. She wanted the fourth
...rhood book [*The Jury*] so her friend could read it to
... I sent it along with a roomful of flowers. You just can't
...orget things like that, ever. And I never will. I like to think
I make people's lives a little happier with my storytelling.
Now, if you want to go in the other direction, I was inducted
into the New Jersey Literary Hall of Fame along with such
notables as Mary Higgins Clark, Peter Benchley, Belva
Plain, and many others (I lived in New Jersey at the time),
and you better believe that was a thrill!

QUESTION: Now that the Sisterhood is still going strong
and topping the bestseller lists with every book, what is
the next thing you can tell readers that you're excited
about? What will 2010 and beyond bring?

FERN MICHAELS: I'm sure not ready as of this moment to put the Sisterhood series behind me, but I do have
other things I'm excited about. Especially my brand-new
series called the Godmothers. Again, some feisty ladies,
led by eight-times-widowed Teresa "Toots" Amelia Louden-
berry, getting their way in the world and having a lot of
great times while they're at it. I think these books are even
more fun than the Sisterhood books, and I hope my readers find them just as entertaining. The first book is *The
Scoop*, in September 2009, and then I have another non-
Sisterhood novel called *Return To Sender* coming in the
spring of 2010. So I'm working on all kinds of things, but
in my off-hours, my brain is swirling with Sisterhood stories. I can multitask.